I0549780

Magic
Once Removed

James Kirst

This is a work of fiction. Names, characters, places, and incidents are products of the author's imagination or are used fictitiously and are not to be construed as real. Any resemblance to actual events, locations, organizations, or persons, living or dead, is entirely coincidental.

World Castle Publishing, LLC
Pensacola, Florida
Copyright © James Kirst 2020
Paperback ISBN: 9781951642808
eBook ISBN: 9781951642815
First Edition World Castle Publishing, LLC, June 29, 2020
http://www.worldcastlepublishing.com

Licensing Notes

All rights reserved. No part of this book may be used or reproduced in any manner whatsoever without written permission, except in the case of brief quotations embodied in articles and reviews.
Cover: Karen Fuller
Editor: Maxine Bringenberg

CHAPTER 1

Rain fell from the heavens on that lukewarm February night like the tears of God. It would take more than mere tears to cleanse this vile city. Nothing short of a biblical flood would suffice.

Tacoma, the cesspool of Seattle, where all of her rejected degenerates come to congregate. It is a place where pot shops are more plentiful than weeds in a neglected flower garden. It is a place where crack heads are able to get their fix with seeming impunity. It is a place where methamphetamine lab explosions are more commonplace than traffic accidents.

As I gazed outside the window to the ground floor parking lot, observing the ravenous fools arriving to get an injection of greasy bread with tomato sauce and cheese, I began to reflect. Here I was, a self-retired cop working as a private investigator on the second floor of an unremarkable grey building on Sixth Avenue, sandwiched between a pizza place and a nail salon, flanked by a retirement center's home office and some programming place.

Business had been slow lately. It suited me just fine, for the most part. I was getting tired of the women who complained about their husband's infidelity and needed me to catch them in the act. It was sleazy work, but one that paid the bills, as meager as that payment tended to be. Yet, for the last week or two, I had been bereft of clients.

Locals call Tacoma the "City of Destiny." The funny thing about destiny is that it works in many ways. It seemed that night, though, that my fate was to try and show an eight-year-old a magic trick, as I had been temporarily assigned the role of babysitter.

"Sorry," I said to the young man sitting in a seat in front of my desk as I returned to my swivel chair behind it. "I guess I didn't hear anything after all."

"Oh, okay," the boy said with a quizzical look on his face.

"Let's continue the trick." I put my right index and middle finger to my forehead and closed my eyes. "I'm getting a strange feeling from the ether. The next card I'm going to pull is going to be your card. Was this your card?" I drew an eight of clubs and showed it to the boy.

The little brown boy in the Seahawks gear sitting in front of me stared at the card for a moment. "No, that wasn't my card."

"It wasn't. You're kidding."

"Nope, it was the four of hearts."

"Really? Dammit, what did I do wrong this time?"

"You said a bad word! You said the 'D' word!"

"All right, all right. I'm sorry, I didn't mean to cuss. Still, I'm not sure what I did wrong." I muttered to myself as I went over the trick again, gesticulating with my right hand while my left hand held the deck of cards. "Hey Darren, each time you pointed at the pile. You're sure you pointed at the correct one, right?"

"What kind of fool do you take me for? Of course, I pointed at the right one."

"Let's try that trick again." I collected the cards.

"That one. That one. That one." The boy pointed at each pile after I dealt the cards during each phase of the trick. I was about to reveal his card once again when suddenly I had an epiphany.

Oh my God, I said to myself. *I'm supposed to make sure the pile he points to is always the middle pile. That's what I've been doing wrong.* "Hey, Darren?"

"You want to try the trick again?" The boy sighed.

"This time it'll work, I swear," I said as reassuringly as possible. The boy simply nodded.

This time, when I got to the finale, after having gone through the rigmarole of acting as if I had "received a message from the ether," though in a much less bold and more rushed manner than I had when I had tried the trick the first time, and dealt the eleventh card in front of him, the card was the one he chose.

"It was the six of spades, correct?" I asked.

"Yep," the boy exhaled as he cheered unenthusiastically. "Hooray, Uncle Pete."

"Sorry about that, little man," I said with a heavy sigh. "I thought I knew this trick back and front. I didn't think it'd give me so much trouble."

"Can I play my video game now?"

"Yeah, go ahead."

The boy gleefully pulled out his Nintendo 3DS. As he played, I was left with little else to do, so I combined the twenty-one cards I had used for the magic trick with the other thirty-one I had placed to the side.

"Another exciting Friday night," I muttered to myself.

After gathering the cards in one hand, I rolled over to my filing cabinets and moved past the one that held my infidelity, due diligence, and miscellaneous cases, and tried to open the albatross that had been hanging around my neck for the past twenty years, a filing cabinet simply labeled "Erin Ross." I stared at the cabinet's contents, leafed through a couple of folders, sighed deeply, put the folders away, and closed the cabinet. I moved back to my desk and began playing a game of solitaire. It was going to be yet another quiet evening.

I was gathering the cards on my desk angrily after a failed third game of solitaire when I heard a knock on the door. "Come in, the door's open," I growled through clenched teeth as I began dealing for my fourth game. A tall man wearing thick, black-rimmed glasses, a white dress shirt with a red and black striped tie, and black pants entered the room.

"Oh, hey Carter," I said to the man. Carter Palmer was a programmer who worked in the same building as I did, and was one of my closest friends.

"Hey, Peter, how's it going?" the man asked.

Darren's face lit up as he looked up from his video game, and his eyes set upon the tall figure. "Dad!" he exclaimed as he leaped out of his seat and moved swiftly towards his father.

"Hey, little buddy!" the man said as he lifted his son from the floor, eliciting a few giggles from the boy. "I hope you didn't give Uncle Peter any trouble."

"I didn't give him no trouble, Dad," the boy replied.

"You didn't give him 'any' trouble, you mean," Carter corrected.

"I didn't give him 'any' trouble, Dad."

"Is that true, Peter?"

"Other than being a harsh critic to my impromptu magic show," I said, eyes glued to my game as I waved my fingers slightly with my elbows resting on the table, "He was perfectly well-behaved, as usual. Sheryl's coming back tonight, isn't she?"

"Yeah, she'll be arriving here in a couple of hours or so, which means I'll probably be headed to the airport after grabbing a bite to eat downstairs with this little guy. Unless you think you can wait until Mommy gets back before eating. How hungry are you, little man?"

"Pretty hungry," Darren said. "But, I can wait until Mommy gets back before eating."

Carter chuckled. "I suppose we'll be headed directly to the airport then. Thanks again for looking after Darren this week. Sheryl and I really appreciate this."

"It's no problem, it's what friends are for," I said as I tossed the cards in frustration.

"School begins again on Monday, so Sheryl will be able to take care of him again in the early afternoon. We won't need you to babysit for the rest of the school year."

"That's good. I mean, I am a private investigator, not a babysitter, right?" I asked.

Carter chuckled in response. "I hear you, buddy. Don't worry, this shouldn't happen again."

"You misunderstood me, Carter, I was legitimately asking. I haven't had a client in so long I'm starting to forget."

"You've just hit a rough patch. I'm sure things will turn around for you soon."

"It's been almost two weeks, man. Two weeks. I haven't had

a dry spell like that in years. The jobs I was getting were hardly pleasant, but they did pay the bills."

"Speaking of which, are you sure you don't want me to pay you for looking after Carter this week?" Carter reached for his wallet.

"Stop it. You're a good friend of mine. I'm sure you'd do the same for me if the roles were reversed. Besides, I'm not at the point where I have to choose between food and rent. Not yet, at least." I stood up and took a long, reflective look out the window. "I don't know, Carter, I think I'm just getting a bit burned out by this job."

"Maybe you just feel that way because of the lack of clients you had lately," Carter suggested to me.

"Nah, I don't think that's it. Even when business was booming — or at least, when business was booming for a guy like me — it wasn't the kind of work I was enjoying. This job's just too slimy at times, you know? Most of the work I was getting was infidelity cases, and believe me, those aren't any fun at all. And that's if I get lucky and the client is relatively sane, you know? I tell you, Carter, I get some crazies, man. I mean, like some serious crazies. One guy came in here telling me that Ron Howard was trying to steal his thoughts or something — it was surreal."

Carter let out a slight laugh before regaining his composure and apologizing.

"Don't worry about it, Carter. It is funny." I let out a deep sigh. "I could live with all of that if I just thought I was making progress. If I had a lead, a clue, a hint, anything, it'd all be worth it. Instead, in spite of all these years invested in finding out the truth, I am still where I was at the beginning."

"Maybe it's time to move on with your life. Find a new career. Make a new life."

"You know just as well as I do, I'm not going to quit." I sighed wistfully and stared out the window. "Not as long as I am still unsure of what happened to her."

"I know, Pete, but it was such a long time ago."

"Nearing the twentieth anniversary."

"And you were still just a child then. After so many years and without many clues, do you still think you can solve this case?"

"I do. I have to. I just can't give up. Especially when I was so close before."

Carter paused for a moment. "Are you sure it wasn't just a strange coincidence?"

I hesitated before saying, "I was sure at one point. I like to think I feel the same way now."

"Excuse me."

An unfamiliar feminine voice wafted from my doorway. Three heads turned immediately to the source. At the doorway was a pale, raven-haired woman who wore heavy black eye shadow and had thin purple lips. She wore a tight black T-shirt with a light red and white guitar in the middle, with the words "Rock Angel" written on the front. The right knee of her blue jeans had a small hole in it, and small black boots covered her feet. A black purse dangled from her left shoulder.

"Yes," I said. "May I help you? If you're looking for the nail salon, it's on the floor above us."

"Is this the office of Peter Cunningham?"

"Ah, yes, it is. I'm sorry. I just didn't expect to get a client. I mean, I didn't expect to get a client so late into the evening."

"I can come back," the young woman said. "It seems like you already have an appointment with someone?"

"Oh no, I was just headed out," Carter said. "I need to get going in order to pick up my wife on time, anyway. Let's get going, Darren." The boy placed the cards in his hand on my desk and stood next to his father. "Say goodbye to Uncle Pete."

"Goodbye, Uncle Pete."

"Thanks again for all of your help, Peter."

"No problem at all. See you later, Carter, and you too, Darren." I returned their waves as the two of them departed.

"Family of yours?" the woman asked.

"Not quite. Carter's just a really good friend of mine, though he may as well be family at this point."

"Oh, I was just a little confused because the little boy called you 'Uncle.'"

"Ah, right. He calls me 'Uncle' because Carter didn't want his son calling me Peter, so he bestowed upon me the title 'Uncle.'"

"I see. That makes sense."

"Please," I said, gesturing and moving towards the chair in front of my desk. "Take a seat, Ms....?" I grabbed the brown swivel chair and turned it towards the woman.

"Abigail," the woman said, smiling as she sat in the chair. "Thank you very much. My name is Abigail Mitchell."

"Abigail," I said with a nod as I sat in the black chair behind my desk. "What brings a woman like you to a place like this, anyway?"

"It's a little difficult to explain," she said, tilting her head coyly. "You look like the skeptical type. I'm not sure you'll believe my story."

"I'm sure it's nothing that strange. In fact, let me guess. You're looking for your missing sister, who is with a man named Archer. Or maybe your millionaire husband has gone missing flying from Tacoma to LA? Or perhaps you want me to surveil your husband, who is a chief engineer for the Tacoma Department of Water and Power?"

"No, nothing like that, though I must commend your taste in movies, even if you did take a few liberties with the cities. I don't think any of those took place in Tacoma."

"So, what is it? Is it a cheating boyfriend or husband? A due diligence case, perhaps?"

"I'm afraid it's nothing so mundane. Would you mind if I smoked? Smoking helps me relax and allows my mind to focus." She reached into her purse.

Unable to hide the disgruntled look on my face, I responded, "Actually, I do mind. I'm not a big fan of secondhand smoke. Besides, I'm sure the building has some sort of policy against smoking."

"It's just one cigarette. I'll be done with it before your building manager notices. Nobody's even in the building right now besides us. And if you're worried about secondhand smoke, don't worry, these are slim cigarettes. They are far less likely to cause cancer than the regular kind."

"What? Since when?"

"Since I made it up a moment ago," the girl said with a modest grin. "I'm sorry, Peter, but I really do need a cigarette to calm myself. Believe me. I think you'll understand when you hear my story." She snapped her right hand, and a small flame was produced from her index finger and her thumb.

"Neat trick," I said in response.

"Magic," she said with a smile. She lit her cigarette with her hand.

"How silly of me—of course, it's magic."

She took a quick puff. "Thank you very much. I think I'm ready to tell my story now. Would you like to hear it, or does my smoking bother you too much?"

"I suppose I can table any talks about your tobacco dependency for a later date. Right now, I'm just curious what kind of crazy story you might have in store for me. It had better be a good one, though. I once had a guy come in here claiming he was a pastel pony, and that the Illuminati was after him because they wanted to turn him into glitter glue."

"A pastel pony, huh?" she said with her voice trailing off as she finished the sentence. "Okay, well, it might not be that bizarre in comparison, but it's still pretty wild."

"I'm dying in anticipation. Please, Abigail, just tell me."

"Here goes nothing," she said, then paused dramatically. "Burning at the stake may have been the end for Joan of Arc, but for me, it was only the beginning." She took another puff of her cigarette and exhaled, which caused me to use my hand as a makeshift fan.

Silence filled the room. After a brief pause, I responded. "You're by far the best looking burnt corpse I've ever seen."

"You sure know how to flatter a girl," she said with a wry smile.

"You were really burned at the stake?"

"Well," she said, taking another hit of her cigarette and giving me a crooked half smile, "I might have exaggerated my story a bit. Obviously, they weren't able to finish the job. They were very close, though. I felt the fire at my feet. The raging inferno was about to encompass me. It was a frightening thing."

"Oh, my God! So somebody really did try to burn you at the stake?"

"Yes, though I admit I did tell you that in the most dramatic way possible. I have quite a flair for the dramatic, especially when I am nervous."

"Okay, well, this is a pretty serious thing, then," I said, leaning towards the woman. "Though I must admit I'm a bit confused. Why would somebody want to burn you at the stake?"

"Are you asking for a potential motive?"

"I mean, that would be good to know, but I'm asking more about why specifically burning at the stake? It seems like a very cumbersome method to murder somebody. A pistol, a knife, a blunt object — hell, even a pointed stick — would be a much easier and more effective manner of killing someone."

"This is where an already complicated story becomes — well, rather nebulous," Abigail said with a heavy sigh and a drag of her cigarette. "Tell me, Petey —"

"I'm sorry. I hate to interrupt, but please don't call me Petey. Peter is my name, please call me that." Only one person was ever allowed to call me Petey.

"I apologize," she said as she leaned forward and used my desk as an oversized ashtray, an action that elicited an involuntary frown and grunt from me. "Yes, Peter." She said this exaggerating both syllables with a slight giggle. "Allow me to try and answer all of your questions by first asking you, do you believe in witches?"

"Where exactly are you going with this?"

"Simply put, I am a witch."

"While I can appreciate the self-deprecation and the implied self-awareness that goes along with it, I'd hardly think that'd be enough of a reason to want to burn someone."

"I'm not sure I know what you mean."

"Wait, you said witch, right?"

"Yeah. What did you think I said?"

"Well, it certainly wasn't the word witch. Wait, do you really believe you are a witch?"

"Yes, I'm definitely a witch."

I gave what must have been a perplexed look as I gazed into her eyes, seeking a hint of irony, humor, or any sort of indication that the statement was meant to be sardonic in any way. I found nothing but earnestness in her eyes.

"Uh huh, sure you are. And I'm a werewolf, and it's getting late, so you probably want to get out of here before I turn." All this for a practical joke.

"Clever. I knew you wouldn't believe me. You're the type that's too cynical for his own good. That's why I was so hesitant to tell you about this. Might I remind you that there are more things in Heaven and Earth than what is dreamt of in your philosophy?"

"Yes, but seeing is believing. The only witches I know of are in fairy tales and badly written supernatural stories. Wait a second—you aren't talking about being a storybook witch, are you? You're talking about one of those modern witches that do holistic medicine, mixing twigs and berries together to find 'cures' or some bullshit like that. Or maybe you're the type that believes Wicca is 'empowering.' What a joke."

"I am not here to debate the merits of modern witchcraft, though I suppose in a certain way I would consider myself one of those too. And I would again ask you to open your mind and not be so judgmental. For the sake of this conversation, though, I will say that I am closer to what you would call, albeit in a derisive and condescending manner, a 'fairy tale' witch than a modern practitioner, although it's much more complicated than that."

"Are you now? Amazing. Stop wasting my time, please, and get out of my office."

"I know you are very busy," she said as she looked around the empty office in a smug manner. "But I implore you, you must listen. Perhaps a demonstration would convince you. My father really doesn't like it when I use magic outside the coven, and to be honest, I can't really blame him. It's gotten me in trouble before, albeit a long time ago. Still, considering the circumstances, I think he'd understand. Also, must you pace around the room? It's very distracting and, might I add, unprofessional."

"Unprofessional?" I shouted, pausing my nervous pacing for a minute, a little surprised that I had unwittingly gotten out of my seat. I muttered to myself. "Unprofessional. She comes in here, giving me a cock and bull story about being a witch, and then calls me unprofessional. So what if I pace? It's just a nervous habit. Why doesn't she just leave already?"

"I apologize. It was not my place to criticize, no matter how accurate my assessment might have been. Still, would you mind simply humoring me and allow me to do a demonstration?"

I grunted. I didn't know where this prank was leading, and my patience was beginning to wear pretty thin. "If I let you do your demonstration, will you leave my office? I really don't want to throw you out physically." I may have my flaws, but I like to think, at my core, I am a gentleman.

"I will leave if my demonstration fails to convince you, yes, but I have no doubt that it will." She took out a cigarette and placed it to her lips.

"I thought you said you were only going to have one cigarette," I admonished, staring daggers at the woman from behind my desk, no longer pacing.

"Cigarettes calm me down," she said through clenched lips. "One more couldn't hurt. I ask that you now simply observe, and please, save your applause until the end." She once again snapped her right hand and produced the small flame from before.

"That trick again," I said, flopping into my chair. "It's impressive—I wish I could do that. I used to be very interested in magic as a kid. You ever do the Great Indian Rope Trick? Kills the audience, let me tell you. At least it did when a friend of mine did it successfully. The neighborhood kids loved her. They didn't love it so much when I tried it, but then again, I wasn't nearly as good as she was. I probably would have burned my hand right off. I could have practiced, though. It takes ten thousand hours to become an expert, right? I would have gladly done that.

"Forgive me, I was reminiscing for a bit. Now I'm a private investigator instead of a magician for reasons I don't care to discuss with you. You have to admit, though, things worked out for me. At the very least, I was able to fulfill my potential." I began spinning around in my chair with my arms extended. "I mean, my dilapidated office is enough proof of that. The second floor over a pizza place is the perfect location for a private investigator." Grabbing the desk, I stopped my spinning and began leaning towards my visitor. "So how did you do it? Flint on your hand? I bet you painted the flint a flesh color. Let me take a —"

"You can be very loquacious, Petey, have you noticed that? Besides, I believe I instructed you to hold your applause until the end. I have not even started yet. Now hush, I will let you know when I have finished."

"Okay," I said, looking smug as I leaned back in my chair and rested my feet on the desk. "I'm on the edge of my seat in anticipation. Please, go ahead."

Abigail closed her eyes and began a low chant, in a language that was completely indecipherable to me, and executed some odd hand movements. A strange sensation overcame me as I began to feel something akin to being on a roller coaster ride. I was stunned as my feet began to hover above my desk.

Slowly, it dawned on me that I was feeling as if I were being lifted by an incredibly strong force. I looked down in a near panic as I realized I was floating in the air. I reached down and moved my hand underneath the wheels of my chair just to confirm it.

"It can't be," I said in utter bewilderment. "It just can't be." I gazed at Abigail. She continued to chant as she began to glow in a faint blue luminescent light. For what seemed like minutes, even hours, I stared at her, my mouth agape, words completely lost to me.

Without warning, my chair suddenly crashed into terra firma and awoke me from my trance. Both the chair and I tumbled over when we landed.

Abigail apologized immediately. "I am so sorry about that! Levitation is an exhausting spell. Well, technically, it's telekinesis, but you get the idea, and it is very tiring. I am literally lifting you up with my mind, and it is hardly my best spell. To be really good at it, you really need to be a specialist. I specialize in healing spells and sensing people in a room. Regardless, I should have put you down far sooner than I did. Are you all right?"

Other than the pain in my rear end, which was sore but didn't feel bruised, I was quite all right, if not a more than a little bit shocked at that moment. I peered over my desk, my ass still on the ground, and noticed that the woman was no longer glowing. I answered her question by nodding softly.

"I'm glad you are all right. Now, do you believe me?" Abigail began to giggle.

Slowly, I lifted myself off the ground. "I...I believe you are one helluva a magician."

"Still aren't convinced I'm a witch, though."

My hands began hovering over the chair's armrests and around the rest of the piece of furniture. "No wires. Did Carter help you out with this trick?"

She shook her head, no. "It was only me, and it wasn't a mere trick. It was magic. I think I can prove it. Check underneath your shirt, on your left side, by your armpit."

"Why would I do that?"

"Just humor me."

I rolled up the sleeve of my dress shirt and bunched it up until my left armpit was exposed.

"What the hell is that?" I screamed as I saw, underneath my armpit, what appeared to be a burn mark of a pentagram. Hesitantly I touched it. I felt nothing.

"Unfortunately, it's the residual effect of having a spell performed against you. Don't worry; it'll disappear within a week."

"Isn't that the sign of Satan?"

"Obviously not! Although Christians may believe such signs are the mark of the one you deem the devil, the truth is our gods and witchcraft, in general, have been demonized to the point our holy symbols are believed to be evil. The pentagram is nothing more than a symbol representing the Earth, Air, Fire, Water, and Spirit—no more, no less. Hardly the only example. Our horned god Cernunnos is not a devil as you Christians believe."

Loathe as I was to admit it even to myself, my skepticism was beginning to break down. I had spent most of my youth studying the art of illusion. Levitation was a fairly common trick, but it was never performed quite like this, with only one person in the audience, without wires, without a plant. This somehow seemed legitimate.

"I'm still not sure if you are a witch, and that was actually magic," I said as I sat down, my breath returning to me, "But I am a lot more intrigued than I was a few minutes ago."

"That's good, I suppose."

"I still have many questions to ask. This story is very confusing."

"I would be surprised if it was otherwise. Please, ask away."

"Have you tried talking to the police?"

"Do you really think I would have had better luck telling my story to the police? As insane as they are, I'm sure the stories you've heard pale in comparison to ones told to an officer."

"I know from experience that you're correct."

"Oh, so you were a cop at one point?"

"Yes, but it feels like a lifetime ago."

"So you understand, then. Besides, there's a segment of our society that does not trust the police or, for that matter, society at large. The history between us witches and the rest of the world is, shall we say, a checkered one. I'm afraid that even asking an outsider like you is potentially a scandalous matter, so to include the police would be much more controversial, to say the very least. I can hide a single private investigator from the rest of the coven. I cannot hide the police."

"I suppose that makes some sense. Why come to me, though? I hate to say it, but I get most of my clients due to my cheap price and willingness to take seedy cases. So why me?"

"Don't you feel like you are capable of better?"

"Don't we all? Why didn't you try Stein and Murphy?"

"Stein and Murphy? I'm not familiar with those names."

"Joe Stein and Leo Murphy? You're really not familiar with those names? They're only the best...um, uh...the private investigators with the best reputations in the entire slate. Even a cursory search on the Internet would have led you to them."

"To be perfectly honest, Petey—"

"Peter."

"Sorry. Peter. I'm not sure why I call you Petey. Perhaps it was because of a young boy I once knew. To be perfectly honest, you're the only detective I've visited. I saw your advertisement, 'Peter Cunningham, Private Investigator Extraordinaire,' and I simply liked the name. Something about it was very pleasant to me, very nostalgic." She cleared her throat and looked to the side for a second, as if lost in thought momentarily.

"Wait, the same advertisement that says, 'Wife or husband cheating on you? Boyfriend or girlfriend screwing around? Call Peter Cunningham, P.I.'? That ad?"

"Yes."

Her frank, nonchalant manner stunned me. I got up from my seat, my perplexed gaze never leaving the face of the mysterious woman sitting in front of me.

"You keep staring at me," she giggled. "Am I that odd to you? I suppose I would be, considering that I must be the first witch you've ever seen—"

"Still not convinced," I said, interrupting the woman as I began approaching her slowly. "At least not entirely. That's not it."

"Perhaps it is my captivating beauty that has bewitched your heart."

"Or maybe you just put a spell on me," I grumpily retorted, my hands reaching down towards her armrests. "There's something familiar about you, but I can't quite place my finger on it. And nothing about this makes any sense to me." Sighing deeply with a small smile creeping onto my face, my grip loosened from the chair, and I returned to my seat. "Well, at least it's a more interesting story than I've heard in a while."

"Does that mean you'll take the case?" Abigail asked excitedly.

"Not quite," I said. "But I am definitely thinking about it." I reached into my top desk drawer, which contained only two items: my notebook and a pen. I pulled them both out and plopped the notebook on my desk. "Let's start from the beginning. When did this assault occur?"

"It occurred about a week ago. Petey —"

"Peter."

"Yes, of course. Peter. Are you familiar with a witch's chanting circle?"

"Not really."

"Of course not, why would you be? As you can probably surmise, a chanting circle is pretty much what it sounds like. A group of witches hold hands and chant around a pentagram. We always dance around to the right — it is imperative to note that it is always to the right." She rolled her eyes.

"Why is that so important?"

"I have no idea. I just remember when I was being taught to be a chant leader, I was told to always say, 'Deosil!' 'Deosil!' 'Deosil!' That's Gaelic for 'right.' It's tradition. Who am I to question tradition?"

"Might I ask what the chanting circle is for?"

"In the past, it was believed to increase the power of witches, specifically the spells they cast. I'm sure some of the witches in our coven still believe that, but I've been doing and leading the chants for a number of years now, and I have not noticed any power increase, nor has anyone else I know. It helps create unity within the coven, though, so it's a good custom. An important one too. It actually went dormant for a long while."

"Why's that?"

"Something happened a few years ago. Something really bad." Abigail let out a sigh. "I don't blame our priest and priestess for their reluctance, but I couldn't just let the circle die. It is a much too important part of our culture. Somehow I managed to convince them, and for the first few months, it looked like everything was going to be all right. We began meeting in Titlow. We originally were in Point Defiance. Somebody allegedly caught us, so we moved to Wright Park. Some witches have suggested we move the circle outside the city, but it's our tradition to do it in Tacoma.

"A good chanting circle needs a drum to keep the beat. In our case, it's a bodhrán, a type of Irish drum. But in reality, any drum would do, as long as it provides a steady beat. A sort of 'tom-tom-tom' is required. One of our witches, a woman who goes by the name Dicana, forgot the drum—hardly the first time. Nor is she the only one who is cursed with the malady of forgetfulness, as unfortunately, it seems to be an epidemic within my chanting circle.

"Anyway, frustrated with Dicana, I angrily volunteered to retrieve the drum from our home. As I headed to my vehicle, it suddenly went dark, and I felt a sensation of being carried. It took me a second to comprehend that a burlap sack had been placed over my head, and I had been apprehended by a couple of brutes. I struggled to get myself free." Abigail placed her arms to her side and mimicked attempting to escape from her bonds. "But unfortunately, the sack had been tied pretty tightly, and I couldn't free myself. I felt them tying me to a wooden fixture, which I naturally assumed was a stake. I heard what I would soon learn was a blowtorch being lit, and soon I felt the fire beneath my feet. At this point, I dare say I might have panicked just a little bit.

"Luckily for me, though, my captors didn't take me too far away from the rest of the circle, who were wondering where I was and began exploring. The women heard my cries for help and came to the rescue. The two men were long gone by the time they arrived. After putting out the fire with a spell, they freed me from my bonds. I owe them a lot. They saved my life."

I scratched my head slightly. "Why didn't you cast a spell to protect yourself?"

"It's a little difficult to cast spells when you are ambushed," she said, giggling slightly. "Besides, one thing you must understand is that casting spells effectively is a complicated procedure. It takes a calm mind, a bit of time, and the proper hand motions." She began pantomiming a bit with her hands before resuming. "And knowing where the receiver of the spell is located. Now, witches do have the ability to sense a person's location, but doing this is much easier when his or her feet are on the ground. Obviously, I knew where my captors were located, but my mind wasn't quite in the right place to cast a spell, and my hands weren't quite able to move properly."

"Do you have any idea who these men were? They knew you were a witch. They set up stakes. They tried to burn you. They were definitely more than mere hikers."

"You'd be correct. I didn't get a good look at them."

"Because of the burlap sack."

"Yes, indeed. We could probably get a description from the members of my coven, though. At least one of them should have gotten a good look."

"Better than nothing, I suppose."

"I have something to show you." Abigail reached into her purse. "One of the men who captured me dropped a coin." She placed it on my desk.

"What's this?" I picked up the coin and examined it closely. Printed on it was a statue of a sleeping man. I had seen the coin before. I was stunned to see it again.

"What's wrong?" Abigail asked. "It looks like you've seen a ghost."

I slammed my hands on the desk. Abigail jerked backward in surprise. "This coin," I stuttered as I frantically reached into my shirt and pulled out a coin that was dangling around my neck on a red string, "Is exactly the same as this one." I took off my necklace and shoved both coins near her face side by side so she could compare the two.

"By the Goddess above, you're wearing the same coin."

I stared down at my desk. The only sounds that could be

heard were my heavy sighs and Abigail trying to regain her breath.

"Okay," I said, piercing the tense silence between the two of us. "I'll take the case."

CHAPTER 2

"Hey Pete, check it out. According to this *Sports Illustrated*, the Houston Astros will win the World Series in three years." The tan mustachioed man wearing a blue dress shirt with the sleeves rolled up, a red tie, and black khaki pants said this to me, eyes glued to a center article of his magazine, as he entered my vehicle and handed me a cup holder holding our two Coca-Colas. It was much too hot that day for coffee. I was still part of the Tacoma Police Department then. The man entering my car on the passenger's side was my partner, Officer Kelly Martinez. It was my fifth year as a detective and his third.

"You actually purchased a *Sports Illustrated*?" I asked jokingly as I took out one of the sodas and handed the holder back to my companion after he had sat down. "You know you can find most of that information on the Internet."

"You know me. I'm an impulse buyer."

"I've talked to you about that, haven't I, Kelly? So they really think the Astros are going to win the World Series in three years?" I placed the soda in the cup holder and started my car.

"Ah, you criticize me, but you're interested, right?"

"It's something to talk about besides work," I said as I began our trip. "I checked the standings this morning. The Astros are currently thirty-six and fifty-four. World Series Champions in three years. That's quite a bold prediction. They can't even get the World Series champion correct on any given year. How on earth can they predict who's going to win it all three years from now?"

"According to this article, the people they got coming up

from Triple-A are really good."

"That would be just the Mariners' luck, wouldn't it? The Astros enter our division two years ago, and in another three, they'll be playing championship-caliber baseball. Remember when everyone thought the Mariners would get an extra thirteen to fifteen wins when the Astros joined their division?"

"And I was nearly one of them, but you set me straight. You warned me things weren't going to be that easy, and you were right."

"I didn't mean to ruin your excitement. I just didn't want you to get your hopes up too high."

"No, don't worry about it. I'd rather know right away than to be fooled later on. I'd rather people just be honest with me with their opinions. Clara is constantly beating around the bush. It drives me crazy."

"Another fight with Clara? Want to talk about it?"

"No—not right now, at least. I'd rather talk about this article. Do you think the Astros will be World Series winners in twenty-seventeen?"

"The prediction seems a little bit too much on the nose. I could see them being contenders by that time. Their farm system does look good. Their management seems intelligent. I think they'll be in the thick of things in three years. But World Series Champions? Even if you make the playoffs, at that point, it's mostly luck. It's what makes predicting a champion from year to year so difficult, much less predicting a champion in three years."

"Hey, do you think *Sports Illustrated* just jinxed the Astros?"

"We can only hope. SI has made these kinds of predictions in the past, and they've never panned out."

"The SI Cover jinx. I remember once they predicted a comeback season out of Ryan Leaf, and you know how that story went."

"So maybe this is ultimately good news for the Mariners."

"It'd be nice to have some good news for a change." Kelly closed the magazine and squeezed it between his seat and the center console.

"Yeah," I said in response. "Not just for the baseball team, but for us as well."

"You haven't quite been yourself lately. The chief gave us the warrant. Normally you're a little more pumped up about making an arrest."

"Something about all of this is bothering me."

"Tell me what's on your mind."

"Everything has just been too convenient for us lately. Haven't you noticed the same thing?"

"How do you mean?"

"With the first five drownings, we couldn't find any evidence at all on the killer. Not an eyelash, not a fingerprint, nothing whatsoever. It wasn't until we, out of sheer desperation, 'leaked' it to the media that we were heavily invested in this case and would spare no resource in finding the culprit that all of a sudden we were able to find clues all over the place. Now our guy is suddenly leaving his wet work coat at one crime scene? He's leaving his fingerprints at another one? A witness is finally able to give us a decent description? It all just seems awfully convenient."

"Maybe Cullen's just getting a bit nervous, or maybe he's trying to get caught. You know how these crazies are. They're ostentatious. He wants the world to know he's a murderer."

"Even then, a serial killer normally has some sort of pattern. This one doesn't seem to have one."

"What the hell are you talking about? All of his victims have been women, and all of them have been drowned. I think that's a pretty clear cut pattern to me."

"They were drowned differently, though. One was in a public bathroom. Another was in the victim's house. These murders seem to be taking place all across the city. The state the victim was in before she was killed differed each time. Some were unconscious, some were wide awake, the poor things. The cause of death was the same, but the method was different, and it was always in a completely different location."

We crossed over the railroad tracks into the heart of

downtown Tacoma, towards the seedier part of town just before reaching the mall. I took a right just past the baseball fields and the auto repair shop and began heading towards an old housing area surrounded by a forest.

"So you don't think Cullen is the one drowning all these women?"

"He could be involved, but I don't think he's the only one. It seems more like a group effort to me."

"Then why are Cullen's prints the only ones we've been able to find at the crime scenes?"

"Perhaps he's taking the fall for another person — or persons."

"That seems like a stretch to me. Don't forget he has a history of domestic violence. He definitely has an issue with women."

"Have you read the arrest record, though? It sounds a lot like there was a squabble, and things got pretty heated — I won't deny that. However, the neighbor who heard the two arguing said she mostly heard the woman screaming. The police on the scene noted that Cullen had larger and more prominent wounds than his wife. He was beaten pretty badly. A concussion, multiple lacerations, multiple deep bruises, et cetera. In contrast, she only had a couple of bruises on her hands and elbows."

"Just because she knew how to end a fight or was really good at defending herself doesn't mean she started the fight or deserved to be hit."

"True, but I'm just suggesting that there may more than meets the eye. We'll never know for sure because his wife dropped the charges before the case could go to trial."

"It's the unfortunate cycle of abuse."

"Still, it's our only corroborating piece of evidence that this guy would even have a motive to kill all of these women — that it is some sort of rage issue. He's only had one arrest for domestic abuse, and the details are, at the very least, murky. You can see why I'm a bit apprehensive about this arrest."

"I don't know, Pete. Normally I'd trust your judgment, but all the evidence points to one man, Cullen Jones. The fact he's been arrested only once might just mean he's very good at evading the law. Don't forget, his wife is currently missing, and he's provided no explanation as to why."

"That definitely doesn't look good, and I admit that's pretty strong circumstantial evidence."

"I hate to ask, Pete, but you're still on board with arresting this guy, right?"

"Of course. If nothing else, the evidence is too strong to ignore. And besides, we can't police on feelings alone. Maybe I'm getting worked up over nothing. It wouldn't be the first time."

"Actually, it might be, but that's okay. I forgive you. It shows that you're human, after all."

"Hey, now, let's not go around starting rumors or anything."

We arrived at the house of Cullen Jones. His house, as were all the houses in this neighborhood, was located on top of a small ridge. All of these houses were in desperate need of maintenance or repair.

We walked up the walkway of the steep hill to the door of the dilapidated bluish-gray house. Its vinyl doorway's white paint was peeling after years of neglect. I rang the doorbell. No answer. I decided to give the door a hearty knock.

"Hello? Cullen Jones?" I called out to the man in a forceful voice from just outside the doorway, hoping he'd hear me. "This is Officer Peter Cunningham with the Tacoma Police Department. With me is my partner, Officer Kelly Martinez. It is really important that we talk to you right now. We have a warrant for your arrest." There was still no answer.

"Maybe he isn't home," Kelly suggested.

"Maybe. I'm going to check around back and see if he's in the backyard or something. You wait here in case he answers the door or arrives home."

"Okay, no problem. Sounds good to me."

I unhooked my holster and hovered my right hand over the gun as I cautiously approached the tall, rotting wooden fence. I reached over and unhooked the gate and opened it slowly in order to enter the backyard.

"Cullen, this is the police. If you are here, we'd just like to talk to you."

As the gate opened, I peered through and saw nothing but dead grass and gravel. I paused for a moment and listened to determine to see if there were any signs of human activity or the movement of an animal, such as a dog or any other creature. Hearing nothing but the sound of a songbird, I concluded that the area was clear and entered the backyard.

I called out to my partner, waiting at the door. "No signs of him!"

"Well, that's just great," Kelly shouted in response, "Should we just wait for him to arrive, or should we call HQ to see if they know of any other potential whereabouts?"

I rebuttoned my holster and headed to the front of the house. "There are other places to search. Maybe we can go over there and ask one of our guys to stake out this place in case he returns."

"I suppose that makes sense," Kelly said as I rejoined him after my triumphant journey and return. "At the very least, we should probably call in first just to see— Wait a second. Did you hear that?"

"No, I didn't. What are you talking—?" My voice trailed as I heard a faint sound coming from the backyard. "Oh wait, you're right. I think I hear it too. It's coming from the backyard. Let me go back there."

My pace was a little bit quicker and bolder as I reentered the backyard, and the sound became a little bit louder and clearer. With what could be described as calm haste, I looked around a bit, searching for the sound's origin. My eyes looked up, and I finally noticed a window slightly ajar near the far corner of the house furthest away from the now open gate. I walked under the window.

A feminine voice rang through the window. "Please, someone, help me!"

"Sh-shut up! N-n-no use strug...struggling," screamed a masculine voice. "I'm...I'm going to get you...you...you witch, you!"

"Kelly!" I shouted as I sprinted like a rocket out of the

backyard and towards the front door, "Our guy is in there, and I think he's trying to kill someone! We got to get in there now!"

"Shouldn't we call for backup?" Kelly protested.

"There's no time!" I screamed. "We have to get in there now!"

"If you say so!" Kelly bellowed in response as he slammed his foot against the door. Immediately after his kick failed, I tried to do the same. We were finally able to breach Cullen's abode after the third or fourth round of well-placed strikes with our feet.

"This is the police!" Kelly shouted as he entered the domicile, holding his pistol in front of him with both hands. "Please come out with your hands up!"

"We don't want to hurt you," I said as reassuringly as possible as I followed my partner into the house. "Please, just surrender."

We frantically searched the house. It was small with a really repugnant smell. The living room housed a small television set that had not been turned off and, strangely, the remnants of tree branches, bark, and other plant-like substances were spread all over the sparse amount of furniture he had. In the kitchen, there was what appeared to be swamp water in jars.

"Please help me." A woman's voice, afraid but strong, was coming from a closed door at the end of the hallway. "We're in here!"

"Sh...shut up!" the man screamed as we heard the unmistakable sound of a hand slapping a face. The woman let out a terrible scream, and it sounded as if her head collided with the floor. "Oh my God," the man said, voice quivering. "I am so, so sorry."

"This is the police!" Kelly shouted as we approached the door. "Come out with your hands up! Now!"

"You better not hurt her, asshole!" I shouted as we hovered right outside the door. For a moment, the only thing that could be heard were the sounds of our breathing and the feminine sobs coming from right inside that door.

"Should we try kicking the door open again?" Kelly asked in a whisper.

"No," I admonished in as low of a whisper as I could muster. "We don't know where the woman is, and we could hurt her if we do that."

"Well, what should we do then? We're running low on time."

"The window's open. Maybe I can climb in from the backyard."

"Are you kidding me? That'll take far too long."

"The psycho could be pointing a gun right behind that door waiting for us to approach it like fools!" I argued.

"We need to do something! He hasn't shot at us yet, and if he takes down one of us, the other can take him down. I'll do it. I volunteer."

"He'll probably kill her if we just bust down the door!"

"At least it'll give us a chance! Time's running out! If we do nothing, she's as good as dead!"

"Maybe," I said, looking towards the door. "Let me try talking to him first."

"Oh, come on, Pete!"

"Hey, Cullen," I said towards the door. "We don't want to hurt you. I promise you things will be much easier if you just come out." No answer. "Okay," I sighed. "Let's do it your way."

Just as I finished that sentence, the door sprang open, and the suddenness of it allowed the perpetrator to push past us.

"Kelly!" I shouted as I ran after the culprit. "You go in there and take care of the woman!"

A feminine voice shouted at me from behind. "Be careful! He's much stronger than he looks!" I silently acknowledged her statement as I ran after the guilty man.

I was able to track him down fairly rapidly in spite of his head start and in spite of my generally mediocre speed. He was barely on his front lawn when I reached him and was able to grab him from behind. Cullen threw a feeble punch that I was able to dodge with ease, and I apprehended the man with very little resistance.

"I confess to everything," the man said. As I reached for the wrists, I noticed that his hands and the rest of his body were covered in a thin, brown, almost sap-liked substance that was sticky to the touch. My olfactory nerves kicked in, and I noticed there was a most unpleasant smell wafting from the man's body. As I cuffed the man roughly, I asked, "What the hell are you covered in, and why do you smell so bad?"

"Um, I slipped in the woods and fell in some sap."

"While you were gathering all that wood, I suppose. I don't think that's sap either. Why were you gathering all that wood, anyway?"

"U…uh, firewood. That's all."

"Do you even have a fireplace?"

"To s…sell, and I had some wood projects, o…okay?"

"If you say so," I said, scratching my head.

"It was me, though. I did it. All of the murders. All of the women. I confess."

"That certainly makes the paperwork easier. You have the right to remain silent."

Reciting the Miranda rights to him was a bit of a chore because he kept interrupting me with declarations that he wanted to confess for his crimes after every stanza.

"It was me," the man continued to say even after I concluded my state and federally ordered obligation. "I confess to everything."

"Yeah, you keep telling me that. I guess that means you are still willing to talk to me about the charges against you."

The man simply repeated, "I confess to everything."

"Look, if you want to confess so badly, can it at least wait until we get you to the interrogation room? We have cameras there, and we have people that can take down your statement."

"Okay, I can wait until then. I can confess then. I did it all. I killed all those women. Just me. Nobody else."

I marched him towards the kitchen, then commanded that he sit in one of the chairs, making sure I placed him so he would still be in the view of both me and Kelly from the end of the hallway. I warned him that if he were to move, I wouldn't hesitate to apprehend him by any means within the legal limits, which might include the use of deadly arms. He nodded in solemn confirmation. He was in no state to argue.

I then headed back to the room where Cullen had been hiding earlier with the woman. I wanted to see how Kelly and the captive were doing.

"You're back. Did you...?" His voice trailed as he looked past me and noticed the man sitting in the chair. "Haha, you caught him, and you were able to capture him alive. Do you think we'll get a medal for this?" Kelly sniffed the air. "Jesus Christ, what is that smell?"

"Cullen apparently had a mishap in the woods, and now he's covered in some foul-smelling sap or something."

Kelly was kneeling down next to a woman who was sitting upright, holding her knees up against her chest and hanging her head down, so the bottom of her face was nearly against her knees. She was wearing torn denim shorts and a small, pink tank top. Her eye shadow was smeared down her face and all over her cheeks, and her dark brown hair was wet and tangled. She was young, too, not much older than twenty, I guessed. Some rope and a white cloth were lying next to her, and seeing the rope burns on her wrists and ankles, it was easy to figure out that the woman was tied up before our intervention.

"Maybe we can wash him off in there," Kelly said as he pointed at the bathtub behind him with his thumb. "The tub's full. Pretty easy to figure out what he intended to do with her."

"How's she doing?" I asked, leaning over slightly to peer into her face as best as I could.

"She hasn't said much to me, but she seems as all right as anybody can be considering the circumstances. Traumatized, I'm sure, though. She'll probably have to talk to somebody about all of this."

"Are you all right, miss?" I asked the poor young lady. No answer. She just continued with her thousand-yard stare. "Has she given you a name or anything?"

"Nah, afraid not. Other than thanking us for rescuing her and implying that Cullen has a sexual relationship with his mother,

I'm afraid she's been pretty closed lipped. Speaking of which, has that jackass said anything to you?"

"Only that he wants to confess to everything, and he's eager to do so."

"Told you he wanted an audience. He probably thinks of himself as a maestro, and that all those women he killed are part of his orchestra. I can't wait until that monster is behind bars."

"Yeah," I said with a sigh. "Me too. We still should probably search this place, though. We might find something. Psychos always hide things in a loose floorboard."

"You say that all the time, Pete!" Kelly shouted jovially.

"Am I ever wrong?" I asked as I made my way back into the kitchen area.

As I searched the room, I felt my right foot kick a small object, which made a metallic ring as it hit the nearby wall. I looked in that direction and realized the object I had kicked was a gray, metallic coin.

"That freak kept looking at that coin." Kelly and I immediately looked back to the woman, who suddenly spoke to us. "As soon as we heard you guys, he kept looking at that coin. When my gag came off, and I shouted to you, he just kept looking at that coin."

"Your gag fell off?" I asked rhetorically. "How does a gag fall off?"

I picked up the coin. What I saw was something I would never have expected.

"What's wrong, Pete?" Kelly asked, noticing I had stopped virtually all movement after picking up the coin. "It looks like you've seen a ghost. It's not one of those really old collector's quarters, is it?"

Without saying a word, I turned around and showed him the coin. He took it. I saw his broad smile turn into a frown. "Oh no, it can't be."

"It is," I confirmed. "It's a statue of a sleeping man. This is the same type of coin I told you about, the one I found as a child."

"It has to be some sort of weird coincidence."

Rage suddenly overwhelmed me, and I ran into the kitchen

and grabbed Cullen. "You bastard! You killed a girl named Erin Ross fifteen years ago! She was only eleven years old, you asshole! How could you do such a thing?"

The shocked man could barely utter a sentence. "Girl? What girl? I didn't kill any girl! I only killed the women, no girls!"

My grip loosened as Kelly angrily pulled me away from the man as forcefully as he could. "What the hell are you doing? Are you trying to ruin this case with your crazy outburst? We've already won, let's not cock it up."

"He killed Erin!"

"How? You read his file. He's five years younger than you! Did he kill Erin when he was seven?"

"That's right," I said, calming myself for a moment, but getting angry shortly after. "But he knows who did it then!" I shouted at the man, "How do you have that coin?"

After a long, silent, and awkward pause, the man said, "Oh. I g…got that coin fr…from an online auction. I'm a c… coin collector. Th…the guy on the coin is a, is a famous man or something."

"A coin collector?" I scoffed. "You heard that Kelly, he's a coin collector. Oh, I guess I was wrong about him. That explains why he has an exact replica of this coin." Despite being locked in a pretty strong full nelson, I was able to move my hands just enough to reach into my shirt and pull out that coin with a hole in it that I had dangling around my neck. "So that's why you have a coin just like this one. Makes sense."

I stopped struggling for a bit. Kelly, undoubtedly confused, loosened his grip on me a little.

"You believe him?" Kelly asked. After nodding to him slightly, I performed a couple of quick and swift motions and was able to free myself from his grasp.

"Bullshit, you're lying!" I shouted.

"Pete, you better not do anything stupid!" Kelly shouted.

"This coin!" I shoved my coin into Cullen's face. "I found this coin as a kid when my friend Erin was murdered! She was just a little girl then! It isn't a collector's item! Who gave it to you?"

"I'm…I'm…I'm going to wa…wait until…until I get a lawyer before I…before I speak to you anymore."

"Bullshit, don't go mum on me now!" I screamed. Before I could do anything to the man, though, Kelly stepped in between us.

"Pete, I'm serious—stop it, right now. Let's call it in and let the courts do the rest of the work."

"But the coin!"

"Pete, there's no way he's involved with Erin's death."

"But he may know something about it! I told you this looked like the work of more than one man. Perhaps he's part of something, and he's just covering it up!"

"Or maybe it's just a bizarre coincidence. Do you really think it's odd to find more than one coin with a statue of a sleeping man on it?"

"Don't lecture me on these things. I'm the one who told you about the coin and Erin!"

"I know, but listen. Do you really think your coin has anything to do with this case?"

"I know there's a link. There's too much here to be a coincidence."

"Okay, let's say there is something more to it. How would assaulting this guy help things out in any way? Let's not mess things up further. This guy is guilty of attempted murder if nothing else."

"Yes," I said, breathing heavily. "That's true."

"When we get back to the station, you can talk to the chief about all of this. Edwards might let you investigate further. I'll admit you did find some strong circumstantial evidence."

"It's a little bit more than circumstantial," I protested. "But, you're right." I closed my eyes and sighed. "Thanks for calming me down."

He smiled. "No problem. I just didn't want you to mess up this case. As I said, I think there's a medal in store for us. Would you like me to call it in?"

The boys at the station arrived almost immediately after

we called, along with the media. The reporters called the killer the "Baptist," so catching him was a huge story. Police Chief Herbert Edwards was especially proud of us. "We just got rid of a beast," the man said to the two of us triumphantly. Our reward: a commendation and a pat on the back. No medals, though.

Cullen's case was incredibly easy to process. He was so eager to confess, and that, along with the earlier evidence, the domestic violence charge, and us catching the man red-handed at the scene of an attempted murder, made it practically open and shut. The man was sentenced to life in prison, as Washington State doesn't have the death penalty.

Of course, the man's confession was captivating. He provided an amazing and conclusive account of how he was able to perpetuate his crimes without being caught.

Something struck me as odd, though. The story never changed, not even a word. It was almost as if it was rehearsed. I think I was the only one who felt that way, which caused part of the friction that came later.

I was constantly getting into arguments with the district attorney. Even though I implored that he look further, it became obvious that he was not going to take into account the coin I'd found for his case, mostly because it wasn't necessary. I then began lobbying with the police chief to investigate further, but he too did not listen to me, even though I threatened to resign if he did not allow me to continue the investigation. He responded gruffly, "See Michelle to fill out the necessary paperwork."

Kelly greeted me as I angrily exited Chief Edwards' office. "He's not going to let you investigate further, eh? Don't worry about it. Let's just concentrate on our next case for now. I'm sure he'll change his mind someday. Hey, slow down, I'm having trouble keeping up with you."

"He made it quite clear that will never happen," I said as I marched swiftly right out the station's door. "That's why I quit."

"You did what?" Kelly roughly grabbed my shoulder.

"I quit. It's not official until Michelle comes in tomorrow, and I fill out the appropriate paperwork, but I've already resigned."

"You're just a bit upset right now. It's been a long week. It's natural, you're a bit tired. Get some sleep, and we'll talk about this more in the morning."

"No, Kelly. I'm not going to get the answers I'm looking for here. I've found the strongest lead I've had since I was a child, and I'm not allowed to follow it. If he won't let me now, he'll never let me. That's why I have to go out on my own."

"What do you mean?"

"I'm going to become a private investigator and search for the truth myself."

"A private investigator," Kelly muttered to himself. "Of all the stupid things. So you're just going to throw your career down the crapper?"

"You don't understand. I have to find out what happened to her."

"I understand. There's something wrong with you, Pete. You're a brilliant detective, and you're going to piss it all away because you can't let go of the past. You wear that coin around your neck like a madman. You have to let it go."

"I won't. I can't until I find out the truth."

"Some maniac poisoned a bunch of apples, and Erin just happened to bite into one of them. It's horrible, but it happens."

"No, Kelly. That man standing outside the window—he was involved. I will prove it to you even if it takes me the rest of my life."

Kelly flashed a condescending smirk. "Fine. I wish you luck." He turned and walked towards his car.

"Kelly, wait!" I followed the man.

He turned around. "Don't follow me, okay! Just get the hell out of my face!" He entered his car and drove away.

The next day I submitted my resignation with Michelle. I looked for Kelly briefly to apologize, but he was nowhere to be found.

I was able to study for and easily pass an exam to get a license to become a private investigator. A place was open in downtown Tacoma, which seemed like as good of a location as any. My initial plan was to do some work on my own, with the occasional visitor providing clues related to Erin Ross or the coin, as the reward I offered was more than a bit enticing. Unfortunately, the only people who arrived were scammers, well-meaning but completely misguided people, or just plain old conspiracy theorists.

Also, being a private investigator is very expensive work. Factor in no external income, rent, and the online and newspaper ads I had purchased, and it is easy to see how quickly things add up.

I had to take more traditional private investigator jobs. I promised myself I'd just take one infidelity case to get me through the month, and then I'd be back to investigating Erin's untimely demise. The case didn't bring in as much money as I had anticipated, as I had to reduce my prices way below market rate in order to get a client. Barely able to pay for food or rent, the harsh realities of being a private investigator began to set in.

Days, months, and even years continued like that, with me barely getting enough business to scrape by. I often thought about begging Police Chief Edwards for my old job back and would have too, if I didn't cling to that little bit of hope, that little firefly in pitch-black darkness. My faith would soon be rewarded, as the answer to all of my questions did appear before me, though it still took some legwork to figure it all out.

CHAPTER 3

"So, you've been wearing this coin around your neck for the last twenty years?" Abigail asked, closely examining the medallion part of my crude necklace.

"Ever since Erin was murdered, yeah."

"How old were you when she was murdered?"

"Twelve years old. She was only eleven. She wasn't even a teenager yet."

"And you've been looking for her murderer ever since?"

"Yep, but I haven't made much headway. See that filing cabinet?" I pointed behind me. "I've probably got articles and notes of every child killer in the state of Washington for the last twenty years, as well as any crime that had any mention of coins of any type during that period of time, and still I've made almost no progress whatsoever."

"And yet," she said, handing me back my coin necklace, "You still haven't given up."

I put the coin around my neck again. "I can't give up. Not until I solve this case."

"She must have meant a lot to you."

I sighed heavily. "Yeah, she did."

"That sort of dedication is unbelievable. I'm sure if this friend of yours—"

"Erin. Her name was Erin."

"Yes. If Erin were here with us today, surely she'd be moved that you've spent so much time trying to solve the circumstances surrounding her death."

"Murder. Just say murder."

"Yes, her murder. At the same time, I'm sure she wouldn't have wanted you to have spent your whole life trying to figure out who killed her."

"If you had known Erin, you'd understand. She was one of the best people I've ever met in my life. Even at a young age, I knew there was something special about her. The day she died was the day I realized just how cruel the world was. That's why I can't give up."

"I'm sure wherever she is now, she'd want you to know how much it means to her that you even remember her."

"Actually, wherever she is, she's probably wondering why I'm taking so damn long to figure everything out. Twenty years is plenty of time."

"I wouldn't say that. Don't be so hard on yourself."

"You're right. If nothing else, I should just focus on the future. There's a reason to be optimistic. You agree with me, right? There is a link between this case, the one five years ago, and Erin's death."

"It certainly doesn't seem to be merely a coincidence." Abigail paused. "Petey, there's something I need to tell you."

"Yeah? What is it?"

Her eyes focused on the coin around my neck. "I'm not sure how to tell you this."

"Just tell me. I'm sure I can deal with it."

"I'm not sure you are ready for this." I leaned in a bit in anticipation. "Those women in your story. The ones that Cullen killed. They were part of my coven's chanting circle."

"What? Really?"

"Yes. We never told the police, but he was the reason we initially stopped doing the chanting circles."

"My God. That seals it. There is definitely a connection."

"It sure looks that way."

"The young lady Kelly and I found. Is she a member of your coven?"

"She was. She has since changed her name, her identity, even moved to a different coven in a different part of the state, anything to try and escape the pain."

"Why continue the circle?"

"Tradition is important, and we must continue moving forward. We can't let bad incidents dictate how we act. We have to pick ourselves up and keep going."

"I agree, and to that end, we should start solving your case. Would I be able to talk to the members of your coven to get a description of the men who attacked you?"

"Are you familiar with the Layton Fruit Market?" Abigail asked.

"The produce place?"

"My friend Dahlia owns the place. She was one of the women who rescued me from the stake that night. She's also one of the wiser members of my chanting circle, one of the few with a working brain. She's also very trustworthy. She'll hardly be excited that I've hired an outsider to assist us, but I'm sure she will be able to help us out."

"Sounds good to me," I said.

"I warn you—she may be a little bit upset at me."

"Why's that?"

"She's really upset about the chanting circle."

"I don't really blame her. You were nearly killed."

"I'd understand if that was it, but even before the attack, a month or so ago, Dahlia started telling me it was too dangerous to revive the chanting circle. This was quite a departure, as her testimony actually played a pivotal role in helping me convince the high priest and priestess to revive the tradition during one of our esbats. Oh, sorry, an esbat is our word for meeting."

"It's definitely something we should talk to her about then," I said. Making sure I had my car keys, my cell phone, and my wallet on me, as well as the pistol that I concealed under my black vest—a firearm I hoped to never use but always carried with me just in case—and a couple of tuff tie and feet restraints hidden in the same black vest—different pocket, just in case—I pointed towards the door. "We should probably get going then." We went to my gray four-door sedan located in the ground floor parking garage. As we began to drive, I asked the woman, "Is the circle really worth all of this?"

"Pardon me?"

"I like tradition myself, but is preserving it really worth your lives?"

"There are some things that deserve to be fought for!" Abigail shouted. "The past should never be forgotten! A millennium of persecution wasn't enough for you cowans! You have to take everything away from us!"

"Cowans?" I asked.

"Our word for non-witches." The woman reached into her purse and moved her hand frantically within. "Where are my cigarettes?" She pulled out her pack. "Ah, here they are."

I rolled down the passenger side window. "You know, if you have to smoke, at least exhale out the window. I really hate the smell of secondhand smoke."

"Duly noted. I will try my best to accommodate your request. It would help if you were far less critical of our practices. You keep doing that. It is really starting to annoy me."

"I didn't mean to be critical. I wouldn't normally say anything, but your coven was targeted before, and you yourself were the victim of a recent attack. Maybe the circle should be abolished."

"We hide so much of ourselves from the world. Most witches are able to live ordinary lives outside the coven, and even have families with cowans, but we do it with a cost. I want something to remind future generations of what it means to be a witch, outside of just magic and spells. The past is worth fighting for."

I nodded silently. "I agree. I apologize for upsetting you. I forget how difficult it is to be a witch in our society. I wish you didn't have to hide so much of yourselves from the world."

"Thank you, but I'm actually hoping that things are about to change."

"What do you mean?"

"Centuries ago, we were monsters, but I think the world, for the most part, is ready to accept us as we are. I think we can be accepted as fellow human beings that just happen to have certain gifts. A lot in the coven disagree with me. Many think we should retreat further and never interact with cowans. Their viewpoint is misguided but ultimately understandable, considering the tumultuous history us witches have with the rest of humanity."

"I can't really blame them. You were just attacked for being a witch, after all."

"Yes, but that is why I feel it is imperative for us to find who is behind all of this. Bringing them to justice would help in the effort to unite the houses of my coven."

"Your coven is divided?"

"The argument of integration or separatism has been going on for a couple of decades now. As you probably guessed, the attack has hardly helped."

"Do you think it was a random attack, or do you think it was by an organized group?"

"Until I met you and found out about the coin, I would have said it was a random attack. Now I'm leaning towards it being part of a grander conspiracy."

As we passed under a green light and I made a left turn, I looked up to see the large, familiar billboard of televangelist Tony O'Stein. Though the street light that normally illuminated his big chinned, large eyebrowed, medium length curly brown haired, goofy, toothy-grinned face had burnt out, it was easy to make out the contents of the sign. True, I had passed it so many times that I had involuntarily memorized it, but even if that weren't the case, the colors were so bright and gaudy it practically lit that intersection all by itself.

"Tony O'Stein's getting pretty popular these days."

"Yes," the woman sighed. "I suppose he is."

"Not a big fan, I presume? Is it because of the checkered past witches have with Christians?"

"Not at all. For me, that's all water under the bridge. Most Christians I've met are nice and pleasant people. There's just something about televangelists that bothers me."

"I think a lot of his 'motivational speeches' are empty platitudes, but he seems like a good enough guy."

"I guess, but I doubt Tony and I would be friends."

"Maybe you would. He's really big into conservation. He wants to protect the rare ximuce tree only found in Evergreen and is leading a protest against deforestation. Aren't you witches really big into the environment?"

"There you go stereotyping us again, Petey — although in this case you just happen to be correct. Yes, I am in favor of preserving the forest for the most part, but just because we agree on one issue doesn't mean we'd be friends."

"I was just teasing you. And please, call me Peter."

Right off the highway's exit sat the Layton Fruit Market, an unassuming place, the kind of place you'd pass by every morning on a commute to work or the local gym. After I had parked the car, we began our search for the owner.

The lights hanging from near the rooftop of the facility were the only illumination of this lonely parking lot. Some fruit stands were open all night, but this one had long but limited hours. We passed under the tents that would normally have scores of tables piled with crates of fruit and vegetables, now empty due to the late hour. Remnants of various foods littered the ground, but otherwise, the entire place had the almost melancholy feel of a typical empty shopping center. I could still smell the faint scents of grapes, apples, pears, and oranges wafting through the air.

"This place seems to be really popular," I said. "I keep hearing about it from all of my friends. Carter and Penelope won't shut up about it. They say the food's really good because it's organic. I don't have the heart to tell them that studies have shown that organic fruits and vegetables aren't actually more nutritious than the non-organic type."

"Maybe the foods they studied lacked a witch's touch," she said with a wink. "Come on, I think I know where she is. She must be in the back somewhere — follow me." Which I did. "Besides," she added as we approached a lone door in the middle of a long wall located behind the shop, in an area covered with trees and the adjacent highway, "The methods that make our fruits and vegetables good and nutritious is a secret to outsiders, one that we would prefer not to divulge to the world at large."

She knocked on the door. No answer.

"Is she not here?"

"She should be. The place has been closed for less than an hour, and she typically works for another couple of hours to put everything away for the night."

I reached for the knob. "Hey, would you look at that? The door's open."

Almost without thinking, I burst through the door into the back room. My brain failed to process the petite slipping fingers on my right arm, and the frantic cries of Abigail until it was too late.

"Wait! Don't go in there!"

I was looking over my shoulder when I bumped straight into a middle-aged, heavy-set woman. Though she managed to stay on her feet, I heard the loud crash of a crate hitting the ground and the shattering of glass. Each of us did a little one or two-step dance in order to avoid a glass shard being embedded into a leg. A detective has to be able to assess a situation quickly, and I quickly ascertained that I had knocked a crate of vials containing a red liquid out of the woman's hand.

"Oh, by the great horned god Cernunnos, look what you made me do!" the woman scolded.

"I'm sorry, ma'am. I'm afraid I got a little distracted." I tried in vain to find a dry and clear spot away from the aromatic crimson river that smelled of apples and was flowing from the broken ampoules.

The apron adorned woman turned abruptly towards me and asked with a scowl, "Who the hell are you? What are you doing here?"

"Hi, Dahlia," Abigail said sheepishly, slinking from behind me. "I brought him here."

"Abigail! You know better than to bring an outsider to the back room without warning."

"I tried knocking, but you didn't answer."

"I was a bit busy, Abigail. I'm sorry if I didn't hear you. You could have knocked again."

"He didn't give me time."

"What's going on over here?" I asked. "What are all these vials for?"

"You never answered my question," Dahlia said, continuing to glare at me. "Who are you?"

"I'm the health inspector," I said sarcastically. "And I'm currently wondering what you were planning on doing with all of these vials."

"He's not really the health inspector," Abigail said, jumping between me and Dahlia. "He's a private investigator I've hired to help us with our little 'witch hunter' problem."

"Now that you mention it, we've never actually discussed payment."

"We'll talk about that later, okay?"

"A private investigator? You employed a private investigator? How much does he know?"

"Not that much. Only that we're witches and that I was the victim of an attack."

"Witch matters should only be handled by other witches. We cannot trust outsiders. Do you know how difficult it is to trust cowans? Even when they seem trustworthy, they could betray you at a moment's notice. You of all people should know that, Abigail."

"I know, but I thought you learned that there are some cowans we can trust."

"Yes," Dahlia said with a sigh. "I know. But trust needs to be earned, and I'm not sure about this one."

"Nobody else is investigating this matter besides me, and I'm going to need some help. We can trust Petey. He's a good man, and very smart too."

"Peter," I muttered and was ultimately ignored.

"Yes, he seems like a genius and a total sweetheart." She began scanning me up and down. "Not bad. He looks kind of familiar. Is he the man from Marysville? This isn't just an elaborate excuse for a date?"

"Of course not. I'm not a kid anymore. I don't do those kinds of things."

"What about that time when we visited Kirkland?"

"Come on, Dahlia, that was five years ago."

"All right," I said, throwing my hands to my sides. "As fascinating as this conversation is, I'm afraid I'm going to have to interrupt. I think we've digressed just a tad. I may not be the health inspector, but I still have to know. What are these vials for? Perhaps poison for the apples?"

"Poison," Dahlia scoffed. "I see—because we're witches, we must be poisoning the apples."

"I didn't mean it that way. It was just the first thing that came to my head."

"Interesting how poison was the first thing that came into your head, though. Very interesting."

"Just answer the question, please. What are all these vials for?"

After bumping the bucket rather harshly against my knees and shoving the broom into my companion's chest, Dahlia said to us, "I figure you two are at fault for this mess. The least you can do is clean up. I'll answer your question as you work, all right?"

"Fine," I said, snatching the mop out of Dahlia's hand. "I'll help clean up, but you better answer me now."

"Okay, Mr. Tough Guy. I'm very intimidated." I glared as I roughly squeezed out the yarn and began brusquely mopping up the floor. "That liquid you are cleaning up—it's a potion designed to improve the flavor of apples and to increase their nutritional value. We have similar potions for all of the fruits and vegetables we sell here."

"Once applied, it's almost undetectable to the human eye," Abigail explained as she meekly swept up the glass of the vials. "The potion is also untraceable by even the most modern scientific equipment. Organic fruits and vegetables aren't really any different than any other types until you apply our potion. We're the real reason why the organic craze started in the first place."

"We had to do something to market our product and to explain why it was healthier for you," Dahlia explained. "The organic label was the best thing we could come up with. Of course, when other companies caught wind that they could charge more for fruits and vegetables by slapping on the organic label, things started to snowball. When a witch charges more for their product, it's to cover the cost of the potions. But for everyone else, it's greed, plain and simple. Then the government got involved and really started muddying the waters."

"Dahlia is the best potion-maker in all the land," Abigail said as she threw some glass away in a nearby recycling bin.

"Maybe not the best, but definitely one of the best. Thank you, Abigail."

Giddy as a child, Abigail set her broom down on the floor and grabbed one of the apples off a nearby table. Abigail, looking at Dahlia, pointed at the apple and then pointed at me, and continued to repeat this process in a pleading manner.

After a pause in which the curly brown-haired woman with lily white skin's temperament shifted from heated anger to almost serenity, Dahlia said, with a warm smile, "Are you sure you can part with one, Abigail? I know how much you love apples." After an eager nod from the girl, Dahlia continued, "Oh, why not?"

Abigail squealed in delight and then shoved the apple in my face. "Here," she said. "Try one."

"No thanks, I'm not hungry."

"Don't you like apples?"

"I used to. A friend of mine used to be crazy about them, come to think of it. I don't think I've had one in years."

She paused. "Come on, just a bite."

"All right," I said, shoving the mop back into the bucket and grabbing the apple. "Just a bite." I bit into the apple. "It tastes like any other apple as far as I remember them," I said, shrugging my shoulders. "Nothing special."

"Ah, but let me apply the potion." She gently took the apple from my hand and grabbed an unbroken vial from the crate on the floor. After pouring a red liquid on it, she handed it back.

"Now, take a bite."

After a short examination, noticing the apple seemed no different than before, I shrugged and took another bite.

"Wow, that was truly excellent," I said to my beaming companion after I was done eating. "I can honestly say I've never eaten such an appetizing apple."

"I told you it would be great. It's good for you too, better than any apple you'd find in the wild."

"And it's all because of that potion?"

"Yes indeed," Dahlia said with a large smile. "To be fair, though, the potion Abigail gave you is mostly saved for fellow witches. We normally make the food slightly more nutritious and slightly more flavorful than the usual fare, but not too much. We don't want to arouse suspicion by having our foods too good, after all. Abigail applied the good stuff."

"You really are a fantastic potion maker," I said. "This was probably the best apple I've ever eaten."

"Well, thank you."

After a quick pause, I said, "I already have a pentagram under my left armpit. Will I get another one after eating this apple, maybe on my right armpit?"

"You know about the pentagram?" Dahlia looked at Abigail with an accusing eye.

With a nervous giggle, Abigail responded, "I had to do a spell on him to convince him that witches were real."

Dahlia sighed. "I suppose it's all right that he knows. He already knows we're witches—he may as well know everything else. First, no, you can't get multiple pentagrams. A person can only be marked with one pentagram at a time. Second, potions work a little bit differently than spells. Pentagrams are not marked on a person's body when a potion is used."

"That's good," I said. "And it should disappear in a week, right?" After both Dahlia and Abigail confirmed this, I continued. "Still, had pentagrams appeared all over my body, it would have been worth it."

Practically glowing, Dahlia responded, "Maybe you aren't so

bad after all. What was your name again? I don't believe we've actually introduced ourselves."

"Peter," I said, extending my hand outwards. "Peter Cunningham."

"Nice to meet you, Peter," the woman said, shaking my hand. "I'm Dahlia Layton. I can clean the rest of this up later." Dahlia gently pushed the bucket and wringer away from me and grabbed the broom off the floor. "The two of you have done a good enough job for now. Well, an adequate job, at least." Dahlia opened a cabinet near the door and pulled out a couple of towels. "Here," she said, handing one to me and one to Abigail. "For your shoes."

"Thank you very much, Dahlia," Abigail said.

"What's on your mind, Peter?"

"I'm here because I wanted to talk to you about the two men who attacked Abigail about a week ago."

"Ah yes, those men," Dahlia said solemnly. "Abigail, must you continue with that nonsense?"

"Of course! Tradition is important! You used to feel the same way. What made you change your mind?"

"You were nearly killed!"

"Even before that, you were telling me you didn't want me to do the circle anymore."

"I did no such thing!" Dahlia protested. "I just told you to be careful that night, that's all. Is it wrong to tell you to be careful?"

"Why on that night in particular, though? You never seemed so worried before. And why did you tell Maxwell, Cassandra, and Joy not to come?"

"I just had a feeling something was going to happen, that's all."

"Why, though?" I asked. "Why that night in particular? It seems odd to me too."

After a moment of hesitation, Dahlia blurted out, "It's because of those men that always hang around the shop! Those two weird men. Remember those punks that were messing around the stand about a week or two ago, Abigail?"

"Who could forget those two weird looking but really well-dressed men? They harassed all the women that visited, tried to steal fruit, and were incredibly obnoxious."

"Were they the ones that attacked Abigail?" I asked. "Please, tell us more about them."

"I don't know," Dahlia explained. "They were incredibly suspicious acting, and would definitely be my first guess, but I cannot say definitively. I was able to get a glimpse of the men that attacked Abigail. Not much more than that, though. I was more concerned with freeing Abigail."

"Completely understandable. Still, anything at all would help us out immensely, even a general description."

"It's funny. They were wearing these long alabaster robes and hoods, something you might have seen a monk wear in the dark ages. I had hoped to see something from underneath as they ran, but unfortunately, I did not get a good look. They smelled awful, too, almost like a rotted skunk, but even that is putting it mildly."

"I thought that smell was the burlap sack," Abigail explained.

"It was them, trust me. I even took a quick whiff of the sack just to be sure."

"What about their shoes?" I asked, "Did you get a good look at their shoes? People often forget the importance of footwear."

The woman paused for a moment. "Now that you mention it, there was something odd about their shoes. They were really fancy, like dress shoes. They reminded me of something." There was a brief silence. "That's right," Dahlia said. "Those two men at the stand. They wore fancy shoes like that. I knew they were trouble. They must have overheard the two of us talking about the chanting circle. That's how they knew where you were."

"It's very likely," I said in response.

"Are we sure it's them, though, Petey?" Abigail asked. "It could all just be a coincidence."

"Petey?" Dahlia chuckled. "Would you prefer to be called Petey?"

"I can't get her to stop," I explained. "I think I'm just going to give up. To answer your question, Abigail, it's possible, but I think for now we should work off the assumption that the men that harassed Dahlia's customers and the men who attacked you are one and the same until we find evidence to the contrary."

"I just thought of something. Frank might know more about them," Dahlia said.

"Oh yeah," Abigail said. "Frank did seem to know who they were."

"Frank? Who's Frank?"

"Frank Cannelli," Dahlia explained. "He's my security guard. He should be back tomorrow morning."

"Sounds good to me," I said. "Hopefully, we can find out more tomorrow. Thank you very much, Dahlia. Sorry about the crates. I'll give you my card. You can bill me at my office."

"Thank you very much, Peter," Dahlia said, taking the card from my hand. "I might have misjudged you a bit. I'm sorry I couldn't help you more."

"You did plenty, and you might have given us a lead. Thank you for that. I guess we'll see you and Frank in the morning."

"Absolutely. And once again, it was good meeting you, Peter. And Abigail, next time, call me before you bring over a strange man, okay? Though it happens so often, I suppose I should expect it."

"Don't hate me just because I'm beautiful." Abigail smiled as she hopped to the ground. "It was good seeing you, Dahlia. I'm guessing we won't see Maxwell, Cassandra, or Joy at the next circle?"

"I'm afraid not, Abigail," Dahlia said solemnly. "They just don't feel safe there, and honestly, I feel the same way. I'll be there, though. Someone has to watch over you." Dahlia then smiled. "Abigail, I'm glad you are all right. I just worry about you, that's all."

"I know, Dahlia. Thank you." The two exchanged a hug.

"Dahlia takes everything that happens to me personally," Abigail said as I drove her back to my office's parking lot so she could retrieve her car. "She's the kind of woman who thinks she can always keep me safe no matter what and takes everything personally. She's like my cool big sister, which I suppose is fitting because she is family."

"The two of you are related?"

"Yep, she's my cousin. I think of her daughter Cassandra as if she were my niece, even if it isn't technically true."

"Oh, so she has a daughter?"

"Just call me Auntie Abigail. Maxwell is Cassandra's husband, and Joy is their daughter. Wait, I never thought about it before, but I suppose that makes me a grand aunt too. Grand aunt. That makes me sound old. I'm not sure how I feel about that."

"Wait a second. If Cassandra has a daughter named Joy, doesn't that mean Dahlia is a grandmother?"

"That's usually what that means, yeah."

"Dahlia barely looks old enough to have an adult daughter, nevertheless a granddaughter."

"She got pregnant at eighteen during her senior year of high school. The daddy disappeared shortly after. Even though Dahlia had to drop out of school for her daughter, her parents were surprisingly supportive after their initial anger cooled down. Unfortunately, they died when she was only twenty-four. Joy was six at the time."

"What happened?"

"A freak boating accident killed them both."

I whistled in response. "God, when it rains, it pours. How awful for the poor woman."

"That's actually about the time I really got to know Dahlia. I knew of her, of course. We just never really talked to each other outside of a few words at a family reunion. My parents offered to help her. Dahlia appreciated the assistance but was driven to make her stay as short as possible, so she no longer had to rely on others to help take care of her daughter. I got to know her very well during that time, and our friendship has blossomed ever since."

"How old were you when you met Dahlia?"

"I was about thirteen or fourteen. God, I just thought of

something. That means we've known each other for almost eighteen years. Time really does fly."

"How about Frank? Have you known him for a while?"

"Only about a year. Sweet old man, though, with a sharp memory even in his advancing age. He, too, is a witch."

"A witch as a security guard. It's nothing that I'd have ever imagined."

"It's not that strange. Witches make incredible security guards."

"Why's that?"

"Witches have the innate ability to sense people around them. We can feel people's presence in the next room, two rooms down, through cement, and so on. No one breaks into an office, warehouse, etc. where there are witch security guards."

"I didn't realize witches could sense people."

"Not every witch can, and it is a skill that needs to be learned and enhanced. A witch really needs to be concentrating on it for it to be the most effective, but it is not an uncommon skill by any stretch of the imagination."

"Do you have this ability?"

"Of course. As loathe as I am to brag, my skills in that sort of extra-sensory perception always achieved top marks in class."

"Is that right?"

"Is that really so difficult for you to believe?"

"No, but tell me—why weren't you able to sense the two men that attacked you?"

Abigail took a long drag of the cigarette she had lit on the way back to my office in spite of my protests. "That's an excellent question. I hadn't thought of that. I did sense something about a step or two before one of the boys literally threw the sack over my head."

"A step or two behind you before you sensed them? Maybe I'm a witch because even I can do that."

"Yes, your sarcasm is always very much appreciated. Regardless, in my consternation over the transpiring events, I hadn't even had time to think about why I didn't sense the young men that ambushed me. Typically I can sense people even when I'm not fully concentrating, but I had no idea they were there. I must have been so frustrated with Dicana that I lost complete awareness of my surroundings."

"Or maybe you're losing your touch."

As we approached a pizza place, she told me to stop, then said, "There are two people in the top right corner, a person sitting by himself near the left middle table, three people in the bottom right corner, a greeter near the entrance, three people in the kitchen, three at the bar, and two people playing pool. That's a total of fifteen people. Now, go in and count them."

The woman practically pushed me inside before I could react. The young greeter there asked from her podium, "Table for one?"

"Actually, I'm just looking to see if a friend is here," I lied.

"Oh, okay. Let me know if I can help you with anything."

I took a look in the room to the right. I counted six. I looked towards the left side of the establishment, where the bar and pool table were. Every person was located as she described. I didn't bother looking in the kitchen. I was already convinced.

"Amazing," I said as I exited the restaurant. "Either you have incredible luck, or you really can sense people around you. You witches are becoming more and more impressive the more I learn about you."

"Thank you, that is very kind of you to say," Abigail said as we headed back to her car. "It feels very good to hear you compliment us rather than lambaste our traditions."

"Yeah, sorry about that," I said as I started the car once again and continued towards the parking garage. "I'll try to keep a more open mind in the future."

"Thank you."

"Still, it leaves us with a mystery—why you weren't able to sense those men."

"Perhaps that is something else we could talk about with Frank in the morning."

"Wait, we? You're tagging along?"

"Of course. Do you not want me to?"

"Most clients don't follow me around. Didn't you hire me to do all the legwork?"

"Not completely. I've pictured our relationship to be more of a partnership. I've hired you to help me with this case rather than solve it on your own. You don't mind, do you, Petey?"

"It's Pete— Actually, you know what? Forget it, I give up. It's a bit unusual," I said as I parked in the garage. "But it sounds like a plan. It'd be nice to have some company, at least. It'll remind me of my days on the force. Still, I'm worried about whether things might get too dangerous for you. These cases can get pretty rough."

"I understand the risks. Besides, I can hold my own. I'm hardly a helpless damsel in distress. I have a few tricks up my sleeve."

"Shall we meet at the produce place in the morning?"

"I don't particularly like to drive. How about I meet you at your office first so we can carpool?"

"Okay. I'll be at my office around seven. I checked the schedule, and your friend's store doesn't open until eight, so you can meet me there at that time."

"Perfect, I will meet you then. It was good seeing you, Petey. I will see you tomorrow."

"It was good meeting you too, Abigail. I'll see you later."

In the rearview mirror, I watched her get into her black, two-door hatch-back coupe that I recognized to be an electric car.

On the way home, I thought about my new companion. There was something about Abigail that intrigued me and endeared me to her. I could not help but think about how silly she was, smiling at her friend and pointing to and from the apple when she wanted to ask her friend to offer it to me. Still, these thoughts were mostly drowned by other thoughts, such as I finally had a potential lead on a case that had been vexing me for almost two decades. For the first time in a long time, I had hope.

CHAPTER 4

"Ah yes, I know them two boys," the wizened, gray-haired security guard whistled through his crooked gapped teeth, stroking his thin, patchy gray and white beard as we talked on a bright cool February morning. "Tommy Stim and Chuck Ericson. Tommy is the tall one, muscular, brown hair, and has a mustache. Chuck is the smaller, skinnier one with auburn hair, and always wears blue jeans. Anyway, my son Dave went to school with them. Do you really think them two boys are the ones that attacked Abigail?"

"We're not sure about that," I admitted to the old man. "Dahlia didn't get a great look, but it appeared that Abigail's attackers had the same taste in shoes. There's, at the very least, a strong correlation between the two events."

"I'm not following," the old man said to me.

"He means that there's a good chance the men who attacked me are Tommy and Chuck," Abigail clarified.

"Ah, I see," Frank said. "Why didn't you just say that?"

"I apologize. Tell me, Frank. Does a brazen assault such as the one they engaged in with Abigail seem consistent with the psychological tendencies of our two suspects?"

"Huh?"

"Do they seem like the type who'd attack me?" Abigail once again clarified.

Why do I have a tendency to do this with people who cannot understand my somewhat expanded vocabulary?

"Why didn't he just say that, then? Well, it's hard to say really. Them two boys was always getting into trouble. Mostly for things like missing class, that sort of thing. They was basically dropouts before they were dropouts if you know what I mean. The two of them are definitely a couple of jerks. Davey would tell me stories 'bout how they used to go around and pick on the weird kids, 'specially the weird girls."

"What did he mean by weird?" I asked.

Rubbing his chin, the man responded, "Not sure, to be honest. Davey would say the kids who looked like they shopped at Hot Topic or Zooms, I think the name was."

"Zumiez?" Abigail asked.

"I guess that was the name, yeah. Not sure what Davey meant by that, but safe to say the two of them were a right couple of bullies. Tommy seems like he'd be an all right guy if he wasn't friends with Chuck. Chuck is a bad influence on him, and definitely the leader of the pair. Tommy ain't too bright, either. Chuck knows this, so that's why he hangs out with Tommy—he's easy to control. For Tommy, better than being alone, I suppose. Neither seems like the type to try and murder someone, though."

"You did have to chase them off for bothering women. That is to say—"

The old man cut me off with a cackle. "I know what you meant. You think I'm some sort of idiot?"

"Anyway," I said, glowering. "They were bothering the patrons of this establishment, right?"

"Now there you go again with your fancy talk," he laughed as he continued. "Yeah, they was. But you know, talking about how big your unmentionables are and implying how much the woman would enjoy doing the deed with you and swipin' a couple of apples isn't exactly the same as tryin' to kill someone. Although…." The man's voice drifted as he looked lost in thought.

"Yes?" I asked impatiently.

"I just remembered something. Them two were arrested recently."

"Really? Do you know what for?"

"Not quite sure. I think it was stealing something from one of those fancy stores that sell those fancy clothes at the mall. 'Least that's what I've heard, anyway."

"How long ago?"

"Oh, I'm not too sure. Six months ago? A year? Of course, not sure if the rumor is even true. Just what Davey told me. Wasn't quite sure himself."

"It's something to go on, at least. Just one more thing," I said as if I were Columbo. "Were either of them rich?"

"Oh, Lord, no! Them two boys were so poor they made me look like JP Rockerfeller."

"Yet they wore expensive clothes and shoes."

"Yeah, it was the darndest thing."

"Any idea where they got that money?"

"I did overhear them talking about some group giving them some cash so they'd look good. Don't know who they was talking about. Maybe it was a gang or something."

"Hard to say, but it is definitely something to look into. Abigail, I've been dominating the conversation so far. Did you have any questions you'd like to ask Frank?"

"Just one," the woman said, her arms moving from the crossed position over her striped purple and white shirt. "Frank, has somebody ever snuck up on you without you being able to sense that they were around?"

"Not that I can recall. Never had trouble like that. I can tell you that there are eight people in this very shop right now. Why?"

"I've had trouble with it recently, so I just wondered if you've ever experienced the same phenomena. Anyway, whatever it was, my abilities seem to have returned. I've been through a lot recently, so maybe I'm just imagining things."

"Okay," I said, putting my notebook away in the right pocket of my brown vest. "I think that covers everything. Thank you very much for your time and for answering our questions."

"It was so good to see you," Abigail then said as she hugged the old gentleman. "I'll see you at the next gathering, yes?"

"I wouldn't miss it for the world. And Abigail, be careful out there."

Abigail smiled. "Don't worry. My knight in shining armor is

here to protect me."

I returned the smile. "I don't think that's part of the deal."

"Where do we go from here?" Abigail asked as we reached my vehicle.

"To the Tacoma Police Station to see my old friend Ed," I said, as I unlocked the car door, and we entered the car. "He's one of the few friends I have left at the station. Since the boys have an arrest record, it's possible we can find more information on the two."

"A private investigator is different than an officer. Will you be able to get that sort of information?"

"Normally, you'd have to make a formal request and have to have a specific reason, such as a background check for a firearm. Even then, there are some restrictions. If I'm a firearms dealer and I'm not trying to sell someone a gun, for example, then I'm not allowed to access that information. Plus, you'd need that person's consent to get that information. Of course, for things like employment, not giving consent is a huge red flag, but it is something that even a corporation would need before getting such a record."

"I highly doubt either of those two would be willing to give us consent." Abigail pulled out a cigarette. Displeased, I opened the passenger side window but said nothing. "Maybe if we asked them nicely enough," Abigail continued.

"Don't worry, Ed and I have a system. He knows how to give me information without actually handing it over to me." I gave her a broad smile and a wink.

Abigail looked at me, perplexed, saying nothing. We eventually arrived at the police station.

"Peter!" the rotund man with receding brown hair and a somber yet gentle face said as he stood up to greet us warmly after we walked up the white steps through the glass door under the sign that had the word "Police" written in dark blue. In spite of the rustic smell and white brick slowly changing to a grungy yellow, there was a bit of a comfort to be found in these old walls. It once had been my second home, after all.

"Ed!" I said, grabbing the extended hand of the jovial desk sergeant of the Tacoma Police Department. "It is so good to see you, my friend."

"It's been a while since I've seen ya," Ed said, shaking my hand vigorously. "I was beginnin' to forget yer face."

"What are you talking about, Ed? Didn't I play poker with you and the boys recently?"

"Peter, that was six months ago," Ed chastised. "And ya only stayed fer an hour."

"I was losing all of my money. I had to quit before you left me in the poor house."

"If ya say so," Ed said. His eyes darted behind me to my companion. "Say, Peter, who's this beautiful young lady?"

"Oh right, how rude of me. Ed, this is Abigail Mitchell, my current client. Abigail, this is my good friend Ed Bergeron."

"Ah, I was hopin' for a second it was someone a bit more special in your life, Peter," Ed said as he shook Abigail's hand. "It is a pleasure to meet you, Abigail."

"Nice to meet you as well, Ed."

"What can I do for you two? Is this a social visit, or do ya have somethin' ya need from old Ed?"

"I'm afraid this is a professional visit, Ed." I pulled out my notebook from my vest and took a look at my notes. "I need to know if you have any information on Tommy Stim and Chuck Ericson. I've heard a rumor that they were arrested recently for shoplifting. Is this true?"

"Ya know, I'd love ta give ya that information, but ya know better than anyone else I can't just give it to ya. Yer going to have ta submit a formal request like everyone else, and yer going to need a good reason. Out of curiosity, what's yer reason?"

"Abigail's been the victim of a recent attack," I explained. "They may have literally tried to burn her at the stake."

"What?" Ed said, leaning back a bit in his seat, dumbfounded. "Really?"

"Yes," Abigail said. "Despite my relative composure, I have to admit it was quite the harrowing experience." Abigail then relayed her story to Ed before concluding. "So, as you can see, we really want to get to the bottom of this case."

"I understand," Ed said, shaking his head and exhaling deeply. "That's quite a story you've told me. Let's put that down in a report."

Abigail turned an even paler white and waved her arms as if she were signaling a missed field goal while mouthing the word "no" to me.

"I'm afraid we can't actually submit a report due to certain reasons that are really too difficult for us to explain at the moment, Ed," I said. "Her family really doesn't trust the police, and she would get in serious trouble if word leaked that she went to them for assistance."

"We really should make a report. I mean, you know the police can be trusted, don't ya, Peter?"

"I'm sorry. It's just something that can't be done."

Ed shrugged. "I suppose I can't force ya to do so. I suppose a family problem's a family problem. Still, I'm afraid I can't just give ya the information. A hunch isn't a good enough reason to give ya information, even if ya do go through the proper channels."

"It's slightly more than a hunch. Come on, Ed. We have history together. We've known each other since I was a pup on the force. Sure, I'm no longer with the force, but I'm still a detective, in my heart and in my soul. Can't you just bend the rules a little bit for me?"

Ed rose from his seat and shouted in a deep baritone. "Ya always do this. All ya ever want from me is information! That's the only reason ya ever come ta me! Yer no longer an officer, yer just going to have to submit a request like everyone else!"

Abigail physically moved backward during this verbal assault.

"So even after all this time, you still won't do a favor for a friend."

"Some friend. All ya ever do is take—ya never give, you know that? True friendship is 'bout a give and take, and all ya do is take, take, take. I'm just doing my job. Some of us still know what it means to serve and protect."

"I'm sure you know all about serving and protecting from behind this little desk of yours."

Ed pointed at the door. "Get the hell outta here! Ya can't say shit like that ta me!"

"I have every right to be here! I'm a tax paying citizen! I've committed no crime! I'm staying here!"

"Stay here then, but I've got work ta do! Unlike you did, I take my job very seriously, and I do a good job — unlike you, 'Columbo.'"

Ed slammed his hands against his mahogany desk as he turned around and headed towards a filing cabinet. I leaned back on it and smiled broadly at Abigail, who seemed aghast over what had just transpired.

"Um, Petey," the woman said meekly, gently placing her thin fingers on the white sleeve of my dress shirt. "Maybe we should leave."

"Don't worry," I whispered with a wink. "This is all part of the ritual."

"Ritual?"

Abigail's eyes looked over to my right, and I reacted with a hop when I heard the slam of folders against the desk. After regaining my composure, I turned and stared at Ed.

"You can stand there glaring at me all day if ya want," the man said as he angrily turned the pages in the folder just out of my sight. "But I still won't give ya anythin'."

"I'm just standing here. I won't bother you while you work."

"Good, because I've got things ta look up for a real officer, not a deadbeat like you."

I stared daggers at the man as he leafed through some papers in the folder. While doing this, I noticed Abigail hesitantly moving towards one of the benches, where she sat down.

A few officers passed us, and even though a couple did look at us askance, they did not say a word. As Ed leafed through the folders, I noticed him take out something from one folder and move it to another one he had previously been observing. After he did this, he rose from his seat.

"My coffee's gone cold," Ed announced, piercing the uneasy calm. "I'm going to get a new cup. I'll be back in a moment. Don't touch anything. Or better yet, just leave."

"I'd still prefer to stay," I said, turning around and leaning backward on his desk once again. "Don't worry, I won't touch anything."

Ed mumbled incoherently as he left his desk to go to an adjacent room. I saw him with his back completely towards me as he began to brew a cup of coffee.

"Abigail," I said. "Please, come here for a moment." She just stared. "I know this looks weird and I seem irrational, but I'll explain it to you in a moment. Please trust me." Abigail slowly rose and walked towards me as if there were large weights attached at her ankles. When she arrived by my side, I whispered to her, "Witches can sense people, yes?"

"Yes, why?"

"Normally I'd have to do some scouting and Ed would have to make several 'coffee breaks' before I can find the information I need, but I think with your help I can do this much more efficiently. Is anyone nearby?"

"There's a couple above us, and a few are in rooms down the hall, but they seem to be sitting down. They aren't moving right now."

"Great, that means we have some time. Could you do me one more thing? Act as if you're talking to me."

The woman complied and stood to my right. She spoke in a harsh tone. "I really wish you'd tell me what's going on. I am so confused right now."

"It'll make sense in a second. For now, just say something, anything."

I leaned further back as I halfheartedly listened to Abigail. She mostly seemed to be talking about her confusion, but my concentration had completely shifted.

Moving slightly, I used my peripheral vision to get a good look at the contents of the folders Ed had conveniently left open on his desk for me—the case reports of Tommy Stim and Chuck Ericson. I had to look at them without arousing suspicion, and out of view of the cameras that were perched in front of the desk.

"The two of them live at the same apartment complex near the Tacoma Dome," I muttered to myself. "Ocean's Terrace on Pacific Avenue, Apartments 25 and 28. Arrested several times. Mostly nickel and dime stuff. Underage drinking, drunk and disorderly, public nudity, vandalism, public urination, and various parking violations. They were caught shoplifting at The Suave Gentleman, the designer clothing shop in the mall. It's a new place, but very popular. A clerk caught them stealing— but the store owner let them go? He believes the two are well-meaning young men with great potential? A couple of ex-school bully dropouts who get naked after drinking. I can definitely see the potential there."

"Petey!" Abigail shouted in a panicked whisper. "Ed's done making his coffee, and somebody is heading this way right now!"

I whispered back, "I think I got everything I need."

A female officer entered the room from the west just as Ed returned to his seat.

"All right!" I shouted. "I've been here long enough! It's obvious you're not taking me seriously!"

"Already?" Ed asked earnestly, breaking character, before suddenly regaining his composure. "'Bout time! Don't let the door hit ya on the way out!"

"Come on, Abigail, let's get out of here," I announced. I took two steps towards the door with Abigail just behind me when I felt a sudden tap on my right shoulder. I turned around.

"By the way," Ed whispered. "Poker game this Thursday if you're interested. A couple of new recruits are going, along with my friend Vince. He's a P.I. like you. I think the two of ya would get along."

"Sounds good, I'll try to make it. Depends on how this case goes. I'm not actually 'Columbo,' after all," I said with a smile.

"Hey, ya said I didn't do any real work," he said, smiling back. "May be true, but it still hurt."

"You know I didn't mean it."

"I know, Peter. You take care now."

Ed gave me a quick pat on the shoulder, and I responded with a nod and a smile. Abigail simply stared, mouth agape. Smirking, I motioned for her to follow me as we left the station.

"A very clever ruse," Abigail said, consuming yet another cigarette as I drove towards the village apartment complex. "But next time give a girl a head's up before doing something like that."

"I did tell you that Ed would find a way to give me that information. It was actually my idea. I came up with it after a poker game, but we both got our roles down to perfection. People are utterly baffled that we're still friends considering how often we 'fight.'"

"I'd appreciate it if you were a bit more specific as to what exactly your crazy plans entail."

"I suppose that's your way of asking where we're headed and why we're headed there, is that right?"

"Not exactly, but it would be appreciated."

"We're headed to Tommy and Chuck's place, an infamous apartment complex known as Ocean's Terrace. Kelly and I made more arrests there than anywhere else. The plan is to break into one of their apartments and see if we can conjure up any clues while there." I smirked when I said conjure, even though I probably used the word incorrectly. I looked at Abigail to see if she noticed.

She took a long hard puff of her cigarette and said calmly, "And you used to be a police officer."

I became slightly perturbed. "When I was with the force, I had access to a lot more information than I have now. If there was a legal avenue for me to get that information, I'd take it. But if I've learned one thing about being a private investigator, it's that sometimes you have to bend the law a bit to catch a break. Do you really think I was always above board when I was spying on cheating husbands?"

Abigail glanced at me and back out the window. "I'm sorry.

I shouldn't be so judgmental. I was just surprised. It seemed like you were an exemplary officer, so it was a little surprising to hear you talking about breaking into a person's home so casually."

"I learned long ago that you have to make your own breaks. These guys may have tried to murder you. There is no need to feel sorry for them."

"Don't worry. If they're the ones, sympathy is the last thing they'll get from me."

We eventually arrived at Ocean's Terrace. It was a drab, wooden, two-story charcoal complex with bright canary yellow doors. The second floor was supported by long wood pillars, and the jet black guard rails were the second floor's only distinguishable feature from the first floor. The paint was already beginning to peel, and the entire complex had an atmosphere of neglect. It was the infamous home of near vagrants, petty criminals, and drifters alike. No questions asked as long as you paid on time. The perfect home for our two suspects.

As it was a workday in broad daylight, there wasn't a lot of activity taking place around the apartment complex. The nefarious dealings usually occurred at night.

"Tommy lives in room twenty-five, and Chuck lives in room twenty-eight," I said as I closed the door of my vehicle. "Both of them probably live on the second floor."

Abigail asked, "Which room should we break into first, then?"

"Room twenty-eight. From what Frank said, and the rap sheet, it appears that Chuck was the 'mastermind' of all the pair's misdoings."

"What are we looking for exactly?"

"Any support for their being involved or anything incriminating—hell, even just some more information at this point. Chuck and Tommy may be our guys, but we have no proof yet."

"Are you just going to barge in there?" Abigail asked. "What if either Tommy or Chuck are home?"

"I thought about that. Most of the time, this would take at

least a few days, if not a few weeks. I'd need to stake out the place, get a feel for the suspect's routine, and make absolutely sure the place is really empty. Can't take a chance of running into a relative, friend, or big dog after ascertaining the suspect is absent. Doing this stupidly is a good way to get arrested or killed."

"And why don't you have to do that now?"

I winked. "I have you as my secret weapon. You can tell me if a room is empty or if someone's there."

"Ah, good thinking. That's actually clear thinking, Petey."

We walked to Room 28. Abigail closed her eyes and extended her hand. After a second or two, she said, "Nobody's in there."

"Great! Allow me to pick the lock." I reached into my vest pocket.

"No need. You forget who's with you."

"Witches can pick locks?"

"Not witches in general, just the more skillful ones. I am one of the few who has this ability, and admittedly it's not quite lock picking. It's more of a short distance telekinesis of sorts, for lack of a better phrase."

I leaned forward in anticipation. "Amazing! You have to show me."

"Of course," Abigail said, covering her mouth as she giggled. "I must admit your enthusiasm is unexpected." I watched as she covered the cylinder and the keyhole with her left hand and pulled out her keys with her right.

"To make it look like I'm opening the door with a key," Abigail explained. "In case anybody passes us as we are breaking in."

"Clever girl."

"Your movie references are an infinite source of enjoyment," the woman sighed.

Abigail closed her eyes, and from her lips came a small murmur. My ear was practically against the door. After a few seconds that felt like minutes, I heard the distinctive sound of a twisting lock.

"Voilà," Abigail said smugly as she threw open the door. "We're in."

"Amazing, Abigail! How did you do it?"

"A magician never reveals her trick," she said with a wink. "Seriously, though, we're lucky this wasn't an electric lock."

"What do you mean?"

"Some witches, like me, are able to use a form of telekinesis at a very short range to control objects. Levitation is essentially the same spell. It was originally designed for self-defense and was used mostly to incapacitate the limbs of an attacker. If you tried to grab me, I'd be able to snap your wrist backward to stop you, assuming I reacted quickly enough." Abigail mimed snapping her hands back to emphasize her point.

"Sounds pretty powerful."

"It is, and specialists can perform the spell at a great distance, which makes it much more useful than it is normally. It does have its limitations, though. Not every witch can do it, and most can only perform the basic version where the attacker has to be pretty close for it to work properly. Even I can't do the spell at a very long range. A lot of witches don't even bother trying to learn it, and frankly, I can't blame them."

"Telekinesis to open a bolt lock. That's amazing, Abigail. Have you been practicing that spell for a while?"

"Honestly, that was the first time I tried something like that. I just assumed it would work."

The sunlight shone through a crack in the blinds of a merely translucent window as we entered the room. It was somewhat dark, but there was still enough illumination that we didn't need to turn on a lamp. The living room was framed by blue-green walls with a large, flat screen television attached to the immediate right of the entryway. A video game console was lying below and connected to the set, and sitting next to it was a large collection of games.

In front of the flat screen was a beat up couch with holes in the vinyl covering such that the yellow foam was visible through the cracks. Next to it was another cheap chair, with vinyl still intact, though lying directly on the floor as it had no legs.

Directly in front of the entranceway, there was an opening in the wall allowing visibility to the kitchen. To the left, down the hallway, was the entryway into the kitchen, and even further down lay the bathroom.

The room was putrid. Abigail pulled the bottom of her shirt over her nose and mouth while I simply used my hand in a vain effort to hide from the smell. "Even for a young man's apartment, this place has a pretty overpowering odor, wouldn't you agree, Petey?"

"Quite a fancy way of saying this place reeks."

Magazines were spread all over the place, as were clothes, including various undergarments of both genders. The less said about the trash, the better. Bills were piled up on the one table in the kitchen. All of them were either marked, "Final Notice" or "Past Due" in bright red letters.

Some of the clothing, as well as the shoes in the entranceway, contrasted with the poor furnishings. The names on the labels were instantly recognizable even to a layman like me. You'd typically see these garments worn by athletes and musicians, not a high school dropout that seemed otherwise to be struggling to make ends meet.

These others were overshadowed by the most distinctive items. Various branches and other strange, plant-like substances, as well as jars of dried mud whose origins appeared to be that of a swamp, were spread throughout.

"I can honestly say that this place, perhaps oxymoronically, is both exactly as I imagined yet at the same completely contrary to what I had anticipated," Abigail said in bewilderment.

"This seems familiar," I muttered. As I began my search around the room, my hand brushed against the couch, making my hand feel sticky. "Sap," I said to my companion as I bent down to get a closer look at the couch, my initial fears of what I may have touched abated. "This couch is covered with it. Must have come from the branches."

Abigail looked over my shoulder at the couch and then began

walking a bit throughout the room. "I think these are ximuce tree branches."

"The ones only found in Evergreen that Tony wants to preserve."

"What would they be doing with these trees? Perhaps they were gathering wood to burn me at the stake, but why take it to the apartment? Also, why ximuce?"

"I have no idea. The muddy jars are puzzling as well." I got up and rubbed my chin as I walked towards the kitchen, my eyes darting between the tree branches and the jars. "Something about this scene seems so familiar to me as well."

The memory hit me with the strength of a colliding truck. I stopped in my tracks at the entrance of the kitchen, unaware that Abigail was right behind me.

"Oof!" she exclaimed as she nearly tripped over me.

"Ow!" I regained my balance before I fell on my face.

"Sorry about that. Why did you stop?"

"Cullen Jones," I said as I turned and faced the woman.

"You stopped because of Cullen Jones?"

"Remember the man who Kelly and I busted during my last case as an officer?"

"Vaguely."

"His apartment was also full of tree branches and swamp water. God, I can't believe I forgot."

"It was several years ago."

"I shouldn't forget a detail like that." A nervous excitement overtook me. "This is big. I'm not crazy. Cullen, these two men, they must be connected. This apartment proves that."

"It really is starting to look that way, and it all but confirms that these guys are the ones who attacked me."

"The correlation is strong, but unfortunately not definite yet. We need to find stronger evidence."

As Abigail searched the bedroom, I pulled off one of the twigs of a tree branch lying next to the couch. Using that twig, I shifted through the magazines lying on the floor. The pile contained mostly pornographic magazines, but there were a few related to video games and men's fashion. I suppose I shouldn't have expected to find the *Economist* or *Popular Science* among these periodicals.

"Hey Abigail, this is kind of weird," I said as I moved aside a video game magazine and looked at a picture I had uncovered underneath it.

"What is it?

"It's a picture of Tony O'Stein. It looks like a stock photograph of sorts, one that you'd find at one of his televangelist shoots or fan outings, something like that."

"I didn't really picture Chuck as being a big fan of a televangelist."

"Exactly. Then again, Tony is getting pretty popular these days. This guy even got Tony to sign the damn thing and write him a little message. 'To our two newest members, I personally welcome you. I am sure you will not fail to do us proud. Learn, grow, and help us all serve our higher purpose. Never forgot how important our mission is to the world. Anthony O'Stein.' Not exactly 'To my number one fan.'"

"That's a very strange message indeed. 'Never forget how important our mission is to the world.' What does that mean?"

"No idea. Probably something related to one of his lectures. I think I'll listen to a couple of them after we're done here to see if I discover any more information."

I continued rummaging through the magazines until I reached the bottom. Buried at the bottom was a thick, leather-bound book with the words *Malleus Maleficarum* emblazoned on the cover. The book was in pristine condition. This, combined with the feel of the pages, along with the text being written in Italian, were dead giveaways that this manuscript had never been read.

Abigail returned excitedly from the bedroom into the kitchen. "I think I've found evidence that these are the men we are looking for."

"How's that?" I asked.

"Follow me," she instructed, and I did so as she led me to

the bedroom closet. Abigail moved aside some designer clothing to reveal, tucked in the back, a couple of alabaster colored robes with hoods.

"These are the robes that Dahlia described, right?" Abigail said with a half-smile.

"That all but confirms that these are the men who attacked you." I pulled out my phone.

"Making a phone call?" Abigail joked.

"I'm going to take a picture of these robes and show them to Dahlia just to confirm."

"Good idea. Don't you also find it odd that the closet is full of designer clothing?"

"I thought maybe he only owned a couple of pairs of really nice clothes for job interviews, but it turns out he has quite a selection to choose from. I have no idea where he gets the money."

"Were you able to find anything else?"

Before answering, I went back to the living room while Abigail went on to look in the kitchen.

"One thing, take a look at this." I handed the book to Abigail through the kitchen window. "What's a high school dropout doing with a thing like this?"

"Oh my God," Abigail said as she gazed at the cover. "The *Malleus Maleficarum*. The Hammer of Witches."

"Hammer of Witches? Are you familiar with this book?"

"It's kind of a thing of legend among witches, or at least it is amongst the members of my coven. It's a manuscript that vilifies witches, as well as a guide on how to torture them in order to gain a confession for the crime of witchcraft. It was written by a pair of German monks in the 15th or 16th century, I believe, at the behest of one of the popes. You know the legend that witches have sex with Satan in order to enter a pact with him? It may not have originated from this text, but it sure was propagated widely because of it. It was often used to justify witch hunts and massacres."

"Why would he have something like this?"

"It's odd that it's in Italian. There are English translations. I know because I actually read it once. Like the old adage says, one must know thy enemy. So why would it be in Italian?"

I thought for a moment. "Now this is purely speculation, but a couple of ideas do spring to mind. Perhaps it's symbolic. Chuck hates witches, and this is a manual justifying that hatred, so that may be enough."

"Maybe, but how would he even know such a manuscript exists? I wouldn't say that this is common knowledge. True, this is all information you could read online, but be honest, have you ever heard of this thing?"

"I can't say I have."

"And why would you have? It's not something typically taught in schools, at least not in this country. If you haven't heard of it, what are the odds that someone like Chuck has?"

"That is why this leads me to believe it was given to him. But by whom? A sympathizer who also hates witches?" I shrugged. "If that's true, I'd really like to know how that conversation went."

"Perhaps it was a Christmas gift?" Abigail joked.

"Maybe a well-meaning aunt who knew he hated witches and gave him an Italian version by mistake." I paused and looked up at the ceiling. "My mind works in odd ways, I must admit, but there is something about the police report I read that bothered me. He and Tommy were busted for trying to lift designer clothing from the Nice Garb Express. The proprietor let them go. He said the two men had great potential. I didn't know what he meant by that. Now again, this is pure speculation, but I wonder if the owner is in some way connected with these two. He may even have given him the book."

Abigail shook her head. "I don't know. It seems like a bit of a stretch to me."

"It would explain the fancy clothing you found."

"How?"

"Payment. He may be paying Tommy and Chuck to do his dirty work. Maybe the owner is the one with the grudge against witches. That's my working theory, though I will be the first one to admit I'm currently only working off circumstantial evidence."

"It's not a bad one, Petey. I'm almost convinced. It's just...."
The woman paused and stuck her hand out as her eyes began to
shift towards the door. "Wait, I think I'm sensing something."

"What?"

"Shush, Petey," Abigail whispered harshly. "I believe two
men have just entered the parking lot. They are approaching this
stairway."

"Chuck and Tommy?" I whispered back.

"I'm not sure, but I know they are headed this way."

Just as she said those words, I heard a gruff shout near the
stairwell. "You never listen to me, Chuck, you never listen to
me!"

"I think that just about confirms it," I whispered to Abigail.

"We need to hide!" Abigail whispered, in a near panic.

"Don't you have an invisibility spell or something?"

"Don't be ridiculous, such a thing doesn't exist! Why would
you suggest something like that?"

"Okay, okay. Well, we can't leave, they'd catch us!"

"I know! I know! Where can we hide?"

"The closet. He's not likely to change if his friend is here."

Abigail nodded, and we moved quickly to the closet, pushing
aside a few pants and shirts in order to squeeze inside. It was a
pretty tight fit. Sheer panic mitigated any initial embarrassment,
but we soon realized that the two of us were positioned quite
awkwardly. My pelvis rested against the woman's stomach, and
my legs were placed over and around hers. Her chest was close to
mine, and her hands and arms were extended past my shoulders.
Abigail's face began to glow crimson.

I flashed Abigail a quick smile to try and alleviate her
embarrassment, then placed a hand on the gun I hid under my
vest. A look of horror flashed across the woman's face. "Just in
case," I whispered reassuringly. "I'm not planning on using it,
only if forced."

"It's not that," Abigail said. "Did we remember to relock the
door?"

"Oh shit," I muttered, but the men were already at the door before I had any time to react.

"Why don't you ever listen to me?" the gruff voice said from just outside the door. "We're screwed, dude! We need to get out of here!"

"We're going to be fine, dumbass," a nasally voice said in response. "What do you think they are going do to us anyway?"

"I overheard a couple of the older men talking. They said that the coin means death, that we're a sacrifice! Death, man!"

"They said that just to scare you. If it really meant death, why did they send us on another mission?"

"But they didn't even give us the stuff, Chuck. We had to make it ourselves!"

"So they forgot to give it to us, so what? It could mean anything. We were able to make it ourselves anyway. We're lucky that Commander Keith is so lax in protecting the formula."

I heard the sound of a key entering the lock and turning, but the tumbler didn't move. We both held our breath in nervous anticipation.

"Do you know why I treat you like an idiot?" the nasally voice man said as he threw the door open. "Because you forget to do things like lock the door. I asked you to lock the door, and you didn't do it. Why the hell did we even make the spare key if you aren't going to use it?"

"What the hell are you talking about, Chuck? I locked the door!"

"Whatever. Let's just go inside." The men entered the room and slammed the door behind them.

"We're in trouble, Chuck. We didn't kill that witch. We didn't kill her, and they were mad at us before, so they must be really mad at us now."

"Look, Tommy, I explained to them that there were things beyond our control. They understood. That's why they're sending us on another mission."

"He only said okay, and he paused for a long time. He seemed pissed too."

"He paused because he was thinking, all right? I know you don't know what that is, but some of us do that, you know? We actually use that thing in our head — you know, a brain? And yeah, he was pissed, but not at us, just at the witches, the situation, that sort of shit. I mean, he assigned us another job, right? Why would he do that if he was pissed at us?"

"He never said we had another job, he just said we needed to meet outside the abandoned theatre near the bowling alley on Mildred Street at midnight tonight."

"Yeah, but what else could that mean? We meet at weird places all the time. It's not like they can just meet us out in the open to tell us what to do. It ain't like we're doing legal shit."

"We should run, Chuck, while we still have a chance."

"And abandon all that money and clothes? No way. If it were up to you, we'd have spent the last year in jail. We're making money now. We have a purpose. Do you want to go back to just lounging around drunk off our asses and doing odd jobs to scrape by?"

"We did a really bad thing. She was completely innocent. That's why they're so angry. We really messed up."

"They liked our enthusiasm, though. They know we were just trying to impress them. Yeah, I should have been more careful, but mistakes happen. This is a rough business. Not everybody is willing to do this job, you know? As long as the cops don't get us, nobody really cares."

"I'm scared, Chuck. I knew we shouldn't have accepted the deal. I knew our lives would be constantly in danger."

"Oh, shut the hell up. You know what your problem is? You don't have balls. You have to have balls to win at life."

"Don't make me kick your ass, Chuck! I'll do it!"

"All right, don't get your panties in a bunch — I didn't mean it. Just stop acting like a pussy, all right? We'll be fine. Tommy, I wouldn't let anything happen to you. Have I ever let you down?"

"No."

"Have I?"

"No."

"No, right? They still trust us. Believe me, everything will be just fine, okay?

"I guess."

"Okay?"

"Okay."

"Okay, great. Trixie and Cinnamon are waiting for us to show them around town, and I, for one, don't want to keep them waiting."

"Trixie?"

"Yeah, Trixie, buddy. She said she wanted to see you again. You like her, don't you, buddy?"

"Uh, yeah, I do."

"Who doesn't? And have you seen Cinnamon's ass? Goddamn, I get erect just thinking about it. I just need to grab some cash from the bedroom, and we can get out of here."

As Chuck entered his bedroom, Abigail and I hardly breathed as we heard his footsteps come gradually towards the closet. My hand hovered over my firearm. The handle rattled the rest of the sliding door, and just as the door began to slide, I heard that obnoxious voice say, "What the hell am I doing? I left my money in the drawer."

The door stopped rattling. The footsteps moved away from us.

After the sounds of a drawer opening and closing, the man left the room to presumably rejoin his friend.

"All right, I got the money. Let's get out of here." The door was slammed shut, and as the two men left, Chuck shouted at his companion, "Lock the door, Tommy, and this time do it right!"

"I did it right last time too, Chuck!" Tommy shouted back.

I heard the door lock. Abigail and I stared at each other for a brief period of time.

"Okay," Abigail said, breaking the silence. "I think they're gone."

"Right. Anyway, I think I know what I'm going to be doing tonight."

"A midnight matinee at a theatre, perhaps?" Abigail said

with a half-smile.

"Keep that up, Abigail, and I might think you have a sense of humor. You're right, though. They're meeting someone tonight. Not sure who or why, but I think I can find out more by spying on them."

"It sounded like you may have been right and that the boutique owner is involved. However, it also sounded like they are part of a larger organization."

"It did, but it's difficult to tell. We only got a snippet of the conversation."

"Perhaps we'll find out more tonight."

"We? You're going with?"

"Of course."

"I don't know if you should. This could be very dangerous."

"I understand the risks. As I told you before, I'm paying you to be my partner, not to be the sole detective on this case."

"Now that you mention it, we never actually discussed payment."

"Do you know where the theatre is located?" Abigail completely ignored my comment.

"Yes. Carter and I bowl next to that theatre every couple of weeks or so. It has been abandoned ever since I can remember."

"Perfect. Please take me home, and let us get back together just before the meeting takes place."

I simply nodded in response as we left Chuck's apartment. Abigail used her telekinesis to lock the door again, then we went to my office and on our separate ways to meet later that day at my office.

From there, we arrived early, just before midnight, at the supposed meeting place, giving us time to find a parking spot far enough away to not be noticed, but close enough to walk. We hid amongst the shadows behind some bushes where we could see without being seen. The only illumination came from the alley's neon lights, and the few street lights providing illumination for drivers who were headed to and from the apartment complex behind us.

The evening was colder than we had anticipated. My long, brown overcoat provided adequate warmth, but my companion's sweater wasn't enough. I noticed her shivering, so I draped my coat over her. She smiled to thank me.

The abandoned theatre loomed portentously over the empty parking lot across the road. An outline of the theatre's initials, AMC, indicated that those large letters once hung there, an almost literal sign of better times. The doors of the dim brown building were completely walled up to prevent entry, not that there was anything left to steal.

Everything was in disrepair. The parking lot showed wear and tear, and the lines were all but completely faded from the pavement. The optimism that was once here was now home to melancholy, an eerie feeling of hopelessness. Perhaps it was for this reason that my hand was hovering over my pistol as we waited.

Midnight fell, but nobody had arrived. We waited for five minutes, then ten, then fifteen. Abigail and I looked at each other and, seemingly thinking the same thing, we both shook our head.

I was about to stand when I heard the sounds of a vehicle parking nearby. Immediately I held Abigail by the shoulder and pushed her down towards the ground, as gently as possible, though admittedly, it was a little more abrupt than I had intended. I whispered an apology that went unanswered. We both then fixated on the tan truck as its door opened, and a young man left the vehicle. He began speaking with a familiar nasally voice.

"This is the place, ain't it? Damn if it ain't a dump."

"This place is scaring the shit out of me," the gruff-voiced Tommy said. "We should leave. I have a feeling this isn't going to end well for us if we stay here."

"Wait, this again? I thought Trixie made you a man today, but here you are still about to piss yourself because of the dark. I keep telling you not to worry. Jackson called me while you were out banging Trixie."

"Keith called?"

"Yeah, to make sure we were going to make this meeting.

Why would he do that unless they had a job for us? That guy should be here any minute now."

Almost on cue, a fancy black vehicle entered the lot. I was never good with cars, but it was easy to tell that the vehicle was a Mercedes-Benz. It was driven over to the men still standing next to the truck, Chuck on the driver's side and Tommy on the passenger side. The lights of the Benz were switched to bright, which illuminated the young men, and because of unlucky alignments, shone in our eyes as well, so we had to move a bit to get a better view.

"Holy shit, dude, those lights are bright!" Chuck yelled.

"I can't see a damn thing, Chuck," Tommy said in response.

I heard the sound of a car door opening, but the engine was still running. I tried to adjust my head and block the light with my hand, but despite my effort, I wasn't able to get a good look at the man in the black car. I noticed Abigail had similar issues as her eyes were nearly shut, and she was squirming around.

"Turn those damn lights off!"

A large, lumbering figure exited the car silently.

"Come on, dude, just turn off the light so we can discuss our next job," Chuck said as he continued to cover his eyes.

"Chuck, I don't like this," Tommy whined. "I think we're in trouble."

"Come on, dude, just turn off the lights for us, okay? You're scaring my friend. He's kind of a puss."

The man took two steps forward in response.

"Aren't you going to say something?" Chuck's voice grew more irritated as he spoke. "What the hell is going on?"

The man extended his arm towards the two men.

"Just what the hell are you...?" Chuck's voice trailed for a moment before he began to panic. "Oh shit!" he screamed. "Oh shit! Oh shit! Oh shit!"

"Chuck, what the hell are you —?" Tommy went silent when his head turned towards the lumbering stranger, and his eyes focused on the object that gave his friend such a fright.

A low, baritone voice emanated from the mysterious man.

"Nel tempo del suo Pontificato, la gloria della scoperta di un nuovo mondo."

It took me a second to realize that the man had spoken Italian, though I didn't know why

Gunshots pierced the air. In the bright headlights, I saw the nasally voiced man shot twice in the shoulder, once in the chest, and once in the head. He was dead before he even hit the ground.

Abigail breathed in to scream, and I moved to block her view and mouth as gently as I could. I was used to such experiences, sadly enough, but this was the first time Abigail had seen anything like this. I held her in my arms as the poor woman began to sob lightly.

"Chuck!" Tommy screamed. Tommy took a step forward, but perhaps thinking better of his decision, he turned to run but was immediately struck down with a gunshot to the leg and two more in the back.

As the mysterious man began moving forward, I whispered to Abigail, "I'm sorry, this will just take a second." Abigail continued to weep. I let go of her, pulled the gun out of my vest, and began to move.

I felt a tug, and a feminine voice whispered, "No, don't go! He'll kill you!"

I smiled as reassuringly as I could. Her concern was moving, but I was already late to intervene. I had wanted to act before the coup-de-grace could be delivered, though deep down, I knew it was already too late for Tommy. I gently removed her hands and whispered, "Don't worry. I'll be fine. This is hardly my first rodeo." Tears continued to stream down her eyes as I turned and headed towards the gruesome spectacle.

I frantically dodged towards the truck. Once there, I turned and put my back against it. I slid along the passenger side until I was at the tail end.

The gunman was walking towards the body. I could see Tommy out of the corner of my eye. He was in really bad shape. Moaning horrifically, he tried frantically to crawl away. The sounds slowly became a gurgling noise as if one of his lungs had been pierced. The terror he felt was palpable.

Breathing deeply to calm my nerves, I counted backward from three, preparing to leap out and confront the assassin.

He wore black gloves, black shoes, and a black coat. His face was covered by a gray scarf. The man was clearly in fantastic shape as his muscles seemed to bulge under his thick winter coat. "*Nel tempo del suo Pontificato, la gloria della scoperta di un nuovo mondo,*" the man said once again, pointing his gun at Tommy's head.

I was about to spring from my position when in the distance, a familiar sound was heard. Though barely audible at first, it grew increasingly loud as every second passed. The killer must have heard it too, as he paused only a split second, then turned towards the car. The police were on their way.

"Freeze, asshole!" I said, finally leaping out to confront the gunmen. He ignored me. I fired a shot in the general direction of the man, but the car's headlights made it impossible for me to aim. I heard the bullet ricochet off the ground, followed by the sounds of the car door slamming and rubber burning. The black car sped off through an exit on the opposite side from where Abigail and I had originally settled in for the night. The police car arrived at the scene no more than a few seconds after the black car had left, but it was more than enough time for the shooter to escape.

Already people were beginning to congregate as I stood there, dumbfounded, over two dead bodies. The police car arrived through the same exit that the black car had escaped through, and it stopped with its lights shining brightly in my face.

"This is the police!" shouted a strangely familiar voice from the driver's side of the police car. "Put down that weapon, now!" I complied with the man's orders. "Oh no, it can't be. What kind of mess have you gotten yourself into, Pete?"

CHAPTER 5

"Normally, I'd take you in for questioning."

Kelly began his spiel as we froze to death, sitting on the curb into the early morning. Kelly was courteous enough to provide some coffee and a blanket for Abigail, though he offered no such luxury for me. Abigail was still pretty shaken up. Her arms were over her knees, and she looked down at the ground.

"You were caught with a gun in hand at the scene of the crime. That's pretty damning evidence against you, as you well know."

"I didn't kill them."

"Let me finish. Witnesses told me they saw a black car arrive on the scene, a fancy one — perhaps a Mercedes-Benz or a BMW or some luxury car — there wasn't really a consensus on that one. It almost goes without saying nobody got a license plate number. Multiple shots were heard from what was believed to be at or around the passenger side of the car or the hood, and the vehicle sped off the premises right before we arrived. Considering you're still here, it's not likely that you were the driver of that vehicle."

"Of course not. Besides, how would I be able to afford a car like that?"

"So the private investigator business isn't as glamorous as *Magnum P.I.* makes it out to be, then? No red Ferrari? No helicopter best friend?"

"The Ferrari's in the shop and his wife got the helicopter in the divorce."

Kelly let out a small laugh before regaining his officious demeanor. "I cannot say definitively until we get back to the lab and do a few more tests that you only fired a single shot, but you and I have enough experience to know when a gun's been fired multiple times. I notice that you're still using an STI Lawman, the same piece we use on the force."

"It's the only handgun I've ever used or will ever use."

"You never had a lot of imagination." Kelly pointed at an officer talking to a coroner next to the ambulance parked by the entrance. "Martin nearly tripped over a bullet casing that I think is yours. It's a nine millimeter, the same type of bullet your gun fires. Scoping the other casings we've found at the scene, I'd guess the other shots came from a twenty-two, maybe a Ruger Mark Three or a Browning Buckmark?"

Martin pointed to the two dead men. "Those men were shot multiple times. We couldn't find any other guns, so I think it's safe to say those aren't your bullets in those men."

"We were partners for three years. Do you really think I'd murder somebody?"

"Frankly, no, and admittedly that may be biasing me a bit. I think you are capable of a lot of things, especially betrayal." Kelly paused to let the words linger. "But murder? I don't think you would do something like that. I see no reason to take you in for questioning as long as you answer a few of my questions. Perhaps not standard police protocol, but I'm sure you'd let it go for your old pal Kelly."

"Anything for an old friend."

"What were you doing here in the first place?"

"I tried telling you earlier. You screamed at me to shut up."

"You're right. I'm an asshole. Just answer the question."

"This woman," I said, using both hands to present Abigail to Kelly, "Is Abigail Mitchell. She and I have reason to believe that those two men tried to murder her. We were spying in order to gather more evidence."

"If they tried to kill her, why didn't you go to the police?"

Abigail chimed in, her voice still shaky. "Family issues. My family doesn't trust the police. They don't really trust anybody. I shouldn't have even gone to a private investigator, but I couldn't solve the crime on my own."

"Are there a lot of criminals in your family?"

"We've mostly been the victims of persecution, at least historically speaking. I don't necessarily agree with my family's opinion of police officers, but their paranoia is not completely unjustified."

"How are you doing?" I asked, turning my attention to Abigail. "Are you feeling all right?"

"I meant to ask the same thing," Kelly said sheepishly. "How you holding up, Miss Mitchell? Mrs. Mitchell? Ms. Mitchell?"

"Call me Abigail, and I'm still a little freaked out."

I put my hand on top of hers. "If you had any other reaction, I'd be much more worried."

"I'm freaking out more now than I did when they tried to kill me."

"There's a difference between being a victim and seeing men gunned down in cold blood," I tried to explain. "When you were freed from your captors, there was a sense of relief. It's never easy for anyone to see another human being killed, regardless of who they were. Kelly and I are simply more used to it."

"One of the perks of being an officer," Kelly said sarcastically.

"That wasn't always the case. I remember the first time I saw someone killed. A fellow officer gunned down a man to save my life. It was perfectly justified, appreciated even, but it still took me a while to get over it. I could hardly eat for a week."

"It was only my second year on the force," Kelly said somberly. "I was just walking my beat when I saw an elderly clerk at a convenience store murdered ruthlessly. His hands were up, and the bastard still shot him through the head. Yeah, my instincts and training got me through it. I drew immediately, told the asshole to drop his weapon, that sort of thing, and he did, and I was able to arrest him with little resistance, but the event haunted me. I felt like quitting. Shot down for a few lousy dollars and a pack of cigarettes. Luckily, a friend of mine was able to talk me out of it."

"We would have lost an incredible officer if I hadn't."

Abigail began to squirm. "Cigarettes, that's what I need, cigarettes. Kelly?"

"Officer Martinez, ma'am."

"He gets to call you Kelly, and I have to call you Officer Martinez?"

"I've known the man for too long, Miss Mitchell. It's useless to try and correct him."

"I see. So, Kelly, you wouldn't happen to have a cigarette, would you?"

"I'm afraid I don't smoke."

"My purse has a pack of cigarettes. Where did it go?"

"Martin was taking a look inside it last I checked. Hey Martin! Where did you put the purse?"

"I didn't find anything particularly interesting, so I left it by the bush. Do you want me to get it for you, sir?"

"Please do, Martin."

Martin hurried enthusiastically to the purse, grabbed it, and lightly jogged to Kelly, handing him the purse.

"Thanks, Martin."

"Is there anything else I can do for you, sir?"

"No, thank you very much, Martin." Martin saluted Kelly and returned to his post near the ambulance.

"Good kid," Kelly said. "He was just doing his normal rounds when he saw Tommy and Chuck on their way over here. He gave me a call, and I drove down here as soon as I could."

"Wait a second. Why were you so interested in Tommy and Chuck? You still work homicide, right?"

"That is not your concern. If you were still with the force, I'd let you know, but as far as I'm concerned, you're just another civilian." Kelly handed Abigail the purse.

"Thank you," Abigail said. She reached in, pulled out her package of cigarettes, and place one in her mouth. I noticed that she was about to snap her fingers when she suddenly stopped herself and instead asked, "Does anybody have a light?"

"You don't have a lighter?" Kelly asked.

"My lighter ran out of fuel, so I was down to using matches, but apparently, I have already used my last one."

"I'll ask Martin if he has something. Hey, Martin!"

Abigail quickly lit the cigarette by snapping her fingers while Kelly was distracted talking to his partner.

"If Martin doesn't have a light, I'm not sure who to ask. Wait a second." Kelly noticed Abigail smoking. "Where did you get a light?"

"It turns out I still had a match left after all. I just had to do some digging."

"Okay, that's good, I guess. I sincerely hope it makes you feel better."

"Don't worry," the woman said after a long exhale. "I'm feeling better already."

"I'm glad you're recovering. Now, review time. You hired him because you were attacked by two men, and you wanted to find out who they were. Why did you suspect Tommy and Chuck?"

Omitting certain details, I explained how Dahlia had noticed that Abigail's attackers wore the same fancy shoes as the men that hung around her fruit stand.

"I suppose that all checks out. With your prime suspects dead, I suppose that's it for you then?"

"No, this goes a lot deeper than Tommy and Chuck. They were working for somebody more important than them, an organization perhaps."

"Oh God, are you about to tell me another one of your crazy theories again, Pete?"

"Think about why Tommy and Chuck were killed."

"We still don't know, but rest assured we'll figure it out. Police detectives tend to be better than private investigators at solving these kinds of things."

"Don't underestimate us; we've already discovered a lot. Their house was full of tree branches. And not just any tree, the rare ximuce tree only found in Evergreen. The shopkeeper let them go after they tried to rob him. He may have been supplying them with designer clothing as payment for their jobs. And what's a pair of idiots doing with a copy of the *Malleus Maleficarum*?"

"How do you know any of that?"

"His closet was full of designer clothes. We also overheard a conversation while hiding there." Abigail stared at me, eyes wide open while I moved my hands towards my mouth, trying to push the words back in.

"You saw his closet?" Kelly accentuated every word in that question. "And you overheard his conversation while in his closet? So you're admitting he didn't exactly invite you in."

"Does it really matter how I happened to be there?" I said, smiling sheepishly.

"Okay, how about this? I'm going to pretend I didn't hear you say any of that." Abigail let out a relieved sigh and resumed smoking. "Instead, I'm going to just tell you that even if hypothetically the two were receiving expensive clothes as payment, it could have been for literally anything. Hell, maybe he caught them stealing again, and it enraged him, so he killed them in response. No conspiracy, just a betrayed man."

"Was the shopkeeper Italian."

"Italian?" Kelly asked. "What are you talking about?"

"The killer said something before he shot the men, and I think it was in Italian." I scratched my head and closed my eyes. "Tempo del pontificate, glory nuevo mondo, or something like that."

"I'd have to look into it. But still, whether the shopkeeper was Italian or not, you still haven't really convinced me of a conspiracy."

"Then, take a look at this!" I pulled out Tommy and Chuck's coin that Abigail had given me a couple of days ago.

"Not again," Kelly moaned.

"It matches the one that we found on Cullen five years ago. It also matches this one!" I pulled out the coin I always wore around my neck. "It's the same coin! Whatever these guys were up to, they're part of the same group that Cullen was part of when he drowned all those women—or at least took the fall for their drownings—and part of the same group that killed my friend

Erin Ross!"

Kelly momentarily closed his eyes. "I can't believe you are still wearing that coin. You're just as crazy as ever, Pete!" Kelly snatched the coin from my hand and chucked it away.

"Why the hell did you do that?"

"You threw away your career for a snipe hunt. Erin is dead, and you're never going to find out who did it or why. It sucks, I understand, but that's how the world works. You'll never believe it because you keep thinking the smallest things are a connection to the case. You hear a man sneeze. 'A man sneezed the day Erin was murdered!' A dog barks. 'A dog barked the day Erin was murdered!'"

"Shut the hell up!"

I had stood up and gotten a few inches away from Kelly's face. The coroner, Martin, and a few other officers saw this and were ready to take action, but Kelly called them off with a single raise of a hand.

"How dare you say something like that to me?" I continued, undaunted, and unthankful for his gesture. "I have never and never will reach for clues. If I say there's a connection, it's because there is one. Get your head out of your ass and think!"

"Go home," Kelly growled. "Right now. Get out of my face before you regret it."

"Fine. Come on, Abigail, we're leaving."

Abigail stared silently for a moment before dropping her cigarette and grinding it out. She apologized to Kelly for littering.

Abigail must have been in shock, as she followed me silently rather than protesting I'd ordered her around rudely. As we left the parking lot and headed towards the car across the road, Kelly added caustically, "Don't leave town."

"Ten-four, Detective," I answered. "It was good seeing you again."

The trip back to my office with Abigail was incredibly uncomfortable. She and I barely exchanged words even after the two of us separated to return to our respective homes, but by the next day, all was forgiven and forgotten.

Another pressing issue that Abigail had to attend to and kept us from communicating for a while involved the internal politics of the coven. She didn't really inform me of the specifics, but she did tell me this was something stemming from tensions between two factions she dubbed the separatists and the unionists.

She had already explained that four major thoughts were prevalent in Abigail's coven. Most witches within the coven wanted to maintain the status quo. Witches had lived incognito amongst us, who they called cowans, for centuries, and they wanted things to remain that way.

Others wanted to let the rest of us know that witches were real and wanted to essentially reveal their abilities to non-witches in an effort to promote understanding and acceptance. They felt that humanity at large was ready for this, a thought Abigail was completely supporting.

Though these two approaches were dissimilar, they shared the idea of peaceful coexistence, so Abigail grouped them together as being what she called unionists.

Conversely, there were witches that wanted to separate themselves completely from the rest of humanity, which obviously Abigail called separatists. The majority of them simply wanted to live peaceful lives away from non-witches. They believed that non-witches were simply incapable of living peacefully with witches and, though they admitted it would be a long, generational process to create an infrastructure to allow an insular society away from humanity, they believed, in the long run, it would be worth the effort.

The more radical ones believed that non-witches should either be subjugated or eradicated by witches, thinking themselves to be superior beings and believing non-witches should kowtow to their whims. Others believed it would be reparations for the way non-witches treated them in the past.

Unionists still outnumbered separatists, but with recent events, the separatist movement was beginning to gain momentum. The two witches being attacked after Abigail was assaulted was not helping the unionist cause. One of these two was able to escape relatively unharmed, but the other was reportedly beaten to death. While there wasn't any evidence showing that these witches were being targeted, the separatists simply didn't believe these were random attacks.

Left on my own during this time, I went to speak with the proprietor of the Nice Garb Express, Keith Jackson, a tall, scrawny man with long, black hair and a distinctive, shaggy beard that hung way down his chest. He had an apparent affinity for white business suits, black shirts, and red ties. Keith explained that even though Chuck and Tommy had tried to steal from him, he always saw the good in people and had hoped that those two unfortunate youths just needed somebody to mentor them and that the job would help the duo turn their lives around.

He seemed aghast when I told him they were likely the ones who attacked Abigail and acted horrified to learn that the two men were gunned down. He added that he had no idea why anybody would have wanted them dead. In his words, "They were good boys at heart in spite of it all." When I reminded him they had attacked Abigail, he backed off a bit, admitting they were mistake-prone and lamented that his lessons hadn't taken hold. I had to admit, the man was affable, seemed sincere, and spoke very well. I almost believed him.

With Keith bearing little fruit, I decided to drive out to the Layton Fruit Market after hours. I hadn't heard from Abigail for a while, so I hoped her friend Dahlia could tell what she had been doing and where to find her. I was at the back door when I heard Dahlia's voice.

"Can't you just leave us in peace? I refuse to do this for you anymore! They are my friends. My family. I cannot keep betraying them like this…I know. I know. I know! But Abigail is my best friend! I don't care. I'll find a way to protect them. You won't be getting anything from me anymore!"

"Dahlia, is everything all right?" I asked, throwing open the unlocked door.

The middle-aged woman yelped in surprise. Her phone flew up from her hand, but luckily she was able to catch it just a few inches before it hit the floor.

Dahlia glared at me. "For the love of Cernunnos, have you ever heard of knocking, Peter?" She said into the phone, "I have to go. We can talk later." Dahlia put the phone into her pocket and used her fingers as a makeshift comb.

"Is everything all right? That phone call seemed pretty dire."

"You heard that." Dahlia paused for a moment. "Not that it is any of your business, but that was a call from the bank. They claim that I'm currently behind in some payments, but they're wrong. My records are immaculate. I've made all my payments, but they refuse to believe."

"The bank is calling you at this late hour?"

Dahlia paused again. "It's run by a witch. They work late hours because of the nature of their clientele."

"You mentioned something about a betrayal."

"You're so damn nosy," Dahlia snapped. "I'm tired of having to borrow money from my friends and not paying them back. I'm a woman who honors her debts. When I don't pay them back, I feel like I'm betraying them. Is that answer satisfactory for you?"

"Okay, okay. Dahlia. Sorry about the twenty questions. I just wanted to make sure you were all right. I didn't mean to pry."

"It's all right." Dahlia's voice was noticeably relieved. "I appreciate the concern. Take a seat." She motioned towards an empty part of one of the tables. I obediently sat down. "What brings you here? Wait, let me guess. You're here about Abigail, right?"

"Good guess."

"You're not as difficult to read as you'd like to be, Peter Cunningham. What would you like to know about her?"

"I haven't seen her for a while. I wanted to know if you've heard from her lately."

"I'm afraid I haven't heard from Abigail in a while. She's been busy trying to quell the tensions in our coven. Has Abigail told you about any of this?"

"I know about the separatists and the unionists, but I'm not sure how Abigail fits into all of this."

"I suppose there's no harm in telling you. Abigail told me that you didn't even tell your old police partner about witches, and let Abigail say the reason she couldn't go to the police was because of family problems."

"If nothing else, my story would have sounded absolutely crazy."

"Still, I appreciate that. Abigail became the de facto leader of what she dubbed the unionists basically by being the most outspoken—and frankly, the loudest—voice on their behalf in the community. I think part of the reason she feels so strongly is that her father used to share the same beliefs as her when she was a little girl, so this is her effort to convince him to join her side once again."

"What caused him to change his mind?"

"I would rather spare you the details. It's not something I am comfortable talking about."

"I thought you trusted me."

"I do, but I'm not comfortable sharing this story even with my own family. For now, let's just say her father has his reasons, and very good ones, to hate cowans. That's not all that's been on her plate lately. That circle nonsense is also a big point of contention."

"I suppose your coven isn't exactly thrilled with how the chanting circle is going so far."

"At first, it did seem like a success, but the recent attack is making everyone very nervous. The attacks of five years ago are still fresh in our minds. I haven't recommended getting rid of them to the high priest and priestess because I know how much they mean to the girl, but I haven't endorsed them either. I'm not in favor of them anymore."

"I understand, and for what it is worth, I think you're a really good friend for supporting Abigail as much as you can. Is there anything I can do to help?"

"Solving the mystery as to why Abigail and the coven seem to be targeted would help out immensely, which seems to be right in your wheelhouse. How is the case going, by the way?"

"Not great. I seemed to have reached a dead end with my only lead right now."

"You'll figure it out."

"I don't know," I sighed. "My confidence right now is pretty low. I don't know whether Abigail told you this, but I've been investigating a case heavily for twenty years."

Dahlia gasped. "Twenty years? Dare I ask what you've been investigating for twenty years?"

I hesitated. "Murder. Of an old friend."

"Murder. My god, you must have only been a child then."

"She was too. I know Abigail's attack is linked to my childhood friend's murder, but I just can't seem to piece everything together. Deep down, I'm afraid I'm not going to be able to solve these mysteries, and it seems like I've run into a wall once again."

"So, what's next for you?"

"I intend to listen to some old recordings of the Tony O'Stein show tonight. I want to see what the fuss is all about."

Dahlia turned pale. Her expression became suddenly graven. "Please don't mention that man's name in front of me ever again."

I was stunned. "Of course, Dahlia, I won't. I'm sorry."

"He's a real shit stain, to say the least. I absolutely loathe the man."

"Why do you hate him so much? I don't know much about him, but from what I've heard, he's led an exemplary life."

Dahlia turned slowly away from me and placed her hands on a nearby table. "Let's just say I've known men like Tony my entire life. His public persona is certainly not how he is in real life. Men like him are monsters."

"I'm afraid I'm not following."

"I may sound like a madwoman, but there are reasons why I hate Tony. Ones I'd rather not reveal."

"Please do," I implored. "You've helped me so much. Just maybe I can help you with whatever the problem is."

She turned back towards me. "I'm sorry. I truly am."

I tried to conjure up the magic words that would loosen her tongue, but failing to do so, all I could say was, "Okay, Dahlia, but you know where to find me if you ever do want to talk about this. I'll be there for you, and I'm sure Abigail will be too."

"I sincerely thank you, very much. Good luck, and let me know if you need anything else."

A few days after my meeting with Dahlia, Abigail and I finally reunited. Approximately a week and a half had passed between visits, but for some reason, it had felt like ages. We exchanged a pleasant greeting and a hug as she entered my office. I was so happy that I chose to ignore the cigarette in her hand.

"I'm so glad to see you, Abigail," I said as we settled down into our respective seats. "I've grown accustomed to your face."

Abigail giggled. "You really are a movie buff."

"It seems that things have been rough for you lately."

Abigail sighed. "The internal politics of a witch's coven are complicated, to say the least, especially for someone in my position."

"Dahlia told me you're the leader of the unionists."

"She told you that?"

"I didn't mean to rat her out if she shouldn't have shared."

"No, I'm glad she told you. You deserve to know what's going on."

"What are things like in the coven right now?"

"These recent attacks have set both sides on edge, though I think things have settled down enough that neither side's about to do anything. It's a very uncertain truce, so honestly, it isn't much different than it was before. It couldn't have come at a worse time, though. Many witches are still upset over the chanting circle's return."

"The recent attacks support their claim that the tradition should be eliminated."

"That sentiment, unfortunately, is only growing. The discussion has been tabled for now, which is good. The chanting circle is still allowed to continue, but the issue will come up again in a meeting in May. At least the nightmares are starting to dissipate."

"Nightmares?" I asked.

"Tommy and Chuck may have deserved it, but it was still horrifying to see them die. I hope I never have to see anything like that again."

"I'm sorry. I wish I could have protected you from having to see that."

"Don't beat yourself up over it. You warned me things could get dangerous, and I assured you I knew the risks. Sometimes bad things just happen no matter where you are. As much as you try to insulate yourself and put up a shield, things like that have a way of finding you."

"By the way, Dahlia seemed upset when I mentioned Tony O'Stein. She seemed genuinely angry at me for bringing him up. Do you know what might have caused this kind of reaction?"

"Oh, you mentioned Tony. Yeah, she's definitely not one of his fans. You know how I feel about him, right? If you magnified my hatred a hundredfold, you'd only be about halfway towards realizing her true feelings towards the man."

"She seemed to genuinely think he is an evil man and the way she said it made it seem personal somehow."

Suddenly, our conversation was interrupted by a large crash as my outer office door was banged open. A voice in the outer room intoned, "*Nel tempo del suo Pontificato, la gloria della scoperta di un nuovo mondo.*"

"Oh my God, he couldn't have found us, could he?" Abigail asked, her voice slightly quivering.

I pulled out my gun. "I don't know, but I'll check it out. You stay here, okay."

"Be careful." I nodded and smiled briefly, then approached the entryway with my gun held in front of me. I moved quietly and carefully until about halfway there a figure popped up before me.

"Holy shit, Pete!" the man said as he raised his hands over his head. "I know I was an asshole to you, but there's no need to shoot me!" It was Kelly.

I quickly lowered my piece and responded, "For the love of God, Kelly, can't you knock like a normal person? I thought the assassin had found us. Why the hell are you greeting us like that rather than saying hello like a normal person?" I turned and shouted to Abigail, "It's just Kelly!"

"That's good," Abigail shouted back. "But why is he here?"

"That's a good question," I said, turning back towards Kelly. "Why are you here?" I holstered my gun and made a motion to him to follow me to the main room. He silently complied.

"Well," he said. "The state of Washington now agrees with me that you aren't the murderer, so you are no longer a suspect. Forensics has confirmed everything I assumed at the scene. Congratulations, Pete!"

"Great. Is that the only reason you're here?"

"Not exactly. I wanted to apologize."

"I somewhat accept, and I admit that's very big of you. Thank you. Still, I can't quite get past some of the nasty things you said."

"That's not exactly what I was apologizing about."

"Oh? What then?"

"I said you were crazy for believing that all of these cases were somehow connected."

"Yeah?" I leaned forward in anticipation of what I thought he might say.

"I can't believe I'm going to say this, but I'm starting to think you're right. I think the cases may be connected."

"About time. Don't get me wrong, I'm thrilled you agree, but why the sudden change of heart?"

"You mentioned an Italian phrase. You butchered it, but it seemed so familiar. I just couldn't get that notion out of my head, so I had to find out why it seemed so recognizable. When you mentioned Cullen Jones, it started to jog my memory a bit. Did you follow the newspaper reports or the court proceedings at all?"

"Not really. I was preoccupied beginning my private investigator business at the time, and reading about the affair made me sick to my stomach."

"There was something odd about his trial. I mulled over Cullen's files and found a newspaper report where, after his sentencing was announced, the judge asked if he had anything to say for his crimes. Cullen responded with *'Nel tempo del suo Pontificato, la gloria della scoperta di un nuovo mondo.'* Does that sound familiar to you?"

"That's what the assassin said!"

"Exactly. Another thing is that Cullen was murdered in prison a couple of years ago, in year three of his sentence. Nobody is quite sure of why, either. He was found bleeding to death all alone, no witnesses — or at least no witnesses willing to snitch. The warden who found him asked who attacked him, and he reportedly responded, *'Nel tempo del suo Pontificato, la gloria della scoperta di un nuovo mondo.'*"

"What does the phrase mean?"

Kelly pulled out a notebook from his pocket and read, "It means 'During his Pontificate, the glory of the discovery of a new world.'" As Kelly put the notebook back into his pocket, he continued, "Have you ever heard of Pope Innocent VIII?"

"I have," Abigail interrupted. "He was a terrible pope and a terrible man. He did many sinful things, but among his most grievous crimes was the persecution of witches."

"Impressive," Kelly said, nodding. "You sure know your history."

Abigail nervously shrugged. "I read a lot."

"That phrase is the inscription on his tomb. Nobody is quite sure what it means. Historians seem to believe it refers to Columbus, but Pope Innocent VIII died a week before his three ships reportedly went off to discover the so-called 'new world' — though some believe that just means he sailed earlier than what was recorded."

"Why would Cullen or the assassin say this phrase? Why would they be talking about Columbus or a late fifteenth century Pope before they killed someone, were sentenced to jail, or were murdered?"

"I don't know, but the specificity of that phrase and the strange context in which it was spoken makes me think that you're right, the cases are somehow connected. Also, remember this?" Kelly reached into his pocket, pulled out a coin, and flipped it to me.

I caught the coin with both hands. "It's that coin you threw away."

"I looked for it the next morning. I'm not even sure why. I knew you already had a copy, but still, I looked for it with Martin's help, and he actually wound up finding the thing. Finding the coin was very beneficial because I was able to find out something very interesting. That sleeping man on the coin? He's not sleeping, he's dead. Who is he? Take a guess."

"No way."

"He's Pope Innocent VIII. The picture on the coin is Pope Innocent VIII's tomb. Now isn't that a highly specific thing to be passing around?"

"What does this all mean, though?"

"For now, it means that you're right. There has to be a connection between all of these cases."

"After all these years, you finally believe me."

"Don't gloat, Pete. It's so unbecoming to gloat."

I beamed. "I can't help it. I'm almost giddy; you finally believe me! Yet I have to admit this whole ordeal has left us with more questions than answers. Our only leads, Tommy and Chuck, are both dead. Which reminds me—what made the Tacoma PD so interested in them?"

"Heather Edwards."

Kelly handed me a picture of a young teenage girl no older than seventeen, her jet black hair tied in pigtails, her face covered with black makeup. On her neck she wore a black choke collar, and the picture of her from the waist up showed her wearing a Gothic-style dress.

"Her name and face seem vaguely familiar to me."

"I'm not surprised. Her death made national headlines, and not just because it was a pretty white girl or because she's so young. It was the manner in which she was murdered that made her a countrywide sensation."

"Wait a second, I remember this now. She was tied to a chair and drowned in the middle of the Puget Sound."

"Steilacoom Road specifically. Since it's adjacent to a small, rocky beach, it's a good place to practice scuba diving, especially for beginners. I say this only to tell you that a couple of divers found her body. The look of horror on the girl's face was enough to haunt even the most jaded veteran on the force."

"Meaning it disturbed even you, Kelly?" I asked.

"Yeah," Kelly sighed. "I mean it even disturbed me, Pete. Anyway, from interviews with friends and classmates, we were able to determine that Tommy and Chuck were the last people seen with Heather, which made them persons of interest. It seems like it was a recent friendship. The duo knew of a local dive bar that is very lax when it comes to carding people, and served really cheap drinks."

Abigail winced. "Inviting an underage girl out for drinking wasn't enough to get them arrested? They even had a criminal history!"

"For mostly nickel and dime stuff like shoplifting and public intoxication. Also, they may have been adults, but they too were under the drinking age, which mitigates things a bit. Besides, we had no proof, only hearsay. We don't even know what bar they allegedly entered. Their names just kept coming up with all of her friends, especially her boyfriend, Cyrus Pontem."

"Cyrus Pontem?" Abigail asked. "You talked to Cyrus Pontem?"

"Hmm? Do you know the young man?" Kelly asked Abigail.

Abigail paused. "No, nothing like that. It's just such an unusual name that I didn't think I heard you correctly."

"It's certainly no John Doe, that's for sure. But weird name or not, he did tell us a lot, enough to believe it was either Tommy, Chuck, or her father, Joseph."

"Why is her father a suspect?" I asked.

"A religious conflict of sorts. Joseph held beliefs worthy of the Dark Ages, including an irrational hatred of witches."

"Witches?" Abigail asked, perking up a bit. "He hated witches?"

"Yeah," I said, winking at the woman. "Strangest thing I've

ever heard. How about you, Abigail?"

"Oh yeah, of course, Petey. How very odd."

"It's sad because they seemed to have been very close at one point, especially after her mother died of cancer, but his dogmatic views eventually drove them apart. He'd have been the prime suspect for his daughter's murder, except he does have an airtight alibi. He bowled the night of his daughter's death in front of dozens of fellow league bowlers. Also, the way he broke down upon hearing about his daughter's death wasn't something that could be faked, at least according to the department's psychiatrists."

"Did Joseph know about Heather's friendship with Tommy and Chuck?" Abigail asked.

"Not as far as I could tell. At least, her friends didn't seem to think so."

"He could have found out about them and murdered them in revenge," I suggested.

"The same thought crossed my mind. I think I will pay Joseph another visit."

"I'm going to keep digging around myself. Perhaps a private investigator who only has one case to deal with will find something you missed."

"I don't have to tell you that the entire department is stretched pretty thin right now, so that's a good idea. I'll let you know what I find. I hope you will do the same for me."

"Of course. Thanks again, Kelly." I extended my hand towards the man. "I can't believe after all these years, Cunningham and Martinez are back together again."

Kelly's hands remained in his pockets. "Yeah, let's not go that far. I'm willing to help you out, but that doesn't mean I want to bury the hatchet. When you left the police force, you abandoned all your brothers in blue. That's not something I can forgive. I'm mostly doing this because I believe we have a rather important case to solve, and nobody on the police force believes me or is willing to help me out. I'm not doing this so we can be friends again."

I lowered my hand. "I see."

Abigail leaped from her seat. "He just wanted to shake your hand. Why the hell do you have to refuse it like that?"

"Abigail, it's okay," I said.

Abigail ignored me and move within inches of Kelly's face. "No, it's not okay! He's been nothing but polite, and this is how you treat him! No wonder people hate cops!"

"Abigail, that's enough!" Abigail turned to give me a death stare. "I mean," I said, coughing a little bit, "Abigail, I appreciate your concern, but I understand Kelly's perspective."

"But Petey, what kind of person doesn't shake a man's hand?"

"Petey?" Kelly asked.

"Kelly has his reasons."

Abigail stared at me for a moment and then glared at Kelly.

Kelly shook his head in disgust. "I should get going. Do you still have my number?"

"You didn't change it, right?" As Kelly walked towards the door, I said with genuine feeling, "It was good seeing you again, Kelly."

"Thanks," he answered without inflection as he continued on.

"Even though that man's helping us out," Abigail said as Kelly shut the door behind him, "He's still an asshole."

I plopped back down on my seat. "Kelly's not an asshole. He never was, and he never will be. I understand his anger."

"I don't. He needs to get over it."

"Realize you're talking to a man who wears a coin around his neck he found from something that took place twenty years ago."

"That's a little bit different, though. That was from a murder. You didn't kill anybody. You quit a job, big deal. A lot of people quit jobs."

"It's a little different when you're a cop. The people you work with, they become like your brothers and sisters. Quitting the force is like quitting on your family. Kelly viewed me as his favorite older brother."

Abigail's expression softened quite a bit. "He still could have been a bit nicer to you, or at least shook your hand."

"I believe he's still coming to terms with everything. He's been angry at me for years, and suddenly I reappear in his life. And not only that, he's now learned that all my seemingly obsessed and crazy ramblings were true. It's perhaps a bit overwhelming."

"I suppose you're right."

"Besides, we have more important things to think about."

"It's hard to believe how big this thing has gotten. When I came in here to hire you, I really didn't anticipate the size of the problem."

"Well, we're still speculating. Kelly and I have our suspicions, but they're only suspicions."

"Still, this seems big, you know. Like, perhaps even a bit over our heads?"

"I have to see this thing through to the end, though, Abigail. For Erin's sake."

"Yes," she sighed. "I understand. For Erin."

"You're welcome to leave, though," I said as gently as possible. "I don't mean that as a criticism, either. We don't know what we're getting into, so I'd understand if you wanted out now."

"So, what? Just pay and leave?"

"Now that you mention it, have we actually ever discussed payment?"

"I can't leave, Petey, not without knowing more. If there's even a chance there's a conspiracy against our coven, I have to know about that."

"We should probably discuss where to go from here. By the way, do you know Cyrus Pontem?"

"I've known him since he was a child. He's the son of Archon Pontem, one of the leaders of the separatist movement. I was his babysitter. Remember Dicana?"

"Vaguely."

"He's her younger brother. I didn't know he had a girlfriend, though. I wonder why he didn't tell me."

I scratched my head. "Is his father another leader of the

separatists?"

"We haven't actually divided ourselves up into two factions. Who we call the leaders of the movement are actually, for the most part, de facto leaders. They are the ones who have been around the longest, or simply carry the most respect for one reason or another. We're still bound together as witches, though we have some ideological issues. Oddly, a railroad track divides the two groups, but that happened more or less organically. We don't force people to live on one side or the other as far as I know."

"Technically, at least according to what you've told me, no one seems to hold much real power. Correct me if I'm wrong, but it's not as if there's a document truly granting them any sort of control."

"I suppose now you'd like me to arrange a meeting between you, Cyrus, and the rest of the Pontem family."

"Would that be possible?"

"I'm not sure. Though he and my Dad are good friends, Archon really hates cowans, so he'd probably refuse to meet you. That attitude is probably why Cyrus hid Heather from his father."

"Makes sense. I doubt that Archon would know that much about this anyway. The one we need to talk to is Cyrus."

"That should be possible. Visiting Archon in and of itself shouldn't arouse suspicions. We are on generally good terms, thanks to my father. If I can get Cyrus alone, I can tell him about you and arrange a meeting. In spite of her attire, he did date a cowan after all, and will probably be more than happy to speak to the detective that's trying to find out more about his girlfriend's murder."

"There's logic in that."

"We have an all-hands monthly esbat coming up in a couple of days. Everyone in our coven should be attending. I can talk to them then and let you know what they say."

"Perfect. Thank you very much, Abigail."

She winked. "A good boss should help out her employee every now and again."

"In the meantime, are you very familiar with social media?"

"Not particularly. Witches like to keep a low profile, after all, and social media is kind of the antithesis to that."

"I'm not either, but a friend of mine certainly is. He's a guy who excels at these sorts of things, and he's an expert hacker. I think I'll give him a call."

CHAPTER 6

"I really hate it when you call me a hacker," Carter said to me while Abigail and I looked over his shoulder as he logged onto a social media page on his home computer set up in the corner of his living room. "I'm a programmer. Hacking is a very specific skill. Most programmers don't know or need to know how to hack."

"But you were a hacker," I said.

"When I was a teenager, but I haven't done that in years. You're making me look bad in front of your friend."

"Technically, she's my client too. Although now that you mention it, I'm not sure we ever discussed payment."

"Hollywood always makes hacking look so glamorous, but in truth, hacking is a long, laborious process that mostly involves running some tools and finding exploits. Most hackers aren't even malicious. Do you know what's even more dangerous than a hacker when it comes to finding out information?"

I sighed. "A man with a clipboard."

"That's correct. A man or woman that looks authoritative is much more dangerous than a hacker. How did you know that?"

"We learned basically the same thing in the police academy."

"Then you understand better than most that hacking is largely unnecessary when it comes to finding anything out."

"You found all of her information in a day. How did you do that without hacking?"

"Elementary, my dear Abigail," Carter said with a wink. "Though it's trivia time. Sherlock Holmes never actually said 'Elementary, my dear Watson' in the original books. I think it started with Basil Rathbone's depiction of the character."

"Fascinating. Would you please answer how you were able to gather the information?" I growled.

Carter turned towards Abigail. "Touchy, isn't he?"

"Just ignore his sardonic comments—I do," she said. "I enjoyed that bit of trivia even if he didn't."

"To be fair, I've probably told him that a hundred times—he's just tired of hearing it. To answer your question, finding information online is hardly a Herculean task. Most people post everything about themselves without restraint. All it takes is somebody who knows what they are doing and has a bit of time. Luckily, I had the day off today. Let me show you what I found."

Carter showed us Heather Edward's social media page. Practically everything about her life for the last eight years was on full display.

"It's funny," Carter said as I perused the site. "In George Orwell's most famous piece, *1984*, he discussed an elaborate government surveillance system used to spy on the citizens in order to gather personal information. Now, people can't wait to reveal intimate details online on a public forum."

I studied the deceased girl's profile page. Her latest picture showed her in a similar fashion as the picture Kelly had shown me. She wore dark hair, pigtails, a choke collar, and a gothic dress. She appeared to be at a concert of some sort. Below her profile picture, there was written text, and a lot of pictures of her and presumably her friends.

We combed through her photographs and saw many that showed the inside of her house. Every room was incredibly tidy, including a pool room. I couldn't help but notice that the pool table was empty, and the rack lacked cues. It struck me as rather a waste to have an unused pool table. Perhaps it was a gift.

"The whole place is immaculate," I said to Abigail. "It's like the polar opposite of my place."

Abigail gave me a wry smile. "To be fair, that is an incredibly low bar if your office is anything to go by."

Carter turned from his gray swivel chair and, looking

discomfited, said, "It was tough at times reading everything that was on her page. She was so young and had so many plans and goals for her life. All of it snuffed out in a second. It was heartbreaking. A couple of times while reading this, I had to pause and give Darren and Penelope a long hug. Of course, they had no idea why I did that."

"Sorry to put you through all that, Carter."

"It's okay, I know it's for a good cause. Anyway, you can see from these pictures she was happy enough and went all over the place with her dad. Normal in most ways, and a healthy eater. See the pictures where she was younger and with her dad?"

We nodded.

"Unfortunately," Carter continued, "Things seemed to change about three years ago."

Carter then showed us a myriad of posts that chronicled the fraying relationship between father and daughter. Joseph's religious views became more and more extreme. Apparently, Heather wasn't particularly religious, and his trying to convert her to his beliefs created a lot of friction between them.

One post that leaped out at me was one related to the Salem Witch Trials. Heather believed it was a travesty, and his original comments seemed to be in agreement as Joseph called it a mistake. However, he also wrote, "One mistake shouldn't destroy a worthwhile cause," "Evil still exists because of human error," and "Sacrifices sometimes have to be made." She stated that his comments only confused her.

The one thing her father made clear was that he intensely hated witches. He went so far as to ban television shows or movies that had witches as characters.

Heather claimed her father had a cult-like devotion to his beliefs, and added that her father abandoned going to his regular church in order to dedicate himself more to a different organization she also referred to as a cult. She indicated that she suspected he might have been with that organization for years.

"It seems recently Heather had started to rebel," Carter explained as he got near the end of looking through her posts.

"She died her auburn hair jet black and wore gothic styles of clothing. She may have been trying to emulate a witch. Take this post, for instance."

Carter showed me a familiar picture—the full shot of the photograph Kelly had handed to me a day before. Underneath the photograph was a caption reading, "If Dad hates witches so much, I wonder what he will think when I start dressing like one…a more modern one, at least. Dad probably won't recognize it, though, unless I wear a pointy hat."

"Ridiculous," Abigail scoffed. "Why would witches dress any differently than anyone else? Like most everyone else, I dress the way I do because I want to, not because I have some special reason. Witches would probably be like that."

Carter nodded. "I agree. It seems as though people have a tendency to conflate witches, vampires, and goths together as if they are all part of the same group when nothing could be further from the truth. That's popular culture for you."

"Let's try and stay focused," I said. "Was it only her clothing that changed?"

"Everything about her changed," Carter explained. "From the books she read to the music she listened to, her personality did a complete one-eighty. She was a cheerful daddy's girl. She became the stereotypical Goth. Cyrus Pontem may have played a role in her transformation."

"Her boyfriend."

"Yes, do you know the young man?" Carter asked.

"Kelly told us about him," I said, winking at Abigail. Technically it wasn't a lie.

Carter nodded. "Heather met Cyrus at a concert when her Gothic transformation was still in its infancy, and the two apparently started dating shortly after. However, her posts simply stop after that. No posts for three months."

"Well, how could that be?" I asked. "Maybe with a boyfriend, she just found better things to do?"

"A teenage girl abandoning her social media page? Unlikely. Take a look at Cyrus's page."

Carter entered a name in a search bar and clicked on a picture of Cyrus with Heather.

"Take a look at all of his friends." Abigail and I glanced through the list of friends and family, mostly teenagers and a few adults, but we didn't notice anybody or see anything particularly noteworthy.

"You didn't see it?" Carter asked as Abigail and I gave him back his mouse and shook our heads. "Okay, just let me type in the name in the search box."

He typed in the name Abigail Mitchell in a small search box above a list of all of Cyrus's friends. A picture appeared of a young teenage girl with jet black hair that wore heavy black eye shadow and had thin purple lips. She wore a tight black T-shirt with a light red and white guitar in the middle with the words "Rock Angel" written on the front. The right knee of her blue jeans had a small hole in it, and small black boots covered her feet. A black purse dangled from her left shoulder.

"Abigail. Is that you when you were a teenager?" I asked facetiously. "I thought you didn't have a social media page."

"I don't, and that girl isn't me!" Abigail protested.

Carter laughed. "I thought the same thing at first, Peter. It's actually why I clicked on the profile in the first place. But if you look closely, I think you'll realize that the girl isn't Abigail. It's Heather."

"You're right. But why is she going by the name Abigail Mitchell?"

Carter clicked on the picture and scrolled to the bottom of the fake Abigail Mitchell's page. "Take a look at her first post."

It read, "I'm no longer Heather Edwards. My new name, my new Wiccan name, is Abigail Mitchell. Cyrus came up with the name. He was very insistent on it, and I'm not sure why. I like it, though. If my Dad doesn't like it, he can rot in Hell."

"Cyrus," Abigail said in an exasperated whisper. "He was the one responsible for all of this."

"She even began dressing a bit like you," I muttered.

"She probably mixed up witches and Goths. It happens more

often than you'd think. It wasn't just her attire that changed, though—her entire masquerade as a witch became more nuanced and sophisticated. As Heather Edwards, she simply regurgitated things she learned about witchcraft from popular culture. It was, for lack of a better term, the 'theme park' version of a witch. After she became Abigail Mitchell, she began to make references to history, and not just the facts you can find with a quick Wikipedia search. Heather began citing obscure facts like how a witch would create a temple, initiation rituals, and names of Wiccan gods such as Cernunnos and Arawhon."

"Cyrus probably had a hand in shaping her later views towards witchcraft," Abigail said with a hint of disdain. She glared at every photograph of Heather as Carter scrolled through the page.

"All the other non-witch posts seemed normal enough. Here's the last post she made. I think you'll find it interesting."

It read, "Going bar-hopping with my new friends, Tommy and Chuck! They found a place that doesn't even card. I'll let you know if the place is any good." Those sentences were followed by various emoticons of beer steins, happy faces, and a face that appeared to be vomiting.

Several comments were posted below. The cleaned up version is that her friends questioned going to the bar with two strange men, but Heather countered by saying she was merely meeting them for drinks and had no intention of engaging in anything further. Since Cyrus was afraid of getting caught for underage drinking outside of certain bars in Tacoma, he opted to stay home.

"This is excellent information, Carter. Thank you very much."

"No problem. I'm glad I could help."

"I should probably give Kelly a call sometime to let him know what we've found."

"You won't tell him everything, will you?" Abigail said, emphasizing the word "everything." It took me a second to figure out what she meant.

"Oh, of course. I won't tell him about Heather masquerading

as Abigail. Kelly doesn't need to know such embarrassing information."

Abigail sighed with relief. "Thank you. An asshole like him should be happy we give him anything at all."

"I guess Officer Kelly won't be on Abigail's Christmas card list anytime soon," Carter said. "I take it your meeting wasn't exactly an amicable one."

"If you're trying to say that I think he's a veritable asshole, then yes, I'd have to agree with you."

Carter chuckled, then said, "I respect that you speak your mind without constraint, Abigail. It's no wonder Peter speaks so highly of you."

"Oh?" Abigail's expression and demeanor brightened perceptibly. "You speak of me favorably to your friends, Petey?"

I began stuttering. "It's not like I'm singing your praises or anything like that. I'm just telling Carter the truth, and it just happens that the truth about you is very positive for the most part."

"Aw, Petey, that was almost sweet of you to say."

"He can be a charmer, even when he doesn't mean to be," Carter teased.

Their joking was interrupted when a beautiful brown young woman walked in wearing blue jeans and a sweater with the purple initials "UW" emblazoned on the front. A little boy with a bag of colored boxes in his hand darted past her.

"Hi, honey!" the woman said.

The words "Hi Penelope" barely escaped Carter's lips before the boy was practically leaping into his father's lap, dropping the bag onto the floor.

After a few hugs were exchanged and pictures were taken by Penelope, documenting the cute scene in spite of Carter's gentle protests, the boy finally noticed me. "And Uncle Pete's here too!" The boy then jumped off his father's lap and gave my right leg a firm embrace.

"It's good to see you too, Darren."

The boy looked up at Abigail. "Who are you?"

"My name is Abigail. We've met once before, do you remember me?"

Darren took a closer look at my companion before flashing a shy grin and burying his face into my leg a bit. The boy then showed his right eye and looked at the woman bashfully as he said, "You're the pretty lady from before."

"Aw, thank you, Darren," Abigail said, smiling at the young man. She turned towards Carter and Penelope, who had moved next to Darren. "He's quite the charming young man."

"It must come from Penelope's side of the family because he certainly didn't get it from me," Carter joked.

Looking at me, Abigail said, "You certainly could learn a thing or two from him."

"What did you have in that bag?" I asked the boy quickly, changing the subject.

"Oh yeah!" the boy said, releasing his death grip from my leg.

"I bought Darren a magic kit from a board game shop at the Tacoma Mall," Penelope explained. "He's really getting into magic."

Darren knelt on the floor and pulled out the already opened kit. "I want to show you a trick, Uncle Pete!"

"The guy working at the shopping counter showed us his favorite trick from the kit," Penelope explained. "Darren picked it up right away. He's so smart."

"What trick did you learn, Darren?" I asked.

"The cha meal ion silk trick," the boy said, showing me a red handkerchief.

"You mean the chameleon silk trick," I corrected. It was a trick I hadn't thought about in years. Hearing the name again brought back a flood of unpleasant memories. I clutched the coin around my neck.

"Are you okay, Petey?" Abigail asked.

"Yeah, you do look a bit pale," Carter noted. "Are you all right?"

"I'm fine, but I just remembered that I need to be somewhere right now and have to get going immediately."

"Oh," Darren moaned. "But I wanted to show you all of my new tricks."

"Some other time, little man," I said as I knelt down next to the poor boy. "I'll be back soon to see your magic show, but I really have to get going now. I'm sorry, Darren."

"Can't you just stay for one trick?" Darren begged.

I hugged the boy. "I'm sorry. I just can't do it right now, but I promise you I'll be able to later."

"Okay," the dejected boy said as he hugged me back.

I got back up to my feet and looked at my concerned friends. "Carter, if there anything else you find, would you mind texting it or e-mailing it to me?"

"Actually, I think that's about all I'll be able to find out about Heather, Joseph, or Cyrus. I'm sorry there's not more."

"Thanks again, Carter, you helped immensely."

"I guess we should leave, then." Abigail shrugged, looking at Penelope, who had wrapped an arm around Darren. His bottom lip was curled over his top lip as he stared glumly towards the ground. "I'm really sorry we're leaving suddenly like this."

"It's okay," Penelope insisted as we headed out the door. "Just visit again when you can, okay, Pete? You too, Abigail."

"Of course," I said as I waved to the family who, except Darren, reciprocated as I closed the door behind me.

"Now, what the hell was that about?" Abigail asked as we entered my vehicle that was parked at the curb in front of Carter's laminated yellow house with white trimmings.

It took me a minute to gather my thoughts. "It was about a month after I had returned to school after Erin's murder."

A tinge of horror was in Abigail's voice as she said, "Oh my God. I'm so sorry, I didn't realize it was related to Erin."

"Strangely enough," I continued, "I wasn't actually absent for very long, only for about a week. And even then, I didn't seem to be too shaken up by the event. I was so calm my parents were worried that I was taking it too well."

"It sounds like you were repressing the incident."

"I knew what death was, and recognized that bad things happened to good people, but I think that was part of the problem. I kept thinking to myself that in order to be a man, I had to handle this on my own."

"A foolish thought that, unfortunately, many boys still have after they've grown up."

"One weekend, I was home and didn't have much to do. Erin was really my only friend. I had always been a loner, and so was Erin, really. Probably the reason we got along so well."

"I was a bit of a loner too when I was young."

"I suppose that being a witch and the inherent secrecy you are burdened with makes it so. I really didn't have that excuse. I just had difficulty getting along with others."

"I'm sure you were very nice and a good friend to have, just a bit shy."

"True, I was shy, and I had a hard time being around other kids. Not with Erin, though. She understood me. She was always there when I needed her. So it was the weekend, and I was bored out of my skull. I began sifting through my closet and lo and behold, I found a tube that was used for the chameleon silk trick. My grandmother got it for me for Christmas, and I had chucked it back there after a fit of frustration with it. I could never get it out of the tube properly, and it always fell out of my hand."

"I can definitely see that happening for a novice."

"So, you're familiar with the trick, too?"

"A little bit. It is a classic trick, after all."

"It certainly is, but it's one that I always had trouble with. That day, though, I was bored and decided to give it another shot. This time everything clicked for me. On the first or second try, I was able to perform it adequately well. With a couple more attempts, I was practically an expert. I don't know why it was suddenly so simple for me, but I was really excited. I wanted to show the trick to a girl who loved magic almost as much as I did."

"To Erin Ross," Abigail said, her voice fading to a whisper.

"Erin was always a better magician than I was—a lot better— but I wanted to show her that I was able to do a complex trick too—well, complex for a twelve-year-old. I was practically out the door when I remembered I couldn't show Erin that or any trick ever again. My hand was still on the door handle when I broke down and suddenly started bawling uncontrollably. Both of my parents had absolutely no idea what triggered it, and had a helluva time consoling me."

"You poor, poor thing." Abigail put her hand on my knee. I looked at the woman and sighed.

"After that, I gave up on magic, or at least the performance part. I'd still read about it every now and again, but I lost the passion. It wasn't until I met and became friends with the Palmer family, or more specifically their son Darren, that I began to pick it up again. I just didn't want him sitting around playing video games all day when I babysat him."

"I've read somewhere that you don't truly miss someone until you have something you want to tell them or show them, and you realize you can't anymore."

"That's certainly what happened to me. That was the last time I cried, too." After a slight pause, I continued. "I've never told anybody about this, outside maybe my parents. Not Carter, not Penelope, not Kelly. You're the first one I've ever told. I probably should have told Carter and Penelope rather than just marching out of the house like a lunatic."

"We all have different ways of responding to things like this, Petey, and there's never a right or wrong way. I'm just happy you were able to share this with me."

"I appreciate it, but I need to start handling these things better. I need to face these problems head-on. Bad things happen to people all the time. Sometimes we need to get knocked down so we can get back on our feet and continue moving forward." I patted the smiling woman's hand. "Thank you very much for listening to me, though. I do appreciate you being here. Let's go back to my office. I still need to give Kelly a call, but like I promised, I'll omit the parts where Heather dresses like you."

"I'm really angry at Cyrus. Though I knew he had a bit of a crush on me, I didn't think he'd go so far as to emulate the

Pygmalion story with Heather."

"You mean the original Pygmalion story about a man who falls in love with his statue?"

"I'm using it metaphorically to describe Cyrus 'sculpting' Heather into me." Suddenly Abigail went pale and reached into her purse to pull out a cigarette.

"Everything all right, Abigail? I wouldn't worry too much about Cyrus. I'm sure he's just a dumb kid who can't express his emotions properly."

"It's not that," Abigail said as she lit her cigarette. "I just had a terrible thought. What if Heather was killed because Tommy and Chuck thought she was me?"

"Oh, I see what you mean. But—"

"She went by the name 'Abigail Mitchell.' She looked like me. She acted like a witch. Perhaps…well, you can see what I mean."

"Don't be ridiculous," I scolded. "How could they have known about you? The first time the three of you ever 'met' was when they attacked you. It's all just a coincidence."

Abigail just stared at me silently, seemingly unconvinced.

"Even if Tommy and Chuck mistook Heather for you, it's not your fault that she was murdered. Tommy and Chuck were responsible. Besides, you didn't tell Heather to dress up as you or to go by Abigail. Cyrus did. Not that he's responsible either, but you get my point."

After a few more puffs of the cigarette, Abigail calmed down. "You're right. I'm being silly right now. I just really feel bad for poor Heather, and I really want to talk to Cyrus. I'm going to give him a piece of my mind."

"I'm sure you have a lot to talk about with him, but so do I. We have to get to the bottom of this. Is your esbat tomorrow night?"

"The day after tomorrow, actually," she responded. "I should be able to meet Cyrus and Archon then. I'll let you know how that goes."

"Perfect," I said as I started up the car. "Do you feel all right,

Abigail?"

"I'm fine, or at least I will be. Thanks for asking, and thanks for snapping me out of it." She gave me a half smile.

"Of course. Shall we get going then?"

CHAPTER 7

"There was once a witch who claimed she could do all sorts of magical things." The voice on the radio atop my desk blared loudly with the voice of Tony O'Stein. I was kneeling down with a metal strip in my hand, looking at a safe I had placed underneath my desk, and to help pass the time while waiting for a phone call and a visit, I decided to listen to his show. Listening to the show was becoming a more common pastime for me recently, and though I constantly told myself that I was only listening to him "ironically" and for criticism, deep down, I was becoming nervous that I was slowly turning into a fan.

"She did things like poison cow's milk, turn people into frogs, and make men go insane with violent thoughts and actions," the voice on the radio continued. "The good-hearted townsfolk complained. They told her that if she continued to act in her evil manner, she would face divine punishment. She laughed at them and told them her powers were even greater than God's, so she feared no one."

Is this supposed to be the story of the 'Witch on Trial'? I thought to myself as I placed the metal piece into the right slit of the safe. *That's what he said, but this isn't the version I remember.*

"One day, though, emboldened by the spirit of God, the moral people of her village accused her of heresy and condemned her to death. Their righteous hearts overcame her evil. As they were leading her away, a little boy turned to her and said, 'You claimed to be higher than God. Why were mere mortals able to stop you?' She then turned to him and said, 'Pure and virtuous hearts can always overcome evil.'"

"Wow, he really butchered that story," I said as I reentered the code on the safe's keypad after I was able to find and hit the reset button with the strip of metal in my hand. "Not only did he tell it wrong, but he got the moral wrong too. The original story was a fable showing people the dangers of making big promises they cannot keep. He got the moral of the scorpion and the frog tale wrong too. 'Never trust someone upon meeting them for the first time.' Not even close. Oh well, at least it's better than that speech he always makes about sacrifice."

A short and catchy marimba song played at the top of my desk. Having reclosed the safe, I placed the metal strip down by my feet and answered the phone. It was Kelly.

"I talked to Joseph Edwards, but I'm afraid he refused to answer any questions related to Tommy and Chuck. His alibi of being home alone isn't great, but at the same time, it is hardly implausible. There's a small chance that I'll be able to get a search warrant, but I'd really need to sweet talk the DA. The potential motive is pretty strong, but it's not enough without evidence."

"How long do you think it'll take for the DA to get you a warrant?"

"Assuming I'm successful? No telling how long it would take. You know as well as I how these things tend to get bogged down."

"Yeah, I know, which is why I'm a bit worried. Say, would you mind if I talked to Joseph?"

"I don't think that'd be a good idea."

"Why not?"

"I have a feeling you're going to do a little bit more than just talk to him."

"All I want is a conversation with the man, I swear. Besides, he might be a little bit more open with someone who isn't a police officer."

"This is probably a bad idea, but I'll let you talk to him. I'll text you the address. You better keep your word, Pete."

"When have I ever betrayed you?"

Kelly mumbled incoherently before hanging up. Shortly

after, I received a text message of the address, along with, *Only talk to him, OKAY!*

I texted back *np* and set the phone back on the table. After pulling a magnet off the top of the safe, I tried a different method of opening it.

A knock came from the front of my office, followed by the sound of a door opening. "Petey? It's me, Abigail. Are you in right now?"

"Yeah, I'm right here, Abby," I said as I placed the magnet back on top of the desk and rose to my feet.

"Do you mind if I ask you what you were doing down there?" Abby asked as she approached my desk.

"Not a whole lot. I was just killing some time until you arrived, practicing breaking into safes."

"Underneath your desk?"

"Yeah, absolutely—take a look." I motioned her so she could see the large, dark gray safe.

"Why are you doing that? Did you lock something in there, or are you changing careers and becoming a thief?"

"People hide documents and such in safes. That's what I'm interested in. It's something I had to learn as a PI. When I found a safe as a police detective, I took it to HQ, and they typically just blew open the lock. I had to learn a lot on my own after quitting the force, and I've even had to pay for my own self-defense and disarmament courses. It's worth it, though. I've found a lot of evidence of cheating husbands breaking into safes. Fought off a lot of them, too."

"Why don't they just get rid of the evidence?"

"Perhaps they're just more sentimental than you'd think."

"I suppose you're right. I noticed you're working on only one type of safe. Are all safes built the same way?"

"Not at all. Safe-T-Tech is the most popular brand in Tacoma and Seattle, and since I could only afford one to practice on, that's the one I bought—not that I don't read up on other types of safes. Anyway, is this a social visit, Abby?"

"I'm afraid not. Archon and his wife Mathilda adamantly

refuse to allow you to see their son."

I sighed. "I'm not surprised."

"I explained to him that speaking to Cyrus wasn't just important to us, but to the entire coven. I told him that you have been nothing but trustworthy and haven't revealed our secret to anybody, not even Kelly, who's been helping us out." Abby paused. "And that is where I made my mistake. I let it slip that we had a police officer helping us. That ended the conversation immediately. Almost immediately. I did receive a long lecture from the man." Abby's voice deepened as she imitated Archon. "'Involving cowans is going to bring about destruction to the coven.' He explained that he wouldn't stop me, but hopes he and I won't regret that decision."

I smirked. "Is that really how Archon sounds?"

"It's a close facsimile. If you ever heard the man's voice, you'd realize my impression is spot on."

"So Archon sounds like a chain-smoking drag queen."

Abby glared and gave me a swift slap on my shoulder. She reached into her purse and pulled out a cigarette. "The merits of my impersonation aside, I'm afraid we won't be able to meet with Archon."

"Don't worry about that, Abby. Kelly called, and we have another lead. He talked to Joseph but didn't really get anywhere, so he gave me permission to talk to him, albeit reluctantly. We're headed to University Place."

South of Tacoma, the town of University Place, is like a lot of small towns. A nice community baseball field next to a skate park greets people as they enter the humble municipality. Its downtown area, which most cities would call a very large park, is populated by the typical chain stores and restaurants with a bit of local flavor here or there, but not enough to make the town special in any way.

At the bottom of a large hill is the rather large and elaborate Chambers Bay Golf Course that was built in an area that used to be home to a railyard. Trains still travel on the track on the far side of the course.

For a short period of time, Chambers Bay flirted with fame. It once hosted the US Open—quite an impressive feat considering that the town's population is just over thirty-three thousand. To contrast, Augusta, Georgia, home of the Masters, has a population of nearly six hundred thousand people.

Fans, players, and tourists there to see the spectacle quickly soured on the event. Golfers, who had the misfortune of competing on the course, complained about the brown grass and the overall poor playing conditions. The lack of any sort of nightlife or even in-town hotel accommodations meant that people had to leave town in order to find entertainment or even a place to stay. Although the PGA did their best to speak highly of the town, it came off as empty, and it was clear that there wouldn't be any major events returning anytime soon.

Though University Place was able to shoulder the economic pain of the failed event, it was clear that there were ramifications for this action, and some of it could be reflected in the homes, such as the one that Joseph lived in across the street from the infamous course. His home was a small and gloomy cobalt vinyl building. The paint peeled in several places. His patchy, yellow, weed-strewn lawn was a poor facsimile of a front yard.

A gray door and a coal-colored rooftop did nothing to mask the dull and dreary look of the home. Two windows visible from the front of the home were covered with blinds and shades and added to the reclusive feel of the abode. At the bottom of the home, there was just the sliver of a basement window overlooking a barren area of the yard.

After walking across stones half concealed by weeds, we arrived at the man's front door. I pressed the doorbell. No sound. I then gave the door a firm and loud knock.

"No answer," I said to Abby after knocking a second time.

Abby leaned forward and placed her right hand on the door and closed her eyes. After a few moments, Abby moved away and said to me, "I felt no presence whatsoever, not even a dog or frog or any sort of sentient life in there."

I began pacing. "What should we do? I promised Kelly that

all we'd do is talk to Joseph, but he isn't here right now. Should we wait for him to arrive?"

Abby answered my inquiry by opening the door. "Would you look at that? The door just happened to be open. I suppose our good friend Joseph wouldn't mind if we just walked in and made ourselves at home."

"You were a step ahead of me this time, or you can read my mind. Regardless, you can stop acting—nobody is around right now, so I doubt anyone will notice."

"I just want to make sure people know that Joseph is our good friend," Abby practically shouted as we entered. After closing the door behind her, Abby said, "It's getting a bit disturbing to me that not only was it easy for me to unlock the door, but I was also able to do it without any hesitation. It's because you were dropping unsubtle hints, which just confirms that you're corrupting me, Petey!"

"I'm doing no such thing. I'm a detective, and you're practically my assistant at this point, so it's expected of us. I think there's a de facto law that says we're allowed to break into people's homes."

She gave me a coy smile. "It is kind of thrilling to be in here searching for clues."

"That's the spirit! Shall we start?"

Joseph's home was absolutely filthy. Dirt, dust, and stains were all over the carpets and furniture. Food wrappers were spread throughout the house, including some from a couple of things I might have eaten once; Hostess products like Twinkies and Zebra Cakes.

An old computer sat on an even older computer desk in the living room next to the entranceway. Next to one of the windows was an old loveseat, and a decrepit couch with torn seats was to our left. A flat-screen television missing its power cord was placed above the fireplace in front of the couch.

Abby pointed at a painting next to the television set. "This certainly is charming." It depicted a large fire burning three unfortunate individuals to death as smoke rose from the flames.

A bearded man in white and orange appeared to be gleefully adding wood to the blaze from a stack next to him. Two men covered completely in black looked on, one on foot and one on horseback. Three men in black hats and white shirts also observed the slaughter.

"It's the *Burning of Three Witches* by Johann Jakob Wick," Abigail explained. "Or that is to say, it is a poor replica of that painting. The original is relatively famous. I think it's on the Wikipedia page of witch hunts."

"Were you a history major in college, by any chance?"

"Is it that obvious?" Abby said with a smile. "I'm actually a teacher's assistant with a Dr. Samuel Hawthorne at the University of Washington, Tacoma. I hope to become a professor one day."

"You'll make a good one because you certainly know your stuff."

"Well, thank you."

"Anyway, while the painting serves as a good Rorschach test into his mind, it's not very incriminating, legally speaking at least."

"I agree. Let's see what else we can find."

We waltzed into the kitchen, which was located just beyond the living room. On top of an old wooden table lay the remnants of a microwavable breakfast sandwich that was bitten into once or twice. I placed my hand on top of the sandwich. It was practically room temperature.

"Something must have caused Joseph to leave in a hurry," I explained. "He must have left it a while ago, too, because it is practically cold."

As we passed by the mostly empty, though terribly stained, kitchen counters, my attention was drawn to the sink. I moved the dishes carefully in order to be able to look without making it obvious what I had done and found something of interest amongst the dirty cups and plates.

"Hey, take a look at this, Abby," I said after wiping off my hands with a dirty towel I found underneath the sink.

After closing some cupboard doors, she replied, "What did

you find, Petey?"

"Take a close look at this," I said, holding the jar I found so she could get a clear view of the bottom. Inside there was a speck of brown dirt. Abby carefully placed her finger inside the jar and touched the substance with her finger.

"It's sticky," she said as she pulled back her hand, "and it smells awful. There's something familiar about it, though."

I thought about it for a moment. "You're right. It kind of smells like Chuck's apartment."

"It's also how Tommy and Chuck smelled when they attacked me."

"This suggests to me that Tommy, Chuck, and Joseph are either working together or are part of the same organization."

"We don't know that yet. The mud could just be a strange skin product for all we know."

"That probably isn't true, but let's keep looking around."

In the garage, we found a gold, four-door sedan, not the black car we had hoped to find. After a quick look around, I was, unfortunately, unable to find anything of particular significance.

As we headed back through the door, I looked out through a small opening of blinds that covered the glass and saw something in the backyard. I opened the blinds to get a better look.

"Hey Abby," I said, motioning her over to me, pointing at a large number of holes in the yard scattered around two large trees and the perimeter of thorn bushes and empty patches of dirt. "Take a look at this."

"Strange," she replied. "Why so many shallow holes?"

"My parents have decorative stones around their trees and decorative bricks around their garden," I said. "I'm assuming Joseph had the same thing. What I'm not sure of is why they were removed."

We walked around the equally patchy and weed infested backyard, taking a closer look at the holes that now served as its chief decoration. Kneeling, I reached down to feel inside one of the holes.

"Still wet. The bricks and stones were removed recently."

"But why?"

I sighed and shook my head as I rose to my feet. "I don't know. It's a lot of effort, but for what gain?"

"Maybe he moved them to the other side of the house?"

"It's worth a look."

At the side of the house was what appeared to be a small garbage pit. A pile of debris, including a stack of old newspapers and empty paint cans were piled in the area, but as I looked down, I noticed something else.

"There's a bicycle under here," I said to Abby, pointing at the tire with my foot as I removed things off the bike.

"Joseph probably doesn't ride it anymore, so he put some stuff on top of it and forgot about it," Abby suggested.

I pushed aside the newspapers and paint cans to reveal more of it. "Are you sure? The bike is in excellent shape."

"Oh, you're right. Why would he hide his own bicycle in his backyard?"

I shrugged. "Maybe it's the only thing of value he has."

"Even if that were true, which I doubt, why wouldn't he have hidden it in his house or his garage?" Neither of us had an answer, so we went back through the living room to one of the rooms we hadn't yet seen.

To the left, a pair of glass doors led to a simple room with a wooden floor, which contrasted with the dirty white carpet in the rest of the rooms. The main feature of the room was a pool table, which had not experienced a game in some time. It was piled with clothes and used plates, and all the billiard balls were pocketed. I didn't see a cue ball or any chalks. A nearby pool rack was full of broken or warped pool cues that seemed to be used mostly as makeshift coat racks.

"The table seems to still be in close to mint condition," I said. "If he's not interested in pool, why doesn't he just sell it?"

"Maybe you can ask him when you see him."

"Yeah, right, I'll do that. Something about this room bothers me, but I can't quite place my finger on it." I paused in thought, then said, "We might as well check out the two rooms we haven't looked at so far. Maybe something will jog my memory."

With a nod, Abby and I continued past the living room and walked towards the upper left corner where the two bedrooms were located. The feminine décor of the smaller one made it readily apparent this was the late Heather Edward's room. It had a disquieting effect on us, as the room seemed to have been left untouched since her death.

The laptop on her dusty desk was uncovered, but nothing appeared on the screen when I hit the "On" button. I guessed that the battery had died as the machine was not connected to a power supply. At my feet near the entrance of the room was the unconnected power cord. I wondered why it was left like that.

Various stuffed animals piled on top of the bed contrasted sharply with her black gothic-themed comforter, bed sheets, and pillowcases. Drawers that she would never open again were at the front of the bed, and Gothic style clothing she would never wear again hung in the closet.

"I'm not sure Joseph's even entered this room since Heather's death," I said as I looked around. "Perhaps we should just leave?"

"I agree one hundred percent," Abby said, noticeably relieved. "Let's get out of here."

We moved down the hallway to Joseph's room. In complete contrast, this room was a complete mess. Many drawers were left open, some of which were barely half filled with clothing while others were virtually overflowing. The bed was unmade with a dirty brown comforter, and gray pillowcases and sheets scrunched together. Joseph's closet contained ordinary clothes for a man—blue jeans and dress shirts. Most of these clothes were strewn haphazardly on the floor. The man's undergarments decorated the floor so well that the white carpet was almost invisible. Other than the obvious, we saw nothing worth noting.

"It's just so frustrating," I complained as I reached for the knob. "It's like having most of the pieces of a puzzle, but not being able to understand the picture until we solve it. Not the perfect analogy, but you get the idea."

"What pieces could we be missing? We've searched

everywhere in this house — there's nothing more to find."

This triggered something. "Wait a second, Abby. I don't think we have searched everywhere. Do you remember going into a basement?"

"No, probably because we didn't."

"And that's what's been bothering me."

"What do you mean? Does this place even have a basement?"

"It does," I confirmed as I released the knob to stand directly in front of her. "I saw the top of a window peeking from the ground as we entered this place. There must be a basement somewhere."

"You're right, but how can we get to it?"

"There didn't seem to be an outside door, and we couldn't find one inside. So I guess he's hidden the entrance, so obviously, he has something that needs hiding."

"You think perhaps something like his connection to the group that attacked me."

"Whatever it is, it must be pretty big if he went to all this effort. Now I think I know where the entrance could be." I pointed towards the pool room. "I'd bet it's there."

"But, we didn't find anything there before."

Since I then had a more specific goal, I was able to better analyze the place and notice something I had missed earlier. Though it would have been a little extreme to call it a path, the pile of clothes, rags, and other like items had a noticeable demarcation that led me towards the pool table. It was as if a couple of people had walked through the clothes and reached down and shoved them out of the way.

This led me to under the table. I lowered myself to the ground, holding the table as I bent over to poke my head underneath. I noticed that the floor was surprisingly clean. I got down on my knee and moved my hand across the floor. I felt a small ridge.

Pulling out my cell phone, I shook it lightly to turn on its flashlight. I could then see the outline of a trap door. Not finding a handle or knob, I began looking for some other means to manually open the door. Using the light, I carefully examined the bottom and sides of the table. I missed it the first time, but after a second and more careful examination, I saw a very small red button, which I pressed.

Slowly and almost silently, the trap door began to rise. I nearly fell backward in surprise, still being on top of it. I was able to roll out of the way in time, to the great amusement of my client, who had been watching me from just outside the room. I looked down the opened trap door and saw a stairway leading to another room.

"There's the basement," I said to her.

"Wait a second," Abby said, slowly waggling her index finger in the air. "Do you hear that?"

I listened closely and heard a gruff voice that rose from the bottom of the stairway.

"Why don't you make it easy for yourself and just admit that you're a witch?"

A much higher pitched and raspier voice replied, "And let me guess—as soon as I confess, you'll let me go, right?"

"Some people are certainly down there," I flatly stated.

Abby responded in an exasperated whisper, "I don't understand. I concentrated hard this time. I swear there was nobody down there."

"Cute," the gruff voice said. "You don't quite understand the shit you've gotten yourself into. Confess, then tell me about your coven."

"I think I need to be down there." I pulled my pistol, and while holding it with both hands, led the way as we walked down those steps as quietly as we could.

We were about halfway down when I motioned to Abby to stop. The two of us positioned ourselves so that we were just out of view. My eyes had locked on the scene below.

It was a gray-walled basement with a damp and musty gray concrete floor. The illumination of an old-fashioned single light bulb turned on and off with a pull chain, showed cabinets lining the right wall, a work table full of an assortment of tools, and what looked like some sort of power cord strung along the wall directly in front of us. Most arresting was the sight of a young blond-haired man tied spread eagle to a black table. A large flat stone was placed on top of the young man's chest, and piled on top of that were a few decorative stones.

Next to the young man was a large pile of these stones, as well as a large and evidently heavy stone. A tall, thin-mustached man with a mix of brown and ashen hair stood next to the pile, his arms and face covered with brown mud. In each hand, he held one of the bricks. The cruel and sadistic nature of the man was reflected in his brown eyes, which fixated on his victim.

After placing a couple of more bricks on top of the pile, the older man spoke. "Tell me about the circle."

"That's like a square, but without the pointy edges," the young man wheezed.

The older man added more bricks. "Any more wisecracks, or would you like to confess now?"

With a heavy, exhausted breath, the young man wheezed, "I need more weight, old man."

"You will regret that," the torturer replied as he picked up two more bricks.

"We have to do something," Abby furiously whispered. "I think I can cast a levitation spell on him."

"Good idea," I whispered back. "Try to lift him up and drop him as you did me, only make it harder. It'll probably hurt a lot on concrete."

"I'll do my best."

Abby closed her eyes and began a low chant. I leaned forward with gleeful anticipation. After a few seconds, though, I heard a frustrated grunt from my companion.

"I don't get it," she said angrily. "I can't seem to lift him off the ground. It's like I can't cast a spell on him for some reason. This has never happened to me before."

"Don't worry about it, Abby," I said. "We can figure it out later. I've got a few tricks up my sleeve as well. Stay here until I give you a signal otherwise."

As the older man continued to place the bricks on the young

man's chest, I lunged off the stairs and shouted, "Freeze! Drop the bricks now!" I aimed my gun directly at the man's back.

"Am I correct to assume that you have a gun pointed at me right now?" the man asked in a gruff voice as he lifted his arms over his head, both hands still containing a brick.

"I told you to drop the bricks," I repeated sternly.

"Somehow, I think you're bluffing," the man said smugly as he began to slowly turn towards me.

In response, partly out of fear, I did something you are never supposed to do in such surroundings. I fired my gun, much to the chagrin of everyone else in the room. Abby screamed. The young man gasped a weak, "Holy shit." Nobody was more rattled than the older man, who immediately dropped the bricks and went down to his knees. That is to say, he dropped the complete brick from his right hand and the remnants of the one in his left. I actually hit what I was aiming at for once.

"I think everything is now under control," I said to Abby as I secured the man's arms and hands with the tuff tie cuffs I always carried with me.

"Next time warn me before you fire that thing," she said as she darted past me and moved towards the young man. She paused, turned towards me, and smiled. "Although I must say, that was an excellent shot."

"Better lucky than good," I grunted back, trying not to smile.

"That was pretty cool," the young man gasped. "You're like an action hero."

Both the older man and the one under the stones were covered with brown mud. With Abigail's inabilities and remembering the substance I had found earlier in a jar in the kitchen, I guessed what the mud was all about.

While Abby removed the bricks, the blond man said, his voice slightly stronger with some of the weight being lifted, "Holy shit, is that you, Abigail?"

Moving a strand of hair from her face, she bent over to take a closer look at the boy. Abby's head moved backward sharply. "Oh my God. Is that you, Cyrus?"

"Yeah! It's me, Abigail! What are you doing here?"

"More to the point, what are you doing here? Why the hell was he placing those bricks on top of you?"

"Oh, wonderful," I said. "So you're Cyrus. Do you think Archon would mind if I spoke to you right now, maybe ask you a few questions?"

CHAPTER 8

"Well, it's a lot easier now than it was about ten minutes ago," the skinny young teenager in a black T-shirt and torn blue jeans said as he rubbed the dirt off his hands and arms with a towel I brought him while he sat resting on the table. "I'm still having a little trouble breathing, though. My chest really hurts, and a couple of my ribs are sore."

"You probably have at least some bruising, and your ribs might be cracked or even broken," I said authoritatively as if I knew what I was talking about. I grabbed the towel from his hand and threw it on the workbench. "I'd definitely recommend that you see a doctor after we're done here."

Abby muttered, "That's strange. All of a sudden, I can sense Cyrus again."

Before I could respond, Cyrus continued. "If my injuries aren't too bad—like, you know, a rib isn't poking into one of my lungs or something—Abigail could always apply one of her potions on me and cast a heal spell. She's one of the best healers in the coven, aren't you, Abigail?" Cyrus then flashed Abby a smile and a wink.

Abby folded her arms in front of her chest and moved away from him "Don't wink at me. I'm not happy with you right now, and I'm in no mood to play your sort of games."

Cyrus shrugged. "I was just trying to say you were a good healer. I guess I could go to Doctor Jack Galahad instead." Cyrus explained, "He's a witch doctor. Well, not a 'witch doctor.' You know, he's not like from Africa or an Indian, I mean Native American or a shaman or anything like that. He's a witch who happens to be a doctor. You know what I mean."

I sighed, and the young man continued.

"The funny thing with Doctor Jack is he doesn't really know much magic, he's just a regular medical doctor. He used to be a much respected medical examiner for the police department, and he did the job for many years. Unfortunately, too many kids wound up on his examining table. It just became too much for him."

"I'm actually not familiar with an ME by that name," I said. "He must have predated me by quite some time."

"He's definitely been out of that game for a while," Cyrus said. "He's ancient, but his mind's still very sharp, and he's phenomenal. Still, a magical healer like Abigail can do things that men like Doctor Jack can only dream of."

"Doctors and healers aren't mutually exclusive," Abby explained. "Healers don't have the ability to heal sicknesses or big stuff like broken bones or large cuts."

"But after we're sewn up, or our bones are set," Cyrus continued, "Healers can do their thing." Cyrus shifted in his seat in order to turn towards Abby. "Which is why we might as well cut out the middle man, and you can do your thing when we get out of here."

"I said that I'm not in the mood to play your games, Cyrus. I am really upset with you right now, and I don't feel like talking with you."

"Geeze, what's your problem?"

"Her problem is your little Pygmalion act that you were pulling with Heather Edwards," I said, surprisingly rather perturbed with Cyrus's awkward attempts at flirting.

"What the hell are you talking about?" Cyrus asked, seemingly bewildered. "What the hell is a Pygmalion anyway?"

"I thought everyone knew it's the story about a man who falls in love with his creation. It's kind of a metaphor to how you made Heather look, dress, and act just like Abby."

Cyrus turned towards me. "Making Heather act like Abby?" he said. "Who's Abby? Oh, you mean Abigail? You call her

Abby? Wait, oh no, no, you've got it all wrong. I didn't make her act like Abigail. She told me she wanted to be a witch, and once I start talking, I just can't stop. She asked me about witchcraft, and after some prodding, I told her about what I knew, and, you know, maybe Abigail came up once or twice. Sure, I told Heather about how you dressed and everything. I might have suggested Abigail Mitchell as a name when she wanted a witch name—not that there's such a thing—but it just slipped out!"

"You told her about the coven?" Abby scolded. "You gave away our secrets?"

"Nothing specific, Abigail. I left out specifics and didn't tell her any secrets. Don't you believe cowans and witches should share things together anyway?"

"It has to be judicious, Cyrus, with people you trust, and only at the right time."

"Heather was somebody I could trust. She was somebody we could all trust. That's why I was so hell-bent on bringing him to justice." Cyrus pointed at the man still brooding angrily where I had left him in the right corner of the room, the opposite side of the stairway, his arms and legs still cuffed.

"I didn't kill my daughter!" the man shouted gruffly as he struggled with his restraints. "I regret that I wasn't able to kill you!"

"Calm down, moron!" I shouted. "And stop struggling, you'll only make yourself tired!" I turned my attention back to Cyrus. "You think Joseph murdered his own daughter?"

"I know he did. He thought his daughter had turned into a witch, and he hates witches. I needed to gather evidence on him, so I was here almost every day."

"Did you find anything?" I asked.

Cyrus sighed. "Not really. I looked all over this house. I can't believe I missed this place, though. I didn't even know this house had a basement, but I did find something. It was the *Malleus Maleficarum*. Do you know what that is? It's a pretty important document in witching circles," Cyrus asked, looking at me.

"Yes, Abby told me all about it. Do you have it on you?"

"No, I hid it at home. It's very suspicious that he had it, though, right? I'm telling you, he hates witches and wants to kill and torture them. He's insane, that's why I had to come in here and prove to everyone he's a murderer!"

"Wait a second," Abby said, utterly exasperated. "You broke into the home of a man you suspected of murder? What made you do something so incredibly insane?"

"It's not like I ever broke in when Joseph was home," Cyrus explained. "When I sensed he was here, I turned around and rode my bicycle back home, and when he wasn't, I went so far as to hide my bicycle. I always kept my visits short too. Also, I never left any evidence that I broke in."

"How were you able to do that?" I asked.

He explained he used a telekinesis spell to unlock then relock the door.

"Very clever. Hey Abby," I said, smiling at the woman. "He basically used the same trick you did."

"Oh, so that's how you guys got in. Great minds think alike, eh, Abby?"

"Something like that," she said.

A thought crossed my mind. "If you always turned back home when you sensed that Joseph was here and kept your visits short, why were you caught this time?"

"I was home when this fool tried to break into my house!" Joseph growled. "I have done nothing wrong! A man is allowed to defend himself against a home invader, especially when he is a witch!"

"I think piling bricks on top of somebody in a secret basement is a bit more than mere self-defense," I replied. "Why not just call the police?"

"He's telling the truth, though. When I broke in, I walked to the kitchen, and there he was eating a breakfast sandwich. I tried to run, but the asshole caught up and tackled me, then tied me up with his television power cord. Then he marched me down these stairs into the basement. He is a helluva lot stronger than he looks. He tied me to this table," Cyrus said, patting the table.

"The freak rubbed me with that same mud, or whatever, that he rubbed on himself. Maybe a strange fetish or something. It smelled so bad, it actually made me feel physically weaker if that makes any sense."

"Why would he do that?" I wondered aloud.

"That's not the worst of it, not even close. He kept me down here and took his time, grabbing a bunch of stones or whatever from his backyard. The smell and fatigue prevented me from getting too scared. For a while, I believed the anticipation was going to be worse than the punishment, but when he started piling bricks, I thought, 'Nope, this is much worse.'"

"Why break in when he's home?"

"That's the weird thing—I couldn't sense him. That kind of thing never happens. Still, I thought the protect spell would save me even though I was caught."

"Protect spell?" Abby asked. "What protect spell? We don't have a protect spell, do we?"

"Of course we do. You know, the spell where you bury a coffee jar and fill it with sharp objects—broken glass, old razor blades, rusty nails, and screws, pins and needles, that sort of thing—and then…well, pee in it to fill it. After that's done, seal the top of the jar and bury the thing in the ground at least a foot deep, right? As long as it remains undisturbed, it should protect you, right?"

"You really did all of that?" Abby asked.

"Yeah, but it didn't work. Maybe the dog got to it or something. She's always digging up things in the backyard."

"Where did you get that information?"

"From a book I read in my dad's study."

"I think you misread the book," Abby explained. "That spell is not designed to protect witches. It is designed to protect your crops."

Cyrus stuttered, "Are you sure?"

"Look on the bright side, Cyrus," Abby said with a small, wry grin. "At least your backyard won't be infested with locusts anytime soon."

"I suppose that explains why the spell didn't do anything," Cyrus said with a slight grimace. "Still, it doesn't explain why I wasn't able to sense Joseph. Has anything like that ever happened to you, Abby?"

"Abigail," Abby corrected. "You still call me Abigail." Abby pointed at me. "Only he's allowed to call me Abby."

"Okay, 'Abigail,'" the young man said, rolling his eyes. "Have you ever experienced anything like that before?"

After a silent pause, Abigail said, "Yes, it's happened to me several times recently, including just now. I thought this place was completely empty when we entered. There were no signs of life. I can sense you now, Cyrus, but I still can't sense Joseph. I'm starting to see a pattern, but...."

Following her thought, I picked the malodorous Joseph up and asked, "Now then...Joseph, right? It's time for you to talk to your good buddy, Peter Cunningham."

"I've got nothing to say," Joseph growled.

"Now that's a poor attitude to take. Don't sell yourself short. I'm sure you have plenty to tell me. I'll be sure to ask nicely." The smell was starting to get to me a little bit.

"All I'll tell you is that I did not murder my daughter! I loved her in spite of her choice of lifestyle!" A couple of tears fell from his eyes even as he clenched his teeth.

"You know something? I actually believe you. Yeah, that's right. I know you didn't kill your daughter. It was Tommy Stim and Chuck Ericson. I have a feeling you know more about them too. Would you mind sharing?"

"I've nothing else to say," Joseph spat out at me.

Abby startled me by saying, "Peter! Look what I found!" I turned to peer into the drawer she had opened. Most notably inside was an alabaster robe identical to the ones that Tommy and Chuck had worn when they attacked Abigail. Of seemingly lesser note were various posters and other sorts of paraphernalia advertising Tony O'Stein's show, as well as some recognizable charms and amulets that supposedly provided protection from witches.

"That cinches it, then!" I shouted while I shook Joseph. "All three of you were somehow involved in whatever led to the attack of this beautiful woman!"

"Beautiful?" Abby asked.

"Beautiful?" Joseph said with much more contempt. "She's nothing but a witch."

He piqued my curiosity. "What makes you think she's a witch? For that matter, why do you believe Cyrus is a witch?"

The man threw back his head to laugh, then said, "We have our ways." Glaring at Abigail, he added, "You are a particular infamous and iniquitous creature amongst the people I know. Your name is often spoken in soft tones. But to me? You're nothing more but Satan's dirty whore."

I snapped my gun from its holster and pointed it at the man's head. "Don't you dare call her anything like that! Now, start giving me some damn answers, or I will blow your goddamn head off, so help me God I will!"

Abigail gasped and squealed, "Don't do it, Peter! He's not worth it! You're not a murderer!"

The man scorned, "She's right, you know. You won't kill me. You don't have it in you."

"Oh yeah? Mock me. That worked out really well the last time you thought I was bluffing."

"Shooting a brick and shooting a man are two vastly different things. You talk tough, but I know you won't do it. Even if you did kill me, death is preferable to betraying our principles."

My hand began to shake. "I'll do it. I swear I'll do it."

The man smiled at me, contemptuously. "Do it, then. I'm waiting."

I sighed and placed the gun back into my holster. "You're right. I can't shoot a man in cold blood. I do have a good friend on the police force, though, I'll give him a call and make sure you get the worst possible cell at Pierce County Corrections." My olfactory senses were becoming overwhelmed by his hideous stench.

He laughed again. "What do I care about prison? You expect

me to betray our cause because of a threat of being locked up for what, a few weeks at most? I may have been, shall we say, a little overzealous. However, I'm a grieving father, after all, so perhaps my mind isn't in the right place. And both he and you are guilty of breaking into my house, Mr. Cunningham. To implicate me would be implicating yourselves as well."

"Yes," I admitted. "That's true. But Kelly is a good friend of mine, and I can probably talk.... I mean, we can probably make a...." I paused as my train of thought was beginning to escape me. "Abby, could you do me a favor and grab that towel off the tool bench? The stench is starting to kill me. I can't even concentrate."

"Oh yeah, no problem," Abby said as she moved towards the tool bench.

The man squirmed feverishly and shouted in a near panic. "No, don't you dare wipe this off me!"

"Relax, all I want to do is to clean you up so I can concentrate a bit better, that's all."

He screamed, emphasizing every syllable. "I said, don't you dare!"

"Now, why the hell would this bother you so—?" My voice trailed mid-sentence as my mind began to race. My suspicions came to fruition. "Abby," I said as I grabbed the towel from her hand. "After I wipe this stuff off, tell me whether you can sense this man."

The man struggled greatly as I began wiping the mud off his arms and face. "Would you hold still already?" I shouted in vain. In spite of his wriggling, I was able to slowly and gradually wipe all of the strange goop from his arms and face.

"Oh my God, it's like my senses have returned," Abby said in a surprised tone.

"Yeah, I can sense him too," Cyrus said as he continued to sit on the table. "It's like being blind but suddenly able to see, or at least how I'd imagine it."

"It seems that mud which was spread over Joseph and Cyrus's arms and legs blocks witches senses and thereby blocks magical spells. Try your levitation spell again."

Abby nodded, closed her eyes, and began that chant. I let Joseph go, and he began to float in the air. Joseph whined with fear and horror then, without warning, the man fell and crashed, landing hard on his rear end.

"Sorry about that," Abby said sheepishly. "I'm not great with the spell."

I smiled. "You just need to work on your landings. Now then," I said, lifting Joseph back onto his feet. "Without that mud, you can't stop her from casting spells, right?" The man stared at me, dismayed. "I'll take that as a yes. That levitation spell is just a taste of her true power. She's one of the most powerful witches in all the country, perhaps even the world. It'd probably be in your best interest to answer my questions now." He gave me a surly nod.

"Be sure that you're honest, too," Abby said as she moved to my side. "I can tell if you're lying or not."

"You can do that?" he asked.

"It's an ability I picked up by sensing people's heartbeats. It took practice, but now I'm something of an expert. Based on how quickly or slowly your heart beats, I'll be able to figure out whether or not you're being honest."

"Told you she was one of the best witches in the country," I said. "So you probably don't want to mess with her. All those stories you heard about what evils witches do and the tortures they like to do to people? All true. It turns out all those old wives were right. And lucky you, two of them are in this room, and now there's nothing protecting you, and she can tell if you're lying or not. Consider all of this when I ask you these questions."

Joseph stuttered. "I...I already told you that I understand. I'll...answer you...honestly...."

"Okay, then, the first question. How did you know that Cyrus and Abby were witches?"

"Him, I just assumed," Joseph said, motioning with his head towards Cyrus. "I knew I had an intruder. I found his student ID card in my kitchen."

"Dammit!" Cyrus growled. "So, that's where I left that damn

thing!"

"That was pretty stupid," I muttered.

"When I noticed that the only things stolen from my house were the *Malleus Maleficarum* and a few amulets I had accidentally left in my room," Joseph continued, "Items that a typical teenager would have no interest in, I simply guessed that a witch was involved."

"I assume that's why you started covering yourself with mud."

The man's silence was his confirmation.

"How did you know Abby was a witch?"

"She is infamous in our congregation. She is, after all, the daughter of a man that leads a movement against non-witches."

"How were you able to find that out?"

"You give me far too much credit," the man responded harshly. "I'm not familiar with any specifics. They only tell me what I need to know, and I didn't need to know that. Just know that we have excellent spies."

"Uh, Abby, is he telling the truth?"

"Hmm? Oh yes, yes, he is."

"Good. What sort of concoction is the mud that it allows you to hide from witches and suppress their powers?"

"I don't know that either. Only a few do because the fewer who know, the less likely the secret will be revealed. It's just provided on a basis of need."

"Only a select few, huh," I said, lost in thought for a moment. "Somebody like Keith Jackson, perhaps?"

"Don't know that name."

"Abby, he's lying, right?"

"Already beginning the chant."

"All right, I recognize the name. He owns a local boutique, and the two of us have talked on occasion. That means what?"

"I'm just connecting dots," I answered while thinking about the three white robes. Tommy and Chuck weren't bright, but their employer, Keith, seemed smart enough. I guessed that either he had told his odd employees how to create their own mud, or they managed to learn it from him on their own. So far, I knew that the mud included ximuce trees found only in Evergreen, and that it smelled horrible. I mentioned my suspicions about them to get Joseph's reaction.

"I knew those two were trouble from the moment I met them. Useful idiots, Keith called them. How he expected a couple of lowlife thieves to assist us is far beyond me. The worst part is that they had delusions of grandeur, especially Chuck. A fool with ambition is a dangerous man."

"Tommy and Chuck murdered Heather, didn't they?"

After a short pause, Joseph continued. "Yes, they were the ones responsible for her death. It seems they thought she was a witch. They thought that killing her would impress leadership. Those idiots. They tied her to the chair and threw her in the ocean, thinking they were 'dunking' a witch."

"Dunking?" I asked.

"I think he's referring to the torture during the witch trials," Abigail explained, "Where you placed a witch in water to see whether or not she'd float. Floating equaled witchcraft."

"Needless to say," Joseph continued, "They got it completely wrong."

"So you killed the two of them in revenge," I guessed.

"No, I didn't, but I wish I had! Leadership thought they could still be useful to us, so they gave them one last chance!"

"One last chance? What are you talking about?"

"Her!" He barked while staring towards Abby. "Our unquestionable leadership thought those two could provide some use for us by knocking her off."

"Me?" Abby asked. "Why am I so important?"

"It was not so much you as it is what you represent. The daughter of a prominent witch? Oh, killing you would have sent shockwaves down your clan, would it not?"

"Wait a second," I said. "So, you were fine with Tommy and Chuck killing your daughter as long as it helped your cause?"

"I wasn't fine with it!" Joseph shouted. "And the plan was that Tommy and Chuck would be killed during the attack! They didn't know that, but we knew how cruel witches could be and assumed they would not only have been caught but also tortured and killed. We didn't even give them any of the protective salve we normally give our soldiers. They somehow found out about it and created their own batch. They were supposed to die!" Joseph's voice weakened. "Sacrifices, the leadership called them."

"Then you killed them after they failed?"

"No," the man said, with tears beginning to form in his eyes. "But I should have. Leadership thought it'd be better if we had our typical 'problem solver' do it, but it should have been me. I wanted to kill them. I begged them to let me do it. I've been a member of the Benevolent Arms congregation for over a decade, and they still didn't let me do it."

"The Benevolent Arms Church? You mean the one on Eighty-Fourth Street? What do they have to do with any of this?"

Joseph ignored me and started to wail. "Kill me!" the man begged. "Whatever you do to me can't be any worse than what I feel now! I'm already in hell! She was my little girl! I loved her more than life itself!" His body went limp, and he slipped through my hands and fell to the floor. "All those years we fought, all those years I wasted! For what? Torture me! I don't care anymore! They took my girl away from me, and wouldn't even let me get revenge! Smash my head for all I care! Shoot me with your gun! Make my head explode! Just end my suffering! Life is meaningless to me now!" The man began crawling as best he could towards Abby. "Witch, I implore to you. Bring her back to me."

"What?" Abby asked, clearly perplexed.

"Use your magic and bring my little girl back to me."

"I can't do that," Abby said, stammering a bit as she said it. "Nobody can. It's impossible."

"I know I don't deserve it, but please bring my little girl back to me. Do whatever you want to me. Kill me, torture me, do whatever you must, but please, just bring her back to life! I don't even care what form. Let her be a witch—a demon, even. Just bring her back! I want to see her one last time!"

Tears began to form a bit in my eyes as I watched this broken man. I glanced over at Cyrus, weeping softly as he moaned, "Oh God, Heather. Why did this have to happen to you?"

"No, you don't understand. I really, literally can't do that," Abby said as she turned her head away and desperately tried to choke back her tears. "No witch can do that."

"No. I heard witches can bring back the dead. You have to bring back my daughter. Take my life if you must, use my body as a vessel, anything. Just please bring back my daughter."

"I can't," Abigail said, voice cracking. "I honestly cannot. Witches cannot bring back the dead. We don't have that kind of power."

"Oh God," the man wept. "Then she really is gone, and there is nothing I can do about it."

For a while, the only things that could be heard in that pain-filled room were the anguished wailing of the man on the floor, Cyrus weeping into his hands, Abby fighting back the tears, and my own sniffling. Regaining some composure, I said to Joseph, "I only have one more question for you, and I hope you can answer it."

Joseph looked at me expectantly but said nothing, his sobs momentarily stopped.

I clutched the coin hanging around my neck. "Do you know the name, Erin Ross?"

The man responded earnestly. "I'm afraid not." After a short silence, he continued, "She was someone important to you?"

I choked back the tears. "Yes, she was."

The man silently read my face. "How old was she when she was killed?"

"She was eleven years old."

"Dear God, only eleven years old. What a terrible, terrible world we live in." He then asked, "Were you — were you able to get vengeance?"

"Not yet. Still need to find out who did it."

"I sincerely wish you luck."

"Cyrus," I instructed, "I believe there's a knife on that table of tools over there. Would you mind bringing it to me?"

"Why?" Cyrus asked as he abruptly raised his head from his hands. "What are you planning on doing?"

"Letting Joseph free."

"What? Why?"

"He's not going to tell us anything more. Besides, he's suffered enough."

"Do it, Cyrus," Abby said with streaks of makeup down her face. "I trust Petey. If he says let him free, let him free."

Cyrus grimaced as he rose from his seat and limped over to the table as instructed, picked up the knife, and walked over to hand it to me.

Cutting him loose, I said to Joseph, "You're free to go. Leave town and never return."

The man looked up at me, incredulously with tears still flowing down his cheeks. After he understood that I was serious, he stood up slowly, then awkwardly increased his pace until he managed to sprint up the stairs and out of our sight.

"Are you sure that was a good idea?" Cyrus asked.

"No, I'm not. I don't believe Joseph will bother us anymore, but I certainly believe he knows more than what he told us. But at the same time, I didn't know what else to do. I wasn't going to kill him. The three of us are trespassers, and while he underestimated how severe his charge would have been, I doubt any of us wanted to spend the night in jail."

"Fair enough," Cyrus said. "But what if it was all just an act so he could escape?"

"Then his acting rivals even Hollywood's greatest stars. Which reminds me, excellent bluff, Abby."

"Bluff?" Abby stumbled over her words. "What do you mean?"

"I was a cop for almost ten years. Even if you can read a person's heartbeat, in spite of what movies might tell you, it takes an expert to read a polygraph, and even then, polygraphs are not permissible in court. They are notoriously unreliable. Admit it, you can't really tell if a person's lying."

"I can't believe you doubt my ability."

"So you knew that Carter was lying when he said I've praised you often."

"He lied about that?"

"Gotcha."

"God, I really hate you sometimes, you know that?" Abigail pulled a cigarette out from her front pocket and lit it with her finger. "You always know the right thing to say to piss me off." After a deep puff, she continued. "But you are right. I was merely bluffing." She flashed a grin. "It was a pretty good bluff, wasn't it?"

"It was a topnotch acting performance."

Cyrus then chimed in by saying, "I certainly would have given you an Oscar, Abigail."

"Where do we go from here?" Abby asked. "Joseph mentioned something about being part of the Benevolent Arms Church. Should we check them out?"

"It's certainly something that needs to be looked into," I said. "But for now, we have someone else to investigate."

"Okay," Abby said, a bit confused. "Then what do you want to do?"

"First," I said, offering Cyrus my arm as I had noticed he had begun to wobble a bit. "We are going to get this guy into triage, so we get his wounds taken care of."

"Yeah," Cyrus said in response as he placed his arm across my back and grabbed my right shoulder. "I'm starting to feel a bit light-headed."

"Well, we definitely want you healthy, kid," I said as I helped Cyrus up the basement stairs, with Abby leading the way. "Because I have big plans for you if you want to help us out."

"Of course I want to help you out—you did rescue me, after all. What's the plan?"

"It's a matter of grave importance," I said, the gears turning in my head as a plan began to formulate, a crude one at that point, but one that was slowly coming into fruition. "It not only involves you, Heather, Abby, and even me but your entire coven as well."

"Are you sure you want me?"

"I'm sure. You're going to be playing a vital role in my plan."

CHAPTER 9

"Cyrus, I must commend you. You've done a fantastic job thus far," I said to the young man sitting in front of me in my office. I had just finished listening to the recording he had given me from his day of work. "You've gone well above and beyond the call of duty at this point, much more than I could have reasonably asked for, and we definitely got some good information to work with."

The young man really had exceeded all of my expectations. A few days after we found him, and after getting healed, he rode his bike over to my office. After promising Abby he'd follow my instructions, I sent him to start working for Keith Jackson at the Nice Garb Express. I forged some credentials and pretended to be a former employer on the phone when talking to Keith. The combination of Cyrus's skill at using racial jokes reformatted to target witches, and Keith's need for a new employee after losing two of his, helped to get Cyrus hired.

Name any perfectly legal private investigator tool that can be used to gather evidence, and I'd tried it. So I decided it was time for a less than legal method. To that end, I lent Cyrus a cell phone with charger, and instructed him to give my phone a call, put it on speaker, and just go about his day, hoping we could record an incriminating conversation involving Keith Jackson.

With Carter's help, I was able to hook my phone to my laptop, so I could record the conversations I was hoping to hear with sufficient amplification to keep them clear. It was essentially a poor man's wire and the kind of contraption I'd had to resort to ever since leaving the force.

I also didn't want to use a conventional recording device,

because a cell phone was just a phone, but if someone caught Cyrus carrying a bug, I knew I could not react fast enough to ensure he wouldn't get hurt. Still, I drove him to work every day because I wanted to be nearby in case anything went wrong.

Cyrus gathered a lot of good information, albeit in trickles, as the young man was adept at positioning himself in the right place to eavesdrop without actually being involved. It still took hours to sift through all of the conversations, though, for every tiny nugget of real information was surrounded by a metric ton of fool's gold. One such gem was Keith Jackson's obsession with Evergreen.

His desire to protect these woods was only rivaled by his hero, Tony O'Stein. Throughout the myriad of recordings of Keith, I heard the same parable repeated, often in bits and pieces. Anyone who had listened to more than one lecture of Tony O'Stein would instantly recognize it as his favorite one to tell.

Since time immemorial, chickens have always been hunted by foxes, but there was a period of time when chickens tried to change their fate. They went to the king of the animals, Leo the Lion, to beg him to make a decree that would ban foxes from attacking them.

Leo was a fair king, and he listened to the chicken's plight. He asked the rest of the animal kingdom how they felt, and they all agreed that it was unfair that the chickens were hunted by the foxes. Leo offered the chickens a deal; as long as they remained peaceful creatures and never antagonized the foxes in any shape or form, he would use his magic to prevent the foxes from attacking the chickens. Naturally, they agreed; chickens have no reason to attack foxes, so of course, they could remain peaceful. Thus, it was done.

The foxes, though, missed the taste of their prey, and they had to figure out a way to make the chickens attack them, thereby breaking the spell. The foxes scared them with their growls, stole their feed, and kept them up all night with their howls. Frustrated over the foxes' behavior, the angry chickens decided to attack. The spell was now broken. Foxes were again allowed to eat chickens to their hearts' content.

The chickens begged Leo and the rest of the animal kingdom for help, but they refused. The chickens had attacked the foxes. They had broken the deal. Their reaction to minor grievances led to much greater torment.

Another thing that was quite clear in the recordings was that Keith was starting to grow very fond of Cyrus. He constantly made allusions that Cyrus should join his organization that operated after hours. Naturally, this piqued my interest, but not necessarily in a positive way.

"Hey, thank you very much, Peter," Cyrus replied to my compliment. "It means a lot coming from you."

"You are an incredibly brave young man. I had reservations about asking you to do this and would have understood if you declined, so I really appreciate the job you're doing."

"I'd rather be doing something than thinking about how I lost Heather. It doesn't hurt as bad if I'm doing something."

"You really loved her."

"I really did. I wasn't playing some sick game using Heather as my Abigail. Heather asked me about witches, so I told her. She dressed how I described Abigail, which was hot but never my intent. Sure, I had it bad for Abigail for a little while, but that doesn't mean anything. Just because I used to look up adult videos involving babysitters and the men they used to babysit every night, and one thing led to another—"

"Okay, that's enough. If that's what you're into, Cyrus, I won't judge you for it. Well, actually, I will silently, but it's fine that you like those kinds of things—just keep it to yourself."

"Oh, sorry. Those feelings went away when I met Heather. She was perfect for me in every way. It was magic. Not witch's magic. A more powerful magic."

I sighed. "I understand, and that's what makes this so hard for me to say."

"What are you talking about, Peter?"

"You've gathered some great information for me, and I am very grateful for it. Once you graduate from school, please find me. I'd love to have an assistant like you. However, it's now time for me to work alone."

"What do you mean?" The young man rose to his feet and slammed his hands on my desk, "How can you fire me after all I've done for you? You said that I'm doing a great job!"

"Cyrus," I said calmly. "Keith Jackson told you that in order to join his little cabal, you need to kill a witch. That was his entrance exam. Are you really planning on killing a witch just to keep your cover?"

"No, but—"

"Besides," I said, interrupting him. "Just having a recording of him saying this is pretty damning in and of itself, isn't it?"

"Yeah, but technically he didn't say it, I did. Listen to the recording again." Cyrus pointed at my phone, sitting on the edge of my desk. "He told me that due to the actions of less competent members, they had to increase the standards of the exam. It was up to the applicant to come up with the test on his own. I'm the one who foolishly said, 'You mean like killing the witch,' and all he said was like, 'That would indeed be a bold thing to do.' I mean, you and I know what he really meant, but that's hardly a smoking gun. Somebody who didn't know what was going on would probably say that's a joke. He's got plausible deniability, at least."

"Yeah, I know," I said, rubbing the back of my neck. "He never actually told you what organization he wanted you to join, either. He was probably purposely vague just in case. Still," I continued shrugging, "It does confirm that he's involved."

"But the goal was for me to find something big. I've stumbled into it. Let's not back off now."

"The goal was to find evidence of his involvement," I corrected. "And I think you've adequately done that."

"Let me continue for a few more days."

"I can't believe I have to say this." I stood and leaned towards him. "He wants you to kill a witch!"

"Oh that," the young man replied calmly, sitting back down on his seat. "Don't worry, I have a solution for that."

I gave the boy a jaundiced glare. "What exactly do you have

in mind? If you tell me you are planning to sacrifice one to save one hundred, I'm kicking your scrawny little ass out that damn door."

"No!" the young man said sharply. "I'm not what you'd call an expert conjurer. Other than the levitation or telekinesis or whatever, I really can't conjure up anything else. However, I am great with potions, and one of the potions I can mix together is a 'bas fake' elixir."

"What is that? A fake death spell or something?"

"Yeah, just a fancy way of saying fake death. I think it's Gaelic, and I think it's called bas fake. My memory and my Gaelic have never been good. Abigail taught it to me when I was a little boy. She learned it from her friend Dahlia."

"Is teaching children how to fake deaths a common practice of witches?"

Cyrus laughed. "Nah, nothing like that. Abigail was babysitting me, and I heard from my friend Timothy that it was possible to revive the dead. She told me that it was impossible to actually raise the dead, and the closest thing she knew of was faking death and having them wake up again as if you were raising the dead. Abigail then let it slip that Dahlia had taught it to her not too long ago. So every time she came over to babysit, I begged her to teach me. I did it so much she eventually just broke down and told me. Actually, she recited the ingredients really fast and told me how to do it really quickly, so that she could technically say she told me how to do the spell and for me to stop bugging her. But I kept asking her to repeat and was eventually able to record everything in my notebook."

"Knowing a spell and actually casting it are two different things, I would think. I've read about the Chinese linking rings trick, but I could never execute it properly. I imagine actual spellcasting even with potions might be similar."

"It is similar, and I'd be more worried if I hadn't performed the spell before."

"You've done it before?"

"To my friend Timothy. Did it to him a couple of years ago

to win a bet. He looked so much like he was dead that it scared the hell out of his mom. Deep down, it scared me a bit too. His mom would have killed me, but Doctor Ellis confirmed he was still breathing, albeit incredibly slowly, and under a deep trance. Sure enough, a few hours later, Tim was wide awake, unaware that the spell had been cast."

"Is the spell dangerous?"

"Not at all. Nobody has ever died using this spell. You ever hear of those fairy tales where the evil witch makes the princess sleep for ages? This spell is similar, but it only lasts a few hours."

"I guess it's feasible," I said, sitting back down as I tried to absorb all of this information. "But who would we use as your victim?"

"Why not my friend Tim?"

"He'd be willing to go under again?"

"Of course! He's my best friend. Besides, he owes me. I fronted him the money for Gen Con, which is some nerd convention for board games or something in Indianapolis, about six months ago."

"So Tim would be the 'body' used as an offering to join the cabal." Cyrus nodded to confirm. "This could get really dangerous. Are you sure you want to do this?"

"I understand the risks. Besides, won't you be listening in anyway? You can always come in if things get too heated."

"I think you put too much faith in me. I'm just one man."

"I already saw you in action, remember? You're like an action hero. An opportunity like this might never happen again." Cyrus then moved forward and looked me directly in the eyes. "Besides, Heather was my Erin. I will do whatever it takes to avenge her."

This somehow made me decide to tell Cyrus about Erin and me. She and I grew up in Dupont, a small city just north of Olympia that's more like a speed trap with houses built around it. The two of us wanted to be stage magicians. Erin was the prodigy, while I couldn't even guess the right card. To illustrate, I told him my favorite anecdote.

She was performing in front of the kids in our neighborhood

using my parent's front yard as a makeshift stage. Erin placed a sheet over her dog and made him levitate.

Gary, a fat kid with a slice of pizza in his hand, came up to the front and announced that he had seen the Masked Magician, and knew that the sheet contained wires that helped perform the trick. He was dismayed when he pulled the sheet away only to find that it was an ordinary green sheet. Erin had somehow replaced the trick sheet with the real one without anyone noticing.

I also told him about Erin's father running out his front door, screaming that something terrible had happened to his little girl. I told him how I ran to Erin's house, somehow sneaking my way in past the adults. I told him how the jubilant little girl who had befriended me when nobody else would, the one who understood me more than anyone else, the only one who was ever truly my friend, lay there lifeless, her favorite food, an apple, not far from her hand.

My parents grabbed and dragged me from the scene as I hysterically explained that I had seen a mysterious man a few nights before sneaking around Erin's house. I had seen him when I looked out the window while practicing magic tricks I hoped would impress Erin. I told her about it, but she didn't take it seriously, and after her death, my parents thought I was just overwrought and imagining someone to blame. But I was certain he was real and probably behind her murder.

The medical examiner, Doctor Jonathan Tristan, whose name I had only learned after looking it up when I became a detective, concluded that the cause of death was cyanide poisoning. According to the police, some maniac had poisoned random apples via a syringe, and Erin's family was just unlucky enough to have purchased them. The girl's midnight snack induced in her a deep sleep that no handsome prince could wake her from.

The morning after the murder, I checked under Erin's window where the man had been looking. The latch of the window was broken. As I continued to examine the area, I kicked something across the grass. The object's shine in the sun drew me to it. I picked it up, and in my hand was a coin. I would decades later learn that the sleeping man printed on it was actually the representation of the tomb of Pope Innocent VIII.

I followed the news closely the next week, thinking there would be some sort of panic due to the poisoned apples. There was none. There wasn't a rash of deaths occurring due to cyanide either. It was as if Erin had been singled out, and the mysterious man and coin only augmented that theory.

When I told him about all of this, Erin's father claimed that the window had always been broken, the coin could have come from everywhere, and that the police must have been able to get rid of the poisoned apples before a widespread panic could occur. It was easy to believe he just dismissed my claims due to my youth, but it was more likely that he was merely a grieving father who didn't want to listen to me.

He and his wife moved shortly after the murder. The thought of living in the same home where their daughter had died was just too painful. According to one rumor I heard, the two didn't live long after they moved away, having died of grief or something more self-inflicted.

Finished with my story, I said, "I guess you win."

"Does that mean...?"

"Let's fake your friend's death."

We shook on it.

***

"I don't know, man." The short, stocky teenager with brown hair, wearing a dark blue shirt and black denim pants, sat on the forest floor on a cool Wednesday evening. A small animal rustled the forest debris nearby, which made the three of us jump.

We were gathered at the bridge closest to the entrance of Swan Creek Park, a 373 acre greenspace nestled on the boundary of East Tacoma. With its salmon-bearing stream, wooded canyon, upland forest, paved and natural trails, a new community garden, and new mountain bike trails, this was supposed to have become a popular attraction for the local community. It didn't work out that way.

Before being developed into a park, it was a place for low-income housing designed to shelter the families of those who worked by the docks in downtown Tacoma. However, by the fifties, the homes were deemed unfit by the state and were torn down. The park that was built in its stead actually became a hotbed of illegal activity.

Much of the park was beautiful. The main entrance had a huge and beautiful community garden, and the old blacktop roads provided an excellent walking path. The dirt hiking paths extending off the main course gave visitors a means to walk deeper into the forest.

Yet, there was something eerie about this place. Perhaps it was the old eroded curbs and fire hydrants along the grid patterned streets that contributed to this atmosphere. Perhaps it was the old telephone poles tangled up in the forests that made it seem like humanity had long abandoned this place, though that could not have been farther from the truth. Perhaps it was all the scorch marks in the old blacktop, where people had made improper campfires that provided unprovoked thoughts of apparitions haunting the place. Regardless, there was no denying the unease that we were all feeling. But at the same time, it felt like the perfect place to stage a murder.

"I'm beginning to have second thoughts about all of this," Tim continued.

"It's a little bit too late now," I explained, hovering over the young man next to my blond haired friend. "Cyrus has already made the call to Keith, so he and his crew will be here any minute now."

"What's the problem, Tim?" Cyrus asked. "You know you're not really going to die. It's all pretend."

"I know that," Timothy responded irritably. "But those men you called are witch hunters, right? Do you know why we stopped using this spell?"

"I don't know. We used to do it to show how powerful we were to cowans like we really had the power to raise the dead. But after witchcraft fell out of favor, we probably wanted to hide such powers from them."

"Yeah, maybe we did that a million years ago or something, but witches used to do this to fake their death and avoid being burned at the stake, you know? Like you can't kill me if I'm already dead. Only problem was they'd just burn the body anyway. Didn't want the 'disease' to spread."

"You were all in ten minutes ago," I admonished. "When I asked if you were ready, you said, and I quote, 'Yeah, dude, I was born ready. Let's do this!'"

"I was just trying to psyche myself up. I'm actually very scared."

"We're doing this for the greater good of the coven. Doesn't it make you excited?"

"I'd rather be home playing Blood Bowl."

"What about the money you owe me?"

"I'll find another way to pay you back."

My head was throbbing. "Look, Cyrus told Keith he just poisoned a witch and has his body sitting here in the forest as evidence. He could be here any moment now. I think if he found a teenager sitting here that he thinks is a witch, he'd give him a fiery greeting if you catch my drift."

"You'll make sure they won't do anything to me when I'm unconscious, though, right?"

"Yes, I'll do my part," I said exasperatedly.

"Fine," Tim sighed as he lay down on the forest floor. "I hate lying in the dirt. It's so cold and dusty."

"At least it's not raining like last week. See, no mud."

"Lucky me. Go ahead, Cyrus. Do your thing."

Cyrus smiled as he pulled out a jar from his coat pocket. Opening the lid released an almost almond-like smell mixed with some sort of citrus sweetness.

"What's in that potion anyway?" I asked.

"Believe me, you don't want to know," Cyrus said as he kneeled next to his friend and began wiping the substance all over his friend's neck and head using his thumb.

"Believe me, I don't want to know either," Timothy said as he closed his eyes and grimaced throughout the process.

After Cyrus had applied the concoction to the neck, head, and chest of the brown-haired young man, he waved his hand over his friend's face. Closing his eyes, Cyrus chanted a few words in what seemed to be Gaelic.

"Would you hurry up, already?" Timothy said, "I hate having this stuff on—"

Before he could complete the sentence, Timothy was out cold and appeared to be comatose. The substance on his face had disappeared.

"There," Cyrus said. "That should do it."

I stared at his body in bewilderment. "He looks dead. Are you sure he's all right?"

"He's fine," Cyrus said, closing his jar. "He's still breathing, just really slowly."

I knelt next to the young man lying on the ground and grabbed his wrist. A chill went down my spine. "He doesn't have a pulse, Cyrus."

"Yeah, the spell really makes you believe he's dead. His pulse is really slow right now. His entire body is moving in slow motion. In a couple of hours, he'll be awake as if nothing happened, as if by—well, magic, funnily enough. It's why I wanted to call Keith first to ensure he gets here while Tim is playing dead."

I sighed nervously. "If you say so."

"You'll be...uh...you'll be nearby, right?" Cyrus asked.

"Of course," I said, tapping the gun I had hidden in my thick track and field warm-up jacket I had just picked up at local sporting goods store. "Hopefully, I won't have to use it, though. I'll probably be within listening distance, but just in case, how about you give me a call now so I can listen in to your conversation." I tapped the Bluetooth in my ear. The young man did as instructed and dialed my phone. After giving him a confirmation that his voice was going through, I gave him a quick wave as I hid just out of sight—once again close, but not too close.

For a short while, silence filled the air, with the only sounds being the creatures in the woods. Various woodland creatures made seemingly haunting noises while the air grew thick with anticipation.

It was almost a relief when the sounds of footsteps amid forest rubble could be heard. Even in the twilight, I was able to make out the visage of a sharply dressed man approaching the staged scene from the entrance. It was Keith Jackson.

Cyrus nervously greeted the man as he arrived. Keith ignored the young man and went down onto one knee next to Timothy's head and placed his hand on his neck to check his pulse. After a few moments, a malevolent smile spread across his bearded face.

"Excellent work, Cyrus," the man said as he rose to his feet. "You have adequately fulfilled the necessary requirements to enter our prestigious organization." As he said this, I realized that I was still within hearing range and, because I was getting an annoying echo in my earpiece, I decided to hang up the phone.

"Thank you very much."

"How were you able to accomplish this task?"

"Oh, well, so I've been spying on this guy for a while," Cyrus said, pointing at Timothy on the ground. "And I knew he came here every week to do some casting circle shit or something—you know, some sort of evil, witch thing or something—so I created a witch's bottle and buried it deep next to this bridge, so when he tried to cross it...well, that was it for him." He pointed at a random nearby pile of dirt and made a throat slash gesture with his hand.

Although he improvised a little bit, obviously a bit nervous about the situation he was currently in, I'd say that he recited what I told him to say fairly well. I'd found that information with my cursory research, and the idea of how to fake Timothy's death germinated from there.

"Ah, the witch's bottle, that is very inspired," Keith said in response. "To be honest, I thought that was merely a myth and didn't even think to try it. However, the proof is right there." He pointed at the body. "The best part is that it leaves no evidence. You read about it all the time, a mysterious death of an otherwise healthy individual. Probably a witch killed by the bottle. Regardless, this is truly outstanding work." The man began circling the body, chuckling maniacally. "The ramifications of this are massive. Disposing of witches may become a much easier task than we had ever anticipated. We need more men like you rather than the two idiots I had mistakenly employed before."

"It'll just be nice to be part of a community that shares the same interests I do—which just happens to be, you know, killing witches and stuff." He was beginning to lay it on pretty thick.

"I think you're going to be one of our rising stars." Keith knelt next to Timothy. "Now, the question is what to do with you?"

"What do you mean?" Cyrus asked.

"We could just leave the body here. Leaving him here could be an excellent means of intimidation, a symbol that we are ready to attack, a declaration of war if you will."

"That's a good idea."

"At the same time, burning is much more traditional, is it not?"

I blanched a bit at the suggestion, and even in the moonlit sky, I could tell it had the same effect on Cyrus. He stammered, "Burning? Are you sure that's a good idea? Burning him would probably leave some residual evidence lying around, right?"

"True, but we want to make sure that witches know we mean business."

"But, we'll probably be caught if we do it."

"So be it."

"What?"

"The cause is greater than the two of us. Using him as a symbol is much more important. Of course, such things take time. I have to make a few phone calls. Luckily, this place seems to be mostly empty."

I took that as my cue. I found a nearby jogging trail and began jogging while pretending to be on my phone with my imaginary wife. "Yeah, honey, I'm still on my jog," I began, making sure every step I made was as noisy and deliberate as possible. "I always take a jog at the park after work. What do you mean it's taking longer than usual? What are you talking about? Cheryl just works for me!"

As I jogged back and forth along the same stretch of land trying to buy time and not actually intrude on the two individuals hovering over Timothy, I heard Keith say, "It looks like our plans have to come to an abrupt end. I suppose leaving him here will do. We'd better split up for now. Find me after work, and we'll begin the initiation process."

Cyrus's relieved sigh was still audible over my loud jogging in place. "Okay, sounds good to me."

After waiting a couple of minutes after they had left to ensure neither man would suddenly return, I walked and knelt next to Tim, waiting for him to recover from his trance and hoping furiously that nobody would happen upon the two of us. Nobody did, and I was able to keep watch until the young man awoke.

"...on my face," Timothy said. His eyes then darted around frantically in apparent bewilderment.

I flashed a large grin, relieved that the spell had worked properly. "Welcome back to the land of the living."

Timothy stared at me for a moment, still lying on the ground, eyes as wide as saucers. "Can I go home and play Blood Bowl now?"

"Yeah, of course. Will you need a ride home?"

"No thanks. I drove here. Will you need a ride?"

"No, I drove here too."

Suddenly I heard the sounds of marimba music playing in my pocket. I answered my phone.

"Hey, did Tim wake up yet?" It was Cyrus.

"Yes, he has. Would you like to talk to him?"

"Just let him know I'm waiting for him by his car, and I'm ready to go home."

"Wait a second. You're still here?"

"Yep. After we left, I told Keith I lived nearby and could run home. He believed me, so I just ran in some random direction. Then I waited around for a while just to make sure Keith had left, and then I got a little bit lost."

"Hey Tim," I said, pulling my phone slightly away from my mouth. "Cyrus is still here. Would you mind giving him a ride home?"

"Oh, I guess that's no problem."

"He says he'll give you a ride home."

"Thanks, man." After a short bit of silence, Cyrus continued, "That went pretty well, don't you think?"

"Couldn't have gone better. Excellent work, Cyrus."

"Thanks, Peter. By the way, as we left, Keith mentioned that the ceremony would take place at his home tomorrow night. Maybe you could follow us over there?"

"Absolutely, sounds like a plan. I'll give you a ride to work tomorrow, and we'll see where it goes from there."

"Sounds good. See you later."

"Take care, and thanks again."

The following day I was doing what I had been doing for much of the previous few weeks, sitting in my car in the parking lot of a lone store across the street from a gas station in downtown Tacoma, a small place about a minute or two away from the Tacoma Mall, eavesdropping on all of Cyrus's conversations while he was at work. Rain poured from the heavens as if God had forgotten to turn off the faucet, making loud noises as it splattered against my car as if a thousand little hands were pounding on it.

Expecting a slow day, I tried to entertain myself by playing with a deck of cards, hoping to learn a new card trick to show Darren. Nothing of significance was expected before the ceremony, but I still wanted to be on hand just in case.

I was interrupted by a knock on the window. The noise nearly made me leap from my skin, but a familiar face greeted me as I rolled down the window.

"Pete, what are you doing here?" the voice asked, barely audible over the rain and wind.

"Kelly, get out of the rain and get in here now!" I demanded as I lunged over in order to open the passenger side. "I'll explain everything when you get in!" Kelly slammed the door as he entered my vehicle. "So what the hell, Kelly, did you walk here?" I asked as the man leaned next to my heater in an effort to dry off.

"No, dumbass, my car's parked over there. You didn't notice me when I waved at you from across the street while I was getting gas. You apparently were too engrossed with your cards, and what the hell is that voice I keep hearing from your backseat?"

"Allow me to enlighten you," I said. I explained to Kelly everything that had transpired since we had last seen each other. I summed up finding Cyrus then recruiting him, and explained how it led to me being there, including how Cyrus was about to be initiated into the organization I suspected of being part of a large conspiracy. I omitted all details that referenced witchcraft, such as fake death spells, levitation, and the suppression of magical powers, for obvious reasons. Kelly didn't have to know everything.

To explain what Keith and his coconspirators were up to, I indicated that they were after people they thought were witches, and I feigned ignorance as to what made them think witches were real. Though to be fair, I didn't know that either. I did tell Kelly that the group was after the descendants of those who were thought to be witches, which was true, from a certain point of view.

Kelly slammed his hands against the seat. "Why didn't you come to me with this earlier? I told you to come to me if you found anything."

"I'm sorry, Kelly, it slipped my mind."

"That's the problem with you, Pete. You can never trust others to help you out with your problems."

"What are you talking about? I've put a lot of trust in Cyrus."

"Oh right, yeah, that makes me feel great. You'd prefer trusting some punk kid rather than your old partner."

"Cyrus has been more than just a punk kid. He's almost been like an assistant to me."

"If you're learning to trust, then try trusting the system a little bit more. Remember? The police are here to help."

"Oh yeah, I'm sure you would have helped me out quite a bit. Be honest with me, Kelly. Would we even be at this point, had I gone through the proper channels and trusted solely in the police force?"

"We could have certainly provided better equipment than what you have on your backseat. Of course, we police use proper channels, like getting a search warrant to make sure we're legal."

"Look, Kelly, I'm closer to solving a case that has been plaguing me for over twenty years than I would have ever been if I had stayed with you guys. Doing things my way is what got me here, and I'm going to keep doing things my way until this case is solved."

"You can only get so far though, Pete, unless you learn to trust." Kelly pulled out his cell phone. "Sorry, I've got to make a phone call. Hi, Clara. I'm going to be home late after all. No, don't worry. I'm not working right now. I just decided to meet up with a certain old friend. Yep, that's who I'm with right now. I knew you'd understand. Yes, absolutely. I love you too. See you tonight." Kelly hung up the phone and placed it in his pocket. "Surprised we're still together?"

"No, not really," I lied. "How are the two of you guys doing?"

"Fantastic. In fact, our sex life couldn't be better. I mean, she's learned this new technique that just makes me — "

"Okay, that's enough!" I yelled. "Why do people feel so comfortable sharing information like that with me?"

After a small, awkward pause, he continued. "We are doing well, though. Married life for me right now couldn't be better."

"I guess things do change." I stared out the window, pretending to be entranced by the rainfall.

"Yeah, I suppose they do," Kelly echoed as he too looked out the window. "You don't mind if I stay here and listen along with you, do you?"

"Do whatever you feel like, Kelly."

"They did it, you know," Kelly said, piercing the uneasy silence that had formed between us.

"Pardon me?"

"The Astros won the World Series in 2017, just like the *Sports Illustrated* article predicted. It was the first time I can remember anything like that ever happening in sports."

"Oh yeah. I had forgotten about that article. I'm surprised you remember it."

"I nearly gave you a call when they won. I had nobody else to share it with — or at least, nobody else who'd understand the full impact of what had happened. Clara was willing to listen and act like she cared, but I knew better. There are baseball fans down at the precinct, but they aren't like you or I. They like baseball. We love it. We breathe it. I've never met anybody as knowledgeable as you either. It kind of dampened the experience for me."

"I wouldn't have minded if you called me. I would have really appreciated it."

"I know, but I just couldn't call you. We were a team, and you abandoned us. We were the envy of every clown at the station. We were like a couple of buddy cops in a movie or television show. We were living in a dream, and you had to ruin it all by leaving."

"I didn't mean to ruin anything, though. You know why I left."

"Yeah, I know," Kelly said with a heavy sigh. "I just wish you put a little bit more faith in the system, in the police force…in me. I thought you trusted me then. I wish you'd trust me now."

A voice crackled from the phone in my backseat. "It is time, young man, for you to join us."

"Was that Keith Jackson?"

"Quiet!" I scolded. "I need to hear this."

Cyrus's phone was heard on the phone. "Great. I'm excited. I can't wait."

I heard Keith chuckle. "That's the attitude I expect from you. Come, it is time s to go. I'm sure you won't mind if these gentlemen follow along with us."

"Oh, yeah, sure, no problem. Should I follow you guys over there?"

"No need. I'll give you a ride. Don't worry, we shall return."

"Cool. Just let me make sure I've got my phone."

"I'm going to follow them," I said to Kelly. "Would you like to come along?"

"Do you even need to ask?"

I nodded, then pulled out of the boutique's lot over to the gas station to park so I could get a good view of the entrance and use proper following techniques without Keith and his band of merry men noticing us.

Keith exited the store with Cyrus next to him, two men flanking them, and another man leading the way. They jumped into a silver van and took off, with us not far behind.

We maintained our distance and followed just far enough away to avoid suspicion. Admittedly a couple of sharp turns here or there caused me to worry about losing them, but Kelly's experienced eyes kept me on track.

A short while later, the van pulled into a pristine home at the end of a lonely road in the outskirts of Tacoma. Its white paint was fresh, and the crimson roof tiles were brand new. His flowers, his trees, and his bushes were all vibrant, healthy, and well cared for, unthreatened by a single weed. It was a fitting place for a man who owned a fashion boutique.

We drove past the driveway and pulled over to the side of a nearby road about a block away. For the time being, we were just observing, not confronting. No laws had been broken thus far, and there was no clear or present danger.

The rain had died down to a mere sprinkle, making it much easier to listen to the phone. Neither of us could determine exactly where they had taken Cyrus in the house, but we did note that Cyrus had said something to the effect that he "...did not expect to find such an elaborate place down here."

From comments heard it was apparent that Keith had to wait for some phone call and confirmation to proceed, but was incredibly vague about the details. He was, after all, not a leader, but merely a subordinate working as a recruiter. He explained to Cyrus that in time, he'd be able to earn his way to meet the one true leader. Keith then handed Cyrus a copy of the *Malleus Maleficarum* and explained that it was written in Italian in order to preserve the original messages. Having it was a symbol that a member truly belonged. Sacrifice was mentioned numerous times, as well as the importance of sacrificing oneself for the greater good. Keith often sounded just like Tony.

One of the topics Keith introduced was the Salem Witch Trials. He believed the cause was just, but humanity, in their effort to persecute, made a grave mistake. It struck me as odd. True, he said the cause was benevolent, but he also said the persecution was a mistake. Not only did it seem contradictory, but it also seemed shockingly sympathetic to witches.

The man then told Cyrus that Tony's preservation efforts were vital because the ximuce trees in Evergreen were the key ingredients in the witch repellant, along with swamp water that was also found in those woods. The other ingredients were easy enough to find, though they caused the horrid smell. He explained that the liquid not only suppressed witches' powers, but when applied to witches, it would weaken them both physically and spiritually.

"What a load of crap," Kelly said. "These guys are insane."

"The Evergreen deforestation protest is one of Tony O'Stein's pet projects," I said. "Do you think he's involved with this group?"

"I doubt it. A lot of celebrities are involved in that thing. He probably just wanted to get on their good side. He's trying to market himself as a 'progressive religious figure,' whatever that means."

"You're probably right," I conceded.

Keith apparently decided to tell a story, maybe to pass the time.

"Great," I said exasperatedly. "This again. I am getting so sick of hearing about the chickens and the foxes. It's like Keith's favorite parable."

"You recognize the speech he's giving?"

"It's from one of Tony's lectures. He recites it all the time."

"Sounds like you're quite a fan."

"I'm not a fan."

"You're beginning to memorize Tony's speeches."

"I've only listened to him for research purposes."

Kelly smirked. "No need to be so touchy. If you're a big fan, it's cool. I won't judge you too harshly. If you are interested, I could possibly arrange a meeting between the two of you. He's giving a sermon over at the Tacoma Dome Sunday. I could pull a few strings so you can talk with him, seeing how you're a super fan."

"I'm not a fan." I calmed down and added, "Though I am interested in talking to him. Doesn't he normally give speeches at The Paragon?"

"Not doing a good job of convincing me you aren't a fan, but you're correct. The Tacoma Dome is just a special event. I think Tony's trying to go a little more mainstream by reaching out to a larger audience."

"The last three men I've investigated have all been Tony O'Stein fans. It's one of their major links. James Bond—rather, Ian Fleming—once said 'Once is happenstance, twice is a coincidence, three times is a pattern.'"

"Isn't it 'three times is enemy action'?"

"I don't know. Carter taught me that expression, so you'd have to ask him. Regardless, I'd like to talk to Tony to see if I can detect a link between him and the people we're after, not because I'm a fan."

"All right, I was just kidding about you being a fan. It'd just surprise me because I thought you were a devout atheist."

"I'm an agnostic, and even then, I don't think that's quite appropriate. I do believe in a higher power, in God, just not one that's necessarily bound by a religion. And I definitely don't believe in a God that needs heavy financing."

"We're on the same page on that one. My humble little church of forty people is enough for me."

Suddenly some techno music was playing over my phone, albeit faintly. Keith responded by interrupting his own conversation. "Ah, I'm sorry young man, I have to take this call. Hello. Yes. So you weren't able to locate it? Have you dug everywhere? I see."

"Is everything all right?" Cyrus asked, laughing nervously.

"There was no witches' bottle," Keith replied, his voice low and resonating with the ferocity of a thousand storms. "You lied to us. I never saw a news story about someone finding a body at Swan Creek Park, and it's because the whole thing was a ruse. You never even buried the witches' bottle."

"What the hell are you talking about?" Cyrus asked, voice cracking, his façade beginning to crumble. "You just didn't dig in the right place!"

"They dug up half the park. If there was a bottle to be found, they would have found it by now."

"But you saw the man. He was dead!"

"I've heard witches had the power to bring back the dead. Perhaps you circled back after we departed the park and revived him. It was certainly witchcraft. Of that, I am sure."

"I hate witches. You've heard me talk. 'The only good witch is a dead witch,' right?"

I started the car and raced to Keith's home. It took seconds to get there, while Keith said, "Perhaps your tongue will loosen under a pile of stones."

"Oh no, not again," Cyrus said.

We jumped out of the car, and Kelly shouted, "Wait! I need to call for backup first! We should wait until they arrive!"

"There's no time!" I shouted back.

Kelly ran next to me as I was scanning the entranceway of the door. "There's never any time. Why don't you ever let me call for backup? You're not even an officer anymore, and you're still telling me what to do. And for some reason, I'm still listening."

"Hey, look over there!" I said, pointing towards the side of the house. "Footprints, many of them, fresh and thick from the mud." I began running and heard a heavy sigh as Kelly followed.

We arrived at an outdoor basement door padlocked shut. "Another basement," I muttered to myself.

"Move," Kelly instructed, and I obediently moved to his side. He placed the barrel of his gun against the padlock and shot it open. "It probably alerted them that we're here, but like you said, time is of the essence right now."

"Yeah, good job," I said as I opened the basement doors.

"Let's not just dash in there. Let me go first." I nodded and let Kelly lead the way downstairs. As he went down, I noticed, out of the corner of my eye, a stream of water coming from one of the trees. Time was running low, so I kept it to myself as we slowly walked down the short stairway, both of us with our firearms in front of us.

When we reached the bottom of the stairway, we were greeted by a large, plastered wall painted gold with a vermillion door in the middle of it. We kept low and approached the door quickly but cautiously. Shaking off any confusion, I reached up to the handle.

"Locked," I said. "Unsurprisingly."

Kelly pointed the barrel of his gun towards the handle. "If they didn't know we were here before, they certainly will now."

I moved behind him and waited for him to fire. The shot tore through the handle, leaving nothing but an open hole as the remains of the front half of the handle fell to the floor. Kelly, while remaining covered by the side of the door with me now right next to him, opened the door slowly and took a peak. He immediately ducked away.

"Shit!" he exclaimed. "All of them have guns, and they're pointed at us!" Kelly looked towards the door as he shouted, "This is the police! Drop your weapons and come out with your hands up!"

He was answered with a barrage of bullets that flew through the door, missing us entirely.

"What about Cyrus?" I asked as loudly as I could in order to speak over the gunfire and Cyrus's terrified screams. "Is he all right?"

"He's tied to a board on the floor!" Kelly shouted. "So, it should be okay if I do this!"

Rapidly and without hesitation, Kelly stood up, threw open the door, aimed, and fired several shots in the direction of the men who were firing at us. Kelly's training and excellent marksmanship skills—always among the top of our unofficial leaderboards down at the firing range, while my scores were always good enough to pass, but just barely — allowed him to do what I couldn't.

After ducking to quickly reload, Kelly opened the door again and released a second barrage. After this second assault, all return fire had ceased.

Throwing the door open the third time, Kelly quickly scanned the room, pointing his gun forward. "Looks like the room is all clear."

"Excellent shooting, Kelly!" I said. I patted my ex-partner with my free hand. "That was amazing!"

"Well," Kelly said with a relieved smile as he entered the room, putting his gun back into its holster. "I don't know about you, but I've been keeping up at the range."

The room we entered was ornate, the walls painted a royal gold, and the floor an opulent purple. Ornate royal purple bunting decorated the walls near the ceiling. A podium of sorts was near the back wall.

A black and gold carpet led from the podium to the entrance of the room. Cyrus was tied to a blackboard in the middle and the three men who Kelly had fired upon all lay dead, forming a triangle shape around the horrified young man. Ignoring the bodies, the entire room looked like something you'd find in a royal chamber.

"It looks like what a certain radio host's bedroom must look," I said. "The one who's a big Husky fan though he never attended the University of Washington?"

"Yeah, well, go Cougs," Kelly said sarcastically, referencing his allegiance to his alma mater, Washington State, and at the same time, pointing out the shade of crimson that now decorated the walls, carpets, and ceiling.

A stack of books was in each far corner of the room. The left side had new copies of the *Malleus Maleficarum*, while the other had manuscripts related to alleged witch chicanery, means to hunt witches and other similar propaganda.

"All of them are dead," I said with my gun still out.

"Well, sorry," Kelly said, kneeling next to Cyrus as he began untying the ropes. "I didn't really have a choice."

"I didn't mean anything by it, I was just commenting. But Kelly, we have to stay frosty! I don't think that's everybody."

"What are you talking about?" Kelly asked without looking at me. "I shot them all, the room is clear."

"The basement door had a padlock on it. If these guys are inside, that means they couldn't have— Kelly, look out!"

As if on cue, a brown-haired, gruff looking man with a five o'clock shadow and wearing a fancy suit kicked open the red door, causing it to crash against the side of the wall while aiming his gun toward Kelly. Without hesitation, I aimed and fired.

The bullet penetrated the man's throat before he could pull the trigger. His gun fell slowly to the floor. A nauseating gurgle escaped the man's throat and lips as he fell to the floor, dying slowly after an agonizing attempt to breathe and speak.

"Holy shit!" Kelly shouted as he turned towards the door. "I thought I got them all!"

"Kelly, the only way the door could have been padlocked is if someone from the outside had locked the door. I figured there must have been a guard out there."

"Well, he sure as hell wasn't guarding anything when we got here!"

"I think he might have been taking a leak against a tree."

"What makes you say that?"

I admitted, "I might have seen him peeing against the side of the tree."

Kelly gave me an accusing stare. "Then why the hell didn't you tell me about that?"

"It didn't process until just now. It didn't dawn on me that the stream of water I saw was urine."

Kelly's expression softened a bit. "Do you think there might be more of them?"

"Probably not. I think I only saw four men enter the van, and I doubt we could have gotten here so easily if there was more than one guard."

"Let's just wait a few minutes just to be safe."

Kelly pulled out his gun and aimed at the door with me doing the same. We waited several minutes, ignoring Cyrus as he begged to be released from his restraints. Once we were certain nobody else was coming, Kelly put away his gun and finished untying the young man.

"Please cover me while I do this," Kelly requested. I nodded to confirm I was doing just that. As Kelly untied the whimpering young man, he said to me, "Dammit, now I owe you for saving my life."

"Not at all. It's nothing you wouldn't have done for me, though I didn't mean to kill him."

"I still appreciate it."

"Don't worry about it. Hell, you're the one who wanted to call for backup, and I didn't listen. As far as I see it, I owe you."

Kelly stopped untying Cyrus to glare at me. "Goddammit, I really hate it when you're like this. Your whole bravado of 'I'm just doing my job' and 'anybody would have done it' and 'if anything, I owe you' shtick. It is really annoying."

"But it's how I really feel."

"I know, and that's what makes it so irritating. For anybody else, it'd be false humility. But I know you're being genuine, and that's what kills me." Kelly resumed untying Cyrus. "There we go!" Kelly said triumphantly when he finished. "I finally got that last rope untied. You're free at last, young man."

"Cyrus!" I asked. "Are you all right?"

"Peter," Cyrus said as he sat up from where he lay. "Do you mind if I tell you something?"

"Not at all. What is it?"

"I don't want to be your assistant anymore."

CHAPTER 10

"Since time immemorial chickens have been hunted by foxes, but there was a period of time when chickens tried to change their fate," bellowed Tony O'Stein to a dome full of captivated fans as he strode from end to end on a large golden stage. Blue lights illuminated the backdrop where a large, hollow golden globe of the Earth spun around. Artificial trees and other sorts of fake vegetation flanked the stage in an attempt to evoke the natural feeling of the Pacific Northwest.

"Great," I muttered to myself as I sat in the upper levels of seats in the Tacoma Dome playing with a handkerchief and a coin, much to the chagrin of the elderly man and young woman who sat next to me. "This story again." It didn't help that I had spent the last three days doing nothing but watching online videos of the man's lectures in preparation for my post-sermon interview.

Of course, it had looked for a while like I might not have the opportunity to do this. Being in a room with four dead bodies is not normally conducive to freedom, even if it is with a police officer. Luckily, Kelly still had a silver tongue to go along with an immaculate history that made him a highly respected member of the force. He convinced the police chief and the district attorney that Cyrus got in a little bit over his head. Kelly claimed that Cyrus thought the men were involved in a live-action role-playing team. After all, who in their right minds would believe that actual witches that can cast actual magic exist in this world?

I did a very good job of biting my tongue when Kelly told this to the police chief and the district attorney, both of whom were thrilled to see me again when I was dragged with him to their offices for questioning. We claimed that when the young man realized that these men were serious about their fanatical anti-witch hatred, he called the closest adult friend he could trust, me. Kelly elaborated that the young man met me through a client, for whom I was searching for information related to issues involving her family and some others.

Kelly told them that he and I just happened to be in the area, reminiscing about good times when we received a phone call letting us know something was wrong. Cyrus didn't speak but merely kept the phone on so I could overhear the craziness these men were espousing. We arrived on the scene, and though Kelly admitted he probably should have called for backup, the circumstances were dire, and the two of us handled the situation in a way we both felt was necessary, believing correctly that Cyrus's life was literally on the line.

Playing them a few select snippets of my recordings, along with the testimony of Cyrus himself, confirmed our story and ultimately exonerated us, though neither the district attorney nor the police chief seemed to believe that I just happened to accidentally click record on my phone at the right time.

Because we stuck to a limited truth, the investigation by Kelly's fellow officers pretty much corroborated our story. This, combined with Kelly's high standing in the police force — along with my, in spite of the way I called it quits, mostly positive career as an officer — and the evidence said the events mostly went down as we told it. The positive spin the press put on the story made it almost impossible for them to do anything but exonerate us and even give us verbal commendations.

"Don't make me mouth half-truths like that ever again," Kelly said to me after we were released. "I'm starting to feel like a corrupt cop, and I really don't want to be a corrupt cop."

The news reports were excellent PR for my private investigative firm, something I would have killed for months ago. Unfortunately, I felt I had to turn down most of those potential clients in order to remain focused on this case. However, I did take a couple of odd jobs just to keep food on the table, lights on, and make ends meet, because somehow Abby and I still hadn't discussed her payment to me.

One I chose to take, for example, was a missing child case that turned out to be nothing more than the boy hiding at his father's house in a crazy parent trap scheme to get his divorced parents back together. Another one was of a young woman that wanted me to find her missing cat. It turned out the mother, while her daughter was on vacation, accidentally ran over her cat while housesitting, and then told her daughter that he had run away. In spite of the sad ending, more or less — admittedly, I'm more of a dog person — it paid surprisingly well.

Abby wasn't particularly happy with me after finding out what had happened — and for that matter, neither were Cyrus's parents, who I learned found out about the incident after it had become a big local story. Partly Abby was angry because I didn't tell her, but mostly because Cyrus had been in more danger than we had anticipated. Moreover, though his parents acknowledged I saved his life the first time, they were very angry that I endangered their seventeen-year-old son the second time around. I was told this incident actually aided the arguments of the separatists.

In a rather depressed state, I watched Tony O'Stein's videos, and even though I noticed that for a televangelist, he focused very little on actual religion, such as the role God plays in life, and more about self-help and personal affirmation, somehow they made sense to me. He mostly spoke of generic topics, such as the importance of confidence and doing good deeds not just for others but also for yourself.

The man talked a lot about himself, his family, and his ancestry, and how important they were and how important it was for him to preserve his history. His father, Jerome, had died ten years ago of a heart attack. His older brother, Nicholas, had gone missing twenty years ago and had been declared dead for thirteen. His mother, Penelope, died of cancer just two years prior to his big event at the Tacoma Dome.

I lost count of the number of times he talked about his great grandfather, a humble man who built a fortune almost literally building parts of Tacoma as an architect. It was from him that Tony learned the importance of patience.

Another habit of his, as noted earlier, was reciting parables. While most he told were uncredited myths and tales of yesteryear, some he simply made up, like the one about the foxes and chickens that had grown completely wearisome to me. His audience seemed enamored with them, even though he always seemed to get the moral wrong even with his own stories.

I noticed a few of Tony's idiosyncrasies while watching his lectures online. A nervous habit of his was rubbing his upper lip and chin while he recited a parable. He paused frequently in order to highlight or emphasize certain points. His arms would flail at the end of his tales or lectures in order to close in a dramatic fashion, which always coerced his audience to cheer.

Tony would often look to the right and above when speaking of his family's legacy or about his grandfather, or even his father. It appeared he was looking towards Heaven, which was odd because even in his old lectures fifteen years ago, he would do this while talking of his father, even though the man was still alive at the time. It may have just been a look of reverence, but he didn't do it every lecture or even very often. He only did it when he was at his home church, The Paragon, where he started his performances and where he still did most of them.

After a period where she did not contact me, I was very happy when Abby finally called me. "It's not because I exactly forgive you for what you've done," she said. "And I am not inviting you because I have any special feelings for you, of course. It's just that, a member of my circle is getting married. Do you remember Dicana?"

"I vaguely remember you telling me about her," I admitted. "She's Cyrus's older sister, right?"

"Yes, good memory. She invited me to her wedding. While I am still incredibly beautiful and young—well, young-ish—many of the women in my coven and in my circle are getting married, and there is some concern that I am slowly turning into an old maid. I must admit that the fact that Dicana is only nineteen years old is making these same thoughts creep into my head, although I keep telling myself she's making a mistake and is much too young. Sure, if I do become an old maid, I'd be the most beautiful one in existence, but still, it'd be nice to quell that talk momentarily and at least have a date to the wedding. Not that you should feel obligated. Declining my invitation will not affect your payment in any way."

"Now that you mention it," I said. "We—"

She cut me off. "I know, we've never actually discussed payment. Regardless, would you like to accompany me to this wedding?"

"Sure," I said, stumbling over my words. "I'd love to go with you."

"Oh, Petey, that's wonderful!" she exclaimed, before regaining her composure. "I mean, yes, that's great. Thank you very much."

"Are you sure it's okay for me to go, though? Won't some object to an outsider attending, and won't that rankle some of the brass at the coven?"

"Normally, yes, but I have already got the couple's permission, and as this is a unionist event, they have a much more lenient mindset towards cowans than separatists. Additionally, even though I still am quite perturbed with your rash actions, you are becoming something of a folk hero among the unionists, and even among a couple of the separatists. It's unprecedented to find a cowan who has actually risked his life twice for a member of our flock, which makes your behavior with Cyrus a little more acceptable in my mind. There may be a bit of consternation, but for the most part, it should be fine."

"I'll be there, then. Oh, will I need to rent a tuxedo?"

"No need. A witch's wedding is often less formal than a cowan's, so a suit will suffice. By the way, there are a few differences between a cowan wedding and a witch wedding." As she explained, my mind began to wander, as the differences between the two weddings hardly interested me at all. I was thinking more about how it made me feel being on Abby's good side again. I didn't realize I wasn't paying attention until Abby said, "I think that's about it. Do you think you can remember all of that?"

"Oh yeah, no problem, I was hanging on every word," I lied.

"Just stick to me, and I'll get you through it," Abby said, a bit of frustration in her voice.

The coin I was idly practicing a trick with slipping out of my hand and falling into my neighbor's lap woke me from my near trance and reminded me that I was listening to a lecture at the dome. With a look of contempt, the man handed me the coin back silently as I sheepishly thanked him for returning it and carelessly stuffed the coin and the handkerchief in my front pocket.

After watching countless videos, listening to Tony's stories again was much like watching a greatest hits compilation, perhaps because this was one his first forays into the mainstream. This broadcast would have more than a statewide viewing. I did notice that when he talked of his family's legacy, he did not look up and turn to his right.

After what seemed like an eternity, his lectures finally ended. Tony still had to meet with fans, do a short Q & A, and other such things. After all that was over, I had to wait until much of the cleanup was done before I had a chance to speak with him in a makeshift backstage area. From the time I'd initially arrived at the dome to the time I was able to interview him, eight hours had elapsed. It was akin to doing a complete shift at a full-time job where all I did was listen to a man speaking banalities. Now I know why Dilbert is irritated all the time.

After I was vetted by Tony's thin, brown-haired handler who was wearing a white T-shirt and blue jeans, I made my way to greet the man. As I approached him, Tony's gold suit began to seer into my eyes. It had seemed bright from my seats, but it didn't actually physically hurt to look at until I was only a few feet away from him. My eyes averted downward to his shiny black shoes just to give my ocular lobes a well-needed reprieve from the bright color.

This dark haired man greeted me with his hand extended while flashing a big, toothy grin. "You must be Peter Cunningham," he said as we shook hands. "The private investigator, your friend Detective Martinez told me all about. It is such a pleasure to meet you."

"The feeling is mutual," I said as earnestly as I could while squinting. "Fantastic show. You had the audience eating right out of your hand."

"It was decent, I suppose," Tony replied in a display of false humility. "Not my best, but hopefully it captured the hearts and minds of the audience and earned a few new members to the flock."

"That's what I wanted to talk to you about. A client of mine and her family, along with Kelly and I, have been having issues with a couple of members of your flock."

"Ah yes, I've heard from your friend, Detective Martinez, about the incident at The Nice Garb Express. I still can't believe that Keith Jackson was involved in such a dire thing. I am glad that you were able to escape that incident unharmed and rescue that poor young man. You are a hero and a man to be admired, Mr. Cunningham."

"Thanks," I said brusquely. "But I'm afraid I've also had other issues with members of your flock."

"Whatever do you mean?"

"Two of them tried to burn my client to death, another tried to crush a teenage friend of mine, and a couple of your biggest fans drowned a teenage girl after tying her to a chair and throwing her into the Puget Sound."

The man gasped and wiped some sweat from his brow with the purple handkerchief he had in his pocket. "Dear God in Heaven! That is truly awful! May a flight of angels take that poor girl's soul into Heaven, and may He dispense His judgment on her killers and on those who did injustice to you and your friends."

"Kind of a pattern building, though. Everyone we've

encountered so far has been a devoted fan of yours. We found your pamphlets and such in the homes of all of the individuals who attacked us. That's more than a little coincidental, wouldn't you say?"

"I would say it was all just a coincidence," the man said with a large shrug. "Not to brag, but the fact of the matter is I am quite a popular man, especially here in Tacoma. People regard me as something of a folk hero if you can believe that." He chuckled. "I can no more be blamed for their actions than a soccer team could be blamed for the crimes committed by their hooligans. Surely I can't be blamed for the actions of people I don't even know."

"One of the men we had the displeasure of meeting talked about forest preservation up in Evergreen, which is your pet project."

"Forest conservation is an issue that affects everyone, Mr. Cunningham, not just any particular group. That is one of my primary messages, the importance of protecting God's green earth—along with the good word and some advice to help a person succeed, of course."

"Maybe your devotees are getting the wrong message from you. You said earlier, you want to 'reach the hearts and minds of the audience.' Were these attacks what you meant by reaching their hearts and minds?" I was admittedly reaching a bit, trying to fluster the man.

"Obviously, we cannot rule out the possibility that they were fans in name only, collecting my wares because it is the popular or trendy thing to do," Tony said, completely unfazed. "But if these were people who listened to me regularly, then they weren't listening carefully. I truly wish they'd sought me out for answers to their questions, or they could have asked one of the leaders of my congregation. At least they should have looked at my webpage that provides a lot of guidance through Q&A, and appropriate quotes. I'm trying to reach out to many people."

"Do you think a lot of people were watching this broadcast?"

"I would like to think so, at least. This broadcast is going to almost the entirety of the continental United States, after all, so hopefully, it resonates with people, because it's imperative that I gain at least some traction." Tony's smile faded, and he stared upward while raising one hand slightly. "Mr. Cunningham, do you believe that one man can change the world?"

"I suppose to a degree it's possible," I said, a bit confused. "But history doesn't bear that out. Take, for instance, the Civil Rights Movement. Martin Luther King, Jr. definitely had an impact on this country, but was he truly alone in his endeavors, or were the people involved in the movement equally responsible? Did Rosa Parks not play a role, or even Jackie Robinson, Larry Doby, or Branch Rickey? Not to mention his followers. The unnamed followers of King's lessons surely played a factor as well."

Opening his eyes and lowering his hand a bit, Tony flashed a smile as he turned a bit to face me. "It seems you've given this a lot of thought."

I shrugged. "Being a private investigator means you have a lot of downtime. Your mind tends to wander."

"I liked what you said about followers. Without followers, a movement cannot be created. And that is definitely what I am trying to create here, a movement, for I do believe that one man can change the world. He can change the world if his message rings true, if his message resonates with the people, if his heart and mind are just and true, if his soul cultivates benevolence." Tony looked again towards the heavens, wearing a solemn expression on his face. "I don't have to tell you that we are living in a dark age, Mr. Cunningham."

"I don't know about that. I admit the world's hardly perfect, but considering we have things like fresh water and relatively clean air that we take for granted, I don't think things are so bad."

Tony looked at me, dismayed. "You cannot possibly really believe that, Mr. Cunningham, not with all the horrors in this world. Why, a man in your line of work must have seen more than his fair share of injustices."

"Sure, I've seen that side of life. However, I don't think one man can change this. Some of these problems have been with us since the beginning of time."

"I must respectfully disagree. My great granddaddy did not feel that any task was beyond the scope of one man. Why, when he moved here from his home in Danvers — that's a small town in Massachusetts — he saw nothing but opportunity here in Tacoma. The railroad was coming in, so a civil engineer like himself would have plenty of work. At the time, they called Tacoma the 'City of Destiny.' I always liked that, 'The City of Destiny.' It always seemed apropos. It definitely was my great granddaddy's destiny to shape the city in his image."

"You certainly admire him, don't you?"

"Jakob O'Stein was truly a Renaissance man. The impact he had on this city is immeasurable, and the scope of his plans exceeded even his lifetime, some of which I am continuing to this day. He practically built this city, and much of what he helped build still stands today. He knew the importance of sacrifice, too, a trait that is lost on so many people today. He made countless numbers of sacrifices in order to build something greater than himself. Do you know the importance of sacrifice, Mr. Cunningham?"

"You mean to sacrifice your own ambitions for the greater good?"

"Something like that, Mr. Cunningham. I may get carried away talking about him, but that's how I am. Did you know he was an excellent painter as well? Sadly, other than one painting that gained some attention at an exhibition, he did not get the recognition he deserved."

"Actually, you must be like him. I've heard you're also quite the Renaissance man. I saw the online videos of you firing your piece on the range. It looks like you are quite the shot."

Tony smiled broadly. "Well, thank you, Mr. Cunningham. I suppose I am all right."

"Still, it's unfortunate what happened at Edmonds."

"Whatever do you mean?"

"Oh, come on, Tony. Remember the shooting competition you were in? You didn't even make it out of the preliminary round. Were you even able to hit the target? Be honest, those online videos were doctored, right? You can tell me."

"Mr. Cunningham," Tony said crossly. "The reason for my failure at the competition was because they wouldn't let me use my daddy's gun, even though they promised me I could. I always do my best shooting with his gun."

"It sounds to me like you have a confidence problem, Tony. I have some breathing exercises that might—" I stopped speaking as something fell from my pocket while I was gesturing too strongly. "Sorry," I said sheepishly as I picked up the objects.

"A coin and a handkerchief?"

"I've been trying to pick up magic again," I confessed. "It's something of a hobby of mine."

The man blanched. "Magic, as in the art of illusion, trickery, the devil's kind of work, yes?"

"That's not how I see it," I said, giving him a jaundiced look. "I'd say it's mostly harmless fun."

"Sorcery is hardly innocent. 'The greatest trick the devil ever pulled was to convince the world he didn't exist.' Thomas Aquinas said that."

I looked at the man, a bit puzzled. "That was a line from *The Usual Suspects*."

"No, I must disagree, it was Thomas Aquinas," the man said confidently. "But it truly doesn't matter. The point is that evil does exist in this world."

"Do you mean evil as in evil people or evil actions?" I asked. "Because I tend to lean towards the latter more than the former. Some people do evil deeds, but truly evil people are very rare, in my opinion."

"I'm afraid they are less rare than you may believe," the man said in a deeply depressed tone. "Most people are like you, naïve to the fact that there's true evil, not that there is any shame in that. The world just needs people like me to expose the evil ones. It's my vision to save the world by bringing us to a new age devoid of such evil!" Tony raised his arms as he shouted these words. For a moment, Tony held that pose, perhaps waiting for me to react.

I obliged by laughing loudly. *Talk about delusions of grandeur*, I thought to myself, saying instead, "Sorry to laugh, but leading people to a new world devoid of evil? That's quite a leap from telling people parables about chickens and foxes."

Though I was expecting anger, Tony simply lowered his arms, smiled, and adjusted his tie. "I admit that my plans are ambitious and far from being ready to be fulfilled. The general populace isn't ready for the big message yet. As the old saying goes, you must teach children to crawl before they can run. First, I gain a foothold by teaching the basics, then I can teach the grander messages. My great granddaddy did teach me the importance of patience, after all. I think of this broadcast as merely being a good first step."

"But, your ultimate goal is to create an army against evil?"

"It's not so farfetched, Mr. Cunningham. Not when you've found the source of evil and have a plan to eradicate it."

Frowning, I asked, "What exactly do you mean by that?"

With a conceited chuckle, Tony said, "Why, I'm afraid even you aren't ready to be privy to that kind of information, Mr. Cunningham. You'll learn in due time what I mean."

"Tony, do you believe in witches?" I asked worriedly.

The man paused and rubbed his upper lip and then his chin. "I can't say that I do, at least not in this modern age. Glorified herbalists exist, but not witches. Why do you ask?"

I breathed a relieved sigh. "No reason. It was just a strange thought, that's all."

Tony replied solemnly, "How awful it would be if there were true witches who could perform actual witchcraft by entering into a pact with Satan. The evil they could do and spread as tools of Lucifer himself. Such a thought chills my very essence. Thank the Lord that such a thing is mere fantasy."

"Yeah, I suppose it is good that hocus pocus witches are completely mythical."

"Is there anything else I can do for you, Mr. Cunningham?"

"Just one thing. I have a wedding coming up that I need to attend, and I hope you don't mind me saying this, but you have excellent tastes in suits. Do you know where I could pick up a nice one?"

The man laughed and patted me on the shoulder. "Thank you very much, Mr. Cunningham. It is indeed my favorite suit, but I'm afraid I picked it up at the Nice Garb Express. Needless to say, that isn't the place to pick up such fine garments anymore. It's a shame too. They did have an excellent selection of suits."

"Unfortunate too that they were involved in criminal activity, yes?"

"Yes," the man said sullenly. "Quite." After a pause, Tony continued. "I'd try the Jos. A. Bank in Gig Harbor."

"I will do just that," I said, extending my hand. "Thank you very much for your time."

"Oh, it was no problem at all, Mr. Cunningham," he said, shaking my hand.

"It was a pleasure speaking with you," I lied.

"The feeling is most definitely mutual," Tony said in what was likely also a lie. "If you ever need to speak with me again, please be sure to talk to Detective Martinez to try and arrange another meeting with me, though I must warn you I am a very busy man. I also hope you continue to listen to my sermons. I'll have Suzy, the one you spoke to over the phone to arrange this meeting, give you a calendar, and you can always access this information on our website. Oh, and please take an autographed photo and a mug, compliments of me."

I thanked the man, and after talking to Suzy, collected the items, though I had no use for them. Perhaps someone might pay a little for them online, I thought to myself, but I had more pressing matters. With only about a week before the wedding, I really did need to pick up a suit, but more importantly, it was time to see what sort of legacy his grandfather left for Tony, and what kind of individual Tony was aspiring to become.

CHAPTER 11

"My, don't we look handsome," Abby said in her most seductive voice as she entered my office. The bright light shone through my windows on that hot day at the end of May. A perfect day to get married.

Wearing a Hugo Boss three-piece suit in a textured weave with a notch lapel, two-button front with a welt pocket at chest level, along with flat-front trousers, shiny black dress shoes, and what I considered to be a fetching red tie, I had to admit, I looked pretty good.

As I looked up from my notes that were spread all over my desk and my laptop, my eyes nearly bulged from their sockets when I saw what Abby was wearing. I always found her quite attractive in her usual attire in spite of the lack of skin shown by those outfits, so seeing her in a comparatively skimpy dress was pleasantly jarring to me.

That navy blue dress with a V-neck and back exposed parts of her that I had never seen, and accentuated her somewhat petite but gorgeous figure. Her slender legs were exposed by the side slit in her dress. Her silver high heeled shoes were a sharp contrast to the black and white tennis shoes I had grown so accustomed to seeing her in. Even the silver pentagram pendant she wore around her neck, though fitting as it may have been for a witch like Abby, would have been a bit incongruous if worn with her everyday clothes. Not that I was complaining.

A part of her remained the same. She still wore her usual dark makeup, which definitely pleased me. It just wouldn't be Abby otherwise.

"Wow. You…you look absolutely gorgeous, Abby," I stammered.

Abby smiled coyly. "Thank you. I was wondering when you were going to say something rather than stare at me creepily. Do I really look that much different than usual?"

"No," I lied. "You look the same as usual, absolutely beautiful. I'm just not used to seeing you in a dress. Um, you look really good in that dress."

"You look good yourself, though you always look a little bit formal with a dress shirt and a vest. I hope you didn't spend too much money on the suit."

"Luckily, Carter and I are about the same size, so I just borrowed one of his," I admitted. "He was more than happy to let me do it too."

"That was very kind of him. Speaking of which, I got the wedding gift."

I looked down at the woman's hand and realized she was carrying a plastic bag full of some sort of cloth.

"Bed sheets?" I inquired.

"To be specific, a Percale Venice Bedding Set."

"Sounds expensive."

"It was. I've also got a gift basket of meat in my car that we'll need to take with us. Part of the cost will be taken out of your final paycheck, as I feel those are gifts from both of us. I hope you don't mind."

"Wait," I protested. "It was your idea to attend the wedding. And besides, we haven't exactly discussed payment yet."

Abby covered her mouth as she laughed. "I know, I was just joking around. Sometimes you take me much too seriously, Petey."

"Yeah, well," I grumbled without finishing my thought. "Oh, Abby!" I exclaimed after thinking a bit. "I have a lot to tell you about what I've found this week!"

"Oh yes, how did your research go? It sounded like you were very busy."

"Yes, I looked into Tony O'Stein's family history, especially his great-great-grandfather Jakob O'Stein. Tony told me he was a civil engineer and a painter, and that he supposedly left him a great legacy, whatever that means. I tried looking it up online but, unfortunately, there is nothing but generalities about Jakob O'Stein and Tony's family history. I decided to try and find out more by looking up old newspaper articles."

"How did that go?"

"Slowly and laboriously. The newspaper archives only go as far back as 1989, or at least that's the case for the Tacoma News Tribune. Carter confirmed that to be true. With no choice left, I went to the library to find old newspaper articles on microfiche. Then I had to go to the Washington State Library in Tumwater and look everything up there. Searching through the files was far from fun, but I found some good information. This is some of it." I motioned her over to me so she could take a closer look at my laptop, which held the fruits of my labor. "These are just some of the articles I was able to find," I said, flipping through the photographs on my machine.

"Dare I ask if you were allowed to take these pictures, Petey?"

"I didn't even ask. I figured it was one of those situations where it was better to beg forgiveness than to ask permission."

"I suppose if they didn't say anything, it must have not been a big deal. What were you able to find?"

"Most of what I was able to find didn't come from the Tacoma News Tribune, but from the Ledger, though I'm pretty sure that was just its old name. Tony wasn't lying about his great-grandfather's line of work or his history with this town. He was mentioned in quite a number of articles, although the doting grandson, Tony, somewhat exaggerated his impact. So he was pretty important, though not actually the father of Tacoma."

"Or infamy," Abby suggested. "Like if a person is a murderer."

"True, but as a civil engineer, you'd have to be pretty well known to get a quote in the paper, even if otherwise you are mentioned briefly. A quote here is about a building project in progress. A quote there related to future plans and city development. The mentions were sporadic and mostly ordinary."

"Hardly surprising given his line of work."

"Absolutely, which is why even the paper seemed surprised when he was scheduled to host his own art exhibit. Take a look at the headline of this article."

I showed her one of the last photographs on my machine. It displayed a microfilm reader displaying a newspaper article whose headline read simply, "Civil Engineer to Host Art Show."

"I found it on the back of an arts and entertainment section of the paper," I continued. "The article is dated August 9, 1916. I'll give you the gist. The tone and tenor of the article is one of amazement. It expresses surprise that a civil engineer, especially one of such high repute, was able to not only find the time to paint but had enough talent to warrant such an event."

I paused for a moment as I flipped through some of the pictures that Jakob O'Stein had painted in order to give Abby a better look at this man's aptitude for art. Paintings of old buildings of Tacoma, scenes of a park, and one of his family with their dog flashed onto the screen.

"These paintings are fine from a technical level," Abby said while perusing the man's works of art. "Good but unimaginative, none particularly special. I'm hardly an art critic, though. Perhaps I am missing something an expert would notice."

"Your assessment seems to actually be pretty much spot on. The article admits that most of his paintings, while technically sound, were also mundane and fallow."

"Fallow?" Abby said with a teasing smile.

"That's what the article said," I admitted. "Just a fancy way of saying uncreative, I guess. Of all his work, there seemed to be one lynchpin painting that justified the entire gala and the real reason anybody went to see his work. Tell me if this painting reminds you of anything."

The newspaper's black and white photograph of the painting made some of the details difficult to make out. However, it showed a large group of women clad in black holding hands as they appeared to be dancing in a circle around a large bonfire. Anger was reflected in their pernicious faces. The woods in the background were depicted with overgrown trees and decaying leaves. A large, domineering moon illuminated the mostly dark background. The critic described the painting as having a manic style that was both primal and enraged as if his innermost thoughts had seen this vision, which needed to be expressed lest he be tortured by the image forever.

"My word," Abby gasped. "It's a painting of a witches' circle. I wonder what made him paint something like this."

"Jakob never answered that question. Contemporaries speculated that his trip to Salem and seeing the sites where witches were persecuted inspired him to paint such a piece, or so the article goes on to suggest."

"He went to Salem? Was it a sight-seeing trip?"

"He went there to collect an inheritance. His family originated from Salem, but most of them moved away, leaving his great aunt as the lone family member still there. When she died, she left her estate to Jakob, her oldest remaining living relative. He apparently sold her house and fled right back to Tacoma."

"Of all places, Salem, home of the infamous witch burnings. It makes me shudder, even thinking about that place."

"There's more," I explained. "Tony said his family was from Danvers, not Salem. I wonder why he would make something like that up. Maybe he was worried his reputation might get tainted—whatever. I don't believe it was Salem that inspired him to do this painting. Take a look in the background."

I pointed towards the top left corner past the woods. I zoomed in a couple of times to provide Abby a better look at what I was referring to. Just above the top of the trees, in a small opening in the left-hand corner, it was possible to make out a distinctive object. It was a roof poking just above the woods, having the distinctive features of the top of a Japanese pagoda. "Recognize that?"

Squinting a bit as she spoke, she said, "I suppose that could be the top of a pagoda if you use your imagination."

"Not just any pagoda, the Pagoda, as in the one in Point Defiance. Take a look at this." I showed her a picture I had quickly doctored up in Paint, where I laid an old photograph of Point Defiance over Jakob's painting. The curve of the painting's pagoda was more exaggerated, and its chimney-like structure was much thinner and shorter, proportionally, than it was in real life, but the resemblance was definitely there.

"Assuming I agree with your assessment that this is a painting of the pagoda in Point Defiance, something that I'm not one hundred percent certain is true, what does this ultimately mean? Why would he paint the Pagoda?"

"Remember you told me a few months back that your coven used to have the circle in Point Defiance?" The expression on her face told me that even as I said these words, Abby had figured out what the painting meant.

"Goddess above, this is a painting of my ancestors."

"Yep," I confirmed. "This wasn't inspired by Salem. It was inspired by something he had actually seen."

Abby gently moved me aside so she could sit down at the seat beside me in front of my laptop. With a look of consternation, she habitually reached for a cigarette, but upon realizing that her purse was on the other side of the desk, apparently decided she didn't need to smoke at the moment.

After a minute or two, Abby said, "What does this mean, though? I mean, Jakob saw us, but how does that fit into everything?"

"Unfortunately, I don't have definitive answers to those questions," I admitted with a heavy sigh. "It might suggest that Tony knows more than he is saying and that maybe this whole thing with your coven goes back further than we had anticipated. I'm afraid I need to keep digging."

After a few more moments of silence, Abby mustered a smile. "All of this going to have to wait. Today is Dicana's wedding day, after all. We can always get back to this tomorrow."

I nodded and smiled. "You're right. It's about time to go, anyway. Luckily, Titlow Lodge is only a short drive away from here." Just before we departed, I patted the object I was wearing underneath my suit. *Yep*, I thought to myself. *I should be able to reach my gun easily enough should something happen.*

"Dicana is marrying a young man named Noel Pederson," Abby explained as I drove her to the wedding. "He and the rest of his family are strict unionists. You can imagine how 'happy' Archon is that his daughter is marrying a unionist."

"So it's a regular *Romeo and Juliet* type of wedding," I quipped.

"It's an apropos metaphor, but luckily we are not quite at that point yet. Both sides are definitely uneasy with each other, but, for the most part, we are still unified."

"Who are the separatists of your circle?"

"Archon and Matilda, as you know, are staunch separatists, and are definitely major players in our political circles. Cyrus, even at his young age, exhibits an acute awareness of the machinations that govern our coven and, just between you and me, seems to actually be leaning towards unionism, though he used to mimic his father's beliefs. I think you may have played a role in that, actually."

"If that's the case, I'm glad I could help. How about Dicana? What are her political views?"

"Frankly, saying she's agnostic when it comes to political matters would be giving her too much credit. She mostly just defers to Neal for an opinion. She hates to think for herself."

"It seems like she's hardly a credit to modern feminism."

"She's hardly a credit to sentient lifeforms," Abby said. Her cheeks turned red, and she quickly followed up with a flustered, "Oops. I didn't mean to say that aloud."

"It's okay. I understand."

"She's a very sweet girl, and I hope nothing but the best for her, but unlike her father, mother, and younger brother, she's just, to put it bluntly, not very bright."

"Will Archon and Matilda be there?"

"I'm afraid so, but I wouldn't worry about it too much. The parents have much more on their mind than you right now, and even though they aren't thrilled with her choice, they are the kind of parents that will be there for her regardless of what decisions she makes."

"They actually don't sound like too bad of people."

"They aren't. They love their daughter and would do anything for her."

We arrived at Titlow Lodge, a wooden building located in the middle of the Titlow Beach Marine Preserve, a beachfront park on the Puget Sound near the Tacoma Narrows. The design of the lodge was almost reminiscent of a stereotypical child's drawing of a house, with its triangle-shaped roof and square body. A stairway led to its black glass doors, and windows flanked the doors and could also be seen on the top of the roof. Next to the stairway flanking both sides and all around the lodge was a wooden fence about half as tall as the average man. Pink and white azaleas planted in pots hung from the rafters, and flower beds of red and white rhododendron were in flower beds in front of the cabin proper.

A gathering of people was already located in the bright green grass behind the structure. Abby informed me that the lodge would be where the reception would take place, but the actual marriage ceremony would take place outdoors, where witch weddings were traditionally held.

Abby took the basket of meat from the car and instructed me to carry the bed sheets into the lodge with the rest of the gifts. Abby schmoozed with some guests in the upper part of the back of the lodge whom I presumed were part of her circle. Navigating through a sea of tables and chairs, I noticed many banners congratulating the couple, including one that hung prominently over a table of gifts on the left-hand side of the lodge.

After setting the gift down, I walked out the back door and saw a familiar face, Cyrus, who stood next to a tall, middle-aged, and attractive dark-haired woman in a black dress whom I presumed to be his mother. After seeing me, the youth gave me a sheepish smile and a wave, an action that I reciprocated. His mother, on the other hand, did nothing but glare.

Ignoring her death stare, I looked around to observe the other guests. To my surprise, I recognized some of them. I didn't actually know any of the people personally, but I did remember seeing them traveling around town, and some had been clients for various cases I had engaged in over the years, both as an officer of the law and as a private investigator.

One woman was a bartender at a dive bar I once visited as part of a police investigation for a robbery. Another woman was a receptionist at an office I once visited as part of a due diligence case. I recognized one guy specifically, since I had passed him every day the last week along the road I used to go home every night while he and his crew did their road maintenance. One lady I was really glad didn't recognize me, or at least she pretended not to because she was the woman one of my client's husbands had been cheating with.

The fact that I recognized even a couple of these faces made it really hit home how witches truly lived amongst us.

After saying a few more hellos and nodding to a couple of more faces I had seen at some point in my life, I walked over to Abby. She was talking to another familiar face. This time it was somebody I knew personally.

"Hello, Peter," Dahlia said as she gave me a hug. "It is so good to see you again. It has been far too long."

"It has been far too long," I replied. "I should stop by your shop sometime. I've just had my mind on a lot of things lately."

"I understand. How is the investigation going?"

"I feel like I have a lot of pieces to a puzzle, but I can't quite fit them all together."

"You will. I have faith in you." She smiled warmly. "Peter, I'd like to introduce you to some people that are very important to me."

She motioned in the direction of a brown-haired man with a thick flowing beard, glasses, and a dark green suit, as well as to a brunette woman wearing a red and white dress and a red headband. The woman held the hand of a little girl wearing a white dress with a flower in her hair.

"This beautiful young woman is my wonderful daughter Cassandra," Dahlia said. "This handsome young man is her husband, Maxwell, and this little bundle of fun is my granddaughter, Joy. Everyone, this is Peter Cunningham, the private investigator I've told you about."

Each of us exchanged handshakes and "hellos" as Dahlia introduced us, and I placed my hands on my knees as I smiled at the young girl in pigtails, who reciprocated the motion along with a cute little smile.

"Abigail," Dahlia addressed her as she approached us. "I have to show you the gift Cassandra got for the newlyweds. It is just the cutest thing in the world."

"Mom," Cassandra whined. "It's not that great."

"No need to be modest, dear. You thought of something incredibly creative. Follow me, Abigail, let me show you."

"Would you excuse us for a moment?" Abby asked. After a quick adieu, Abby followed Dahlia to the lodge, leaving me alone with a family I had just met.

"What did you get?" I asked Cassandra.

"One of those canvases that displays the dates of when the couple met, when they got engaged, and when they got married," she replied in a subdued tone.

"I bought a couple of robes," Maxwell said flatly.

"Those sound like really good gifts," I replied.

"Yeah," Cassandra said with a sigh. "They're okay."

"What do you do for a living, Maxwell?"

"I'm a compiler engineer at Intel."

"Is that like a programmer or something?"

"Yeah, something like that."

"You wouldn't happen to know a man named Carter Palmer, would you?"

"I don't know any Carters."

"I guess there would be no reason for you to know him. How about you, Cassandra? What do you do?"

"I'm studying to become a kindergarten teacher."

"Oh, that's wonderful. The world could always use more teachers."

"Yeah."

"So you're a private investigator, Peter?" Maxwell finally

said after a long, uncomfortable silence.

"Yes!" I replied enthusiastically, eager to have something to talk about. "That's right!"

"And Abigail is your client?"

"At this point, she's more of a friend than a client," I admitted.

"Are you still investigating who attacked her?" Cassandra asked.

"Oh, so you know about that?"

"Yes, Mom told me all about it."

"I see. Well, Abby and I are pretty certain we've figured out who attacked her, and that threat is pretty much dead — er, quite literally, now that I think about it — but this investigation has escalated quite a bit."

"I'm glad Mom warned us not to go that night."

"Something must have happened," Maxwell said. "She used to talk about how much fun she was having, but then one day, she started warning us how dangerous the circle had become."

"It was those two men at her fruit stand, right?" I asked, "That's what made her think the chanting circle could be dangerous?"

"Two men?" Cassandra asked. "Oh wait, are you talking about those two men who attacked Abigail? No, I didn't even hear about them until after the attack. What did Mom say about two men?"

"She said it was two men that caused her to worry about your safety," I responded. "She really didn't tell you about them?"

"She could have just forgotten," Maxwell suggested. "Do you find that odd?"

"I suppose not," I said, though something about it struck a discordant note to me.

I didn't have much time to ponder this, though, as a heavyset woman in a gray gown walked out of the lodge and interrupted our conversation by announcing loudly in a screechy voice that the ceremony was about to commence. Abby and Dahlia exited the lodge shortly afterward, and my date gently grabbed my shoulder and moved me next to a couple of strangers.

The crowd formed itself into a large horseshoe shape. A tall man with a thin build and long black hair, wearing a cobalt suit, stood beaming in the middle of the horseshoe, along with the woman in gray who appeared to be presiding over the event. Behind her and to the right was a giant cauldron containing a bright hot flame, and next to it stood a broom and a small jar full of sand.

Music began to play, and from the inside of the lodge came a tall, muscular blond, middle-aged man in a black suit and tie and white shirt, walking with a beautiful young woman wearing a bright purple and gold dress, her right arm wrapped around his left. Abby whispered what I had already inferred, that the man was Archon, and the young woman was Dicana.

The pair walked into the horseshoe as the crowd moved to close the circle. The father walked his daughter next to the husband to be, and then gently, with a proud smile, let her go to her beloved. Matilda moved from the circle next to her husband and stood by their daughter's side. They were soon followed by the parents of the groom, who moved from their parts of the circle and stood next to their son. Both parties exchanged a quick cool glance, but ultimately regained their composure, smiling and standing proudly.

Dicana recited a poem in Gaelic, and her betrothed did the same. It sounded pleasant even if I didn't understand any of it, and considering how much trouble Dicana had reciting her verse, I had a feeling someone else had written it for her, and she was clueless as to what it meant as well. The two then exchanged vows much like they would at a traditional wedding. Neal's was much more eloquent and loquacious than his young bride's, but her words were no less kind and sweet. Both of them made references to their God Cernunnos and the Goddess Arawhon as they both pledged their lives to each other in their name. As was apparently the tradition, the papers were tossed into the cauldron. This was done to send the words up into the ether towards the heavens.

Most of the members of the circle began placing items in the center. Abby later told me this was done to deliver an offering to the deities, which was why she also placed her basket of meat in the center of the circle at this time. Others lay beer, wine, and various other types of food and consumables.

Afterward, the couple exchanged rings. The wedding officiant picked up the jar next to the cauldron as the couple picked up stones from the ground and placed them in the sand. Abby whispered to me that the stones represented the five humors — Earth, Air, Fire, Water, and Spirit.

With the rings exchanged, the couple's hands were bound together with a black ribbon, and the woman in gray said a blessing towards the union of the couple in the name of the Earth, Air, Fire, and Water. Abby would later tell me this was a tradition known as handfasting.

After this, the wedding officiant picked up the broom and placed it in front of the couple. The two held hands as they gleefully leaped over it to a rousing applause. Smiling ecstatically at each other, the newlyweds shared a passionate kiss. A swarm of monarch butterflies soared over the couple as they kissed. I later learned that broom jumping was originally done in place of a traditional ceremony due to witches not being allowed the rights or rites of a legal marriage, but now was done mostly to encourage fertility in the newlyweds should they choose to have children. From there, we began heading to the lodge.

I paused for a moment as I noticed, out of the corner of my eye, something rather odd. In the outskirts of the woods, a vagabond in a faded green hooded sweater and soiled brown pants, and wearing stained and rotted white tennis shoes, stared at us from a distance. Anxiously he rubbed one of his hands over what appeared to be an overflowing wild brown beard speckled with white hair, but I surmised that the brown color was merely stains from whatever was on his worn and faded gloves. In his free hand, he held what appeared to be a vial of some sort full of a dingy brown liquid that the man repetitively and almost compulsively placed under his nose.

"Oh, there you are," Abby said to me from the doorway of

the lodge. "I thought you were next to me until I went inside. Is everything all right?"

Shaking my head a bit, I said, "Everything is fine. I just got distracted looking at that vagrant over there."

"A friend of yours?" she teased.

"Only the best friend I've ever had. Follow me. I'll introduce you to him."

Laughing and moving away, she said, "Come on, let's go inside."

Abby guided me to a table very close to the back entrance doors. These seats literally could not be further from the newlyweds and their family. They all were near the main entrance just under a large banner that simply read, "Congratulations Neal and Dicana Byrne!"

Dahlia was seated at the table, along with Cassandra and Maxwell. Joy was fidgeting in her mother's lap, and a much older, almost elderly couple was standing next to their seats.

"Abigail!" said the woman, who was wearing a light blue Sunday dress with her grey hair tied into a ponytail. Abby and the woman shared a hug.

Abby motioned to her companion and the elderly man with black with grey streaks in his cropped hair and a gray and white goatee, who was wearing a brown sports coat over a dress shirt and tie. "This lovely woman is Iris, and that's her husband, Doctor Nelson Howard."

"Nelson's fine," the man said as he and I shook hands.

"A pleasure to meet you both. I'm Peter Cunningham."

"Ah, yes, so you're the private investigator she keeps talking about," Iris said. "It is good to finally put a face with that name."

We exchanged small talk until our meals arrived. I learned that the professor worked at the University of Washington, Tacoma. Abigail had met the man as a student and was still more or less working under him as an unofficial assistant.

"Abby told me about your case, and it is fascinating," Nelson said. "The parts involving the *Malleus Maleficarum* that decries and justifies the persecution of witches, especially pique my interest. Whoever is behind these attacks must have a vendetta against our kind."

"That seems to be the case," I confirmed. "The robes, the ceremony that Keith Jackson was hosting, and the testimony of Joseph Edwards all point to this being an organized effort."

"I have a couple of books about witch hunting and the groups engaged in such horrors that you might be interested in. I brought them over in case they could help you out, and I have them in my car. These accounts are mostly from the perspective of us witches, and they may mostly be apocryphal. Certainly, you won't find many of these kinds of textbooks outside of the covens. Admittedly, I find some of the stories to be a bit suspect. However, I do think it is all still worth a look."

"Absolutely!" I agreed.

We excused ourselves from the table, and I followed Nelson out the main entrance to his red Chevy Volt. Opening his trunk revealed various textbooks of all shapes and sizes. I picked one at random and began skimming through it, then other texts. There was a lot of information to parse and to absorb. Most stories were both fascinating and horrific, much of which I knew to be true. Accounts describing the atrocities of inquisitors Sebastian Michaelis and Roger Newell reflected mostly what I had come to understand from history. Other books discussed witch hunting organizations such as the Virtuous Hunters and the Witch Eradicators. Although the accounts of their alleged horrific treatment of witches were probably mostly accurate, some of these stories seemed too outrageous to be true.

Many of the descriptions bordered on the supernatural. Some seemed to have a sixth sense towards finding witches and used what could only be called their own version of magic to torture and kill them. The legends of the hunters seemed to mimic the alleged crimes witches perpetrated against the rest of humanity, only this time, the roles were reversed.

Scanning through the stories of various witch hunting organizations and their members, asking Nelson to confirm which were real and which weren't, began to be a chore. It didn't help that most of the information wasn't particularly useful. I had almost given up and was ready to slam a thick black textbook in my hands shut when I noticed, on the very last page of the chapter I was glancing at, a small blurb about an organization whose name captured my attention. The paragraph described a group known as the "Innocent Children," who were affiliated with none other than Pope Innocent VIII.

The Innocent Children were once the most preeminent witch hunting organization in all of Europe, and even the world when Europe expanded into the Americas. The organization received the endorsement of Pope Innocent VIII, and he may have been involved with its creation, along with his two cohorts, the infamous Jakob Sprenger and Heinrich Kramer.

Much of their history seemed to be lost to time. The group was incredibly secretive and enigmatic. They were infamous for performing clandestine operations against witches and were spoken of in hushed tones. They wrote down almost nothing, which made it easy for them to remain mysterious, but also made it difficult for historians to confirm whether they had even existed.

The author of this book believed the organization was prominent for almost a century and a half, but by the mid to late seventeenth century, the group began to lose favor with the pope, though nobody was quite sure why. By the mid-eighteenth century, they were completely gone.

That name again, Pope Innocent VIII. He had supposedly created the Innocent Children. Were the men we encountered throughout this investigation members of the Innocent Children? How could that even be? Supposedly they were eliminated by the eighteenth century.

"Would you mind if I borrowed this book?" I asked.

"Not at all," Nelson replied. "Did you find something interesting?"

"Perhaps. It was just a small blurb, but it could be important."

"Borrow it for as long as you'd like. Just give it to Abigail when you are done."

I thanked the man and put the book in the backseat of my car before walking back to the reception, which was nearly over by the time we made our way back.

Abby was in the middle of the room, talking with a crowd. She waved at me as I reentered, and I waved back. Behind her, towards the back exit of the lodge, were Neal and Dicana. The couple was talking to Iris and a couple of other members who sat at our table. My mind was mulling over the new information I had found as I walked aimlessly in the room. Because of this, I failed to pay attention to my surroundings and walked right into a six-foot-four brick wall that went by the name of Archon.

"Oh, excuse me," I said casually, then realized to whom I was speaking. Cyrus was to his left and looked alarmed, while Matilda was to his right with deep anger in her eyes.

"Oh, it's you," the man said in a deep, stern voice, the kind of voice that commanded fear and respect from those around him. "The cowan private investigator."

I reached my hand out in an effort to be polite. "That's right. Nice to meet you. My name is Peter Cunning—"

Archon interrupted, refusing to shake my hand. "I'm aware of who you are. I don't want to exchange pleasantries with you. Allow me to make something very clear. If it were up to me, you would not even be here, nor would you be assisting Abigail Mitchell. Cowans wouldn't be allowed to interact with witches in any capacity. However, it is not my decision to make, at least not now. Nor would I dream of starting an argument in the middle of my daughter's wedding. I would just like cowans like you to stay away from my family."

People gathered and stared as the two of us conversed.

"I suppose I shouldn't send you a Christmas card this year, then," I said, hoping a joke would lighten the mood."

"Petey is a good man." Abigail had moved swiftly to my side. "Petey's somebody the coven can trust—he's saved your son's life twice! Tell him, Cyrus."

"Uh, yes, he sure did," Cyrus said timidly.

"You call him Petey?" Archon asked in a confused manner,

then continued. "Yes, he saved my son's life twice. I am truly grateful for his first rescue. However, the second time he saved my son's life, it was due to him involving Cyrus in a foolhardy effort that unnecessarily risked my son's life."

"Cyrus chose to assist him. Petey didn't force Cyrus to do anything he didn't want to."

"Cyrus is still a child. He can be easily coerced."

"Dad!" Cyrus protested. "I'm not a child, I'll be eighteen next month! And Abigail is right. Peter didn't force me to do anything I didn't want to do!"

"You do not speak to your father that way," Matilda said, chastising her son.

"Cyrus isn't a child! Witches used to believe that seventeen was the age of adulthood. Eighteen being the age of adulthood is a cowan belief!"

"Be that as it may," the man said in austere and even tone. "You should not have invited him to my daughter's event. You know how I feel about cowans and —"

Archon was interrupted by a series of strident noises. A swift and forced opening of glass doors was followed by a loud crack of the door frames as they slammed against the cabin's walls. A masculine grunt was followed by the sound of a body hitting the floor. Accompanying this was screams and yelling from both young and old. All of this occurred in rapid succession as we turned our attention to the back entrance.

"I'll kill her, and then I'll kill the rest of you witches!" a crazed voice from a large man, whose head and arms were covered by a thick, muddy substance, screamed.

He was the vagrant I had noticed earlier that day. Neal lay on the ground holding a gaping wound in his left shoulder where he'd been stabbed. This vagrant tightly held Dicana captive with his left arm, and held a dripping wet knife in his right, just under the poor woman's throat.

"I blessed this knife with holy water, so it'll work against you witches!" he screamed. "Course, I'd rather drown her, 'cause that's the real way to kill witches."

"Let her go, now!" Archon commanded.

"Archon, you have to do something!" Matilda begged.

A couple of men, including Archon and Cyrus, tried to approach him.

"Uh-uh," the man reprimanded as he made a superficial cut on Dicana's neck, causing her to howl with a mixture of pain and fear. He backed the men off with, "You step any closer, and I'll slice this woman's head off!"

A few of the men and women closed their eyes and began to chant, but soon stopped, looking at each other in apparent confusion. Upon realizing that nobody would approach him, the man cackled loudly as he walked his victim out the back door.

I bolted out the front with Archon following right on my heels. Racing towards the back of the lodge, I drew and pointed my gun at the vagrant.

"Freeze," I commanded. "Drop the knife now."

"Daddy," the crying girl pleaded. "Please help me."

"Honey, I'm here," Archon said to his daughter. "I won't let anything happen to you." His attention turned towards the vagabond. "Let her go now!" Archon shouted.

The man screeched frantically. "You can't blame me! I am blameless! I am innocent! Witches are the cause of all of life's misfortunes! Salem was a mistake! Salem destroyed a hallowed institution! It is the innocent that suffer because of witches! I will sacrifice all to destroy them!"

Salem again, I thought to myself. *And innocence. What could this all mean?*

"I said drop the knife," I told the man. "I don't want to kill you, but I will if I must. Drop the knife and let the girl go." Only about half the man's head was exposed just over Dicana's shoulder. The only other parts of him I could see were his hands and a small part of his arms. There wasn't a clear shot to be had. I had to think of a way to get an opening.

"You," the man said hysterically. "You aren't a witch! You should be on my side! You know witches hate us!"

"Right now, you're giving them plenty of reason to," I said

grimly. "Let her go. It's her wedding day. It's supposed to be the happiest day of her life!"

"Wedding? That means this bitch will have more witch children to torture us! Unless...." The man started laughing madly but was able to keep the blade held steadily near her throat. "Unless I kill her now!"

A thought passed through my head. It was a risk, but it was the only way I could think of getting a clear shot. "You make a compelling argument," I said to the madman, lowering my gun slightly so that my arms were closer to my legs. "Witches really are evil, right?"

"What?" Archon screamed.

"You know the truth, right?" the vagabond asked.

"Yes, but you won't kill her by slicing her throat. There's only one way to kill a witch with a knife."

"You're lying! You're trying to fool me, but I won't let you!"

"I've actually read about this. In order to kill a witch with a knife, you have to do a stabbing motion, but you have to really reach back, you see." I took my right arm off my gun for a moment to mimic the motion, reaching so far back, my arm was practically behind me. I moved my arm downward as if I was stabbing someone in the neck.

"What the hell do you think you are doing?" Archon shouted.

"Like this?" the vagrant asked as he began to extend his arm backward. As he did this, he moved a little more to Dicana's right, exposing his entire head and most of his chest to me. In one quick motion, I resumed my two-handed grip on the gun, aimed, and fired.

I could hear the hideous sound of bone-crunching and sinew ripping as the bullet penetrated the vagrant's chest. A gasp and desperate cry escaped the man's lips as his right arm flailed forward, and the knife fell harmlessly to the grass. His body made a sickening thud as it landed on the ground, and his skull bounced slightly off the ground before the rest of his body jerked upward, then lay still on the ground. His still accusing eyes stared lifelessly into the sky. He was probably dead before he came to rest.

"Shit," I muttered as I put the gun back into my holster. "I really didn't want to have to kill the guy."

Unbeknownst to me, a crowd had gathered to see what had happened. Several of them, especially the younger ones, including Cyrus, had their phones raised above their heads, recording everything that had happened.

Dicana raced into my arms and gave me several small kisses on the cheeks, lips, and forehead, and thanked me very kindly for rescuing her. She held me around my neck for a few moments as I looked over to Abby to offer her an awkward smile.

A look of consternation, and dare I say jealousy, crossed her face, but almost immediately, the expression turned into a smile, perhaps out of relief. After thanking me, Dicana ran into her relieved father's arms. Archon took out a handkerchief and covered her slight wound.

"Daddy, he saved my life!" Dicana exclaimed.

"Yes," Archon said brusquely. "He did."

Dicana began to panic. "Oh my God, Dad! What about Neal? Is he all right?"

A familiar voice chimed in. "He'll be all right," Nelson said as he entered onto the scene. "We were able to patch him up. It doesn't seem like the knife pierced any vital organs and mostly caught his upper arm. He'll need some medical attention to completely sew up the wound, then our healers can repair the rest."

"Daddy, can we?"

"Yes, Dicana, of course. Let's go." Archon walked his daughter back into the lodge while his wife and son followed him. Archon did not even look at me as he passed by, though Cyrus did flash me a thumbs up before he entered.

Abby gave me a large hug. "You are turning into quite the hero."

I closed my eyes as I held her in my arms. For a moment, I thought it'd be nice if this moment lasted forever.

Opening my eyes, I noticed that a small crowd had gathered

around the man with a gaping wound in his chest. I gently moved out of Abby's arms and made my way to the man. I hovered over his body and confirmed what I had already known. The man was dead. I had killed another man.

I pulled out my phone and sighed. "I better call Kelly. And an ambulance to attend to Neal, if that's all right with you, Abby."

"Why wouldn't it be?"

"I don't want to accidentally expose your secrets or anything like that."

"Oh, that. Since we're out in public where everyone can see us, it'll actually be less suspicious if we just call the police and an ambulance rather than trying to hide. It's not like on the questionnaire at the hospital; they ask whether you are really a witch."

An ambulance arrived shortly after I called, and the paramedics rushed into the lodge with their equipment in hand.

Kelly and a modest squad of officers arrived on the scene soon afterward. It took him a little while to reach me, as he was bombarded by other guests who were eager to provide him an account of what happened. Some even went so far as to show him the recordings they had on their phones.

After forcefully yet politely making his way through, he was finally able to meet with me. I was still standing over the corpse, even though Abby had tried several times to move me away.

"You're turning into quite the stone-cold killer," Kelly said as he approached me. I glared and said nothing. "Sorry," Kelly said sincerely. "Bad time for a joke."

"I really didn't want to kill him."

"I know. I'm sorry."

"I'm sure the boys down at the station are enamored with me right now. This is what, the third fatal incident I've been around or part of in the last three months?"

Kelly smiled. "I'd be lying if I told you they aren't a little bit suspicious of you right now."

"Not surprised," I said bitterly. "Dead bodies are piling up around me."

"This one is pretty much open and shut, though. Your friend Cyrus and about a half dozen other teenagers showed me recordings of the incident. It's clear to me that you did everything you could to resolve the incident peacefully, and had no choice."

"It still doesn't mean I wanted to kill him."

Kelly patted me on the back. "I know, but it's like you always told me—it gets easier, but it never becomes fun. And if it ever becomes fun, you need to quit and get yourself some help."

"Maybe if I were a better shot, I could have just nicked him on the shoulder."

"Nobody could have done that, not even me. To even get him the way you did took a helluva shot. I'm kind of surprised you were able to do it."

"Thanks," I said sarcastically.

"I'm just saying it was a bit of a risky shot, so you did great."

"I saw him before any of this happened, standing over there, sniffing some mud," I said as I pointed towards the woods. "Maybe I could have said something or chased him away or something."

"Did you see him carrying a knife?" Kelly asked.

"No."

"If you didn't see the knife, then what grounds did you have for kicking him out? You know better than I, Pete, that it's ridiculous to beat yourself up over these things. Maybe if we were all psychics, we could prevent this all from happening, but since we aren't, we have to let these things go."

"I suppose you're right." I let out a heavy and relieved sigh. "Thanks, Kelly. I appreciate this."

"Anytime, friend."

The lodge's doors flew open. Neal was brought out the door on a gurney, and the paramedics carried him down the short flight of stairs. Dicana followed right behind them, her wound closed, and she seemed, for the most part, fine.

Kelly nodded to the paramedics that they could go, and as the doors closed, Dicana and Neal stared lovingly into each other's eyes. They were shaken, but still a happy pair of newlyweds.

Soon after, the boys from the morgue arrived to proceed with their grim endeavors.

"Any idea of who this attacker was?" I asked Kelly.

"As a matter of fact, I do," Kelly replied as a few photographs of the corpse were taken.

"Don't tell me he was a friend of yours," I moaned as the body was being bagged up.

"Nothing like that. The beard made it difficult for me to recognize him at first, but now I've taken a good look at him. His name was Robert Nomad, a boxer who frequently fought at the Emerald Queen Casino. Robert was an okay fighter who I actually watched a number of times. Another tragic story. Both of his parents were drug addicts who suffered from some form of mental illness, and both were dead by the time he was five years old. Robert bounced from foster home to foster home. His only place of solace was the gym, where he built himself up until he became a decent fighter.

"A while back, I noticed he wasn't fighting anymore. I talked to a friend of mine who works at the EQC to find out why, and I was told that his family's history of mental illness finally caught up to him. He slipped through the cracks, and should have been treated or even institutionalized somewhere rather than being left to his own devices."

"Do you know what he was suffering from?"

"Afraid not. I was getting most of this information secondhand, and the guy I was talking to wasn't the sharpest knife in the drawer. I did hear he was homeless, which was obviously true."

"He was screaming about witches, Salem, and innocence. Do you know what that might be about?"

"No idea, but I'm hardly an expert on mental illness."

"He lived mostly in this area, correct?"

"Yeah," Kelly confirmed with suspicion noticeable in his voice. "What are you thinking, Pete?"

"Nothing much," I lied. "Just that it'd be nice to know whether Robert has anything to do with our investigation, or if he was simply a madman disrupting a wedding."

"He was probably just a madman," Kelly said firmly.

"Still, it'd be nice to rule out any possibility he's related to the case."

"Yes, but how would we go about doing that?"

"How indeed?" I asked rhetorically, a plan already formulating in my head.

CHAPTER 12

"What kind of stupid suggestion was that?" I asked my best friend, Erin. She was only eleven at the time, I was twelve. I lived next door to her, so we visited each other often, and this time she was in our yard because our magic show had just concluded. It wasn't originally designed to be "our" magic show when it was scheduled. I was supposed to the main performer, and Erin had promised to remain a member of the audience.

Much akin to a stand-up comedian whose jokes fail to land with his audience, my tricks were failing to entertain the neighborhood kids. Actually, a bad stand-up comic is still usually able to actually recite his jokes, as unfunny as they might be. I was having difficulty executing even the most basic illusions.

I pulled out the wrong card. Everyone saw the sponge on the bottom of the glass. The pencil flew out of my hand. For whatever reasons, the flower just wouldn't pop out of the pot, and that one was supposed to be spring loaded. Worst of all, when I tried to do the old pulling a rabbit out of the hat trick, I dropped the critter, and the poor thing landed awkwardly on its side. He was so scared he frantically scurried off past the laughing children. To be blunt, I was dying up there.

Erin came to my rescue. She started performing dazzling tricks — dazzling to a bunch of eleven or twelve-year-olds at least. A floating soda can, a cup full of water suspended in the air, the old levitating card trick, and she concluded the show with her usual grand finale, levitating someone, a bit.

Erin bailed me out by making it seem that all of my failures were part of the act and that it was our combined magical powers that made all those illusions happen. It may have fooled the audience, but I obviously knew the truth. She was the master illusionist who had to bail me out of yet another poor show. I was jealous of her skills and ability.

"What's wrong with it?" the dark-haired pig-tailed girl asked as she played around with the straps of her overalls. "You'd still be part of the show."

"Whoever heard of a girl magician with a boy assistant?" I asked grumpily. "It's always a boy magician and a girl assistant. That's how it is!"

"Just because that's the way it's always been doesn't mean it's the way it always should be!"

"I don't want to be the girl. I'm a man!"

"What's that supposed to mean?"

"I...I just want to be the magician, okay?!"

"I know, Petey. I'm sorry. It was just an idea."

"You want me to be the assistant 'cause you think I suck at magic, right?" The girl stared awkwardly and silently. "I knew it. You know, I could have still saved the show. You didn't have to come up on stage."

"But Petey, everyone was laughing at you. You looked like you were about to cry. I had to help you."

"I wasn't going to cry!" I shouted, nearly in tears. "And I had other tricks! I could have still saved the show on my own!"

"I was just trying to help."

"You always have to be the center of attention. 'Look at me, I'm Erin. I'm so good at magic, and Peter just sucks at it! He practices for hours; he tries so hard, but nope! He sucks! Let me rub it in his face.'"

"I just wanted to help you out!"

"'Be my assistant, Petey!'" I continued to mock, "You suck anyway!' Nothing humiliating about that suggestion, no sir!"

"Stop it, Petey!" Erin shouted. "Stop it! You know that's not what I meant! I just wanted to help you out! They were laughing at you! I couldn't let them do that! I...." Her voice began to trail and get meeker. "I just wanted to help."

"Whatever. I'm going inside. Don't follow me." I turned and headed towards home.

I felt a petite hand grab mine as I turned my back to the little girl. "Wait, Petey! I have to tell you something."

"What?" I said gruffly without even turning around.

"Petey, I might be going soon."

"What, like moving or something?"

"Nothing like that, Petey. Not quite. I'm just saying, what if something happened to me? Or…uh…or to you? I don't want this to be our last memory together, you know? I mean, if something did happen to me, or to any of us. Not that I think anything will. I just…I just don't want us to go home mad at each other, that's all. We shouldn't go home mad."

"Is this some new age stuff you keep reading about?"

"No! Come on, Petey, can't you just smile for me? Just before you go."

I pulled my hand from hers. "No," I said bluntly and walked inside without saying another word, leaving the poor little girl in tears.

That same night, Erin was murdered.

Marimba music began to play, a different tune than I had as my ringtone. It was time to wake up. I wiped the sleep from my eyes and muttered, "I wonder if I'll ever stop having that dream."

"Somehow, I always knew you'd wind up here someday, in the gutter, especially after you quit the force," Kelly said to me while sipping a cup of coffee. It was the early afternoon. We were both in an alley between the Indochine Asian Dining Lounge and the Harmon Brewery and Eatery, both restaurants adjacent to the main campuses of the University of Washington, Tacoma. He had found me digging through a dumpster with my hands protected with torn gloves. I wore a tattered green overcoat, and my thin gray perforated sweatpants were stained with various foods, and garbage one would find in the streets. Both of my tennis shoes were stained dirt brown and were practically falling off my feet.

"Alms for the poor?" I asked as I closed the dumpster.

"Alms for the poor? I think you're going to have to update

your lines if you expect to get any handouts. Still, I imagine you've already made more so far than you ever did as a private investigator."

"Not quite. Crazy cat ladies pay a pretty penny when you solve the mystery of their missing feline."

Kelly took a large swig of his coffee cup and drained the remains. "Would you like a new cup, Pete?" I slapped the cup out of his hand. He looked at it as it flopped around on the ground. "A simple no would have sufficed. And you better pick that up before I haul you in for littering."

"Your biggest bust of the week?"

"Other than concerned officers harassing you for no reason, how's life on the streets?"

"Not too bad, considering I sneak home at night."

"At least this time, you're doing the dirty work yourself rather than making a teenager do it for you."

"I didn't think he had the acting chops to pull off this role."

"Have you been able to find anything with all this undercover work you've been doing?"

"I'm making progress. I think I'm beginning to win the favor of a couple of the regulars here, so maybe they can tell me something. One of them mentioned that a weird guy used to bus frequently from here to Titlow. He was probably talking about Robert."

"If you really think this is the way to find out more about information, knock yourself out. I learned something new, though. Do you know Diana White from Komo 4 News?"

"I know of her. Why?"

"She ran a story on Robert recently. It was one of those sad 'Where are they now?' kind of pieces. A little melodramatic, but well done. A social worker named Breanna Jones was especially touched. She made Robert something of a pet project, so I suppose she's a bit of a philanthropist."

"Or she discovered something she thought she could use to become famous."

"You always have to be cynical, don't you?"

"I wouldn't be if I wasn't almost always correct."

"Yeah, almost always correct," Kelly repeated with a sigh. "Regardless, she wanted to clean him up for a job interview, but he absolutely refused. His mental problems were much worse than the news story let on. He showed signs of schizophrenia or something like that."

"Schizophrenia might explain why he saw witches."

"Perhaps. He ranted about nearly everything else, at least according to Breanna. He seemed to have difficulty discerning between fantasy and reality, and was very susceptible to suggestion."

"What do you mean?"

"For example, remember that vampire craze a few years back? After seeing posters for that series of movies, Robert believed that vampires and werewolves lived amongst us and were going to kill him. Aliens, superheroes, monsters, you name it, if it's a movie, Robert believed that they were real. Maybe he saw something about witches on television."

"Maybe. That's all good to know, so thanks for telling me."

"No problem. Let me know if you discover anything while out here, okay? In the meantime, I'm going to do as you suggested and take a closer look at Tony O'Stein. Is there anything specific you think might help this investigation?"

"You might see if there's a connection between him, Joseph Edwards, Keith Jackson, and Robert Nomad. Oh, and that reminds me of something I forgot to ask. Would you mind taking a look into the Benevolent Arms Church?"

"Yeah, okay, but what do you want me to look for?"

"Just see if there's anything suspicious about that church. A couple of months back, when Joseph Edwards let it slip that he was a regular member of that congregation, he freaked out. I have no idea why."

"Sounds good. I'll see what I can find and talk to you soon, okay?"

A few days after that meeting with Kelly, I was sitting on the steps of the Valiant Crusaders Church located two left turns and a straight half mile walk away from the University of Washington, Tacoma. I was reading a newspaper, not that there was anything in the paper that I hadn't read about on my computer that morning, but it was something to do in order to remain inconspicuous.

"The homeless are probably the only ones reading the newspaper," I muttered as I thumbed through the pages. I had only made a few friendly acquaintanceships with a couple of vagrants that I happened to run into on the streets, but it was enough to glean some useful information.

I spoke to a man that only went by the name the fake name of Mallard. A former stockbroker, and a rather successful one if his story was to be believed, he chose to live on the streets after suffering from increasing paranoia concerning the government having all his information, although the "paranoia" part is my own editorializing. Mallard wanted to live off the grid, so he wintered in California but headed north in April, the month previous to the current month, so he could get to a more temperate climate.

I asked him whether he knew Robert Nomad. After I described what he looked like and how he acted, he told me that he did, and though he didn't know him particularly well, he knew enough of him to understand why he had developed a negative reputation amongst the other vagabonds.

"That's not to say any of us smell like damn roses," the shaggy red-bearded man in a camo jacket and ski cap said as I shared a half-eaten hamburger I'd found in the trash with him. "But he smelled particularly bad. Most of us try to keep somewhat clean, but he wouldn't even bother trying."

"Where can I go to bathe?" I inquired.

"You're fresh meat, aren't ya, kid?" he asked in response.

"That part's right, but I'd rather not talk about why I'm here or anything."

"And I don't really give a damn why you're out here either, but I'll give you a little bit of free advice." Mallard wiped the remnants of his meal off his face. "Some of the buildings near the university are open, and usually students don't have the balls to tell you not to bathe in there. Sponges are easy enough to find. Still, you better just get damn used to not bathing every day."

"I'll keep that in mind."

"You don't want to wind up like Robert, smelling like dog shit and worse. It was like he sought out those kinds of smells and rolled in them. Hell, I don't think a dog loved shitty smells as much as he did. He always carried around this bottle that smelled like shit—I mean, like real shit that's been sitting in the sun for days."

"Was he just gathering dog feces and placing it in a bottle?"

"Now that ya mention it, that's the damnedest thing. He claimed it came from a church. I think he was talking about the one in that direction." Mallard pointed in the direction of the Valiant Crusaders Church. "I ain't a religious man myself. Don't think Robert was neither. Never talked about God or any of that shit. Still, don't think a church has that kinda crap. Maybe some kids were into jenkem."

I didn't tell him that jenkem was probably a myth, I just thanked him then loitered around Valiant Crusaders hoping to unearth some new information. I could have guessed what was actually in Robert's bottle.

Thumbing through the paper, I skimmed over an article that discussed how the police force's forensic experts tried to downplay confusion over whether a pentagram was actually burned into a man who had recently died. He was a forty-two-year-old family man with deep religious convictions, who suddenly dropped dead after a sudden bout of depression followed by extreme anger, expressions of deep seeded paranoia, anxiety, and violent outbursts along with complaints of lightheadedness, headaches, and nausea. It was at first thought he suffered from lead poisoning, but an autopsy was unable to reveal that or any other type of poisoning. The pentagram burned into the skin under his armpit of this Christian was the only anomaly they found. Because there was no discernable cause of death, a second autopsy was ordered a week later, but that one only noted that the pentagram had disappeared. "This adds a new wrinkle in the case of the Pentagram Killer," the article concluded.

It worried me because I knew all too well the effects a witch's spell was supposed to have on a human body. Abby had also visited me a couple of days later to discuss the ongoing politics within the coven in the wake of the wedding.

"Even though many witches, not just me, have argued that you are a prime example of 'good' cowans acting for our benefit, it fell on deaf ears. Dicana's kidnapping is being used as an example of how dangerous cowans are," Abby explained as she handed me some food from a basket, not only to make sure I was eating properly but as a cover for why a beautiful woman was talking to a homeless man. "So, some of the separatists are using the wedding as an excuse to attack cowans."

"So I've heard—or should I say, read about," I said to my companion as I bit into an apple. "This is still the best apple I've ever eaten, by the way. They are calling him the 'Pentagram Killer' on account of the burn marks under the armpit. I thought it might have been the ramification of a witch's spell, which is one of the reasons I asked you over here."

"One of the reasons?" Abby asked.

"I did sort of miss you."

She blushed slightly. "That's sweet, though if you weren't playing hobo, I'd be able to see you more often," Abby reprimanded. "You really need a bath, too."

"I know, but I think I'm getting close to finding some solid info about Robert Nomad."

"Regardless, the so-called 'Pentagram Killings' aren't the work of one man, but the work of several of our separatists."

"So, we're not accomplishing a lot, and this is the beginning of the war."

"Petey, there's no need to get melodramatic," Abby scolded. "At least not yet. Many in the separatist community are incensed over this action because they do not want to hurt or kill any of them. So far, the attacks have only come from one or two unidentified people, but once they're caught, our coven will deal with them appropriately."

"Are you sure the murderers are the separatists?"

"Yes. There were four victims. A man who was poisoned, a man who took a swan dive off a roof, a man whose neck was snapped, and a man who was set on fire. Those were truly the results of a spell that poisons the body, a spell that poisons the mind, a telekinesis spell, and a fire spell. The last one is especially difficult, and literally, only one or two separatists can perform it, so that narrows down the number of suspects, so to speak."

"That still doesn't sound good. We've got to figure this all out soon."

"Petey," Abby said remorsefully. "This has gotten a lot bigger than I ever anticipated. I am truly sorry you're involved in this mess."

"No need to apologize, Abby, I want to be here." I clutched the coin around my neck.

Abby gave me a hug and a kiss on the cheek. "Just be careful, all right? I still think there are better ways to gather information, but then you're the private investigator."

"Yeah, don't question me. I'm the expert, right?" I said teasingly.

Feeling the call of nature, I stood up and turned around, facing the large brick building with a stucco roof and green paned windows. As I walked up the steps that lay adjacent to two slopes of green, I looked at the cross placed in the middle of a traditional steeple rooftop that was above the first floor of that building. My intent was to go inside, but the door was locked.

I had begun to become a little bit too accustomed to the liberation of being a homeless man not bound by society's rules, or so I had led myself to believe, as foolhardy as that notion truly was. Peter Cunningham, the private investigator, would have never dreamed of urinating outside, but Peter Cunningham, the vagrant, was getting familiar with the practice, maybe even disturbingly so.

It still didn't feel right to pee against the side of the church, but luckily there were some bushes behind and to the right of the building that served as a sort of fence between it and the gray apartment complex next door. A few large trees provided extra cover for my makeshift restroom. It was from there I noticed a vehicle parked in the back parking lot that I had not been able to see from the entrance.

Standing in the bushes, I overheard the sound of a vehicle entering the parking lot. Finished, I turned around and noticed the vehicle that had parked in the back lot was a red delivery truck with the yellow text "Bert's Deliveries" emblazoned on the side. A muscular man wearing red shorts and a T-shirt with yellow stripes stepped out of the vehicle, holding what looked like a crate of vials with brown liquid inside.

A tall, thin man in a white suit and black tie stepped out of the back door of the church, thanked the man for the delivery, and then reentered the building. Afterward, the delivery driver returned to his vehicle and left. Something about the driver struck me as familiar, though I could not remember where I had seen him before.

The containers of brown liquid were even more familiar to me, which was why I chose to continue my daily vigil at the church. It didn't take long for a peculiar pattern to emerge.

For three days, I went to that church, read whatever reading material I could find, and sat on those steps until late afternoon. The truck arrived at the same time daily, like clockwork, while I hid in the bushes on each arrival.

I met with Kelly in the same alley we'd used since I began my masquerade as a vagrant. He told me that based on the description I provided, the man making the deliveries was Bertrand Davis, owner of "Bert's Deliveries," which he also told me mostly concerned itself with making deliveries to and from local businesses. Davis was willing to take on business deliveries of all kinds, from delivering to local tackle shops to supplying needed items to local game shops. This philosophy, along with relatively cheap prices and efficient deliveries, had helped his business expand and grow. Chain stores began to take notice and forged deals with him. There was talk that his business's reach could be expanding past Tacoma.

Kelly noted that the delivery to a church was odd, for it was hardly a typical customer, and it was stranger still for Bertrand to be making deliveries because Bertrand rarely was seen in the driver's seat at all.

After his usual delivery on the third day, I heard Burt addressing the man in the white suit. "I think this is the last set of vials I'll be delivering to you, for a while at least. I know you're gearing up for an attack, but unfortunately, with our recent casualties, our supply is a bit low, and this is all we have for now. We'll need to wait a few weeks until our men are able to gather enough to spread around."

"Keep your voice down!" the man in the suit said in a hushed but harsh tone. "What if somebody is around?"

"Relax, Jerome. Nobody is around except for a few vagrants."

"Shouldn't we be more careful since the attack?"

"That was an isolated incident. Besides, if they wish to do our dirty work for us, who are we to complain? Whether the attacks come from them or us, the end result will be the same."

"Still, I think we should be careful just in case."

"If you say so," the man said with a sigh.

"Thank you, and sorry. I've been on edge since that homeless bastard brought that unwanted attention to witch hating. But it appears that the police are writing it off as an isolated incident by a madman."

"If you remembered to lock the backdoor, none of this would have happened."

"I've had too much on my mind. Still, I would have thought the smell would have been enough to prevent any thefts."

"It may smell bad, but it does the job."

"Yes, I suppose it does." After a moment's pause, the man continued. "Are you really going to quit?"

"I'm not quitting per se. I'm just reducing the amount of responsibility that I have. My delivery business is getting too big for me to continue what I have been doing without drawing attention to myself. I'll still be around for the meetings, and will be willing to help out when needed on most other things."

"You were the best, though, at taking care of issues within our group."

"Perhaps you're right, but at the same time, it has grown wearisome. I know it's for the greater good, but it's beginning to haunt me. My dreams are now unsettling. I'm seeing each of their faces in my sleep." The man paused and sighed. "I think it's time for me to abdicate my position. Tony asked if I could do one more job, and I've agreed to it, but then it'll be time for me to focus on my delivery business."

"That seems to be where your heart is anyway."

"Business has been booming lately, and I'm quite proud of how much it has grown."

"I will miss you, though."

"As I said, I'll still be around. I still believe in the cause, it's just somebody else's turn to do what needs to be done."

"*Nel tempo del suo Pontificato, la gloria della scoperta di un nuovo mondo*, my friend."

"Yes, *nel tempo del suo Pontificato, la gloria della scoperta di un nuovo mondo*." With that, the two men said their farewells and went their separate ways.

During his pontificate, the glory of the discovery of a new world. I mentally translated the phrase I knew to be written on Pope Innocent VIII's grave. Connecting the dots, I realized that the use of this phrase, which was once the words of the Innocent Children who devoted themselves to Pope Innocent VIII, almost certainly meant either that the eighteenth-century group had not died out, or it had been brought back into being.

Figuring there wasn't anything left to learn as a homeless man, I returned home to thoroughly wash and eat a huge meal. While I slept at home and supplemented my diet of discarded food with some actual food, I had been foregoing showers and eating meager meals for breakfast and supper in order to keep up appearances.

After a discussion with Kelly, he agreed that it would be prudent to pay Bertrand a visit at his business. His corporate office was located not too far from the university, only about three miles north past the Port of Tacoma on the outskirts of Fife. It was about a ten-minute drive from my office. Dressing decently for the first time in weeks, I got in my car and headed there early in the morning.

Driving down the street from the crossroad, I passed two sets of warehouses to get to his business, with two more sets of warehouses on the other side as well. Bertrand's warehouse was a gray and white amongst a sea of white and gray warehouses, each one indistinguishable from the rest. I almost drove past, but I was able to see a familiar large red delivery truck with yellow text painted on its side out of the corner of my eye. I was able to make a quick and tight, if not altogether legal, turn to drive into the proper location.

His place should have been open by the time I arrived because Bertrand worked unusual hours. It wasn't surprising that there was very little activity taking place outside his warehouse — or anywhere, for that matter — as it was still very early on a Sunday morning. Bertrand still should have been there, though.

The first I knew that Kelly was right behind me was when I was halfway up the lot and happened to look into my rearview mirror and saw the man looking at me smugly. I parked between a black luxury vehicle and a couple of red delivery trucks directly in front of a glass door that led to the tiny main office in the warehouse. Kelly parked on the other side of the black car next to a BMW.

"Well, among other things I could cite you for, you didn't use a turn signal before you turned into this parking lot," Kelly teased as he faced me, leaning against his open car door. "And I think you clipped some of the curbs as you pulled in. You're definitely guilty of at least a reckless driving violation, and there's probable cause that you were driving under the influence. Let me get my breathalyzer out."

"Knock it off, Kelly. I admit I didn't make the best turn coming in. Nobody was on the road at the time, so I figured it was still a pretty safe thing to do. I didn't realize you were right behind me."

"You keep this up, and I'll have you in for resisting arrest."

"What if I buy a couple of tickets to the policeman's ball?" I asked as I began walking up the short flight of steps to the glass door, with Kelly right behind.

"Oh, come on, Pete, you know better than that. Policemen don't have...formal dances. You thought I was going to say something else for a second, didn't you?"

"You're getting too clever for your own good, Kelly," I replied.

"By the way, I took a look into The Benevolent Arms Church. It's owned by Tony O'Stein, who also owns another church, the House of Virtue. Guess who some of the members of their congregation were?"

"Just tell me, huh?"

"Keith Jackson and the three lackeys that died along with him."

"Keith and his cronies? So they were attending a church belonging to Tony."

"Tony also owns the Valiant Crusaders Church."

"No kidding. So The Paragon is only one part of a quadrumvirate."

"Quadrumvirate?"

"Like a triumvirate, but involving four people — or in this case, four properties."

"Really? Never heard of it."

"I think I read it somewhere online."

"Good for you. It's clear, though, that Tony concerns himself most with The Paragon. There's no place like home, eh?"

"We know who is or was involved now, right?"

"Joseph definitely was, as were Keith and his men. It seems like Bertrand and that leader of the Valiant Crusaders Church both are. Still, we don't know the number involved, nor the extent of involvement for those we do know of. Perhaps Bertrand will have a few answers."

I tried to open the glass door. "The door seems to be locked, and it appears that all the lights are off inside."

"Really?" Kelly said incredulously as he also tried to open the door. "That can't be right. I checked online, and this place should have been opened for at least half an hour by now."

"Yeah, you're right—take a look at this." I pointed at what was written on the door.

Kelly placed his hands above his eyes as he leaned against the glass. "It's hard to make out in the dark, but I can't see anybody in there. Not even a receptionist."

I pulled out my phone. "Perhaps I should give the place a call?"

"Good idea," Kelly said.

I was about to dial when our conversation was interrupted by a familiar distinctive sound coming from the upper part of the building—two gunshots followed by a loud, blood curdling masculine scream.

Kelly and I pulled our guns as he bellowed, "Use the butt of your gun to break open that glass door, but just tap the glass! That should be enough to break it without alerting whoever's inside."

"Aren't you going to call for backup?"

"Why bother? You'd just tell me there's no time."

I shrugged and silently agreed. I turned my gun around and tapped the glass to create a web of cracks. With an aggressive push, I managed to remove enough to allow me to reach my hand in and open the door.

Carefully navigating over the glass shards, I followed Kelly as he led the way past the reception area up a short flight of stairs that led to a closed door. In a smooth motion, Kelly kicked open the door and swiftly entered, with me right behind him.

"Freeze!" Kelly shouted as he entered the room. The wide eyes of a stunned man staring at us, not saying a word or moving a muscle, greeted us as we arrived. Both of Bertrand's hands were covered with white gloves. His hand literally held the smoking gun.

Blood flowed from the victim's chest and abdomen, and a pool of blood was beginning to form all around the floor. What appeared to be cleaning supplies of all sorts and sizes lie next to him, though this was merely a guess, as the liquids were in clear bottles that did not have labels.

"Put your weapon down, now!" Kelly commanded.

Bertrand did as instructed. As soon as he released the weapon, Kelly rushed and put the man in cuffs. Meanwhile, I raced to the side of the wounded man, knowing deep down there wasn't much I could do for him. I was stunned to see a familiar face.

"Joseph?" I asked, and the man nodded as well as he could. "What the hell are you doing here?" I positioned the man as best I could in my arms in order to make his final seconds in this world as comfortable as possible. His blood stained and dampened my clothes.

"Tony...says...too early.... Wanted to recruit Bertrand. He called me...to talk...but it turns out...I'm a sacrifice...." Joseph struggled to say these words.

"Joseph, I don't understand, what do you mean?"

"Heather, Daddy's... going to see you...soon...."

"Stay with me, you're going to be all right! I'm going to call an ambulance and...." I stopped when I realized the poor man was no longer breathing. I closed those eyes as gently as I could and set him on the floor.

"That Joseph Edwards?" Kelly asked after placing Bertrand down on his knees.

"Afraid so."

"Shit!" Kelly turned towards Bertrand. "Now, why the hell did you have to go and do a thing like that?"

Bertrand scowled and said nothing.

"Hey Kelly, take a look at that gun," I said, taking a quick glance at the weapon lying on the floor. "Doesn't that look familiar?"

Kelly took a closer look at the firearm. "Good eye. Looks like a Ruger Mark Three. That's the gun that was used to kill Tommy and Chuck. It looks like we've got our man on that one. That's three homicides that you're facing, buddy. Look around, Pete, see what else you can find."

Looking around the tiny room, I noticed a rather large oak dresser standing next to a window in the right corner across from the door. I threw open the doors and inside found black gloves, black shoes, and a black coat, identical to the ones the assassin wore on the night of Tony and Chuck's murder. Next to the coat was a hooded alabaster robe.

"Would you look at that, Kelly?" I asked. "The same black clothes the murderer wore on the night he killed Tommy and Chuck, along with the same white robe I've seen the other persons of interest had during my investigation."

"Well, that is interesting," Kelly said. He asked Bertrand, "What do you have to say about that?"

Bertrand growled, "Wait, what did he say?"

"Who?" I asked. "Kelly? He asked you what you have to say about the clothing I've found."

"No, Joseph. Did he say something about Tony?"

"I don't know. I think he said something about Tony saying everything is too early, whatever that means."

Bertrand cursed and muttered under his breath. "Dammit. I didn't want to do the dirty work anymore. My business was going well. He ruined it by forcing me to do the job."

"Slow down," I commanded. "I'm not following you at all."

He ignored me. "What is he waiting for? If he just exposed everything now, people would understand my actions, and what I have done, what we've done. It is for the greater good — of course, they would understand that all I've had to do was for the people, for the world. The attacks have already started. The rest of humanity could learn what we have known for years if Tony would just expose them now. We have evidence of their existence. Why is he waiting? He's gone mad. I should force the issue. If nothing else, if I'm going down, he's going down with me." The man looked at Kelly and raised his voice. "Officer, I'd like to negotiate a deal if I can."

Kelly asked, "What kind of deal?"

"Let's just say it is incriminating information with regards to Tony O'Stein. Does that pique your interest at all?"

Before he said anything more, Kelly read him his rights and followed up Bertrand's last comment with, "It depends on the kind of information you have. What've you got?"

"I'd rather not say anything until we've agreed to some sort of deal down at the station."

"Then I can't make you any promises," Kelly said. "If you don't give us something, then how the hell do we know you aren't just blowing smoke up our ass? We can't even begin negotiations without you giving me something."

"Of course, you need a show of good faith. If you would go to my laptop sitting on that desk over there," Bertrand motioned with his head over to the laptop sitting on a desk on the right side of the room, "I think you'll find something interesting."

"Pete, would you mind taking a look?"

"No problem."

As I walk to the machine, I noticed a stack of coins and picked one up from the top. It had a depiction of the Tomb of Pope Innocent VIII.

"Interesting coin," I said. I showed Bertrand that the coin in my hand was identical to the one dangling around my neck, save for the hole I'd put in mine.

"You may keep that one if you'd like to add another to your collection."

"Cut the crap!" I shouted. "Why the hell do you have these coins? What do they mean? Are you part of the Innocent Children?"

"Who or what are they?" Kelly asked, confused.

"You know of that name?" Bertrand remarked, seemingly stunned.

"I've read up a bit on your little witch hunting cabal. You guys used to be respected, and now you aren't even a memory."

"Are you a Christian?" Bertrand asked.

"Not your business," I responded. "What does that have to do with anything?"

"A good Christian knows that the dead shall rise again. That is similar to what is happening right now."

"Great, a fantastic metaphor," I said sarcastically. "It doesn't quite answer my question. What's with that motto you like to throw around, Nel tempo del something or other?"

"*Nel tempo del suo Pontificato, la gloria della scoperta di un nuovo mondo,*" Bertrand corrected. "Do you even know what that phrase means?" I told him the translation, and he said, "No, what it truly means. It means we're creating a new world. You can figure out the details by yourselves unless we can negotiate ourselves a little deal."

"I'm not guaranteeing a damn thing," Kelly said, a bit irritated. "Not unless you start saying something worth listening to."

"Just take a look at my laptop. It's better than talk."

After staring at his smug face, I gave up on either punching it or hoping the man behind it had something worthwhile to say.

"What's the password?" I asked gruffly after booting up the machine.

"Exclamation point, asterisks, at symbol, eye...." Bertrand began. "Look, now that I think about it, this would be much easier if I entered the password myself because even after I log in, there are passwords for a half dozen applications I'll need to run. So it would be much simpler if I just did it all myself."

"Yeah, I don't think so," Kelly responded. "Nice try, though."

"Look, I know when I'm beaten. All I want to do is show you what's there."

"Okay," Kelly said hesitantly. "But Pete, point your gun at him for me."

"No problem," I said as Kelly removed the handcuffs.

Bertrand then moved his hands in a mimic of regaining circulation, a move I felt was a bit theatrical because, if anything, Kelly had the cuffs on a bit too loosely for my liking.

"That gun pointed at my head makes it incredibly easy to concentrate, by the way," Bertrand said as he typed furiously at his keyboard.

"Don't worry, I won't shoot you if you fat finger a password," I said. "We're just making sure you don't get any crazy ideas about escaping."

"It's sad that people have such a lack of trust these days," Bertrand lamented. At long last, Bertrand had finished his work. "I'm sure your geek squad down at the station could have done all of this without my help, but I hope this will provide you some assurance that I have vital information that you want. Take a look, gentlemen," the man said as he moved away from the machine.

"First, get over here so I can put you back into cuffs," Kelly said gruffly in response.

"If you must," Bertrand whined. "People don't have any trust anymore."

Kelly slapped the cuffs back onto his wrists and walked him over to the laptop and, while still holding him with his arm, leaned over to look at the screen. I stood next to him and did the same.

"This is just a list of names," I commented.

"A list of sacrifices," Bertrand corrected.

"Sacrifices? What the hell are you talking about?" Kelly asked angrily.

"That's something we can discuss over at the station when we negotiate a deal," Bertrand said smugly. I glowered at him before taking a closer look at the list, which was long and mostly full of names I didn't recognize. The ones I did recognize, though, were significant.

"Hey Kelly, check it out," I said, pointing at the screen. Kelly leaned forward in response. "Here's 'Cullen Jones.'"

"And above him is the name of his wife, 'Nicole.'"

"The names Chuck and Tommy are also here, but I'm afraid I don't recognize anyone else."

"How far back does this list go, anyway?" Kelly asked Bertrand.

"Almost twenty years," Bertrand replied.

"Twenty years? There aren't that many names for twenty years."

Bertrand chuckled. "We aren't the Aztecs, Detective. We weren't sacrificing people daily."

"There are a few names listed after Tommy and Chuck's. Future sacrifices, perhaps? What exactly are sacrifices in this context anyway?"

"People he's killed because they've failed in some way," I said as if I had an epiphany. "And these coins are kind of a calling card."

"Makes sense," Kelly said. "So this is a list of people he has killed or will kill in the future."

"Wait. That isn't quite right."

"Why not?"

"Cullen wasn't killed by Bertrand. He was murdered in prison, and he had the coin before he was killed. Tommy or Chuck dropped a coin when they attacked Abby, which also means one of them if not both had the coin before they were killed."

"What about your coin?" Kelly asked.

After a moment's pause, I responded, "Found outside of Erin's home after her murder. Only her name wasn't on the list, which means the coin isn't a calling card." After reviewing the places the coins were found, I added, "The sacrifice is the mission they have to accomplish. A sacrifice for the greater good. Tommy and Chuck were supposed to be sacrificed because they accidentally killed a fake witch instead of a real one—er, should I say, who they thought was a real one—and they were supposed to be killed in the process."

"Only they weren't because witches aren't real," Kelly said brusquely. "At least not in the hocus pocus sense. So those two idiots attacked an innocent woman, your Abby, in order to please some nut jobs who think witches are real."

"Witches are indeed real," Bertrand said. "And the world is about to find out. I never thought the goals of the Innocent Children would come to fruition in my lifetime, but it does seem they will and incredibly soon, even if Tony disagrees."

"It's that kind of fanatical thinking that got those poor innocent folks killed during the Salem Witch Trials. I never thought we'd see it again."

"Salem was a mistake," Bertrand said solemnly. "Something

beautiful was destroyed because of impulse and desperation and an eagerness to terminate a wonderful institution. All of us regret Salem."

"Listen to that, Pete," Kelly said. "Sounds almost like even he agrees that the Salem Witch Trails were unjust."

"I don't think that's what he's saying," I said. "With everything I know about these 'Innocent Children,' I'm certain they do not have any sympathy for the alleged witches of Salem."

"Yeah, I agree." His attention turned to the man. "Why don't you tell us more about this 'Innocent Children' nonsense, huh?" The man remained mum. After a heavy sigh, Kelly asked me, "How do you think this guy is involved, then?"

"I'm guessing he distributes the coins to the members who are to be sacrificed, and if they fail in their assignment, he is there to clean things up."

"Oh, you mean like murdering Tommy and Chuck, that sort of cleaning?" Turning his attention to Bertrand, Kelly continued. "We'll have to check the ballistics, but I'm pretty sure that's the gun that was used in the murder of Tommy and Chuck. With the clothes we found, the Beamer, and the list of 'sacrifices' on your computer, it's a virtual confession."

Bertrand shrugged nonchalantly with a calm expression on his face.

Kelly's eyes brightened. "I just thought of something. Cullen was found guilty of several murders, right? You always thought it was the work of more than one man."

"You're right, good catch. His sacrifice must have been to throw us off the scent of the rest of his organization."

"Any idea what Joseph's sacrifice was all about?"

Bertrand suddenly chimed in, his voice low and seemingly hostile. "Joseph was a personal favor for Tony. He was not actually a sacrifice. Tony believed Joseph was about to betray us, so he was, in fact, a traitor as opposed to a sacrifice."

"I guess that explains that," Kelly added. "How does Erin fit into all this, though?"

"I still have no idea. I feel like I'm so close at times, but I can't quite figure it all out."

"I'm sure you will, Pete," Kelly said in his most comforting tone. "You've figured out so much already. I'm sure you'll figure this out too."

"Thanks, Kelly. I'm sure you're right."

"One thing I don't quite get, though. Why write all these names down? I kind of understand having a list of people who needed to be 'sacrificed,' but why keep their names after they've been 'sacrificed'?"

"Tony was a big believer in recording all of our names, even those who necessitated sacrifice," Bertrand said in that same low and hostile tone as before. "It was all part of what he called his 'legacy.' It's always odd when I think about that coin."

"What do you mean?" I asked.

"It wasn't always a symbol meaning you're to be sacrificed. It was once just a gift from father to son. Considering how many I've given out over the years, it's hard to imagine it ever being a gift."

"What the hell are you talking about, Bertrand?"

"I think I've said enough," Bertrand said with a devious grin. "I think that's more than enough for you to be willing to negotiate a deal, wouldn't you say?"

"I don't know. I think Pete figured out pretty much everything you were going to tell us."

The man threw his head back and laughed. "Hardly—that only scratches the surface. There is much more to tell you than what is on that one little machine. I refuse to say anything more until we get to the station, and we can negotiate a deal."

After pressing him some more, Kelly said, "Okay, we're wasting time. We can talk about this more at the station, and I'll talk to the chief about negotiating a deal."

"Thank you," the man said. "Shall we leave, then?"

As I backed away, I noticed there was a framed motivational message above the laptop. It read as follows:

The foxes attacked because they knew the chickens had discovered the evil serpent's magic and wanted to use it to destroy the animal kingdom. The foxes tried to tell everyone, but they refused to believe because they thought the magic was only a myth. The fox's only hope was to force the chickens to use that magic. Their actions may have seemed unjust and cruel, but they did it for the good of the animal kingdom.

At the bottom of the frame was part of a sticky note cut so thin it did not even hang over the frame. It simply read in capital letters, "NEVER FORGET THE PLAN."

"What's all this about?" I asked Bertrand. He simply shrugged and feigned ignorance. I thought about it as I led the way down the stairs, with Bertrand and Kelly following right behind.

About halfway down the stairs, something dawned on me, "Of course!" I exclaimed, abruptly stopping, which greatly annoyed both Bertrand and Kelly. "I think I've figured it out! I need to see Abby right away!"

"Easy, tiger," Kelly said. "You'll see her soon enough. Let's finish what we're doing here first."

"That's not what I meant, Kelly. I think I've figured out the Innocent Children's plan and what their ultimate goal is."

"Would you mind letting me know, Pete?"

"I want to, Kelly, but I don't think it would mean much to you—but it will to her. She's the one that needs to know because it affects her and her people the most."

"Her people? She's Gaelic, right? Or is she Irish? Scottish, maybe?"

"Gaelic refers both to the Scots and the Irish," Bertrand snapped.

"Who asked you?" Kelly said crossly. "Pete, you can call her as soon as we're done, so please be patient."

I nodded as we headed out to his vehicle in a parking lot that was still mostly empty. We were not, unfortunately, the only ones there.

A shot was fired, striking Bertrand's head, and the man fell limply to the ground. I turned and reached for my gun. A completely hooded and masked figure staring at me from behind a parked blue sedan on the edge of the road fired a second shot.

I felt a hot, excruciating pain in my left side. As I fell to the ground, I heard a third shot, but it apparently missed its target. After falling to the ground, I felt a strange sensation, not unlike a small snake slithering across my neck, and heard a metallic noise as if something hit the pavement.

As I was losing both blood and consciousness, I saw Kelly draw his piece and fire a shot.

"Only nicked him!" Kelly muttered as I heard the sound of a car rapidly speeding away, "In the left shoulder."

The last thing I remember was Kelly hovering over me, taking off his coat, and opening the object he had in his hand as he yelled at me. "You son of a bitch! Why the hell did you have to go and get shot? Look at all this shit you always make me do. And if we had backup, this would have never happened...."

***

"Ah, you're awake." An old, heavyset, nearly bald lab coat wearing man, with white hair on the sides of his head, greeted me as I awoke. "Good to see you are back with us."

"Where am I?" I asked, still groggy from the medication, but slowly realizing that I was lying in a large bed. As I rose to a sitting position, I inadvertently moaned as the stinging pain in my left side woke me.

"You're at the MultiCare Tacoma General Hospital. I'm Doctor Harold Lummox, good to meet you."

"Same," I said softly, trying to avoid further moaning. As I tried to ignore the conversation happening on the other side of the curtain, I asked the doctor, "What happened?"

"You were shot. Luckily for you, the bullet went right through you and didn't penetrate any vital organs. Detective Martinez actually patched you up well enough to slow the bleeding significantly. The paramedics didn't have to do much to make sure you got here in good enough condition for us to put you properly back together again. That detective is responsible for saving your life, Mr. Cunningham."

"Damn. I need to thank him for it. Is he still around?"

"I'm afraid not. He left shortly after he learned you'd be all right. It sounded like he had a lot of explaining to do at the station."

"I'm sure he does," I said, chuckling softly before moaning again.

"He did give me one message to relay to you."

"Yeah, what's that?"

"He called a woman named Abigail to let her know where you were. He also mentioned that you should really learn to password protect your phone."

My heart sank. "I see."

"Even though it's visiting hours, I realize you've just woken up. If you'd like me to dismiss her, I'd be happy to do so."

"It's okay, Doc, I think I'll be all right to see her. How long will I be here, anyway?"

"I'd like to keep you here a couple of days at least to keep you under observation, but after that, I think you should be free to go."

Almost as soon as he got done saying those words, I noticed a familiar sexy figure appearing behind the doctor at the door.

"Hi, Abby!" I said with as much energy as I could muster. She stood there, breathing heavily, fuming with rage. If as the saying if looks could kill worked, she would have finished the job the bullet started.

"I think I'll leave you two alone," the doctor said, apparently noticing the makings of a very awkward moment.

Abby did not even look at the doctor as he passed her, and she continued to glare. She walked around the bed to partially lift the sheet so she could see my wound. She then applied the contents of a vial she had to my side.

"You idiot!" Abby scolded as she applied the lotion. "You complete and utter moron! I can't believe you got shot! How the hell did you manage to do a stupid thing like that?"

"It's not as if I did it on purpose, Abby, I was ambushed."

"I don't care. This keeps happening because you keep doing stupid things!"

"Abby, if you'd only let me explain—"

"Shut up for a moment, all right?" Abby interrupted.

The woman then closed her eyes and began to chant. In spite of everything I had been through, I was still surprised that the pain in my left side began to dissipate. I could actually see the wound beginning to heal. The substance on my side soon faded— no mark, no scar, not even a blemish. My left side was healed to the point that it was as if I had never been shot at all.

"Abby, you truly are amazing."

"Shut up! I don't want to hear it right now! I am so goddamn mad at you right now. I thought it was you calling me, so I was shocked when I heard Kelly's voice. When he told me you'd been shot, I expected the worst!"

"I'm sorry, Abby. I really am."

"Oh, Petey," Abby said, tears rolling down her cheeks as she gave me a large and sudden embrace. "I'm so glad you're all right."

"I am too, Abby," I said, returning her hug. After we released each other, I said, "If I'm healed up, I suppose there's nothing keeping me in bed." I then tried to rise to my feet, but felt dizzy and had to return to bed.

"I think the medication is still affecting you," Abby explained. "The spell should flush it out of your system pretty soon. Let's give it about ten minutes. Actually, let's give it fifteen just to be safe."

"Sounds good to me. By the way, my mind's still a little bit fuzzy, but I remember enough to know there's something I need to tell you. But I think it can wait until we get somewhere a little more private."

"Okay, if you say so, Petey," she said, a bit confused.

We made small talk for a while until the medication wore off, and I was able to get to my feet without any issues. Not knowing what Abby had done for me, the doctor objected to me leaving but eventually caved as I kept insisting that Abby would provide the only medical care I'd need.

They gave me my cell phone, wallet, and keys, then made

me fill out a bunch of paperwork before I could leave. I thanked God that I had kept my insurance paid up, so the bill was not that great of a concern. Sometimes medical care was very important for a PI.

As I got into Abby's car, I gave Kelly a call.

"Hello? Is that you, Pete?"

"Hey, Kelly, of course, it's me. Who else would it be?"

"I'm just a little surprised that the hospital is already allowing you to call me on your cell phone no less. How are you doing, Pete?"

"Good. Practically as good as new, in fact. Kelly, I suppose I really ought to thank you for, you know, saving my life."

"Well, the way I see it, you were doing me a favor, and you wouldn't have been in that situation if it weren't for me—oh wait, I was actually there because of you. Shit, I guess you really owe me then." Kelly laughed at his own comment, and even I couldn't help but smile. "In all seriousness, I'm glad you're all right. How long are you going to be in the hospital, Pete?"

"I'm already out. Abby is giving me a ride back home."

"Damn. You are one tough son of a bitch, Pete."

"I wouldn't quite say that."

"Pete, I know you like to do the whole false modesty thing, but seriously, you just shook off a bullet wound. That is pretty damn impressive."

"There's more to this than I can tell you now. Let's call it client-detective confidentiality."

"All right, I won't press any further. Just don't push yourself too hard, all right?"

"I never do, Kelly. Anyway, is my car still over by the warehouse?"

"Nope, had a guy drive it over to that parking garage near your office."

I paused for a moment so I could tell Abby to drive us to the office. Conveniently, the hospital was a relatively short drive compared to the one to Fife.

"So Pete, where are you going with this next?" Kelly asked.

"I'm already looking into Tony. Because of what we found out from Bertrand's computer, it seems O'Stein might be the leader of the Innocent Children. He may even be the one who shot you and Bertrand."

"Can we visit him tomorrow?"

"No, Pete. I'm sure I have enough for a search warrant, but it'll take at least a few days in order to process it and get it to me, especially since it doesn't seem like it's an emergency or anything. It's not as if Tony's at risk of skipping town anytime soon."

"Kelly, I understand — I was an officer before, remember?"

"I'm just reminding you because you seemed to have forgotten a lot lately. Besides, if you intend to join me, the extra days will allow you to heal more."

"All right. Sounds like a plan. There may be some things I need to take care of on my end, anyway."

"I'll give you a call when things are sorted out on my end. And just to let you know, we may need you to come by the precinct at some point to give your side of what happened today, but it should be routine. Anyway, glad you're all right, and I'll talk to you soon."

"Thanks, Kelly. And thanks again for — you know, saving me and all that."

"Of course. What are friends for if they aren't willing to patch you up?"

After hanging up the phone, Abby looked at me for a moment but said nothing.

"Is everything all right?" I asked.

"Everything's fine," Abby said. "Why wouldn't everything be fine?"

"Okay," I replied hesitantly. "Anyway, Abby, I have some big news. Those men we've been dealing with, Joseph, Keith, Tommy, and Chuck, I think all of them are part of the Innocent Children. I read about them in Nelson's textbooks at the wedding. Bertrand practically confirmed this as fact!"

"Uh huh," Abby said unenthusiastically.

Undaunted, I continued. "I think I know what their plan is

too. We can get the separatists to stop lashing out at non-witches! We just need to inform your coven as to what is happening."

Abby sighed deeply. "Great. That's wonderful, Petey. I'm so happy."

"Abby, what's wrong? I thought you'd be more excited about this."

"I am excited!" Abby yelled. "Why wouldn't I be excited that you can continue risking your life in order to be the big hero?"

"What are you talking about?"

But Abby chose to ignore me until we got back to my office.

"Abby, what's bothering you?" I asked again. "Please talk to me."

Abby looked away from me as she spoke. "Why are you continuing this investigation?"

"What are you talking about?"

"Why is all of this so important to you?" Abby reached into her back seat to grab her purse, pulled out a cigarette, and began to smoke. "Is your life really so unimportant?" The woman turned around suddenly to face me with tears in her eyes. "You were almost killed! You realize I can't do anything about it if you're dead! I wouldn't be able to do anything to save you! We just got lucky this time!"

I tried to hold her, but she moved away from me again. "Abby," I said, flustered. "I'll be careful next time."

"You're taking on an evil witch hating cabal all by yourself!"

"If I can cut off the head, I'll kill the body! Tony's the lynchpin holding this operation together!"

"It doesn't mean you have to be the one to do the cutting."

"If it's not me, then who will?"

"Kelly and the rest of the police force can do it on their own. Besides, this is a witch matter. You don't need to be the big hero."

"Abby, this isn't about me being a hero."

Abby took a long drag of her cigarette. "Let me guess. It's about Erin Ross."

"Yes!" I responded angrily. "It's about her! It's about you! And it's about your whole damn coven!"

"How long do you plan on doing this?"

"As long it takes!" My voice began to tremble. "As long as it takes." I began to reach for the coin only to realize it was missing. I hadn't even noticed that it had fallen off. "Shit!" I exclaimed, checking my pockets even though I knew the coin wouldn't be there. "Where the hell did it go?"

"What are you missing?" Abby asked, more out of curiosity than concern.

"That coin I always wear around my neck. I think it fell off when I was shot. Was Kelly able to find it? No, he must not have because he would have told me about it. The hospital didn't have it, otherwise, they would have given it to me, right? It must still be at the warehouse. God, I hope it is."

Abby looked at me with a pained smile on her face. "You see? It's always about Erin. How come that's your answer to everything? To every tough question, the answer is always 'Erin Ross.' Why is that?"

"Erin…." I began to speak, but needed a second to regain my composure. "Erin was my closest friend. A girl like her deserves to have her murderers brought to justice."

"Justice, huh?" Abby scoffed. "Erin deserves justice. And that will bring her back?"

"Of course not!"

"Her death was a completely random murder. Why can't you accept that?"

"How can you say that?" I snarled. "After everything we've seen? After all we've discovered? How can you say it was random?"

"I know what this is really about, Petey. I know why you can't accept that it was random. You were twelve. You made a mistake. I know you got angry at her, yelled at her and called her names when she asked you to be a male assistant to her magic shows, but you shouldn't feel guilty about it."

"Abby, what the hell are you talking about?"

"You want closure. You want to no longer feel guilty. That's why you've been obsessed with her for twenty years. You have to forgive yourself! You have to move on! Erin would want this for you!"

Words came to me, but left before I could speak them. I don't know how much time passed — maybe minutes, maybe hours, or maybe it was just mere seconds — before I could respond.

"Abby," I said finally. "I have never told anybody about this. Not Kelly, not Carter, not even you. How the hell would you know all of this?"

"What do you mean?" Abby laughed nervously. "You told me this before when talking about Erin."

"No, I didn't. I've never been able to tell anybody that part of the story. I've always left it out, even to you. Those words have never crossed my lips. There's only one person that could have known that." Suddenly I had an epiphany. "Oh my God. The levitation spells. Calling me, Petey. The attack by a man who had the coin. Abby, are you Erin Ross?"

"Don't be ridiculous!" Abby chided. "I'm Abigail Mitchell."

"It explains so much. You looked so familiar to me when I met you. It's why you decided to visit me of all the private investigators. You knew me personally!"

"But you told me you were at her funeral," Abby protested. "A…and, you even told me you saw the dead body."

"Yes, but thanks to Cyrus, I've seen the use of the fake death spell!"

"Oh, that's right, you know about that."

"Erin being a witch, puts a new spin on things! It was because those men were after you, right? You had to fake your death!" Then I had a revelation. "Oh my God, I've been such an idiot. Doctor Jack Galahad, Doctor Jonathan Tristan. Both Galahad and Tristan were Knights of the Round Table. Doctor Jack Galahad is just a pseudonym. Doctor Jonathan Tristan is a witch. He must have been in on it somehow."

Abby said nothing but nodded silently.

"Abby — I mean, Erin — why, though? I've missed you so much. Why didn't you ever try and find me and let me know what happened? Even now, why didn't you ever tell me?"

The woman stammered. "I...I just.... I...I mean...." Abby stared at me, tears streaming down her cheeks. "I've got to go!"

Abby ran out, and I was too stunned to follow. As I sat there thinking, I could not be fully certain whether I was currently living in reality or whether this was all a dream.

CHAPTER 13

"Are you still doing okay, sir?" the waitress asked as she passed by, more out of faux politeness than genuine concern.

"Quite all right, thanks," I said with the same vigor she had given me.

Physically, what I said was true, other than the bandages I wore on my left side, causing my skin to itch. Abby had healed me, but I had to at least keep up the façade that my wound was still there to assuage any sort of suspicion. A few drops of food coloring added to the subterfuge. Mentally, however, I was a complete wreck.

I sat in the most dimly lit part of the bar of an establishment that was as a whole pretty bright. My only companion was the pitcher of beer in front of me, and though I was alone at the two-person table, there were many patrons there that night.

To my left, a group of friends was having a friendly argument over a game of chess. Many people were gathered in front of me with multiple tables pushed together to play a large, intricate board game. In the adjacent room, I could hear loud music and drunken caterwauling in a poor facsimile of singing thanks to it being karaoke night. A couple of the singers prefaced their songs by screeching the importance of preserving the forests of Evergreen, and how proud they were that Tony O'Stein was on their side. I blanched a bit at the irony. It was an unusual bar, but it still one of my favorite places.

Magic shows were often performed in the room where they were holding karaoke night. Most were pretty lame even for amateurs, which assuredly most of the performers were, but every now and again, somebody really talented would put on a show that would astound. Those were always the most fun nights and made this place special to me. There hadn't been a performance like that since I was a police officer.

I was about halfway through my pitcher staring at the game in front of me, wondering what the hell rolling for initiative meant when I heard a familiar voice.

"There you are! I knew I'd find you here. When I didn't find you in your office, and Abigail had no idea where you were, I thought there was only one place you could be. Of course, it would have helped if I typed in the right address. Did you know there was a sandwich place in Tacoma that has a similar name? Luckily, I finally remembered this place was called the 'Magic Cauldron.' I forgot this place was all the way up north here in Evergreen."

"Kelly, what are you doing here?"

"Mind if I join you?" It was more like a declarative statement rather than a question as he pulled out the seat in front of me and sat down. "You don't mind if I pour myself a beer, do you? I'm off duty, so it's okay."

"Go ahead."

Eagerly, he grabbed a cup from a nearby table and started pouring himself a drink.

"I'm probably not going to be good company," I explained.

"Why's that?"

"It's a little bit difficult to explain, Kelly. Let's just say things are a lot different than I had expected them to be."

"Because it turns out Erin's actually alive, right?"

I leaped out of my chair and grabbed the table. The motion startled Kelly slightly and turned more than a few heads. Some of the beer in his cup spilled onto his lap.

"How the hell do you know that?"

"Relax," Kelly said as he grabbed a napkin and wiped himself off. "When she couldn't find you, Abigail — or should I say, Erin? God, this really is confusing — your friend went looking for me at the precinct and then told me all about it. Just to me, though — she said all of this to me privately. I'm glad she knows she can trust me."

"How much did she tell you?" I asked, more out of curiosity than anything.

"She told me a lot about the circumstances that forced her to fake her death, why she did it, that sort of thing. You were right. It wasn't a random attack. It turns out this group, the Innocent Children, have been after her and her family for the last twenty years under the outrageous belief that she's a witch. That's just insane."

"Yeah," I said, chuckling nervously. "It's insane to think she might be a witch."

"I agree, but then again, I suppose the world is pretty crazy."

"I hope you now understand why I just want to sit here and feel sorry for myself."

"For what, though? It turns out that Erin's alive. This should be the happiest day of your life. Would you rather she had been dead?"

"Of course not!" I shouted. "Of course I'm happy she's alive. It's just very difficult for me to explain."

"Then what's on your mind?"

I sighed deeply. "For twenty years, I thought Erin was dead. Now it turns out she's been alive and right under my nose. I couldn't find her, even. She had to find me."

"Kind of makes you think you aren't that great of a detective, eh?" Kelly flashed a wry smile.

"I appreciate that," I said hoarsely. "I'm glad you drove all the way out here just to tell me that, in case I wasn't dwelling on it — which I was, by the way."

"You know I'm just goofing around, Pete. You were one helluva detective when you were with us, and, if the last few days are anything to go by, you still are."

"How could I have not found her? How could I not have known she was still alive?"

"It's not really that strange. You were just a kid when she faked her death. It was not as if you were searching for her the second she went missing. The two of you grew up, changed naturally, and became unrecognizable even if you happened to meet on the street. All this time you were working off the assumption she was dead, not missing. It wouldn't have occurred to you that someone that looked like her, was her."

"Everything you said makes sense, and it's been what I've been telling myself as well. I'm sure one day I'll be able to come to terms with all of that. That's not the only thing that's bothering me, though."

"What else is bothering you?"

"When I was a kid, I wanted to be a magician more than anything else in the world."

"Yeah, I remember you telling me about that."

"The whole reason I became a cop in the first place was to solve the mystery of Erin's death. Now, it turns out she's been alive this entire time. My life, my motivation, everything that I became after that fateful night was based on a lie. It makes me wonder if my whole life is a lie."

"I went through a similar existential crisis myself."

"I wouldn't call what I'm experiencing an existential crisis," I said, interrupting my friend.

"Okay, then I and only I went through an existential crisis."

"What happened?"

"A very good friend of mine, a man I respected both professionally and personally, decided to suddenly quit the police force."

"I'm sorry, Kelly—I can't apologize to you enough."

"It made me question a lot of things," he continued, ignoring me. "The man was like my older brother. Everyone has their reasons for joining the police force, but mine was truly to help others. I thought he believed the same. I thought that was what made him a great detective. I thought that's what would make me a better detective. I thought a lot of things then. If this guy— remember, a guy I had a lot of respect for—could suddenly up and quit, what did it really mean, to 'serve and protect'? Was I the only one who took that oath seriously?

"It's funny. The whole incident actually made me closer to Clara. She really helped me through all of this by helping me come to terms with a lot of things, like my anger and frustration towards my friend."

"You seemed pretty angry and frustrated during our reunion."

"I'm not going to lie and tell you I've completely forgiven him, but at least I didn't punch him, which is what I would have done a few years back. I'd like to think that I at least did everything I could for him, even if it wasn't always with a smile."

"You definitely were a big help," I confirmed.

"Still, there was one question Clara couldn't answer. What do you do when something and someone you believed in wasn't what you thought?"

"So what's the answer?"

"What you do is, you pick yourself up, dust yourself off, and move forward. The reason why doesn't matter. We're all victims of circumstance. What matters is not what happened in the past, but how you respond to it in the future. The lessons I learned from him were still valuable and helped me become a better cop. It's not like they went away as soon as he quit. And not to get too sentimental, the friendship didn't suddenly become meaningless over what ultimately was a disagreement. And you know what the funniest thing is?"

"What's that?"

"I'm actually glad to have met him again. I missed him more than I thought I did."

Suddenly, a bell chimed, and Kelly looked down at his phone and set down the now empty glass in his hand. "Ah, there she is," he said as he rose and waved towards his right. "I was wondering when she'd get here."

"Hi Petey," Abby said as she entered the room and sat down in the seat being offered to her by Kelly. "You are a gentleman, Kelly."

"You're too kind, Abigail. I've got to get going." Kelly walked next to me, placed his hand on my shoulder, and looked down on me with a smile. "Good luck, Pete. I'll give you a call when I get that warrant." After a couple of quick, friendly pats to the shoulder, he took off.

"How are you doing, Petey?" Abby asked.

"About as well as a man can be when he's found out his murdered best friend from childhood has risen from the dead like Lazarus."

"I'm so sorry, Petey. I tried to tell you in my own way. I wanted to tell you directly, but I just couldn't. It wasn't about me. My mom, my dad, my cousins, all of their lives were at stake. I couldn't risk all of that just for a boy I had a crush on. We had to make the death look believable."

"You owe me an explanation."

Abby closed her eyes and sighed heavily as she reached into her purse and pulled out a cigarette. As she was about to light it, the waitress from earlier appeared suddenly to grab it from her mouth. The plump, brown-haired waitress said, "Sorry, but this place is a 'Smoke-Free' establishment."

We both stared at the woman in utter disbelief.

"She's not getting a tip from me," I assured Abby after she left.

"Okay," Abby said after another moment's pause. "I guess I'll do this without a cigarette. You deserve an explanation. Where do I even begin?"

"How about starting with why you faked the murder?"

"That isn't the easiest thing to explain, but then again, none of this is particularly easy to explain. When we were kids, do you remember telling me about a strange man staring into my window?"

"Yes, I remember."

"He broke into my house that night and tried to kill me."

"I knew it!" I shouted, more jubilantly than I intended, before realizing the gravity of what she had said. "Wait, what? He was trying to kill you?"

"Yes, and my father was able to stop him. I've never seen my father that angry before, or ever since. I remember him striking the man a couple of times before dragging him into the basement. My mother stopped me from following him. I half-expected her to scold my father. She almost always admonished him for his angry outbursts, as rare as they were. This time, she nodded silently at my father as he glanced at us before closing the door behind him. I can still hear those terrible sounds that were made below."

"Dear God, I am so sorry, Abby. Nobody, especially not a little girl, should have to go through something like that. I should have done something to help you."

Abby struggled to give me a small smile. "What could you have done? You were only twelve. You weren't quite the hero you are today."

"Why didn't your father go to the authorities?"

"Anger, of course, and fear of the authorities. We witches tend to still be fearful of the police and other government authorities, even though, ironically enough, my dad was a pretty staunch unionist at the time—not that I had come up with that term back then. We were living in Dupont even though our covenstead, or temple, was in Tacoma, where most of our covendom lived. My father wanted to show that living with cowans was possible. That attack really shook him to his core."

"I see. That, combined with the already tumultuous history between cowans and witches, probably made him wary of trusting authority."

"There's that, but also, as loathe as I am to admit this, I think deep down he was afraid the police wouldn't be willing to do what he did to find out why the man attacked me. He used some rather persuasive techniques to interrogate the man. I can only imagine, but would rather not, the kinds of magic he used to extract information, forbidden magic."

"What did he find out?"

"The man knew I was a witch. He saw me use magic. My father blamed our magic shows. I assured him that I was very careful, and everyone believed that my spells were just illusions, but he didn't believe me."

"I certainly was fooled, and if it fooled me, it definitely fooled the other children."

"I now think the man only said that as part of some sort of weird bluff to hide his true intentions. The man assumed because I was a child, I must have used magic in public before. To be fair, technically, I did, but not to anyone's knowledge."

"This coin," I said, habitually grabbing at the coin around my neck before realizing it was missing. "The coin I used to wear confirms your suspicions to be true. He probably said that to hide that he was part of the Innocent Children."

"I think you are right, but I still don't know how they knew I was a witch, or what their ultimate goal is."

"I might have an idea on that latter point, but I would like you to finish your story first."

"Regardless of the real reason he was there, the man planted an idea in my father's mind. The rest of the town, due to the magic shows, knew that his daughter was a witch. My mother and father were too, but neither of them was using their magic in an ostentatious manner, and neither of them had been exposed. Father believed that if we didn't leave town, the attacks would continue. So we left, and that's when he became a separatist as well."

"Nobody in town knew you were witches. I didn't, and you were my best friend."

"I agree. At first, I thought my father was correct, but by the time I was a teenager, I believed that my father had overreacted — though to be clear, he overreacted more in attitude than in action."

"What do you mean?"

"If I'm being attacked at home, it is probably a safe assumption that the place is compromised, and moving isn't a particularly bad idea."

"Good point."

"We moved to Tacoma, where we assumed new identities. We became the Mitchell family, and I became Abigail Mitchell. Dahlia invited us to stay at her place, cramped in a one bedroom apartment while we found somewhere to live. What I told you before might have been a bit of a white lie."

"It was then you had to fake your death."

"Yes. Do you remember Cyrus and me talking about Doctor Jack Galahad?"

"You mean Doctor Jonathan Tristan."

"Yes, of course. He's been a friend to the family for several years. My father then fed me a lot of almonds, as they say, cyanide has a sort of almond smell. This was to throw off the police once they arrived. To add to the deception, my father cast a fake death spell on me."

"Just like Cyrus did."

"Exactly. And now I'm happy that Cyrus told you all about that. After I was taken to the morgue, the good doctor took care of me. Once I revived, he snuck me out without anyone being aware that the 'body' had literally gotten up and left. They found a girl who had passed on who was actually a year older and an inch taller than me but looked close enough that it would pass the eye test. My parents told police they didn't want an autopsy for religious reasons.

"Money in the wrong circles helped us change our identities, and we didn't think about it after that. Doctor Jonathan Tristan quit his job and became Doctor Jack Galahad. He told his superiors that he left because my 'death' was the proverbial 'straw that broke the camel's back.' There may have been some truth in what Cyrus told you about Dr. Tristan seeing too much death, but he mostly left in an effort to maintain the subterfuge."

I paused and hesitated before asking, "What happened to the man in the basement?"

Abby wiped away a couple of tears. "My father 'took care of him.' Doctor Jack then made the issue go away. Please, let's just leave it at that."

For a while, the two of us sat there and said nothing to each other. The only sounds were the ambient noises of people playing their games and a couple of the waitresses taking their orders. Hearing all of this was much more overwhelming than I could have ever imagined. Sentences would form in my head but would immediately disappear. Part of me wanted to grab Abby and never let her go. A lot of me felt shame for earlier getting angry at the poor woman, considering everything she had been through. Largely I was simply shocked that the girl I had thought was dead was sitting in front of me alive and well.

"I am so sorry," I said, barely able to get the words out as I reached for her hand. The woman smiled softly and placed her hand in my palm. "I can't even imagine the torment and horror you must have suffered. I shouldn't have gotten angry at you. I was just shocked, that's all."

"Who wouldn't be shocked? It's been over twenty years, and you thought I was dead. It's probably the only rational reaction to something like this."

"I didn't even stop for a second to consider your feelings in all of this. Your life was changed forever too. And worse still, you were nearly killed as a child. It must have been such a traumatic event, and all I could think of was my feelings."

"Petey, your life changed forever too. All of ours did. A lot of things are happening for you all at once. I wasn't exactly forthcoming to you. It's understandable that you'd lash out."

"Even after all these years, you're still that same sweet person I knew as a child. I didn't deserve you then, and I certainly don't deserve you now."

"Petey, don't say that. Never say that."

"Why didn't you tell me who you were when you saw me again?"

"I was supposed to be dead, and it wasn't as if I could have said, 'Hello. Remember that dead girl from your childhood? She isn't dead, and I'm her. By the way, I'm a witch too.'"

"That's a fair point."

"Besides," Abby said with a wry smile. "I kind of developed feelings for you as Abigail Mitchell."

"Oh, I see. As Abigail Mitchell."

"I was hoping you would develop feelings for me, too, as Abigail Mitchell."

"I kind of did develop feelings for Abby Mitchell—I mean

you. As Abby Mitchell."

"I tend to forget I was ever Erin Ross since I've been Abigail Mitchell for over twenty years, and I was Erin for only eleven. So please continue calling me Abby. You're the only one who does, and it's quite nice."

"That's good, too, because I was probably going to still call you Abby anyway."

Abby sighed. "I wanted to see you again so badly during the last twenty years. I even made some effort to visit you after I graduated. I wasn't quite sure what I was going to tell you, but I didn't really care. I went to your old house in Dupont only to find an elderly couple."

"Yeah, my family and I moved to Tacoma not long after your parents moved away. My father found a better job in this city. My parents are in Sequim now, both retired and enjoying the most temperate climate in the state, supposedly. But Tacoma became my home."

"I didn't know that at the time, of course, but I resigned myself to never seeing you again. Imagine my surprise when I saw your face plastered on the side of a bus while waiting with some friends to go to a Mariners game. You were older and changed, so it took me a minute to recognize you. Naturally, the name 'Peter Cunningham P.I.' emblazoned in big letters next to your head helped me recognize that the man I saw was the same little boy I was friends with as a girl."

"I remember that. I had a really good month, and for a little while, business was booming, so I thought it would be a good idea to advertise. Well, suffice to say it didn't work."

"After hesitating on looking you up, Tommy and Chuck gave me the perfect excuse. I needed the services of a private investigator, and knew there could be no one better."

"It's too bad the two of them are gone," I said facetiously. "Otherwise, I'd send them a 'Thank You' card for reuniting us."

"Petey, you shouldn't say things like that," Abby scolded. "Though I suppose it was serendipitous in the end. Still, even with an excuse, I nearly didn't come see you. That's because I was playing a role. You know me—I always had a flair for the dramatic. It was one of the things that attracted me to magic shows in general. That, and a certain boy who seemed to be in love with them." She sighed and continued. "I wanted to play the mysterious woman with a mysterious past. I played games because even though I was able to recognize you, I didn't think you would recognize me. I have a different name, and we hadn't seen each other in twenty years. And I was right. You didn't recognize me."

"You did seem very familiar to me, though I couldn't quite place you."

She giggled. "I noticed you staring. I assumed it was because I was so beautiful."

"I won't lie and say that wasn't part of it. You've certainly filled out nicely, and something about you was always special to me anyway."

"I thought that you might have not quite forgotten about me, but I never dreamed that I would still be on the forefront of your mind. I thought you would have moved on and had someone else in your life, someone more important than me. Our meeting would have been a fun little reunion, but nothing more."

"No, I could never forget someone like you."

"That was kind of the problem though, Petey. The incident scarred you more deeply than I could have ever imagined. When I saw that you still wore that coin and learned how much my death had affected you, I just couldn't bring myself to tell you who I was and what really happened. I felt guilty, ashamed even. Had I known it would have had such an impact on you, I think I would have tried to talk my father out of it, even as a little girl."

While looking at her, for just a moment, I didn't see the adult Erin's face—I saw the little girl with pigtails, who was my friend all those years ago. The one who befriended me when I was alone and was always there for me when I needed her. It was she who made me feel it was worth dedicating my life to finding out who could have been so cruel as to take her away.

"I can't help but wonder how our lives would have been

different had you never been attacked as a child. I became a cop to solve the mystery of your death. If I had known you were alive, I would have been a magician."

Abby started laughing. "No, you couldn't have."

"What?" I said in a faux rage. "Why not? I think I could have been a great magician."

"I'm sorry, Petey, but no, you couldn't have. You weren't good at magic. Your hand would always pull out the wrong card, or you'd accidentally drop the deck. It was always obvious that your hands were bending the spoon, not your mind, or the coin would fly off into the audience's lap rather than your own. You were simply too clumsy to be a magician. But it's okay. It all worked out in the end. I didn't need a magician—I needed a detective."

I placed my free hand on top of hers and said, "Maybe you're right. I still have an important question for you."

"What is it?"

"Are you hungry?"

"I could eat."

"How about I order something for us?"

"Wait a second. Didn't you have something important to tell me? About the coven?"

"Yes, I did, but it can wait. Spending time with you is the most important thing in the world to me now. Let me see if that waitress is still available. Maybe she'll still earn her tip after all." I raised my hand and summoned the waitress over as we continued our first date.

CHAPTER 14

"Just because I've accepted the fact that your life will be in danger at times doesn't mean I'll ever stop worrying about you," Abby said, sitting next to me as I drove past the train tracks in downtown Tacoma towards the mall and the highway. We were on our way to her coven to seek an audience with their leaders, the high priestess, and priest.

"Is visiting your coven particularly dangerous, though?"

"Visiting the coven normally isn't particularly dangerous, but there are now more witches angry with cowans than have been for decades, and they won't take too kindly to you being there. I might not be able to protect you if someone does something crazy."

"I'll be careful. I promise I won't leave your side."

"Why must you come, anyway? I can easily navigate the politics and tell them the Innocent Children's plans without you. You need to trust me."

"It's not about trust or lack thereof, Abby. It's about a gesture of good faith. The angst witches feel over non-witches is starting to reach a level we haven't seen since at least the Salem Witch Trials. We need a non-witch to tell them these are the actions of an isolated group, not by non-witches at large. I think it would have more impact coming straight from the horse's mouth."

As we drove across the track towards the temple, I recalled what Abby had told me about her coven. They were named the Aoibheann Coven because of a witch of that name born in the seventeenth century Europe that essentially sacrificed herself to inquisitors for the preservation of the rest of her coven. Abigail's clan had moved to the new world shortly afterward, and continued moving west to avoid persecution.

While they were mostly traditional Wicca, some of the teachings of Aoibheann had been preserved, and a few other established customs were ultimately amended. According to Abby, covens customarily only consisted of eight to fourteen people, but Aoibheann believed that was a foolish tradition that led to unnecessary exclusionary practices, and so she emphasized that covens should be as large as a group desired.

She also eliminated the requiring of witches to live within three miles of a specific temple or, to use a more witch-specific term, a covenstead, to be considered part of the coven. This three-mile radius was known as the covendom. Aoibheann thought that a coven was a family, and family should not be limited by geography. That sort of limitation probably would not have worked in the modern world. The covendom became a more generic term meaning everyone within a coven. Most covens actually adhered to these teachings, whether they choose to acknowledge that or not.

One of the major themes of her teachings was of love and sacrifice. Family meant a lot to her, and to her, family was more than just blood.

As we neared the temple, I asked, "Who's expected to be at this meeting?"

"The usual cast of characters. Dahlia will be there, along with Dicana and the rest. Archon, Cyrus, and Matilda will be there too. Members of the circle will be there, along with some family members you haven't met yet."

My blood ran cold. "Are your parents going to be there?"

"Oh, no, thank the goddess they aren't going to be at this esbat today. They are across the country attending to matters with a sister coven. They couldn't have made it even if they wanted to."

"That's good," I said with a relieved sigh. "What is on the docket for the esbat?"

"Your speech to the high priest and priestess will be the opening act, but other topics we'll be discussing include the fate of the chanting circle."

"Oh, right. I suppose it is time for the chickens to come back to roost, so to speak."

We arrived at the temple, located in an area almost completely in the middle of a mall and various chain stores that surrounded it. It was a beautiful site, for the temple was located underneath tall oak trees and surrounded by bright green grass, a woodland oasis in a concrete jungle.

The temple was a lavender wooden building with a traditional tile triangle-shaped rooftop, with many windows providing light into the facility. Two large black doors greeted visitors at the entrance. The building reminded me of a town hall, so completely different than the looming structure I had pictured. It was almost inviting.

Members of the congregation were gathered on the grass. Abby told me no one except for the person delegated to set everything up was allowed to enter before the opening ritual.

Dahlia found us immediately, with the rest of her family in tow. Neal told me that healers had been able to repair his arm quite well, though he'd never be able to pitch at a Major League level again, which confused poor Dicana, who naïvely commented that she never thought he had been able to pitch at a Major League level, forcing him to explain the joke.

A husky man emerged from the back entrance of the temple. He announced, "If you would, please gather here now. The esbat is about to begin with the 'erecting of the temple.'"

"Erecting of the temple?" I whispered to Abby as we headed towards the doors.

Abby whispered back, "It's a name for a ceremony in which the high priest and priestess bless the temple, which in turn allows us to enter without disrespecting our gods. Think of it similar to rituals of mass in the Catholic religion. Granted, that's not the most apropos analogy, but all I can think of right this second."

"Why are we headed to the back entrance rather than the main entranceway?"

"When this place was constructed, a mistake was made, and the back entrance is facing east, and the main entrance is facing south. As part of our tradition, we always enter from the east."

I stood next to Abby as the rest of the crowd gathered around and behind us. A man about my height and of average build, dressed in a flowing black and dark purple robe, silver belt, black loose fitting pants, and a black tunic, entered alongside a tall thin woman dressed in a dark black and purple gown with a flowered headdress. Abby whispered to me that these two were the head priest and priestess.

An elaborate ceremony took place involving candles, a thurible, a bell, a bowl, a goblet, a dagger, and several dishes, some full of salt and oils, as well as a silver sword. The bell was rung. Candles were lit in intervals. Chants were made to the crowd throughout the process.

About halfway through the ceremony, we were allowed into the temple. Abby and the rest of the witches were anointed with some sort of oil. I, not being a witch, was not allowed the privilege, and was instead just politely told to enter.

The interior of the temple was far less opulent than I had imagined. The white walls were practically spotless. Many pentagrams and depictions of what I assumed to be religious iconography were painted onto the walls. They were intricate and adroit, yet the large room still had an air of humility to it somehow. If the paintings on the wall were removed, then this temple would have been no different than a town hall or even a large public dance hall.

After entering the facility, all of us were lined up along the wall alternating between male and female, except for one part where four women were standing next to each other, as we had more women attending this meeting than men.

The rest of the ceremony then continued. Much of the tradition was completely lost on me. Oil was sprinkled all over, the dagger was used to pantomime pentagrams in the air, the bell was rung several times, and there were several chants. Often the crowd would join in, leaving me conspicuously silent.

Towards the end of the ceremony, a goblet was passed around the room. Each witch took a drink and passed it along. The goblet was refilled periodically when necessary. Abby whispered to me to just pass the goblet along and not take a drink, which I did obediently. After this had been completed, the priest rang the bell three times once more.

"Now are we all here and is the temple erected," the priestess announced. "Let none leave but with good reason till the temple is cleared. So mote it be."

"So mote it be!" the crowd shouted back. The crowd moved from the walls and started to gather in a large circle around the priest and priestess, who both were standing by the altar. The meeting could officially begin.

"Who is the cowan who wishes to seek an audience with us?" the high priest asked.

Abby whispered to me that I should enter the circle in front of the altar, and I did just as she instructed.

"I am the one you seek," I announced.

"Please, give us your name," the high priestess said.

"My name is Peter Cunningham."

"Why do you wish to seek an audience with us?" the high priest asked.

"I have something important to discuss related to the recent attacks against your people, as well as a potential solution to the issues you've been having within."

"Very well," he said.

"People of the coven!" the high priestess announced to the crowd. "Who amongst you supports this cowan in his bid to seek an audience with us and to state his case?"

"I will!" Abby announced proudly. "The findings of his investigation have been invaluable."

"I will, too," Dahlia said.

"As will I," Neal said with a beaming Dicana. "He saved Dicana's life!"

"As will I," Cassandra announced with her child in her arms and her husband Maxwell by her side, standing proudly.

A deep voice interrupted the high priestess as it bellowed and echoed throughout the temple. "I will too." A collective gasp was heard from the crowd as they looked towards the speaker. It was Archon. "This cowan—I mean, this man, Peter Cunningham— has more than proven himself worthy to seek an audience of the high priest and priestess. He saved my son's life twice. He also saved my daughter's life at her wedding without hesitation, even though I personally had made it clear I did not want him there. He has done more for us than any other cowan, perhaps even more than any other witch."

"Thank you, Archon," I said, my words barely audible above the murmurings of the raucous crowd.

"Very well," the high priest said. "Cowan, you have received the support of numerous households. I believe you are someone we can trust. Please, state your case."

"Members of the Aoibheann Coven, I implore you to listen to what I have to tell," I announced, remembering the preamble Abby had instructed me to use to show the high priest and priestess the proper amount of respect. "The ones responsible for the actions against your kind are the Innocent Children. This organization, or cabal, is led by Tony O'Stein. They are a sort of reformation of an old witch hunting group dating back to the fifteenth century. By attacking the ones that you have dubbed cowans, you are playing right into their hands."

"What do you mean?" asked the high priest.

"Their goal is to have you harm or kill innocent people in an effort to expose your kind, and give cowans a reason to commit genocide against witches. They want to show the rest of humanity that witches are not only real but dangerous and pose a real threat that must be handled with violence."

A low murmur hummed in the crowd as many began to question my story. Both the high priestess and the high priest raised their right arms, which immediately silenced the crowd.

"Do you have proof of this, Mr. Cunningham?"

"Not quite." Angry taunts and derisive laughter could be heard as a response to this. I shouted over the angry voices. "However, everything I have seen and heard from my investigation should be enough!"

"Silence!" the high priestess shouted as she raised her arm over her head. "Cowan, you make a bold claim. Please explain yourself."

"Everyone I have encountered on this case has been in some way related to Tony O'Stein. Tommy and Chuck, the men who attacked Abigail Mitchell, were employed by Keith Jackson, a member of The House of Virtue. Joseph Edwards was a member of The Benevolent Arms. Bertrand Davis delivered goods and was affiliated with Valiant Crusaders Church. Even the man who attacked Archon Pontem's daughter Dicana hung around Valiant Crusaders Church and likely overheard a conversation between members of the Innocent Children leading him to believe in the existence of witches. All of these churches are owned by Tony O'Stein."

I explained the significance of all of the names I had just listed before the crowd.

"When Kelly Martinez, an officer friend of mine, and I interrogated Bertrand Davis, he made allusions concerning Tony O'Stein being slow to act upon a plan. He further claimed that the attacks have already started, and the rest of humanity could learn what they have known for years if Tony would just expose all of you now. What is it that the Innocent Children know that the rest of humanity doesn't? That witches exist."

"Taking that as truth, how could they convince others of our existence?" asked the high priestess.

"The magical attacks. What happens to a human body after it has been attacked by a witch's spell?"

After a moment's pause, the high priest said, "I see. You are referring to the pentagram underneath the arm."

"What makes you think they want to expose us witches in order to lead humanity in a massacre against our kind?" the high priestess asked.

"That knowledge is encoded in a parable." I explained the foxes and the chicken parable to the crowd.

"Yes, we are familiar with that story," the high priest said. "None of us are fans of O'Stein, but most of us are familiar with at least some of his speeches."

"And isn't the moral of that tale that to overreact to relatively minor grievances leads to much greater torment?" asked the high priestess.

"I used to believe the same thing until something else was found." I told them about the epilogue I had read in the frame above Bertrand's laptop related to the chickens discovering the serpent's magic, and the reason for the foxes' assault was to expose this secret to the rest of the animal kingdom and protect them from the chicken's malevolence. "I believe with his business beginning to flourish, Bertrand posted the epilogue of the tale on his wall as a motivational reminder of what he was working towards. It is clear to me that in the story, the foxes represent the Innocent Children, and the chickens represent witches."

Another loud hum overtook the crowd as the witches began to discuss what I had said at length. The high priest raised his arm once again, and immediately the room was silent.

"Even if what you say is true, his plan is foolhardy at best," the high priest said. "Witches are far more powerful than cowans. It would be akin to playing in a cobra's nest. What hope does a cowan have against a witch?"

"These particular cowans have found a way that had existed in the past to counteract witches. Allow me to ask you a question. What happens to a witch once their magic is removed?"

"I suppose they would become no more powerful than a cowan," the high priestess said, seeming a bit perplexed as to the point of my question.

"Even worse," the high priest interjected, "A witch would become something else. Something not quite a witch, but not quite a cowan."

"If Tony had his way, he would essentially remove your magic, remove your essence, and remove everything that makes you who you are."

"How does he plan to do this?" asked the high priestess.

"By combining the ximuce tree branch and a certain type of swamp water, both of which can only be found in the forests of Evergreen. With these elements and some household solvents, they are able to create a powerful liquid that is able to provide a resistance to witch's magic when they apply it to themselves, and it completely counteracts a witch's magic when applied to him or her, making them physically weak. Abigail Mitchell, Cyrus Pontem, and the parties that attended Dicana and Neal Byrne's wedding, along with the respective bride and groom, will attest to that fact."

There followed a small buzz as various voices spoke out to concur with what I had said before once again growing silent.

"Tony once told me his purpose in life was to change the world. He believed one man could do this. What better way than to expose your kind by forcing you to attack, and when people are panicking due to the perceived witch threat, he would then provide humanity with a solution and be heralded for it? Tony sought to create a problem so that he could provide a solution, and ultimately become the world's savior."

This time the hum of the crowd seemed to reflect a turning in favor of my words.

"There is sound logic in what you have said," the high priest said. "We must think upon these facts you have presented before pressing further. As you may know or have assumed, we have laws against harming cowans. Those responsible for the murders of those cowans will be brought to justice and prosecuted to the fullest extent of our laws."

"However," the high priestess said, "That does not mean we have influence over the thoughts and ideas of every single witch in our clan. Much like with your people, a law or decree can only go so far. It is the ideas that matter. A cowan helping our kind would go a long way, but you will need proof that what you say is true, that the attacks on our kind all stem from these Innocent Children. We will need proof of what you claim."

"It wouldn't convince everyone," the high priest said. "But a metaphorical smoking gun, if you will, would be incredibly beneficial in helping us move towards peace."

"Until that point, though," the high priestess said. "I'm afraid there is little we can do to stop this bloodshed."

"What if I were to bring Tony to justice?" I asked. "Would that suffice?"

"Only if it is in conjunction with proving that the Innocent Children are the ones behind these attacks, their plans are as you described, and Tony is the leader," the high priest said.

I was silent for a while, contemplating whether I could fulfill this request. Despite the noise and the confusion in the room, I had an epiphany and realized where I might find damning evidence against Tony O'Stein.

"I have full confidence I can fulfill your terms."

"Terms is a little bit strong, cowan. I was just merely stating fact," the high priest said. "We do appreciate the sentiment and hope you are able to accomplish this. We sincerely wish you luck."

"Now, because that is decided, we must ask you to leave," the high priestess said. "We have other matters to attend to. You are officially dismissed from the esbat."

"What?" Abby protested. "Since when do we kick out visitors when they have already earned an audience with the high priest and priestess? We have nothing to hide, and traditionally we have given cowans the option of staying for the rest of the proceedings."

"True," the high priestess said. "But considering the current political climate of the coven, it would not be wise to allow him to see the rest of the proceedings. We would prefer to avoid any potential conflict."

"Don't worry about it, Abby," I said as I rose to my feet. "I have other things I need to attend to. It's probably for the best that I leave now."

"Then I'll go with you," Abby said.

"Didn't you say that you have important matters to discuss with your coven today?" I asked.

With a bit of hesitation, Abby said, "Yes, but you're important too."

"It's okay," I said to Abby. "My phone's been buzzing for the last ten minutes anyway. I think Kelly's calling to let me know he's got the search warrant, and we're ready for the next phase of our plan."

"Okay," she said, giving me a warm embrace and a peck on the lips. "Just don't do anything crazy."

"It's me you're talking about. Do you really think I'm going to do something crazy?"

CHAPTER 15

"Abby told me not to do anything crazy," I muttered as I picked the lock to Tony's church. "But, it's only crazy if I'm caught, right?" I admit it was flimsy justification.

It was relatively late at night. Having acquired a warrant, Kelly and his crew were at Tony's home trying to find something that would link him to the murder of Bertrand Davis and the attempted murder of yours truly. I, on the other hand, had decided instead to take a look into The Paragon.

I might not have been going about it in the most legal means possible, but if my hunch was correct, then the ends would justify the means. Of course, if my hunch was wrong, I would be in serious trouble, but I had faith in my instinct. It never let me down — or actually, rarely did it let me down.

It took me a while to find the correct pick to use, but I was eventually able to open the door. Returning the picks to my backpack, I pulled out a flashlight that I had to preserve my phone's battery and placed the bag on my back as I passed through purple doors trimmed with gold trim. I adjusted the bandages on my left side. They'd get in the way if I weren't careful.

Compared to the other facilities where Tony had lectured, this mostly golden and white citadel with a traditional steeple appeared to be, from the outside, modest and unassuming. The exterior belied the lavish interior of the facility. The intricacies of the stained glass windows, the quality of the décor and other religious iconography, everything in that facility screamed wealth and luxury. Ironically, Tony often went to The Paragon in order to remember his "humble" roots.

The main room where most of the lectures took place was across a small hallway used mostly for greets of the congregation as they entered. As tempting as it was to switch on a light and triumphantly yell, "Let there be light!" to that empty room, I had to remain stealthy in case someone else either was there or was going to be there soon, as unlikely as it seemed late on a Tuesday night. To that end, I even double checked that I put my cell phone on "silent."

I went down the eastern and western hallways, and as I walked, my flashlight happened upon various framed paintings and historical pictures mixed amongst more modern photographs of what were likely members of the congregation, a display not unlike what you would commonly find in any church.

Sebastian Michaelis, Roger Newell, Pierre de Lancre, and Johannes Nider. All of those names were of men involved with witch hunting. Most prominent on these walls were Jakob Sprenger and Heinrich Kramer.

When I went down the eastern hallway, I opened each door and found nothing but empty prayer rooms or meeting halls, as I had already done in the western hallway. It dawned on me that there was a large separation between the penultimate door and the final one at the end, almost as if the hallway had been extended from its initial design.

When I arrived at that final door, I tried to open it but found it locked. I shone my flashlight on the door while I felt it with my hand. It was not made of mahogany like the rest of the doors but of steel. It was only painted to blend in and would fool most people not examining it closely. That door was the only way into the room beyond, so the only thing I could do was get out my lock pick and begin to work once again. After only four attempts, I passed that obstacle as well.

The room was Spartan. A large table was placed towards the back wall. It was next to a strange contraption that consisted of a hydraulic press over a flat surface bolted against two long black metallic beams. Circular gray metal pieces were scattered all over. I picked one of them up. It was a blank.

I moved my light towards the strange contraption. There was a switch on the side. I pressed and saw that the red light went on, and the machine started to make a peculiar noise. Underneath the press was a large solid round object, and what looked to be a giant washer around the top. In the middle of the "washer" was one of the blank gray coins. I pulled the lever downwards.

Another strange noise was emitted as the hydraulic press went onto the coin in between the washer. I pushed the lever upwards and turned off the machine. With great force, I was able to remove the washer from the round object, and afterward remove the coin from the washer. On it was the design of Pope Innocent VIII's tomb.

"I guess I know where they press the coins," I muttered as I pulled out my phone and took a picture of the coin in my hand, the blank coins on the table, and the coin press. All good, but not good enough. Leaving the room while making sure to lock the door behind me, I returned to the main lecture hall across from the main entranceway. It was the only place I had not yet searched.

As I had done earlier with the other rooms, I opened the doors to the main lecture hall slowly, only to find the room empty like the rest. This room contained several rows and columns of pews. An extravagant red carpet separated these rows.

This church may have had humble beginnings, but as Tony's popularity grew so too did his church, so this building soon became much too small to hold his entire congregation. However, since his father, a preacher in his own right, started at this church, it held sentimental value for Tony, and he refused to part with it, or so he said.

To accommodate the extra members of the congregation, an upper floor of pews had been installed. Derisively called the bleacher seats by...well, me, these pews were about four rows deep along the entire left and right sides of the main room.

In order to access these floors, doors were placed on the left and right sides near the main entrance. I picked the lock on the left side, an activity that took me an embarrassing six tries before

I was able to succeed and go upstairs.

Tony had begun his career on public access television. It was a small broadcast that didn't get much notice right away, and during those years, he didn't have the eccentric tick that would eventually betray him. He didn't develop it until after he began speaking at larger churches and venues, but strangely he did not exhibit it at those locales. It was only when he returned home after the upper floor accommodations that this odd pattern of behavior began to manifest.

Whenever he spoke of his great-grandfather's legacy or a related topic, he would look up to his right. Interviews he had in this church displayed the same pattern of behavior. To most, it probably just seemed like the man was lost in wistful thoughts, a solemn habit borne out of respect and admiration. But because he only exhibited such a habit here and nowhere else, I felt he was actually looking at something.

I had told Kelly about this, and he agreed Tony might just be hiding something up there. However, his search warrant only applied to Tony's house. He assured me, though, if he were to find anything incriminating in Tony's place, it would be practically superficial to acquire a warrant for The Paragon.

I didn't have time to wait. Witches in Abby's coven were already beginning to attack, and I had to stop it before they gave us cowans reason to retaliate. Of course, I couldn't tell Kelly any of this. I made up an excuse that Tony or one of his minions might be inclined to destroy any important information that might be in that church if they caught wind that Tony's home was being searched by the police. Though he agreed that was a risk, he was afraid there wasn't much he could do for me. He made me promise several times that I would not be there when his team conducted the search. Kelly then mentioned he hoped that I would not go to the church while they made their search, because if I were careful, I could go there, find evidence, and leave without the police ever knowing, which was something he couldn't condone. "I'm getting so dangerously close to being a dirty cop," I heard Kelly mutter as he left our conversation.

As I tapped the walls of the upper floor to determine whether I could find a hollow part, I noticed there was a painting hanging on the wall across from where I had entered—another painting of Heinrich Kramer. I removed the painting and found nothing. After knocking on the uncovered part of the wall, though, I heard a hollow sound. With a little more pounding, I determined it was a false wall. Reaching up and around the sides, I eventually found the edges and removed it to reveal a safe. It was a Safe-T-Tech safe, which made breaking in exceedingly easy.

Safe-T-Tech safes grew in popularity because of their durability, relatively affordable price, and impenetrability. These things could withstand explosions. However, there was one major design flaw. It took some skill and a bit of practice, but if an individual placed a long flat metal object, or any object with similar consistency, in between the right slit, and pushed it in the exact right location, the reset mechanism would be triggered. Instead of asking for the old password, the safe simply asked for a new one.

I did just as I described above. After opening the safe, I could see I had hit the jackpot.

There were scores and scores of old documents—the records that outlined the history of the Innocent Children. Quickly I pulled out my phone and began taking snapshots of every piece of paper, hoping that simply showing the high priest and priestess these photographs would provide enough evidence to end the conflict between the separatists and unionists. After I had completed my amateur photography and spy work, the temptation to read them was too great, so I began to pore over them, enraptured by the history of my adversary.

One document was a letter written by Tony's great-grandfather. He had made a long train ride from Tacoma to Salem in order to take care of the affairs necessary to inherit his family home after his aunt's death. He was looking through her large, elaborate bookshelf, hoping to find something valuable, when a stack of papers fell to the floor.

This turned out to be the family history, which described how centuries ago the Innocent Children, created by Pope Innocent VIII, were the preeminent, most successful, and most secretive witch hunting organization in Europe. His family used to lead this group.

Towards the beginning of the seventeenth century, the public sentiment of the witch hunts began to change, as they were deemed cruel and unethical. People began to question the existence of witches, or whether God would even allow such evil beings to exist. Tony's ancestor blamed this shift in sentiment on stronger, more evil witchcraft.

The Innocent Children wanted to show them the truth and needed something big. That is why in 1692, they went to the New World, to Salem. Mary Walcott, who had become an operative while living in that village, sent word of witches and witching activity to the elders, so it was decided that Salem was the place where they would make their mark.

They wanted to show the church that not only were the Innocent Children necessary to protect others from witches, but they also could be creative and find alternate means of stopping witches. However, the Innocent Children, in their haste, did not properly vet the fourteen women and six men they sentenced to death. None of those twenty men and women were witches. This event led to the demise of the Innocent Children.

The church was already vacillating on the idea of witch hunts and witch trials. Instead of showing people the importance of witch hunting organizations, it only displayed what people believed was cruelty. By the mid-eighteenth century, the Innocent Children were no more. Tony's ancestor believed something beautiful was destroyed by a horrible mistake.

After reading his ancestor's letter, Tony's great-grandfather was skeptical, but the thought of the Innocent Children haunted his mind. However, it wasn't until after he went camping at Point Defiance and was woken in the middle of the night by a witch's circle that he truly began to believe that witches were real.

In his mind, they were trying to summon the devil and end the world, and because a spell was cast on him shortly after seeing what he thought of as a horrific scene, all he could remember was the world fading to black, then waking up the next morning with the only signs of what had happened being some torn clothes and the remnants of a fire.

He painted this scene in an effort to expose the witches to the world. To his mind, if they resided in Tacoma, they might be living everywhere. Tony's grandfather concluded that the Innocent Children must be revived to not only prove that witches existed but to protect the world from their threat.

Tony's great-grandfather believed it would not be easy to expose witches to the world. They were, after all, adept at hiding. That was when he formulated a plan to force the witches to act against non-witches in order to show not only that they existed, but that they posed a terrible threat.

Borrowing from the knowledge of the fifteenth and sixteenth-century Innocent Children, they developed an unguent liquid from ximuce tree branches and a certain type of swamp water, along with certain other elements, to protect themselves from witches.

The rest of the documents had a more complete history of the Innocent Children, as well as details of the plan to get witches to attack in order to expose them to the world. There was even a section that discussed how a pentagram was formed underneath the left arm when a spell was cast upon them.

Having pictures of all that I needed, I returned all of the documents to where I had found them. Tony would be a little confused in the morning when he couldn't open the safe, as I had changed his password, but I could live with that.

I walked down the stairs feeling jubilantly triumphant. After getting off the stairs and putting my hands on the door to leave this lecture hall to the main hallway, I felt something against the back of my head. It was the barrel of a gun.

"Please put your hands up, Mr. Cunningham," a voice said to me. I did as he instructed, dropping my flashlight on the floor in the process. He carefully took the bag off my back and searched my body, finding the gun I had holstered in my vest. The man also picked my pockets to remove my wallet, cell phone, and car keys. After confirming he had removed anything of interest from me, the man continued. "Turn around, Mr. Cunningham. I'd prefer to speak to you face to face." After once again doing what I was told, he continued. "Do you know why I haven't already blown you away, Mr. Cunningham?"

"Where the hell did you come from, Tony?" I demanded.

"Now, that isn't an answer to my question, but because it would be impolite to leave yours unanswered, I'll answer it. When your cop friend told me he didn't know where you were tonight, I thought you might just come here. You were foolish enough to forget to lock the front door, which I'd never do, so guessing you were here, I went in through the back. There are multiple entrances to this place, Mr. Cunningham. Now that I've answered your question, please answer mine. Why do you think I didn't just kill you?"

"Is it because you were captivated by me the first time we met, Tony?"

"It obviously isn't because of your sterling sense of humor."

"You certainly didn't have any qualms about shooting me before. That's right, I know you were the one who shot me."

"Yes, that was me, though I must say my aim was a little bit off."

"I can see why you didn't win your shooting competition, then."

Tony shoved his gun into my false bandage. It took a second for me to process what he was doing, but then I acted as if I were in extreme pain.

"Now, I hope that you won't say something like that again. In truth, they say the Lord works in mysterious ways, and I think He realized, much as I did eventually, that you are far more valuable to me alive than dead. I'm glad I didn't kill you. You can help me by providing me more information about your witch friends."

"Sure. Witches cast spells, and they like cats." I said that even though I knew that Abby told me she was a dog person.

Tony drove his gun into my side, and I feigned pain again. "At some level, I kind of admire your bravado while facing eternal damnation, but you really shouldn't risk your life for those fiends." Tony paused for a moment. "Though I suppose it's all because of that little witch that follows you around. My family has dealt with that kind of temptation before. Succumbed to it too, if I'm honest. But you should understand that it's really not worth it. You shouldn't do these kinds of things for that little whore of yours."

Anger flooded my senses for a moment, but somehow I was able to take a deep breath and calm myself down. "Do you really think some eighth-grade level insults are going to get me to cough up the information you want?"

"I am eternally an optimist."

"I suppose you'd have to be."

"Now, what is that supposed to mean?"

"This was such a slipshod operation. How the hell did you ever expect this plan to succeed?"

"This plan was going to succeed before your interference, Mr. Cunningham!" Tony shouted, his voice nearly cracking. "Do you know how many years my family's been doing this?"

"A century?"

"More or less. It's been a difficult time, to say the least. We've been building up an organization that has been dormant for over four centuries. I admit our plan had a little bit of trouble getting off the ground because to hunt witches, we must first find them. Luckily I was able to find one about five years ago. She was someone I knew to be on the inside, and it was she who told me all about the witches' circles. That gave us a pretty good target to attack. We were so close to success those five years ago, but we ran into a few snags. The heat got a little bit too much, so to speak, and we had to back out. Again, Mr. Cunningham, I say this was fortuitous, as it gave me time to build my personal empire to better broadcast my message."

"What do you mean, you knew someone on the inside?"

"I can't tell you everything, Mr. Cunningham. I will say I've used her recently. The first time we met, all I had to use was charm. But this time…well, let's just say I had to use a little more persuasive methods. Now that I think about it, I'm really only doing what my daddy had begun twenty years ago, with a few ideas modified here or there."

"What happened twenty years ago?"

"There's a big difference between me and my daddy. He was a good man—too good, in fact. The losses of members of the congregation really got to him. He had an opportunity to do great things, but he didn't capitalize on it only because someone had failed him. Of course, I suppose it hit him pretty hard, considering it was his son."

"His son? Wait, that means that your brother—"

"Surprised, Mr. Cunningham? Yes, my father stopped everything just because my fool older brother Nicholas got himself killed. It took my brother quite some time to convince Daddy to do his plan, then another few years to map it all out. He had shamed Daddy and the family and wanted to make amends. Had he just gone after who Daddy originally wanted him to, the woman who ruined our family, he would have had a much easier time. Five years down the drain over sentimental value."

"Your father failed twenty years ago, you failed five years ago, and you've failed recently. It sounds like a pattern of failure to me."

Tony again jabbed his gun into my side, forcing me to feign pain for a third time.

"As I keep telling you, Mr. Cunningham, the Lord works in mysterious ways. Daddy's lack of gumption turned out to be a blessing after all. Daddy didn't have the support or the budget to do what I have done. He had a good idea, but the time just wasn't right. The same was true five years ago. I got a little bit too anxious. I've learned to be a little more patient. Unfortunately, some in the flock didn't learn the same lessons I did."

"Your father wanted to be the world's savior, just like you. You don't really want to protect the world from witches. What you really want is fame."

"I'd be lying if I didn't want some credit for what I've done. My family's been through a lot, and it would be nice if I was able to live up to the legacy of our ancestors, of my great-grandfather. There's nothing wrong with taking credit for your own accomplishment. After all, if the glove fits, I see nothing wrong with being called a savior."

"Then why didn't you expose witches yourself? Bertrand told me you didn't believe it was time to expose them, but I know that you knew about the pentagrams under the left arm, which means you know the so-called 'pentagram killings' were witch attacks. Why did you choose to wait?"

Tony chuckled. "Men like you and Bertrand think much too small. My and my daddy's plan was like cooking a good quinoa. It has to be boiled for the absolutely correct amount of time if you want it to come out right."

"I'll take your word for that one."

"I admit I once did think this might have been the time until I thought of something even greater. I probably should have discussed it more with Bertrand, but you saw what a temper he had. You saw how he reacted when he disagreed with me over when we should expose those demons. Why, he was going to spill the beans to the police and ruin everything! I don't regret shooting him in the head."

"What exactly did you have in mind?"

"I plan to show the world a witch casting a spell on a human on national television."

"What the hell are you talking about? How do you plan on doing that?"

"Well, that's kind of why I still need you. I have someone in mind I could use, but I think she's starting to waver a bit. She used to comply without hesitation, but now she's starting to resist."

"What the hell are you going on about?"

"Now Mr. Cunningham, we all are entitled to some secrets. Witches may not feel emotions, but they can be very territorial, something like a mama bear. You see, they breed like the rest of us, and their offspring are a vulnerability. If I were to take one from her, why, I'm sure she'd be mighty mad, wouldn't you say?"

"You're insane!" I shouted. "How the hell could you do that to a child?"

"Allow me to correct you, Mr. Cunningham. It's not a child, it is merely demon spawn, so it's not unlike capturing a rabid animal. Capturing a witch child does pose the equivalent danger, but I've already accounted for that."

"Are you planning on putting some witch bait out in a trap and hoping they'll bite?"

"Actually, yes, Mr. Cunningham, that is the plan. You are the trap, and their trust is the bait."

"What?"

"You've already earned their trust. You can convince them to come to me. I'm not quite sure how, but you're a smart man. I'm sure you'll think of something."

"You're completely crazy if you think I'd ever help you."

"I had some hope that my explanations about how dangerous witches are might have swayed you, but there are ways I have kept in reserve to use if need be, Mr. Cunningham. I'm sure I can convince you one way or another. I hope to do it the civilized manner, but I have other means of breaking her spell if necessary."

"Even if I did this, then what? Are you really planning on sacrificing yourself for the good of your Innocent Children?"

"Lord no, I'm not planning on sacrificing myself. I have plenty of people who'd be willing to do this even if they sometimes need a bit of persuasion. It can't be me because the Innocent Children need me to show the world the danger of witches. They will become as renowned as the olden days. No, wait—they will become something even greater! I shall lead the Innocent Children to a new age of humanity, a world marked with peace and prosperity! *Nel tempo del suo Pontificato, la gloria della scoperta di un nuovo mondo. No, Nel tempo del mio Pontificato, la gloria della scoperta di un nuovo mondo!* During MY Pontificate, the glory of the discovery of a new world!"

"That plan only proves you have ridiculous delusions of

grandeur!"

"And you have delusions of grandeur, Mr. Cunningham, if you think you are getting out of here alive without providing me the assistance I need."

Tony jabbed his gun into me for a fourth time, but this time I did not react. Tony was momentarily confused, which allowed me enough time to slam my left hand into his right arm, moving it away from my body. I followed up with my right hand to push his gun upward, and as I did this, I dove into his left arm, shoving his shoulder upwards. The resulting scream of pain proved I correctly remembered where Kelly had nicked him.

Using his pain and leverage against him, I was able to wrestle the gun out of his hand. Pointing his own pistol at his head, I shouted, "Down on your knees, now!"

"How?" Tony stammered. "Impossible." With a puzzled look on his face, he complied.

I heard a noise from the back as the two backdoors of the room were thrown open and slammed against the walls. "Freeze!" a voice cried.

The front doors were then opened in a similar manner. "Freeze!" a second voice shouted. "Drop your weapon now ass... hole. Aw dammit, Pete, I wanted to be the big hero for once."

"I'm afraid you're a little bit late," I said as I placed the gun down and put my hands over my head. Two cops, both of whom had entered the back, rushed onto the scene. Kelly stood next to a tall, clean-shaven older black haired man who was balding near the top.

"Yeah, sorry about that, Pete, we lost track of him. He must have snuck out the back. He went missing shortly after we told him you weren't with us. I even asked sarcastically why you would be there, considering you're not an officer anymore. Martin here...," Kelly said, pointing at the man next to him, "Was the one who first noticed he was gone. We immediately knew where he went, even though you had specifically told me you weren't going to be here." Kelly winked before continuing. "I tried to call you, but you didn't answer."

"My cell phone was on silent," I admitted. "To prevent someone from hearing me in here if I needed to hide."

"A lot of good that did you, eh?" Kelly said, picking up my phone and handing it to me, along with my wallet and my keys. "When you didn't answer, we expected the worst, which is why Jones and Brown came in the back while Martin and I rushed in through the front. You were supposed to be in trouble."

"I was, but I had just finished diffusing the situation when you arrived."

"I can see that."

"Arrest this man!" Tony demanded.

"For what?" Kelly asked.

"He broke into my church and then held a gun to my head! He wanted to kill me!"

"He had a gun drawn on me, and I had to disarm him."

"I know, Pete."

"What on earth are you talking about?" Tony shouted. "Why do you believe his word rather than mine?"

Kelly knelt next to Tony. "Many reasons. First, let's talk about motive. Pete, over there knew I would be searching your house during this time, so why would he even think he'd meet you here?"

Tony merely growled inarticulately.

"Moreover, you left your house in the middle of our search. I should arrest you just for that. Beyond that, we found your other gun. It was underneath a floorboard. Like a friend of mine always said, there's always something underneath a floorboard."

"Whoever said that must have been a genius," I said.

Kelly rose to his feet. "That friend was most often wrong then, but he was correct today. The pistol we found fires the same types of bullets that were lodged in Bertrand's skull and passed through my friend over here. We won't know that this gun was the one that was used to commit the murder until we get it back to the lab, but somehow I do think the ballistics will match. Why you just didn't get rid of it, I'm not sure." Kelly glanced at the gun at my feet. "I suppose we should probably check that gun, too, just in case."

"It was my daddy's gun," Tony said in tears. "I knew I couldn't use it anymore, but I couldn't just get rid of it."

"He's wounded in the left shoulder," I said to Kelly, ignoring Tony's blubbering. "That's where you shot the man who shot at us, right?"

"That's right, and luminol tests showed that you had blood in your car. You cleaned it up nicely, but traces could still be found under the spotlight. Unless you have an explanation for how you suffered that wound and why there was blood in your car, we have a lot of damning evidence against you."

"Besides, he confessed his crimes to me while he was here."

"Like anybody could trust your word," Tony sneered. "You are, after all, the tramp who broke into this facility. Who could trust a criminal like you?"

"You're right—Pete did break into this place. But you know what? At most, he's guilty of breaking and entering. The man has an otherwise exemplary record as a police officer, and even as a PI. Besides which, while we were gathering at the entranceways preparing the ambush, we overheard you and Pete talking, and I too have an excellent record. My word is golden."

"He's guilty of theft too!"

"What did he steal?"

"He broke into my safe and looked at my documents!"

"Do you have any proof of this?" Kelly asked.

"Check his cell phone!"

"Illegal search and seizure," Kelly scoffed. "I don't have any reason to do that. The word of a confessed murderer is not probable cause."

"Do you think I could have my charge reduced if I help the police find some more incriminating evidence on this man, such as proof that he was involved in a conspiracy to murder?"

"I think we could all but exonerate you if you did that, Pete. Martin, I think we've heard enough. Would you mind doing the honors for me?"

"Absolutely not, sir," Martin replied as he began handcuffing the man and reciting to him his Miranda Rights.

"You probably should stop by the precinct at some point and address the breaking and entering charges, though, Pete," Kelly said to me.

"No problem," I replied. "You know I'll be there. Thanks for all of your help."

"Hey, just sorry that I didn't get here sooner. I was a bit skeptical of your crazy plan, but it seems like it worked to perfection. Thanks for including me this time."

"Absolutely, Kelly. As harrowing as all of this was, the whole experience made me kind of miss being a police officer. Are you looking for a new partner?"

"I'd love it, Pete, honestly I would, but the truth of the matter is Martin's been a great partner, and I couldn't do that to him."

"Martin seems like a good guy."

"He is. He's far more by the book than you ever were, but hell, he'd almost have to be."

"I wasn't really that bad, was I?"

"No," Kelly said, giving me a playful punch in the shoulder. "You weren't bad at all. I just wish you would have let me call for backup every once in a while." He stuck his right hand out. I reached over, and we shared a heartfelt handshake.

"Is it safe to say that after all these years, Cunningham and Martinez are back together again?"

"Maybe not in its original form, but yeah, I'd say that's true."

After releasing my hand, Kelly began looking around the room, appearing to be a bit perplexed. "I can't shake the feeling that I've forgotten something."

A familiar figure rushed through the doors.

"Abby!" I shouted.

Initially, I felt joy, but soon I felt fear. She had the look of death on her face. She walked right in front of me, cocked her arm back, and slugged me in the face.

"Oh yeah, she was at the house too, looking for you. I thought I'd bring her along. I hope you don't mind."

CHAPTER 16

The sun shone brightly from the heavens on that warm summer morning. The rains of months past seemed like nothing but a distant memory. Basic meteorology could tell you that the precipitation would return again, but it no longer bothered me. It was all part of the rich tapestry that made this fair city great.

Tacoma had its flaws, as we all do. Sometimes, though, we focus so much on the negative that we forget about the positive. It was once voted the "most walkable" city in the country, and another time it was named the "most sexually healthy city" in the United States. It was also home of the first modern American legal marijuana farmers market. Okay, I kid. The city has much more to be proud of than that.

Our Museum of Glass has garnered international acclaim, after all, and our Tacoma Art Museum is often used as a prototype for mid-sized regional museums. I'd be remiss not to mention structures such as the Tacoma Dome, an edifice that has garnered nationwide recognition, or the beautiful public memorials the police department has for its fallen officers. From our parks to our homes, from our infrastructure to our forest land, from our reverence to the past to our forays into the future, it is clear how Tacoma is truly a burgeoning metropolis.

With all that said, to me, Tacoma will always be most notable for being the home to the best coven in the world, though I'm basing that mostly on the fact that it is home to the most beautiful and wonderful witch in the world.

"Oh, hey Abby," I said as she entered my office. Saying nothing and moving swiftly but somehow casually towards me, she came around my desk to give me a kiss. She was sitting in my lap, resting her head on my shoulder before I even had a chance to react.

"It's good to see you too, Petey," she said when she had finally settled.

"You're certainly in a good mood this morning."

"Enjoy it for now, because it's probably not going to last when the nicotine cravings flare up again."

"Isn't that what your patch is for?"

"We'll see how well it actually works. I'm keeping my expectations low."

"I'm just glad that you're trying to quit."

"We'll see if you still feel that way when I'm stabbing your hands with a pair of scissors because you're trying to take away my cigarettes."

"How are things going in your coven?"

"Very good. Sending them the photographs of those documents was just what the doctor ordered. News that Tony was behind bars and that you and Kelly were responsible for his arrest was the icing on the cake."

"The talking heads on TV and online just won't shut up about it. I'm glad because it's doing wonders for my business."

"The chanting circle looks like it'll be in no danger of being shut down anytime soon, now that the major threat has been eliminated and the separatists have pretty much been shut down at the coven as well. It's not that the thought has completely dissipated, but since you and Kelly, a couple of cowans, greatly assisted our kind and put an end to a grave threat, it pretty much killed the notion of separation. You especially should be proud. Kelly didn't even know we were witches. You were the only one who did. You should be rewarded."

I felt the blood rush a bit into my cheeks and face. "I think the reward you gave me last night was plenty."

"That wasn't a reward. I was going to give you that anyway." Abby looked around for a moment. "There's something I need to tell you, Petey."

"What's that?" I asked.

"My parents are going to be coming back tomorrow."

"Oh no," I moaned.

"And they want to meet you — or should I say, see you again."

"Oh no."

"You know, if we ever got married, you'd be the first cowan in the family. Not the first in our coven, as it has happened before, as rare as it is, but definitely the first in the family."

"Oh no."

"I'm not sure anyone in the family even dated one."

"Oh no."

"Don't worry," she said, giving me a peck on the lips. "It won't be so bad. They are very impressed with what you did. I think they're going to be more upset that I've been right about you after all these years, if anything."

"It's going to be so awkward, though, with you being Erin Ross and that whole thing."

"Trust me, Petey. Everything will be all right." Abby studied and noted the look of concern on my face. "Is there something else on your mind?"

I sighed. "I'm still puzzled about many things."

"Such as?"

"The informant. Who was she? Tony talked about her, but we never found out who she was. We also don't know why you were targeted as a child. How did they even find out about you?"

"It's because the guy caught me using magic."

"Did he? I only caught a glimpse of the man, but adults never attended our magic shows, at least not as members of the audience. Perhaps he just happened to pass by and notice us, but even then, how would he have known you were using real magic? You fooled all of us."

"Maybe he saw magic before and recognized it when he saw it?"

"Maybe, but then that raises even more questions, like how was he able to see magic in the first place."

"Petey, does it really matter? The bad guy is behind bars.

We've won. Isn't that enough?"

"It's a loose end. It's something unaccounted for. I can't help but think it might bite us in the ass unless we figure it out."

"Can't it wait a couple of days?" Abby asked with a wry smile. "My parents are coming back tomorrow, and didn't Darren have a magic show today that we promised to attend?"

"His party isn't until this afternoon."

"Do you really think you can find those answers this morning? Besides, I kind of wanted to visit Dahlia for a bit before we went to the magic show."

"You're right. Is she still in a good mood?"

"She's in a fantastic mood! Ever since I told her that Tony O'Stein is going to jail for his crimes, it's like she's been on a cloud. I'm not sure I've ever seen her this happy in my life!"

As she spoke, my blood ran cold. An idea hit me about as hard as a ten-wheeled truck hitting a housefly. I had a stunning epiphany and not a particularly pleasant one.

"You're right, Abby, we should go and see Dahlia." I rose from my seat after gently removing the woman from my lap.

"Is everything all right?"

"I think I figured something out, Abby, and we really need to talk to Dahlia about it." I softly grabbed Abby's hand.

"What did you figure out?"

"I think it'd be best if we waited until we got there," I said as I headed out the door, pulling her along with me.

"Okay, fine, but at least slow down a bit. You're going to pull my arm off."

"Oh, sorry about that."

I drove the two of us as quickly as the law would allow to the Layton Fruit Market. Abby and I hardly shared a word the entire trip. A couple of early morning customers were already there, which made the place far more crowded than I was used to seeing it. Dahlia, though, was nowhere to be found, and instead, one of her employees was manning the cashier's desk. Knowing instantly where she would be, I practically leaped out of the car and raced to the back room, with Abby doing her best to keep up with me.

"Slow down!" she admonished as she struggled to keep up with me.

My preoccupied mind hardly even processed that she said anything, and I continued to race towards the door. I threw it open so hard that it slammed it against the wall.

"For the love of Cernunnos!" Dahlia yelled. She had finished placing the vials on the table, so even though I saw her clutch her chest a bit as I entered the room, nothing was broken. "You really never knock, do you, Peter?" After combing her hair a bit and adjusting her clothes, Dahlia smiled. "I guess I should be used to your eccentricities by now. Is Abigail with you?"

Almost on cue, Abby walked through the back door where I had entered. "Sorry, Dahlia," Abby said, panting a bit. "I don't know what's gotten into him."

"Don't worry about it. Now Peter, what's on your mind?"

"Dahlia," I said somberly. "We need to talk. It's about something pretty serious."

"You have my attention," Dahlia said, still smiling. "What's on your mind?"

"I know that you were tipping Tony and the Innocent Children off about what was going on in your coven, and about witches in general."

"What?" Abby was obviously exasperated by my accusation.

Dahlia turned white as a sheet, and a grave expression washed across her face. She barely managed to stammer out, "What are you talking about, Peter?"

"I know that you had a good reason for doing what you did, but I have to know why. I have to know whoever made you do those things is no longer a threat."

"I'm not going to just stand here and listen to your baseless accusations!" Dahlia yelled. "I'm going to have to ask you to leave! I have work to do!" Dahlia then turned around and began moving vials from one table to another in an effort to look busy.

"Petey, apologize to Dahlia!" Abby demanded. "How can you say such things to her, anyway?"

"I can say such things because it's the truth!" I answered loudly. "Dahlia, I overheard your conversation over the phone. You weren't talking to a bank, you were talking to Tony. That's why you got so upset when I mentioned his name. When he held me at gunpoint, Tony said that he needed me because he didn't have an informant anymore. He told me he learned about witches from someone on the inside. That was you, wasn't it?"

"Stop making up such nonsense!" Dahlia yelled back.

"The Innocent Children have been plotting for decades, but have only started to attack relatively recently. Somebody must have tipped them off! You knew they would be there, that's why you told your daughter not to attend the circle. It wasn't because of Tommy and Chuck, it's because Tony had contacted you and made threats to you specifically!

"That's one of the things that has been bothering me. You seemed to hesitate before you mentioned Tommy and Chuck, like you were thinking of a reason why you suddenly turned on the chanting circle tradition, as if you were hiding something. Cassandra even said you didn't tell her about two men. It wasn't just a mere slip up. Tony threatened you, didn't he? He also contacted you five years ago. You were his informant."

"Dahlia, is what he is saying true?" Abby asked.

Dahlia said nothing and continued her work while beads of sweat gathered on her forehead. There was a loud crash when she dropped the crate on the table, and the vials clanked against the wooden sides. The poor woman grabbed each side of the table and just stood there, her back to us, in an effort to compose herself as tears flowed down her cheeks. "Yes, you're right. It was me. I told them about the circle and where you all would be on the night of the attack."

"Why, Dahlia?" Abby asked, her voice cracking with tears flowing.

"He found me, and he found my daughter and my granddaughter. He threatened to kill them! He showed me pictures of them! He was always watching them, and that kept me from going to the police. I didn't think he'd attack you, though!"

Dahlia broke down and wept on the floor. "I thought he wanted me. I thought he wanted to kill me for what he thought I did to his family."

Abby raced over to comfort her friend. "What could you have possibly done to his family?"

"I think he blames her for, and please forgive me for saying this, 'seducing' his brother and birthing his child. Nicholas O'Stein is the father of your child, isn't he, Dahlia?" I asked.

"Yes, that is correct."

"Who's Nicholas O'Stein?" Abby asked.

"Tony O'Stein's brother."

"I met him when I was only eighteen years old. He was twenty-two at the time. He caught me making potions at one of the places I used to work, a place not unlike this fruit stand. He knew I was a witch, but he didn't seem to mind. I loved him, and like the fool I was, I thought he loved me too. He left me not long after I became pregnant with Cassandra."

"He might have loved you, in his own way," I suggested. "Tony told me that Nicholas could have picked a target with less resistance, but chose to attack you instead, Abby. I'm guessing his father initially wanted to attack you, Dahlia, for he blamed you for 'seducing' his son, but Nicholas refused."

Abby gasped, "So was Nicholas the man who…?"

"I'm afraid so. He was the man who attacked you. He did it to earn accolades from his father, and to begin a plan that was plotted for five years."

"Five years?"

"Whatever Nicholas was doing was only the beginning of a much larger plan. Nicholas's death, though, seemed to sap all their father's motivation to carry out whatever plan he had devised."

"I'm so sorry, Dahlia," Abby said. "My father is responsible for Nicholas's death. He did it to protect me, Dahlia. He didn't know. We didn't know."

"No, no, hush Abigail. He attacked you. He left me. Cassandra never even got a chance to meet her father. I don't care what his excuse was, he deserved his fate." The tears flowed down Dahlia's cheeks even more than they had before, something I would have said was impossible.

"How did Tony find you?" I asked.

"That's a bit of a long story. As much as I want to act as if I'm a learned, hardened woman, the truth is I've always been a sucker for a charming man. Nicholas had this charisma, and Tony, in spite of him being a true monster, had the same charm. I knew that Nicholas had a brother, but I didn't make the connection that the Tony that came into my fruit stand that day was my former lover's brother. O'Stein isn't that uncommon of a last name, and Tony wasn't famous then as he is now.

"His charm wore down my defenses. I began telling him all about witchcraft and witches, and even about the circle. I thought he was a man I could trust. Then one day, he just disappeared. No breakup letter, no phone call, nothing. Shortly afterward, the witches in the circle were being murdered. I didn't really think Tony was responsible. All the newspapers mentioned a man named Cullen Jones, a random crazy man, and the police caught him. There was no connection to Tony. Cernunnos help me, I thought at one point that Tony might have been a victim of Cullen Jones's attacks. I thought maybe he died trying to protect one of those women, which was more a delusion than anything, but it is what I honestly believed.

"That feeling changed when I saw his face on those posters two years ago. When I saw his wide smile exposing those perfect teeth and his chiseled face, I was angry enough to kill. Then he tried to worm his way back into my life. He said he missed me, and the reason he left unexpectedly was because he felt I was too good for him, and he wanted to build himself so he'd be good enough for me. The man is charming, I'll give him that. Still, fool me once, shame on him. Fool me twice, shame on me. I rejected him outright.

"He then started peppering me with questions about the chanting circle and the coven. I realized he wasn't actually there for me. I demanded to know why he really had come back. That's when the threats started. Our chance encounter wasn't so random after all. He had been keeping track of me for years. He showed me pictures of me, Cassandra, even Joy! She's just a child! He told me about all the men he had at his beck and call, about the history of his group, his grand plans, and about how I had unknowingly helped him five years ago by telling him all about our kind and how I could be a benefit to him today. Tony was sure to let me know how thankful he was for my assistance and mentioned that it would be a shame if the witches in the coven found out about my betrayal.

"He told me in detail how his men killed those women five years ago. Tony spared nothing in his descriptions. He made it very clear to me what he intended to do to Cassandra and Joy if I did not cooperate or went to the police. That's why I told him everything. I didn't know what else I could do.

"Tony called me again. The men he'd sent had failed, after all, and he wanted to know when the next chant was going to be held. I refused to tell him. I realized what a horrid mistake I made after you were attacked. You're just as important to me as my daughter and granddaughter, Abigail! I couldn't let anything happen to you!"

"Oh, Dahlia," Abby said as she hugged her friend tightly. "Wait, though. Did you tell Tony that I was an important member of the coven?"

"No, I didn't give him specifics at all, just general information."

"Then why did Joseph tell me that I was an important person?"

"I think I know why," I interjected. "You did tell Nicholas about your family, didn't you, Dahlia?"

"Yes," she admitted. "I didn't really know Abigail at the time, but I did know her parents, and I told Nicholas all about them. I was a fool."

"It's okay, Dahlia, I'm not judging. I think Tony tracked Abby with equal vigor as he did you, Dahlia. I think he did it because he blamed Abby as much as you for his brother's demise. He hated Abby because, in his demented mind, she was responsible for Nicholas's death because of what Abby's father did to him. We know it was in defense of his little girl, but to Tony, it was unjustified. Nicholas just wanted to kill a witch, after all."

"Peter, I wish I had known you before when I was threatened by Tony," Dahlia said. "Then none of this would have ever happened, and Abigail would have never been attacked."

"Maybe. But without the attack, I might have never gotten involved in this, which means I might have never been reunited with Abby. Maybe Tony would still be on the loose, and maybe the coven would have been destroyed by the internal and external pressures it felt. Just perhaps, in spite of it all, everything worked out for the best. Think of this as just being fate."

"Don't ever let this man go, Abigail, he's a keeper."

"Oh, Dahlia!" The two women shared a long hug, crying all the while. I turned around to hide a few tears of my own.

"What are you going to do now, Peter?" Dahlia asked. "Are you going to report my crime to the high priest and priestess?"

I stared Dahlia directly in the eyes and gave her a large embrace. "Thank you very much, Dahlia. I am so sorry you had to go through this."

"Peter...," Dahlia said, seemingly baffled.

"Thank you for protecting Abby when she was young. Thank you for being a good friend to her and for me. Thank you for everything you have done. Oh, yeah, and thank you for all the apples you've given me."

Dahlia asked, "So you're not going to tell the high priest and priestess?"

"I wouldn't do that to you, Dahlia—you were being blackmailed. It's understandable—hell, more than understandable. What parents wouldn't do the same thing for their children?"

"But Abigail could have been killed!"

"But she wasn't, so everything is okay."

"What about those women from five years ago?"

"You probably shouldn't have told Tony about the circle, but that is hardly a crime. He's the one who commanded his men to do those awful things. You didn't pull the proverbial trigger. Your hands are clean."

"I like to tell myself that at least."

"We all make mistakes, but you stood up to him when it was most necessary. All of you were nearly divided in a painful conflict that has only recently been resolved. Telling your coven about this would only be harmful to the recovery. Besides...." I picked up an apple. "Where would I be without my number one potion maker?"

"You forgive me?" Dahlia asked, her voice wavering a bit as she said this.

"Of course."

"How about you, Abigail?"

"Of course, Dahlia, of course, I forgive you!" Abby exclaimed.

"Thank you both! It's as if a giant weight has been removed from my shoulders!"

We all shared a few more hugs before Dahlia sent us on our way. She still had work to do, and Abby and I still had plans. Dahlia assured us that she'd have a batch of apples ready for us in the morning.

Locals call Tacoma the "City of Destiny." The funny thing about destiny is that it works in many ways. Destiny can be bad, but destiny can also be good. Sometimes destiny controls you. Sometimes you're the one that controls it. Most of the time, it's a mixture of both. It's important for people to try and forge their own destinies, but also be flexible enough to deal with whatever fate may have in store for them. My destiny was to spend my life with the woman of my dreams.

"Come on," I said. "We've got a little boy's magic show to attend." As we left Dahlia's storage room linked arm and arm, I said, "You know something funny? We never did discuss payment."

Abby gave me a long, passionate kiss. "What? I'm not enough?"

About the Author

James Kirst lives in the Evergreen State in a humble little abode within the forested city of Dupont. There, he earned his Master's Degree at the University of Washington. Commuting up north to Tacoma, he has worked as a senior programmer and software development lead for almost ten years.

With a borderline obsessive interest in the paranormal, James has conducted intensive study into the subject. To that end, he has visited some of the most haunted places in the United States, including Salem, the LaLaurie Mansion of New Orleans, and his personal favorite, the Shanghai Tunnels of Portland, Oregon.

As an avid fan of mystery both in fiction and in real life, he has done extensive research into police procedurals, the machinations of detective work, and life as a private investigator.

A big sports fan, James, is sure to either be watching or participating in one when not writing about or educating himself in one of the aforementioned subjects. In fact, he has won multiple championships in bowling and slow pitch softball and has made several appearances as a softball All-Star where he was given the privilege of playing in Cheney Stadium. He is still seeking that elusive kickball title, however.

www.ingramcontent.com/pod-product-compliance
Lightning Source LLC
Chambersburg PA
CBHW020256200626
46816CB00001BA/323